# MURDER AT THE LAURELS

Could it have been murder? When old Eleanor
Bridges dies on her birthday at The Laurels
nursing home, no-one except her niece, Fran
Castle, suspects anything. But when the will goes
missing, and Fran's newly discovered relatives
appear to be doing everything in their power to
obstruct investigations, she enlists the help of her
friend Libby Sarjeant. Together, they uncover
sinister events in the past, greed and elements of
witchcraft, all of which provide a multiplicity of
motives, and it isn't until a second body is
discovered that the murderer is unmasked.

# MURDER AT THE LAURELS

# MURDER AT THE LAURELS

*by*

Lesley Cookman

**Magna Large Print Books**
Long Preston, North Yorkshire,
BD23 4ND, England.

British Library Cataloguing in Publication Data.

Cookman, Lesley
        Murder at the Laurels.

A catalogue record of this book is
available from the British Library.

ISBN    978-0-7505-3621-9

First published in Great Britain in 2007 by Accent Press Ltd.

Published in Large Print 2012 by arrangement with
Accent Press Ltd.

Magna Large Print is an imprint of Library Magna Books Ltd.

Printed and bound in Great Britain by
T.J. (International) Ltd., Cornwall, PL28 8RW

For my friend Margaret Waller

# Acknowledgements

I would like to thank Hazel Cushion of Accent Press, Bob, my indefatigable editor, all my friends in the Romantic Novelists' Association and all of my "Friends and Writers".

In the interests of keeping the story moving I have telescoped some of the official parts of the investigation. I hope this doesn't offend any of my readers.

# Chapter One

'How many more do you want, then?' Libby Sarjeant pushed a wisp of damp, rusty coloured hair off her brow. 'I can't turn them out like sausages.'

Guy Wolfe grinned at her from behind his neat goatee beard. 'You can't turn them out at all unless you haven't got anything else to do,' he said. 'You're one of the most unreliable suppliers I've got.'

'Thanks.' Libby tried to look outraged and failed. 'Suppliers, is that what we are? I thought we were artists.'

'To me you're suppliers. Now, *I'm* an artist.' He turned to look smugly at the rows of greetings cards behind him.

Libby snorted. 'That's prostituting your art,' she said.

'No it isn't. It's being practical. Think of all the Laughing Cavalier and Stag at Bay cards that are sold each year.'

'I didn't know you were that famous.' Libby picked up her basket and slung it over her shoulder.

'Only among a certain well-informed set,' said Guy, and laughed as her mouth dropped open. 'I'm teasing, Lib.'

'Oh.' Libby turned towards the door and then remembered. 'You never said how many more you wanted. And if you do, do you want them all the same?'

'I'll take whatever you can produce, and as long as it's pretty, it doesn't matter what the view is. You sell quite well, you know.'

Libby smiled, her turn to be smug. 'I know. Especially–'

'Since you turned detective?'

'No, I was going to say especially that one–'

'The view through the window?'

'With the yellow roses, yes.'

'The punters loved that. Was it from imagination?'

'No, I visited the cottage once.' Libby sighed. 'It was beautiful. I wanted it.'

'Was this when you were house hunting? What was it Peter and Harry called it?'

'The search for Bide-a-Wee. Yes, it was then.'

'But Nethergate's miles from Steeple Martin.' Guy perched on the edge of the old oak table that did duty as a counter.

'When I was house hunting I wasn't looking particularly in Steeple Martin. Just something small and somewhere else.' Libby turned her head and looked out of the window. 'Nethergate was somewhere else, as well as Steeple Martin. Just too expensive.'

'Seaside location, you see.' Guy narrowed his eyes and put his head on one side. 'Wish you'd moved here instead, now?'

Libby sighed again. 'In a way. It's all been very difficult.'

'Murder usually is,' said Guy.

Libby nodded mournfully.

'Look, why don't I take you to lunch? You need

cheering up, and Sophie can mind the shop.'

Guy's daughter looked up from her magazine and nodded vaguely. 'No customers, anyway,' she said.

Guy made an exasperated sound and slid off the table. 'Come on,' he said, taking Libby's arm. 'Let's leave her to it.'

'She's right, though, there aren't any customers,' said Libby, as they walked along Harbour Street towards Guy's favourite pub. 'Don't be too hard on her.'

Guy grinned. 'I'm not really. Sophie works for me and lives with her mother. A remarkably well adjusted child. Just very modern.'

'Hardly a child, and of course she's modern. Did you expect a Renaissance maiden?'

'I'd have preferred it. Look what happens to modern misses. That Paula, for instance,' said Guy, referring to the murder case Libby had been involved with in the spring.

Libby shuddered. 'I'd rather not even think about her, thank you.'

'Well, ignore her, then, but I want to know the inside story. People do ask, you know.'

'What people?' said Libby, surprised, as they went into the cool interior of The Swan.

'Those customers there aren't any of,' said Guy. 'When they see your name, if they're local, they always say, "Oh, she was involved in that murder, wasn't she?" and I waffle and mumble.'

'Carry on waffling and mumbling then,' said Libby sitting at a table. 'How on earth do they know, anyway?'

'Local papers, local radio. It was hardly low

17

profile, was it?'

Libby accepted her half of lager. 'No, but it's still not something I want to talk about.'

'Ah, but it got you together with the lovely Ben, didn't it?' said Guy, slyly.

'Sort of,' said Libby, frowning.

'Only sort of?' Guy looked at her down-turned face and decided not to pursue the subject, despite his normal elephant child curiosity. 'So,' he said, casting round for a new subject. 'How are the kids?'

The telephone rang as soon as Libby opened the door of number 17 Allhallow's Lane later on that afternoon. She fell down the step and answered it, breathing hard.

'Libby, it's Fran. How are you?'

Libby sat down on the stairs with a bump.

'Goodness, Fran, how are *you?* Haven't heard from you for ages.' She fended off the advances of Sidney, the silver tabby, who was determined to convince her he was starving to death.

'No, sorry. I kept meaning to ring you, but somehow... I don't know.' Libby did. Fran felt uncomfortable about the circumstances of their friendship.

'Well, the thing is,' Fran went on, 'I've had a call from my cousin Charles to say it's my Aunt Eleanor's birthday today. Apparently, the rest of the family are all going to see her this afternoon.'

'Yes?' said Libby, puzzled.

'Well, Aunt Eleanor's in The Laurels, just outside Nethergate.'

Should have known, thought Libby. Coincidence upon coincidence.

'So you're coming down, then?'

'Not today, I can't,' said Fran, 'but tomorrow. I just wondered if we could meet up for a drink.'

'Funnily enough, I've just come back from Nethergate. A little gallery there sells my paintings. There's a nice pub there called The Swan.'

'That'd be great. The only thing is, I'm car-less at the moment–'

'Would you like me to pick you up at the station? I could take you to your Auntie's.'

'No, no,' said Fran hastily, 'that wasn't what I meant. I thought, when I've seen Auntie, perhaps I could ring you and we can both make our way there. Or I could catch a bus to you.'

'You'll be lucky, there aren't any,' said Libby, amused. 'No, you ring me when you're ready and I'll meet you at The Swan. And why don't you come back with me and stay the night? We could have dinner at the caff.'

'Are you sure?' Fran sounded wary. 'I wouldn't have thought anyone would want to see me.'

'Don't be daft. You practically saved my life, didn't you? Everyone will be delighted to see you.'

There was a pause. 'What about Ben?' asked Fran. 'Won't he mind me being there?'

'What's it got to do with Ben?' said Libby, pulling a face.

'Won't he be around?'

'Maybe. We don't live in each other's pockets, Fran.'

'Oh. I thought...'

'Yes, well, it didn't quite pan out.'

'But what happened? It all seemed...'

19

Libby sighed. 'I'll tell you all about it tomorrow. Now, have you still got my mobile number? And come to think of it, have I got yours?'

Fran switched off her mobile and stared reflectively at what she thought of as her Betjeman kitchen. When she was a child, she lived in a world epitomised by John Betjeman's business women and their bathrooms stuck precariously on the back of tall grimy buildings, issuing steam into grey morning air glimpsed through a yellowing train window. Of course, she didn't know Betjeman then, but as soon as she heard his overstuffed cushiony voice reading that poem on the radio, she knew she had found a soulmate. She didn't feel quite so at home with his statuesque tennis and rowing girls, their lives bore little relation to hers, but his affection for Metroland and Cornish churches, and dates in tawdry dance halls, was as if her own thoughts had taken form and set themselves to paper.

It all boiled down to nostalgia, of course. As a child, Fran could summon up nostalgia for things that she had never even experienced, for places she had never been. She lived in an ever-changing world of her own, now flying up to those grimy bathrooms in Camden Town, then conveyed in a bumpy carriage through a concealed tunnel in rock to a hidden valley in the West Country, next climbing a small green hill above a sea of cow parsley in the Suffolk countryside. Every book she read was measured for its ability to transport her to the place between its covers and her favourites were, and remained, those that did. There were others, borrowed from the library, that she never owned and therefore never read again, but their atmosphere lingered round the edges of her memory like coloured smoke.

She supposed that was part of the reason that she became an actress. She wanted to write, but the words eluded her. She could never transport herself to one of those magical places, so she became other people, able to live in their lives, in their penthouse apartments, seedy bed-sitting rooms, country vicarages, nuclear shelters. She had children of all ages, many husbands and lovers and several different parents. Along the way, she acquired a real life husband and three children, but she was never really comfortable with them. They were too real. Her real husband got fed up with her constant search for the magical place and left her. The children stayed and helped her attain a sort of reality, partly because then she had to stop moving. Until the money ran out and she finally ended up in Betjeman land with a stuck-on bathroom three floors up looking out over the criss-cross railway lines of central London. Somehow, the Betjeman flat wasn't as romantic as she had thought it might be. The blue and white lino in the kitchen was cracked and the window sealed up with blistering grey paint, while a plastic ventilator whirred dustily in the top right hand corner of the glass. The geyser probably pre-dated Betjeman and dribbled occasional hot water from a reluctant rusting arm, and Fran clung on to her dreams.

In a world that owes its existence to dreams, those that don't conform to the stuff of those dreams are soon edged out to the perimeter. There were women with slimmer figures than Fran's, prettier faces and fewer years than hers, and they were there for every audition, every part. Eventually she admitted defeat, and that was when she'd met Ben.

And through Ben she'd met Libby and got peripherally involved in the murder investigation that had devastated the village, and particularly Ben's family.

The phone on the landing began to ring. Fran had given up thinking it might be for her months ago and made no move to answer it, knowing that her downstairs neighbour would be there before her anyway. Sure enough, she heard Dahlia's broad voice, as distinctive as her broad hips, in cheerful conversation with the unseen caller.

'Miz Castle. Phone, Miz Castle.'

Surprised, she pushed herself away from the table. Most people used her mobile, except, she remembered, as she went downstairs, cousin Charles.

'Charles?' she said, as she lifted the grubby receiver.

'How did you know it was me?' He sounded surprised.

'You're the only one who calls me on this number,' said Fran. 'Where are you? I thought you were going to see Aunt Eleanor today?'

There was a short silence.

A muffling blackness descended on Fran and she dug her nails into her palm hard to force her mind to clear.

'She's dead, isn't she?' she said.

'Fran, you're scaring me,' said Charles. 'First,

22

you knew it was me, second, you knew she was dead. What's going on? Were you down there today?'

Fran took a deep breath. 'No, of course not. I told you, you're the only person who rings me on this number, and I doubt if you'd have rung to tell me how she was as I'm going myself tomorrow.'

'You won't go now, surely?'

'No? Oh, I suppose not.' Fran frowned. 'But I've already made arrangements to stay with an old friend. I might as well go down.'

'Why don't you go and stay on the night of the funeral instead? I assume you'll go to the funeral?'

'When is it?'

'Not sure yet. I'll give you a lift if you like.'

'Thank you, I'd appreciate that.'

'I'll ring you nearer the time, then, shall I?' said Charles, sounding more normal.

'Yes, great, Charles, but you haven't told me what happened. When did she die? What was it? Heart?'

'I suppose so, but no one seems to know. Barbara got there first today and was actually sitting with her without realising she was dead.'

'Who's Barbara?'

'Remember I told you? My sort-of cousin? Barbara Denver.'

'Oh, right. Yes. Well, Eleanor was quite old, wasn't she?'

'Over 90. She—'

'Don't say it,' Fran jumped in quickly. 'Please don't say she had a good innings.'

'No clichés allowed, eh?' said Charles, sounding amused.

23

'Sorry. It's so belittling. But how awful for you all. Especially Barbara.'

'Well, yes. She wasn't too happy. Anyway, I thought I ought to let you know.'

'Very kind of you, Charles. Thank you. And I'll give you a ring later in the week, shall I?'

'Fine. At least you've saved yourself a trip tomorrow,' said Charles.

Bloody prat. What a thing to say. Fran climbed back up to the Betjeman flat, absolutely certain that, tomorrow, she was going to The Laurels.

## Chapter Two

The rhythm of the train began to take effect, and Fran's mind began to drift into that peculiar half sleeping, half waking mode where external sounds can still be heard, yet a whole new scenario begins to unfold to accompany them. Faces slid in and out of Fran's consciousness, places revealed themselves and Fran herself was once more a guest at Uncle Frank and Aunt Eleanor's wedding. It was funny how she had forgotten Frank. Yet there he was, looking over Eleanor's shoulder, an Eleanor shrunken with age, her pretty bright hair and pale prettiness faded and wrinkled, her blue eyes opaque and bewildered. But it wasn't Frank after all, and she was looking up at the face now, while the blackness descended, muffling her nose and mouth ... she couldn't breathe...

Fran opened her eyes and found herself looking

24

into the concerned face of a middle-aged woman sitting opposite.

'Are you all right, dear?' asked the woman. 'I thought you were choking.'

'I'm sorry.' Fran struggled into an upright position. 'I was having a bad dream. How embarrassing.'

The woman smiled. 'Oh, don't worry about it. I think we should have reclining seats, like they do on aircraft, for these long journeys.'

'Oh, I'd never wake up in time to get off, then,' said Fran. She smiled and pushed her glasses back up her nose, picking up the magazine which had fallen closed on the table. She looked out of the window, and then at her watch, before settling back in her seat to gaze out of the window, determined not to let herself drop off again. Dreams could be very unsettling, but not usually embarrassing, although occasionally she had mistaken a dream for reality and shocked her nearest and dearest into the middle of next week by telling them things they would rather keep to themselves. Mostly, her 'moments', as the family called them, took the form of a scene unfolding in her head, which she frequently put down to imagination, always being very dubious when they turned out to be right. 'Just think,' she would say, 'how many times I've seen pictures and they're wrong.' Dreams were more like the odd facts that she found herself thinking about that turned out to be true, of which, on further investigation, she could have had no knowledge. The whole business was very disturbing, and she dwelt on it as little as possible, especially when it was as unpleasant as the recent dream.

But it had led to a new career working for an upmarket estate agent, who sent her to ferret out nasties in the woodsheds of some of their top properties. And then she had met Ben, the architect, who, in turn, had introduced her to Libby, with whom she'd tried to solve a murder. The police, naturally enough, managed it without them, but in a funny way, Fran had enjoyed herself. There was something about the village community that appealed to her, although she did wonder how welcome she'd be when she turned up again, as she might provide an unwelcome reminder to some of those more closely involved.

The view outside the window was increasingly beautiful. Summer had clothed the country in a matching set of greens, with brown and cream accents. She loved the country. As a young actress she had adored touring seaside towns in summer, with their slightly raffish air of faded grandeur and tacky amenities, and large, industrial towns in winter, with comforting and fattening food specialities; all of it had charmed her. But the best part had been the tours to small market towns with Shaw and Ibsen and Rattigan revivals, surrounded everyday with beauty, both man-made and natural. Market towns had changed a lot since Fran's young days. Now they had an outer shell of new building, and Fran often thought you could age a town by its rings, much like a tree. The outer ring would comprise low rise industry and thoughtfully designed new housing in village-style developments, the next the little boxes of the sixties, with huge plate glass windows and unimaginative plastic extrusions, then the smart red brick Thirties villas, a smattering of ornate Edwardian edifices, rather more Victorian monstrosities – large and small – and finally the red, black, white and gold of the local stone and brick that looked as though it had been planned and set there from the beginning of time.

For a change, the sun was beating down with an intensity suitable for August as they drew in. A venerable Ford masquerading as a taxi waited near the ticket office and proved willing and able to transport her to The Laurels, the imaginatively named nursing home where Aunt Eleanor had breathed her last, and which had, in fact, not a laurel in sight. It stood, mellow and welcoming, at the end of a slightly sloping, curved drive. Fran peered out of the taxi window at the well kept grounds, noting the absence of shrubbery or dense vegetation of any description. In case the inmates tried to hide, she decided, trying to imagine little old ladies in long winceyette nightdresses flying across the lawns in a futile game of hide and seek.

The wide and curving stone steps were divided down the middle by a smooth ramp. Fran walked up beside it and pushed open the swing doors. Odd that they weren't locked, or was there an inner door to prevent the prisoners escaping?

'May I help you?' A woman looked up from behind a high counter.

'Er – yes.' She suddenly realised she had given no thought whatsoever to what she was going to say when she arrived at The Laurels. She swallowed hard and returned the interrogative gaze of the woman behind the desk. Was she imagining it, or was it a suspicious gaze?

'Eleanor Bridges. I'm her niece.'

The woman's immaculately made-up eyes widened and she stood up.

'But Mrs Bridges–'

'Died. I know.' Fran finished for her. 'I just–' she paused. 'Well, I just wanted to–'

'Her immediate relatives were here, you know.' The woman's tone was frosty.

'I know. That would be Mr Charles Wade, wouldn't it? He's my cousin by marriage. My name is Fran Castle.' Fran tried a winning smile and was gratified to detect a slight thaw in the woman's expression.

'Marion Headlam.' The woman held out her hand. 'I'm the owner of The Laurels.'

'Not the Matron? You don't look like my idea of a matron.' Fran shook the proffered hand and relaxed.

'No. I have qualified nursing staff here, obviously, but I look after the business side of things.'

And very lucrative it must be, thought Fran, looking round the well appointed hall.

'So.' Marion Headlam came round the desk. 'You wanted to see where Mrs Bridges died?'

Fran was taken aback. 'Well, yes, actually.'

'Relatives often do. Particularly,' added Marion Headlam, with a minatory look, 'when they haven't been in the habit of visiting regularly.'

'I didn't even know she was in here,' mumbled Fran in apology. 'We'd – er – lost touch, rather. There was a – well, a family disagreement.'

'Ah, yes.' This seemed to explain everything to Marion Headlam. 'Guilt. You'd be surprised at how much guilt a death generates. Now–' she reached over the high counter and picked up a telephone. 'I'll just get – oh, Nurse Redding? Could you come to reception, please? Thank you.' She replaced the receiver. 'Nurse Redding was one of the staff who looked after your aunt. You'd probably like to talk to her.'

'Thank you, yes.' Fran was grateful that things had been taken out of her hands.

'I'll show you into the visitor's room and send her in to you.' Marion Headlam opened a door on her right and held it open for Fran. 'Would you like some tea? Or coffee?'

'Tea would be lovely, thank you,' said Fran, feeling suitably humble. After the door had closed, she looked round the room.

It was quite a small room, decorated in a rich yellowy cream with blue and cream curtains at the long window, which looked out over the drive. A selection of up-market glossy magazines lay on a well polished table and a strictly arranged vase of flowers and seasonal vegetation stood on another. No roses in here, thought Fran. They might be badly behaved enough to drop their petals.

She moved to the window and stared out at the manicured grounds. It wasn't surprising that Marion Headlam had wondered why she was here. She wasn't sure herself. Just ... the strange feelings that had assailed her from the minute cousin Charles had telephoned her with the news. And then the train journey. She still hadn't recovered from that.

A brief tap on the door heralded the entrance of a dark-haired woman in the royal blue of a nursing sister's uniform. She was much the same age as Marion Headlam, but there the resemblance ended. This woman wore no elaborate eye make-up and wouldn't even when she was off duty, if her unplucked eyebrows and aggressive moustache were anything to go by.

'You wanted to see me?' She stood just inside the room, hands held rigid at her sides.

Fran tried another winning smile. This time it wasn't so successful.

'Nurse Redding? Or should it be Sister Redding?'

'Not here. When I worked in a hospital, I was.' Her tone was flat and unemotional, as though it didn't matter either way.

'Right.' Fran's smile was becoming determined and a little manic. 'Shall we sit down?'

Nurse Redding almost shrugged, but not quite, and sat on an upright chair by the wall. Fran took one of the high-backed, wooden-armed chairs grouped around the magazine table.

'I believe you were with my aunt when she died?'

'No, I wasn't.' Her expression didn't alter one jot.

'Oh. I thought Mrs – is it Mrs? – Headlam said you were.'

'I was one of the team looking after Mrs Bridges. That's what Mrs Headlam would have said.'

'Right.' Fran nodded immoderately. 'And how was she?'

Nurse Redding looked surprised. 'I don't know what you mean,' she said, peering under her beetling brows.

Fran felt herself break out in a gentle sweat.

This was more difficult than she had thought. 'I mean, was she happy? You know, contented?'

This time, Nurse Redding did shrug. 'None of them are happy. They're all here waiting to die. Most of them try and pretend they're not, if they've still got some of their marbles. The others don't know what's going on anyway.'

'And which was Aunt Eleanor?'

'I thought you'd know. Mrs Headlam said you were a niece.' There was definite suspicion in the voice now.

'I am, but I hadn't seen her for years. I didn't know she was in here. Charles Wade only told me yesterday.' Fran hoped that the introduction of Charles's name would allay the suspicion.

'She was confused. Wanted to go home.'

'But not ill?'

'You can never tell. Didn't seem ill. But she had a bit of heart trouble. No surprise that she died.'

Fran thought about this. 'But Charles did seem surprised when she died. He wasn't expecting it.'

'Nobody expects it. It's always a shock.'

Fran was beginning to feel as though she was swimming through treacle.

'Did she have many visitors?' she asked in desperation.

'Mr Wade, Mrs Denver. And Mr Denver.'

Fran caught the imperceptible change in the flat voice. 'Mr and Mrs Denver? I don't think I–'

'Mrs Denver. Mr Wade's cousin. Paul Denver's her son. Thought you'd know.'

'Oh, yes, well,' Fran, remembering just in time, felt the hot flush spreading again. 'Barbara Denver. I'm Mrs Bridge's niece by marriage.'

31

Nurse Redding said nothing.

'Um, I know this might sound a bit peculiar, but do you think I could see her room?'

Fran was aware of the first slight hesitation. 'I don't know... I'd have to ask.' Nurse Redding stood up.

'I'll come with you,' said Fran brightly, following suit. That Nurse Redding was displeased was very apparent, but she had no choice but to leave the room with Fran behind her.

Marion Headlam didn't seem in the least surprised that Fran should want to see the room where her aunt had died.

'Of course. You'll see that it's a very pleasant room with every facility.' She handed Nurse Redding a key. 'We keep it locked, of course, until a new client takes it over.'

Client? thought Fran. Not patient? She came to a halt behind Nurse Redding, who had stopped at a door towards the back of the building. A small metal holder held a card, which, on peering closer, Fran read: E. Bridges. Nurse Redding unlocked the door.

Almost immediately, Fran was overwhelmed by black suffocation. From a distance, she heard a voice saying 'Are you all right?' and felt a hand on her arm. Panic gripped her, and she tried to push the hand away, but she was overborne, and thrust gently into a sitting position, her head forced forwards towards her knees.

'Poor thing,' she heard a voice saying. 'It takes people the strangest ways, doesn't it? Must have been fond of her old Auntie after all. I'll see if that tea's ready.'

Fran's head began to clear and she sat up slowly. She was in a large, bright room that seemed to be a cross between a hospital ward, with its high metal bed, and a well furnished hotel room. Nurse Redding stood in front of her, a frown on her heavy face.

'Sorry,' said Fran, weakly. 'I don't know what came over me.'

Nurse Redding managed her almost shrug again. 'Shock,' she said succinctly. 'Mrs Headlam's gone to see about tea.'

'Thank you,' said Fran, wondering if she dared ask to be left alone. Nurse Redding settled the question by moving to the chair the other side of the bed and sitting down, feet neatly crossed at the ankles. Fran sighed and looked round the room.

'This was her furniture, wasn't it?' she said.

'No. Mrs Denver kept it all in storage.'

'Television? Was that hers?'

'No. She did have one, but ours had a bigger screen.'

There was a video recorder, as well, and something that Fran thought was a decoder for cable television. On the bed table lay a formidable array of electronic gadgetry: three remote controls and a white item with red buttons.

'What are those?' Fran stood up shakily and picked up the white object.

'The call button. Different buttons for different things. This one–' Nurse Redding pointed, 'for calling domestic staff, and this one for Nursing staff. This light flashed if there was a message for Mrs Bridges, and a buzzer sounded.'

'What sort of message?' Fran looked round for

33

a telephone. There wasn't one.

'A visitor, or a phone message. She would buzz back if she wanted to take the message, and someone would either bring the mobile phone in, or come and tell her who the visitor was.'

'So no one could come and see her unless she wanted to see them?'

'Oh, no. The reception desk is manned at all times when the front door is unlocked.' Nurse Redding turned her gaze to the french windows.

'And when is that?'

The other woman looked back at Fran with a frown, and Fran wondered if her questions had gone too far.

'The door's unlocked between 10.30 and 12.30 in the morning and 2.30 and 5.30 in the afternoon. That's when we encourage visiting.'

'Like hospitals.' Fran smiled, hoping to defuse the palpable hostility emanating from Nurse Redding. She failed.

There was a knock on the door, followed by the entrance of a small blonde in a blue and white striped uniform with an old-fashioned starched nurse's cap. She carried a large tea tray set with a delicate bone china cup and a plate of biscuits. She smiled nervously.

'Mrs Headlam sent some tea,' she said.

'Thank you,' smiled Fran going forward to take the tray, but Nurse Redding was too quick for her.

'That'll do, thank you, Nurse Warner.' The tray was set firmly on the bed table and Nurse Redding picked up the sugar basin. 'Sugar?' she asked.

'No, thanks,' said Fran, watching Nurse Warner slide uncomfortably out of the room. There was something there, she thought. Something had come in to her head while that girl was in the room. Fear. Not as strong as the suffocating feeling, but quite tangible. A high-pitched sound intruded in to the silence and Fran looked at the white device on the table in front of her. However, Nurse Redding felt under her cardigan and Fran saw that she wore a pager attached to her belt.

'Excuse me. I'm wanted,' she said, and without any further ado, left the room, leaving the door open behind her.

Fran stood still for a moment, wondering if anyone else was likely to come in and chaperone, but it seemed that she was to be trusted, for there was only silence in the passage outside. Carefully, her heart beating like thundering hoof beats, she moved to the door and pushed it closed. The click as it latched sounded deafening, but there was no answering commotion from outside and Fran let out her breath and began to snoop.

The room contained nothing. The efficient Mrs Denver had obviously cleared everything of interest and only a few forlorn garments were left. Fran picked up her tea and sat down in the chair Nurse Redding had vacated at the side of the bed.

'Mrs Castle?' The voice came from outside the door, and Fran realised that she had shut it and no one without a key could get in.

'I'm sorry,' she said, smiling into the worried little face of Nurse Warner. 'The breeze must have caught it.'

'I came to see if you'd finished with the tea things.' The young nurse scurried over to the table and picked up the tray, casting a nervous glance around the room as she went.

'Did you look after my aunt?' Fran asked, as she prepared to follow the girl out of the room. Nurse Warner stopped suddenly, and the cup rattled in the saucer.

'Er – sometimes,' she said.

'And did you think she was happy?'

'Happy?' The big blue eyes turned on Fran in sheer astonishment. 'Why should she be happy?'

It was Fran's turn to be astonished. 'Good heavens, what a peculiar answer.'

Nurse Warner blushed. 'I'm sorry. It's just – well, how can they be happy? They've no life left.'

'They have every comfort, though, don't they?'

'Oh, yes.' Nurse Warner nodded vigorously. 'And the food's very good. And the doctor comes round every day.'

'Does he?' mused Fran. 'So did he think it was only to be expected that Aunt Eleanor died?'

'I don't know.' Nurse Warner looked down at the tray and shuffled her feet. Waves of something – was it fear? – were coming off her, and Fran couldn't think how to get to the reason for it.

'Sorry to leave you.' Nurse Redding appeared from round a corner and Nurse Warner, with an air of relief, shot off in the other direction.

'That's all right.' Fran began to walk beside the other woman back to the reception area. 'At least I know where Aunt Eleanor spent her last days.' To her own ears this statement sounded like the worst sort of maudlin falseness, but Nurse Redding seemed to accept it.

Marion Headlam was waiting for them in the reception hall.

'Feeling better, now?' She smiled brightly at Fran. 'It's the shock, you know. Mrs Denver fainted right away. Didn't she, Nurse Redding?'

'I'll get back now,' said Nurse Redding, without answering the question. She nodded briefly to Fran and disappeared back the way she had come. Fran thought she heard Mrs Headlam give a little sigh.

'Do you know if there's a bus service that I can get back to Nethergate?' she asked.

'Well, there is, but it's a bit of a walk down the lane to the left.' Mrs Headlam looked doubtful.

'How far, would you say?'

'Ooh, a good twenty minutes walk, I should think. I could call you a taxi?'

Fran put her shoulders back. 'No, I think the walk would do me good. And it's so pretty round here, isn't it?'

'Yes, we've got lovely surroundings.' Marion Headlam looked round complacently, although Fran thought she probably thought more of her interior surroundings than the exterior. 'Well, see you at the funeral, I expect.'

'Oh?' said Fran.

'We always attend clients' funerals.' Marion Headlam smiled and held open the door. 'Good-bye, Mrs Castle.'

Fran, a relieved surge of adrenaline washing over her, walked as briskly as she could down the steps and set off down the drive. By halfway down, she wished she'd left her jacket at home, by the time she reached the lane, she wished she'd worn flat shoes instead of her favourite courts and by the time she was in sight of the bus stop, half

37

hidden by a mass of vegetation, she wished she'd taken a taxi or, when she'd called Libby earlier to arrange their meeting at the Swan, agreed that Libby could come and pick her up. Her mobile had no signal, so she couldn't even call her now. The sun beat down remorselessly on her unprotected head and her forehead and the back of her neck were dripping. It occurred to her that she hadn't bothered to find out how frequently the buses arrived, and, of course, there was no timetable attached to the bus stop. There were no houses nearby, either, which argued that this was possibly one of the one-a-day variety, which, after a quarter of an hour, Fran was convinced was true. Although, she argued with herself, if that was the case, surely Marion Headlam would have told her? She didn't, she realised, even know whether she was waiting on the right side of the road, although she had taken an educated guess judging from the direction the taxi had come. She couldn't see a corresponding stop on the other side of the road, and was beginning to feel quite desolate when the welcome sound of a diesel engine rose above the buzz of insects and call of birds, and round a bend in the road lumbered a double-decker bus. Greeting the surprised driver with a heartfelt smile, she climbed on thankfully.

# Chapter Three

The Swan was near the market cross in the very middle of the little town. A black and white building notable for its carved wooden beams, it presented two faces to the world. One was a sophisticated face that spoke of en-suite bathrooms and colour television in all rooms, the other more rustic and homely, supplying a variety of real ales to a discerning body of rather insular regulars. The restaurant attempted, occasionally successfully, to marry the two faces and was a favourite venue for tourists. Fran didn't hold that against it.

Libby hadn't yet arrived, so she hoisted herself on to a tall stool with regrettably low foot rails and, smiling diffidently at the barman, large, bald and shirt-sleeved, whose sausage-like fingers hovered over the till buttons, ordered a half of lager.

'Good heavens,' said a voice to her left. 'A woman who will drink by herself in a bar.'

The first thing Fran was aware of were two very bright, very dark brown eyes fastened on her own. She blinked.

'I'm sorry. Perhaps your unconventional behaviour precludes conversation with an unknown male.'

Fran felt an unaccustomed warmth creeping up her neck. 'Possibly,' she said.

'Pity.' The man standing next to her was leaning

on the bar, his arms folded. Above the brown eyes, tightly curling dark grey hair topped off an interestingly creased, tanned face with a neat goatee beard.

'We haven't met before, have we?' He turned sideways, still leaning on the bar.

'No.' Fran picked up her lager and faced him, armed.

'Not local then? I could have sworn I'd seen you before.'

'I'm meeting a friend.'

'Oh, who?' He raised an eyebrow.

'Is it any of your business?' said Fran, irritated.

'Sorry. Curiosity is one of my besetting sins.' He grinned. 'May I buy you a drink to make up for it?'

Fran raised an eyebrow. 'Are you trying to pick me up?' she asked.

'I don't think so.' He signalled to the barman. 'I'm not trying to pick this lady up, am I, Tony?'

'Just friendly, that's you.' The barman picked up Fran's glass. 'Same again?'

'No thanks.' She smiled at him. 'I'm sorry if I sounded rude.'

'Not in the least. A woman has to protect herself these days. I shouldn't have butted in.'

'No, you shouldn't,' said a voice behind Fran. *'Have* you been trying to pick up my friend, young Guy?'

Fran beamed delightedly. 'Libby!'

Libby, looking like an animated carnival tent, stretched up on tiptoe to kiss Fran's cheek.

'Sorry, Libby. If I'd known she was a friend of yours I wouldn't have dared speak to her!' Guy grinned down at the little woman eyeing him with amused tolerance.

'You want to be careful with him, Fran.' Libby hauled herself on to the stool recently vacated by Fran. 'He likes to think of himself as the local Don Juan.'

Fran took refuge in her glass.

'Well, you can buy me a drink, Guy Wolfe, then we are going to huddle in a corner and eat before returning to the rural delights of Steeple Martin.' Libby beamed at the barman. 'Lager, please, Tony.'

'My pleasure, Mrs Sarjeant.' Tony beamed back.

'So, how are you?' Libby looked Fran up and down. 'You look a bit pale.'

'That's living in London.'

Tony put a glass in front of Libby and Guy handed him the money. Libby fumbled in a capacious basket and pulled out a battered packet of cigarettes.

'Haven't you given up yet?' asked Guy. 'You'll have to soon, when the ban comes in.'

'Police state,' muttered Libby.

'We'll have a nice outside area with heaters for you, Mrs Sarjeant,' said Tony, 'don't you worry. And I bet there'll be more folks out there than in here.'

'Thank you, Tony,' said Libby, 'and why do you always call me Mrs Sarjeant? Nobody else does. Come on, Fran, let's eat.' She slid off the stool. 'Can we have a menu, Tony?'

'I hope I wasn't rude.' Fran turned to Guy and held out her hand.

'Not at all, it was good to meet you.' Guy

41

smiled and took it. 'I hope I see you again.'

'Yes,' she said vaguely.

'Come on, then, Fran.' Libby stretched up and kissed Guy on the cheek. 'See you, lover boy.'

The table in the corner of the bar lurched a welcome as they squeezed into the old oak settle behind it.

'So who's Guy?' asked Fran, after peering round to make sure she wasn't overheard.

'The Wolfe Gallery, just down Harbour Street.'

'As in picture?'

'As in all things artistic. Pricey.'

Fran studied the menu. 'And is he really a Don Juan?'

Libby pulled the menu down and looked into her face. 'Fran! Don't tell me you're actually interested in a man.'

'I just wanted to know.' Fran was defensive. 'In case he tries to lure me in to see his etchings.'

'Actually, he's not, a Don Juan, I mean,' mused Libby, 'although he could be. He's divorced, financially secure and reasonably attractive, if you don't mind the ageing-gorilla look.'

'Gorilla?' Fran chuckled. 'Long arms and cave-man tactics?'

'No, his face. Didn't it strike you? Perhaps more chimp-like.'

'Can't say it did.' Fran sat back on the settle and finished her scotch. 'I'll have the mushroom stroganoff.'

Libby squinted sideways. 'You're not coming over all vegetarian, are you?'

'No, I'm still a healthy carnivore. I just feel a bit delicate, that's all.'

'Delicate? In what way, delicate?' Libby looked alarmed. 'You can't be pregnant, you're too old.'

'No – it's just that I had this dream–'

'Ready to order ladies?' Tony appeared round the corner of the settle. 'Guy said to say good-bye.'

'Oh, right. Yes, thanks, Tony, we'll have a mush-room stroganoff and a chilli jacket. And I'll have a mineral water.' Libby smiled winningly.

Tony raised an eyebrow. 'I'll shout when they're ready, your highness.'

'Mineral water?' queried Fran.

'I'm driving us back to Steeple Martin, aren't I?' Libby lit another cigarette. 'Never believe I was trying to give up, would you? Right, so what was this about a dream?'

Fran told her. Trying to describe the feeling it had engendered defeated her, and the story dribbled to an inconclusive finish.

'Well,' said Libby after a pause. 'Normally I'd say it was just a dream brought on by something you've seen on television, but as you can describe it in such graphic detail, I suppose it must be one of your famous moments.' She squinted at Fran through a haze of smoke.

Fran fidgeted. 'Don't call them that. Anyway, I don't have them any more.'

'It seems that you do.' Libby stubbed her cigarette out. 'Was that Tony's dulcet call just then? Come on. Let's get our food.'

# Chapter Four

Steeple Martin lay snugly in a shallow valley a few miles from Canterbury. A busy little stream skittered over a stony bed parallel with the main street, before turning sharply to the right on its way to join the River Stour.

'You're in your usual room,' said Libby, as she let them in. 'Can you take yourself up? I'll make us some tea.'

Fran climbed the steep, narrow stairs and turned left at the top. Just in time, she remembered to duck as she stepped down into Libby's little spare room and promptly tripped over the aggressive rug that lay in wait by the bed. Rubbing her leg, she went to the window.

The view from this room soothed her. She looked up the lane to where it petered out at the edge of the woods bordering The Manor lands, and wondered whether Ben was still living there with his parents, and what had gone wrong between him and Libby.

'Fran? I've made the tea. Are you coming down?' Libby shouted up the stairs.

Libby's colourful and voluminous apparel was indistinguishable from the various blankets and shawls disguising the shortcomings of the cane sofa on which she was curled up.

'This place is in a time warp,' said Fran, collapsing into an armchair similarly disguised.

'It's like a village in a Golden Age detective story.'

'We like it that way.' Libby leaned over to hand Fran a mug.

'Doesn't it make everyone a bit narrow-minded?'

'Why should it? Just because we all choose to live somewhere beautiful doesn't mean that we aren't exactly the same as everyone else.'

'Only richer.'

Libby laughed. 'Not necessarily. I'm not. I just happened to sell a large house. There's a lot of people like that. Mind you, if I hadn't had to give Derek his share I would have been able to afford something a bit bigger.'

'And a lot of local people have to leave because they can't afford to buy.'

'Well, yes,' Libby conceded. 'And we do have a lot of weekenders.'

'There you are then.' Fran nodded wisely. 'You're all a lot of nimbys.'

'I think I should be offended by that,' said Libby. 'But I can't be bothered. Now, tell me all about Charles and Aunt Eleanor.'

'I've told you, Charles told me about Aunt Eleanor, then she died and I came down anyway. And had the dream.'

'Yes,' said Libby, extracting a packet of cigarettes from somewhere inside the sofa, 'but who exactly is Aunt Eleanor? And cousin Charles, come to that.'

'OK, well, Aunt Eleanor married my father's brother, Frank, just after my father died. When I was little, we lived in a flat in a big Victorian house in London. When my father died, Frank took over the house and we had to move out. I assume my father had left it to Frank, or perhaps it was jointly owned and it passed straight to Frank. I don't know. I was only about twelve, so all I knew was that we had to leave.' Fran stared into the empty fireplace. 'It caused a lot of bad feeling.'

'I can imagine,' said Libby, indignantly. 'Why couldn't they just live in the other flat?'

'Frank did. It was after he married Eleanor that we had to go. I don't really understand what went on. My mother wouldn't speak about it, and we didn't have any further contact with them from then on.'

'So what about Charles?'

'He was Eleanor's nephew. I vaguely remember him at their wedding. It was a huge shock to hear from him.'

Libby looked thoughtful. 'Why, do you suppose? I mean, after all these years – thirty or so, I suppose – should she decide she wanted to see you?'

'It's more than forty years, actually, and I really have no idea. In fact, Charles didn't say *she* wanted to see me. Perhaps it was his idea.'

'I'd ask him. Will you go to the funeral? You'll see him then, won't you?'

'Oh, yes, he's offered to give me a lift. Funny, I haven't even met him, yet.' Fran leaned down to put her mug on the hearth. 'But I shall speak to him when I go back tomorrow, because I just have this feeling that everything's not quite – right.'

'Because of the dream? And the feeling in her room?'

Fran frowned. 'I suppose so. And I want to find out about this Barbara Denver, who Charles says

46

is a sort of cousin.'

'Barbara Denver? Good grief!' Libby sat forward.

Fran looked up, surprised. 'Do you know her?'

'We all know Barbara Denver. And her precious son.'

'Great!' Fran settled more comfortably into her armchair. 'Tell me all about them.'

Libby stared up at the ceiling. 'She was small and pale. Fair hair and slightly buck teeth. Wore her hair in a single plait. Terribly neat. Barbara Stone, she was then.'

'You've known her a long time, then?'

Libby nodded. 'Known *of* her. Since we moved to Kent. She modelled for a bit, but not very successfully. Still, it brought her into contact with old man Denver, and she would never have met him otherwise.'

'So who was he?'

Libby finally lit her cigarette and blew out a long ribbon of smoke with relish. 'Old man Denver owned Blagstock House. 'Course, he wasn't so old, then, but he was a good twenty years older than Barbara. He was something big in the city.'

'So how did he meet Barbara?'

'His wife organised a charity fashion show.'

'His wife?' Fran was surprised.

'Oh, yes, he was married then. Large committee woman. Did a lot for charity. That's why she organised the fashion show, and, as a local girl, Barbara was included.'

'So what happened?' Fran prompted, after Libby had fallen silent. 'Did she divorce him, the wife?'

'Eventually. He got Barbara pregnant.'

47

'Heavens! So he did the decent thing?'

Libby shook her head. 'Not really. He tried to keep it quiet – offered Barbara money for an abortion, you know the sort of thing. But she wouldn't have it and kicked up a terrible fuss. I don't know the details, but the upshot was that he moved out of Blagstock House and set up home with Barbara. His wife divorced him after the statutory two years, or whatever it was then, took a huge settlement and moved to France.'

'So they moved back into Blagstock House? With the baby, presumably.'

'Young Paul, yes. And then she insisted he married her.'

'Which he did. And is he still alive?'

'Good lord, no!' Libby laughed. 'She wore him out years ago. The trouble was that his first wife took such an enormous settlement that he only just managed to keep Blagstock House going. I gather Barbara had a little money when he died, but that's gone now.'

'They still live there, then? She hasn't sold it?'

'No. I haven't heard of Barbara Denver for years. But I suppose she might sell up to one of the conglomerates. The house is ideal for a hotel. I'm surprised Paul hasn't already done it.'

'The son?'

Libby nodded. 'An estate agent.' She sniffed. 'That's where the last of the money went, or so the story goes. He used to work for one of the local firms and then decided to set up on his own, so Barbara funded him.'

Fran nodded slowly. 'So son Paul would be in an ideal position to sell Blagstock House to the right people.'

'Not really.' Libby threw her cigarette end into the fireplace. 'His business never took off. He liked the trappings of the business rather than the business itself, or so I gather. The lunches and the golf club. That sort of thing. He's still got a small shop in Nethergate, but it isn't often open.'

'Well, I suppose they'll come in for something from old Auntie. Don't know what the relationship is, though.'

'Ask Charles.' Libby stood up. 'More tea, vicar?'

'No thanks, I'm still awash with lager from lunchtime. And anyway, forget all my stuff, you still haven't told me what happened with Ben.'

Libby hesitated, then sat down again, fumbling absently for another cigarette.

'I think we got it together as a sort of what-do-you-call-it, a reaffirmation of life. After all the traumas. For a few days after the arrest we were inseparable.' She smiled wistfully. 'It was fantastic. Especially with me looking like an upholstered rugby ball. I haven't felt like that since I was – ooh, I don't know – in my twenties. And then it all began to fade away. Family, mainly. After all, his poor family were right in the thick of it all. He was at home with his mother and his sister more and more, because his father took a turn for the worse.'

'And how is he now?'

'Old Gregory, or Ben?'

'Well, both, but I meant Gregory.'

'He's recovered, but for how long I don't know. Susan's still living there, so after a bit Ben moved back to his own flat in Canterbury.'

'And what? Nothing? Doesn't he phone? Take

49

you out?'

Libby frowned down at her hands still holding an unlit cigarette.

'I think I said a few Wrong Things.'

'Oh, Lib! And he withdrew again? Like before?'

'Yes.' Libby sighed and looked up. 'Pete and Harry say he's uptight because of the family situation, but Pete's got more cause for that even than Ben, hasn't he? And he's not uptight.'

'I know, but he's got a solid relationship with Harry. And by the way, what about Pete's mother? And James?'

'James is back in his flat, and his mother's back up at Steeple Farm with a paid companion. I think Pete and James are paying for her between them, but there's talk of selling the farm and putting her in somewhere like the place Uncle Lenny was in.'

'Not like The Laurels, then.'

'Well, no, that sounds more like a nursing home. I saw Uncle Lenny's, remember. It was like a luxury hotel.'

'And is he still down here living with Mrs Carpenter?'

Libby grinned. 'Yes, happy as a couple of newlyweds, they are, bless them.'

'Well, that's good. And after all, when the trial's over, everything'll be forgotten and you can go back to normal.'

'Whatever normal is,' said Libby. 'Don't forget, I didn't really get to know Ben until *The Hop Pickers* was in rehearsal, and things weren't really normal then, were they?'

'As I didn't know you until then, either, how do

I know?'

Libby sighed. 'Oh, well, I've probably blown it, anyway. At one time I thought I had a chance. But, as we've both discovered, being over forty reduces your chances of romantic entanglement by about 95%.'

'It's being over *fifty*, dear, and an upholstered rugby ball or, like me, a bolster on legs.' Fran smiled sadly. 'The older men get the more they want to mate with young female perfection. It's something to do with perpetuating the genes. It isn't their fault.'

'Then we don't stand a chance.'

'Not unless we find men whose intelligence overrides their survival instinct.'

'It couldn't possibly be that men are taken in by a pretty face and figure and find it flattering to be with a younger woman?'

Fran shook her head. 'It pains me to say it, but no. Look at how many men whom no one would believe would leave their wives or have affairs suddenly fall head over heels with a girl young enough to be their daughter? It happened to Mr Denver – whatever his name was. It happened to my husband.'

Libby snorted. 'Old Robert Denver didn't fall in love with Barbara. He just wanted a quick bonk.'

'Shame she got caught, then. His first wife could have put up with a quick bonk. It's the falling in love that you can't forgive.'

'I know. And it still bloody hurts, doesn't it?'

Fran sighed. 'Even if you know why it happened, it still hurts.'

'Hey, you're not saying your break-up was your

fault, surely?' Libby looked indignant.

'I couldn't cope with real life, Libby. I was a hopeless wife and mother. I don't really blame him.' Fran stood up. 'Anyway, that's enough of that. What time are we going to The Pink Geranium? Have I got time to have a bath?'

'Help yourself,' said Libby. 'They won't be busy tonight, so we can tip up at any time.'

Peter, who had been slightly suspicious of Fran when Ben had brought her down to help during what Harry referred to as 'The Troubles', was surprisingly pleased to see her.

'She was worried about coming,' warned Libby, 'so be nice.'

'I'm always nice.' Peter looked down his patrician nose at her and tossed back the lock of fair hair that fell rather limply across his brow.

'Oh, yeah?' Harry, in chef's whites, appeared behind them. 'I could tell them a thing or two.' He grinned down at Libby. 'Where is she, then?'

'Over there on the sofa looking scared,' said Libby.

Harry surged across the restaurant and took Fran in an enthusiastic bear hug. Peter followed, to give Fran an affectionate peck on the cheek as Harry released her.

'Lovely to see you,' he said, settling her on the sofa in the window.

'Donna! Bottle of red wine over here,' called Harry. 'On the house,' he added to Libby, who raised her eyebrows at him.

'So, just down for a visit?' Peter sat on the arm next to Fran, while Libby wriggled backwards into the other end of the sofa.

'My aunt just died. She lived near Nethergate,' explained Fran, accepting a glass of red wine from Donna, Harry's uncomplaining assistant.

'Oh, I'm sorry,' said Peter, patting her shoulder.

'No, I didn't really know her. Hadn't seen her for years.' Fran looked uncomfortable, a familiar look to Libby, associated with their adventures during the production of Peter's play *The Hop Pickers*. With a stab of guilt, she realised she hadn't really told Fran anything during their conversation that afternoon. Perhaps she should have made things a bit clearer, if only to prevent Fran putting her foot in it. After all, Peter's mother Millie was almost bound to come up in conversation–

'How's your mother, Peter?' asked Fran, right on cue.

'As well as can be expected,' said Peter, smoothly, 'back at Steeple Farm. I'm sure Libby told you. And now, would you like to order?'

When Harry and Peter had left them alone with two large menus, Fran gave Libby an apologetic glance.

'Sorry. Did I upset the atmosphere?'

'Not at all. You were bound to ask him, it was only good manners. I'd give Susan a miss, though, if I were you.'

'You mean, don't ask about her?'

'Yes. Poor woman. It isn't her fault, but it tends to be a bit of a thorn in the flesh, if you see what I mean.'

Fran did see. Ben's sister Susan would be a reminder of the events stirred up by *The Hop Pickers* that had led to murder a few months previously.

'Steer clear of all of it, then,' said Fran, peering at the menu. 'Can't remember, what was Hongo Quesadillas?'

It hadn't been as bad as she'd expected, she thought later, as she took a last look at the view from Libby's spare room window. Much to Fran's relief, the conversation stayed away from family and murder, and Peter, deep in writing a brand new pantomime for the Oast House Theatre, merely asked a few technical questions regarding length and timing, which caused Libby to go off into paroxysms of lewd laughter. There was no mention of Aunt Eleanor or Barbara and Paul Denver and Fran's uncomfortable mental investigator had been lulled into somnolence with red onion tart, accompanied by an excellent Sancerre spirited from an unnamed source by the heavenly Harry.

Unfortunately, the Sancerre had worn off a bit and the mental investigator had woken up. A loop tape in her head repeatedly played the dream, but what made Fran sit down suddenly on the bed with a gasp was the addition of two more faces, as clear as if they stood before her, neither of which had she seen before. As her breathing slowed to normal and her heartbeat stopped sending messages to outlying parts, she realised that it must be her overactive imagination supplying pictures of Barbara and Paul Denver. After all, it could just as easily have thrown up the faces of Nurse Warner, Nurse Redding or Marion Headlam, but she had actually seen them in the flesh. Barbara and Paul were so far still, if not figments, existing only in her imagination.

Suppressing an almost irresistible desire to go downstairs and top up the Sancerre with a large slug of whisky, Fran climbed into bed and put her head under the pillow.

## Chapter Five

### 1964

Margaret turned from the mirror and took a deep breath.

'Fran, are you ready?'

Fran appeared in the kitchen doorway. 'Yes, Mum.'

'Let's have a look at you, then.' Margaret pulled her daughter further into the room.

'Socks, Fran? I thought you wanted to wear your new stockings?'

'The suspenders are uncomfortable, Mum.' Fran pulled a face. 'Couldn't I have a roll-on like yours?'

'You're only twelve, darling! I've given in on stockings, but that's as far as it goes.'

Fran pulled a face. 'Socks, then. Anyway, they look better with my sandals, don't they?'

Margaret looked down at the maroon sandals. Frank had bought them. She looked up hastily, smoothing down her cotton skirt.

'Of course they do. And you look very nice in that dress, too. Green suits you.'

Fran stroked the satiny finish of the dress. 'I like

it. Thanks, Mum.' She reached up and kissed Margaret's cheek. 'You're really clever.'

'Come on, then. We'll be late if we're not careful.' Margaret picked up her handbag and gloves from the kitchen table and led the way out of the flat. It was high summer in Mountville Road, and the huge lime trees were dusty and lifeless. She turned right and began the long walk towards the High Street, where they were to catch the bus.

'Why couldn't we go in the car with Uncle Frank?' asked Fran, trailing along behind her mother.

'Because he's the bridegroom. You can't go in the car with the bridegroom. There wouldn't have been room, anyway. Mr Wallace was with him.'

'Well, I wouldn't have liked to squash up against Mr Wallace.' Fran wrinkled her nose. 'I really, really don't like him.'

Margaret sighed. 'And you certainly let it show,' she said. 'Try and be more polite when you meet him today.'

'I don't know why he had to be Uncle Frank's best man. You'd have thought he could have had anybody. Why couldn't he have had you?'

'Because they don't have "best women", Fran. You know that perfectly well.'

'But you're his best friend. At least, I thought you were, till he met the Elephant.'

'Stop calling her that, Fran. One of these days you're going to say it to her face.'

'Serve her right for marrying Uncle Frank.' Fran looked warily at her mother's set face, wondering if she'd gone too far.

'It's hardly appropriate, anyway. She's tiny. And you mind your manners. I don't want everyone thinking how badly I've brought you up.'

'Sorry, Mum.' Fran slipped her hand into her mother's. 'And you've done a brilliant job of bringing me up. So's Uncle Frank.'

'Uncle Frank hasn't actually brought you up,' said Margaret, her smile wry as she looked into her daughter's eager face.

'He helped, though. Living upstairs.'

'Of course he did.' Margaret gave Fran's hand a little squeeze. 'So we'd better not be late for his wedding, had we? Come on, or we'll miss the bus.'

It wasn't the fairy-tale wedding Fran would have liked. For a start, the bride was wearing a little suit not unlike the one her mother was wearing, although Margaret had made her own and Eleanor's was obviously shop bought and much more expensive. They both had little boxy jackets with enlarged peter-pan collars, though Margaret's skirt was full and feminine, whereas Eleanor's was straight and sophisticated. Eleanor wore a little pill-box hat with a bit of blue veil matching her suit, and carried a prayer-book and a small sheaf of lilies. There were two brides-maids, one a girl of about her own age with long, straight, mousey hair and another younger girl with bright red curly hair and a scowl. They wore plain pink cotton dresses and white lace gloves. Fran had hoped she might be asked to be a bridesmaid, but seeing these two in their plain, uninspired outfits, she was glad she hadn't.

The reception was held in the church hall next door, and, as it was such a hot day, they were allowed to spill out into what Fran was told was the "garth" behind. The garth was just a large enclosed, grassy area, where someone had set up a wallpaper table with a variety of bottles and glasses.

'Bar's open, folks,' shouted Uncle Frank, as he appeared with his bride on his arm. 'On me.'

Fran found her mother a seat, then looked up to see a good-looking boy of about fourteen offering a tray.

'Wine or fruit cup?' he said.

'Thank you,' said Margaret. 'We'll have fruit cup.'

Fran would have liked to try the wine, but smiled at the boy anyway, and took two glasses of fruit cup.

'I'm Charles, Aunt Eleanor's nephew,' he said.

'I'm Margaret Bridges,' said Margaret, 'Frank's sister-in-law, and this is his niece, Frances.'

Charles politely offered his hand to them both. 'I hope I see you later, then,' he said, and moved away with his tray.

'Nice boy,' said Margaret, peering after him.

'Bit of a square,' said Fran.

'Because he has nice manners?' Margaret raised her eyebrows.

Fran shrugged. 'And his clothes.'

'I expect he's dressed in a suit because it's a wedding. Wasn't he one of the ushers?'

'Was he? I didn't notice,' said Fran, sipping her punch, which, predictably, was warm.

And then Uncle Frank was there, pushing his

bride in front of him, smiling at both of them.

'My three favourite girls,' he said, trying to sound hearty, but Fran knew him too well, and knew he was as uncomfortable as she and her mother were.

Eleanor, small, pale and fragile-looking, smiled tremulously. Fran saw her mother smile back and tried to do the same.

'I'm so pleased to have a sister,' said Eleanor, in a breathy little voice. 'And a new niece, of course.'

'Sister-in-law, actually,' said Frank. 'Margaret was married to Herbert.'

'Oh, I know, darling, but at least Frances is your real niece, isn't she?'

Frank winked at Fran. 'I hope so,' he said. 'Enjoying yourself, Franny?'

'Yes, thank you, Uncle.'

'Good, good,' he said, and taking her elbow, turned Eleanor away. 'Must circulate, you know.'

But he looked back at them as he walked away, and Fran saw his face. She looked at her mother, whose own face was as closed as she had ever seen it.

'We don't like Eleanor, do we?' she whispered.

Margaret looked as if she'd come back from a long way away. 'Not much. But we mustn't be rude.'

'No, you've said that already,' said Fran. 'But I'm going to hate having her in the house.'

'She won't be with us. She'll be with Uncle Frank in the upstairs flat. We'll hardly see her.'

'Does that mean we'll hardly see Uncle Frank, either?'

'Well, not as much. We can't expect to, can we?

Not now he's got a new family.'

'Family?' Fran was horrified. 'He's not going to have children, is he?'

'I don't know. Eleanor's older than me, but she's still able to have children, I'm sure. And most women want babies.' Margaret looked across at the happy couple, now the centre of a group whom she took to be Eleanor's family. She saw the boy Charles look across at Fran.

'Oh, Mum, I can't bear it.' Fran sank down on the grass at her mother's feet. 'Not babies. Uncle Frank's always had me.'

'He still will have,' said Margaret, patting her daughter's shoulder. 'Don't worry. Things are bound to change, but we'll cope.'

'Christmas won't be the same,' mourned Fran. 'He won't be with us, will he?'

Margaret sighed. 'No, darling, he won't.'

Fran looked across at the group of Eleanor's family. 'I hate them,' she said, 'and I hate it here, too. Can't we go home, now?'

'After the speeches,' said Margaret, who didn't look too happy herself.

'Why don't we know anyone here?' asked Fran, after a moment. 'Where are all Uncle Frank's friends?'

'Coming later, perhaps,' said Margaret, with another sigh.

Sure enough, a little later, Uncle Frank's friends from the Conservative Club and the golf club appeared, looking as uncomfortable as Margaret and Fran. They formed a circle round them and Fran felt more secure. Why Uncle Frank couldn't have chosen one of these nice men she'd known nearly all her life as a best man instead of that awful Wallace person, she couldn't think.

At last, Eleanor's father made a speech, Mr Wallace made a worse one and finally Uncle Frank said a few, a very few, words. Then they were free to go.

'Come on littl'un,' said Joe, the secretary of the Conservative Club. 'I'll give you and your mum a lift home. All right, Mrs Bridges?'

'Thanks, Joe,' said Margaret, smiling gratefully. 'Have you got room? I wasn't looking forward to the bus.'

'Got the Humber, haven't I? Plenty of room for me and the missus and you two. Come on then. Let's get cracking.'

'Shouldn't we have said goodbye to Uncle Frank?' whispered Fran, as they made their way through the church hall, where a quartet of ageing musicians were desperately trying to play a Cliff and The Shadows medley.

'Better to just slip out,' whispered back Margaret. 'We'll see him when he comes back from honeymoon, won't we?'

Fran felt undignified tears behind her eyes and a horrible lump in her throat. She nodded, unable to speak, and followed her mother out of the hall.

# Chapter Six

'Charles? It's Fran. I've just got back from The Laurels.' Fran eased off one shoe holding the receiver under her chin.

'Oh. Right.'

'And I'm sure I'm right.'

'What do you mean?'

'There's something wrong.'

Fran heard Charles sigh. 'Look, Fran, I was there, I told you. It was a perfectly normal death.'

'I know. But apparently there was somebody else there as well?'

'Yes, Barbara and Paul Denver. My cousin and her son. I told you.'

'Did you always go together?' Fran finally kicked off the other shoe with a sigh of relief.

'No – it was because it was Eleanor's birthday.'

'Did you take her a present?'

'Yes, I took flowers. I don't know what Barbara took. Why?'

Fran thought for a moment. 'Just wondered. I don't really know much about Eleanor, do I?'

Charles laughed. 'Or me, come to that. I could have been anybody, phoning the other day.'

'Oh, no. I knew who you were.' Fran had been quite certain as soon as she heard his voice. 'And we had met before, after all.'

'Forty years ago, yes.' There was a pause. 'Look, why don't we meet and I can fill you in on the details. It would be nice to see you again.'

'We'll see each other at the funeral, won't we? You offered me a lift.'

'And what about meeting before then?'

'When did you have in mind?'

'Are you too tired this evening?'

Fran looked at the clock. 'No – but I've only just got in and I haven't eaten yet.'

'Dinner then. There's a very nice little bistro near you. I've been there several times.'

'The Poule au Pot? Yes, it is good.' Fran didn't say that she had never been able to afford to eat there, but had gazed longingly through the windows on several occasions. 'What time?'

'Half past seven? Shall I collect you?'

'No, I'll meet you there.' Fran scowled at the cracked lino and the wheezing gas fire.

'Fine. Seven thirty then. Will we recognise each other after all this time?'

'No idea,' said Fran cheerfully. 'Should be interesting, shouldn't it?'

'Very.' Charles laughed. 'See you later.'

Fran put down the receiver and went to the window. It was dark now, and the wet pavements were gleaming with reflected light. Through the ill-fitting frame came the hiss of tyres on the road, the sound of returning workers at the end of a long day. What were they going home to, wondered Fran. Family gathered around the television? Children glued to computer screens? A microwaved meal while the other partner rushed off to aerobics or creative writing classes? She smiled and drew the thin cotton curtains across the glass. Or were they going to have a bath in a rusting tub and get ready for a meal out with a cousin they hardly remembered?

Meanwhile, the sudden emergence into her life of long-lost relatives, even dead ones, was a welcome diversion. And a change from beans on toast for supper.

The Poule au Pot was a hangover from the late sixties. It still had red and white checked table-cloths, candles stuffed into straw covered Chianti bottles and a menu redolent of the era. Prawn cocktail, beef bourguignon and Black Forest gateau had been retained at the behest of the clientele, despite several changes of ownership and the fads and fancies of fashionable cooks and cooking. In fact, Fran knew from reading the magazines while she lurked in the paper shop, it was coming back into fashion, as, indeed, her rather down-at-heel area of London was itself. Nowhere would escape if it boasted a London postcode, which unfortunately meant that the prices were rising almost daily. When her land-lord caught on, she knew she would no longer be able to afford even the Betjeman flat.

Charles was sitting at a table at the side of the room, underneath a large and somewhat roman-ticised depiction of French peasants disporting themselves in a cornfield. His grey head – grey! – was bent over a menu.

'Hello, Charles.' She sat down opposite him as he tried to struggle to his feet. 'Don't get up.'

He subsided and sat back in his bentwood chair. 'Fran,' he said. 'You haven't changed much.'

'Rubbish. I was a child then, and now I look

like my mother.' She looked at him consideringly. 'You've changed. Your hair's grey.'

He looked amused. 'You're very direct, aren't you?'

'Not always.' Fran looked down at her hands. 'I can dissemble beautifully if I have to.'

'Oh? And you feel you don't have to with me?'

Fran looked up and grinned. 'I don't do I? I knew that. But I did at The Laurels.'

'Before we go into that, have a look at the menu.' Charles handed it over. 'What would you like to drink?'

When they had given their order and both had a glass of a robust red vin de table in front of them, Charles started again.

'Now. Tell me all about The Laurels.'

Fran took a sip of wine and leaned back in her chair. 'Do you mean tell you exactly what I did there and who I met?'

'Yes. And try and explain again why you went.'

'That's difficult.' Fran frowned into her glass. 'It just came over me when you phoned. I felt suffocated. And then there was this absolute conviction that I had to go there. That's all I can say. And then...' she looked up, 'I got the same feeling again. When I was in her room.'

'Which feeling?'

'The suffocating feeling. I made a fool of myself I'm afraid, but they put it down to shock and grief. I felt a complete fraud.'

'Start at the beginning.' Charles leaned forward and rested his chin on his hands. 'I'm fascinated.'

Fran told him everything from her arrival at The Laurels to her departure, including her

65

dream on the train. When she had finished and the waiter had served their respective starters of pâté and soup, Charles poured more wine into their glasses.

'Did you say that Barbara had cleared the room?'

'Yes.' Fran spooned up some onion soup. 'Except for a few dresses in the wardrobe.'

'The bureau wasn't there?' Charles was frowning.

Fran shook her head and swallowed. 'Nothing. Even the television belonged to The Laurels.'

Charles stared absently at the French Peasants above him. 'No bureau. That was quick.'

'No bureau.' Fran put down her spoon. 'Is it important?'

'Her will was in the bureau.'

'Ah. Fairly important, then.'

Charles shrugged and spread pâté onto a corner of toast. 'I expect there's a copy at her solicitors' office – whoever they are.'

'Don't you know?'

'No, I don't, although I ought to. The solicitors wrote to me when she told me years ago she'd made me her executor. I think she was old-fashioned enough not to trust Barbara because she was a woman and at the time, Paul was too young.'

Fran pushed away her soup plate and rested her chin on her hands. 'Is there much to leave?'

'The Mountville Road house.' Charles looked up at her and grinned. 'Where you grew up.'

Fran raised her eyebrows. 'Did it still belong to Uncle Frank, then? Old bugger. Must be worth a

66

fortune now.'

'A three-storey Victorian semi in a sought after inner London suburb? I should say so.' Charles was crumbling his last slice of toast. Fran gave him a shrewd look.

'So that's why you're anxious about the will? To see what she's left you?'

Faint colour appeared along Charles's cheek-bones. 'Not entirely.' He sat back in his chair and picked up his wineglass. 'I'm the executor. I need to know what I've got to execute.'

'So, do this Barbara and Paul get anything?'

'I would imagine so. Eleanor always treated Barbara and me equally. She spoilt Paul, though.'

'You sound bitter.' Fran topped up her own wine glass.

'She didn't do anything for my daughter. I suppose I am.'

Fran was surprised. 'I didn't know you had a daughter.'

He looked up with a smile. 'Kate.'

'Goodness.' She chuckled. 'What a lot I don't know.'

'Have you any children?'

Fran nodded. 'Jeremy's in New York being terribly high-powered and Chrissie's married. Lucy was married, and has two children, Rachel and Tom.'

'Lucky you.' He looked up as a waiter appeared with an armful of vegetable dishes. Their empty starter plates were whisked away and Fran was soon inhaling the fragrant beef bourguignon in the rustic *marmite* before her.

'Do you know Nethergate well?' Fran speared a

piece of meat and closed her eyes as she put it into her mouth. Delicious.

'Very well. That's where our side of the family come from. I lived in Steeple Mount when I was a child and went to school in Nethergate until I was eleven.'

'Steeple Mount? Near Steeple Martin?' Fran's eyes were wide. 'I don't believe it.'

He grinned and Fran noticed how his blue eyes seemed to grow warmer. Ridiculous. She'd always scoffed at the idea of the eyes containing expression. It was merely the arrangement of the skin around them.

'It's the Nether valley. The river Wytch runs through the valley from Steeple Martin to Steeple Mount, then on past Up Nethergate at the top of the cliffs and comes out at Nethergate at the bottom.'

'That's where I met my friend Libby yesterday. I didn't see much of it, though.'

'It's lovely.' He grinned at her. 'Pure storybook stuff. Sand and tea shops and caves. Just the place for the grandchildren.'

'I didn't think children were into that sort of stuff these days.' Fran helped herself to more broccoli. 'I thought they just wanted theme parks and computer games.'

'You'd be surprised. Anyway, the adults love the nostalgia of it all. The whole place is in a bit of a time warp – you must have noticed.'

'I know. Libby lives in Steeple Martin. That's where I stayed last night. I was only saying to her that she lives in a Golden Age detective story.'

Charles looked slightly puzzled.

'Anyway, that's why you put her down there instead of London, is it?' Fran sat back to make room for another mouthful.

'That and the fact that Barbara and Paul live near there.'

'So I understand. And my friend Libby knows them. Or of them, anyway.'

'Really? Coincidence.'

'Isn't it?' Fran pushed a pea around her plate. She didn't want to get in to Libby's descriptions of the Denver family.

'Yes.' Charles put his knife and fork neatly together. 'So now you've caught up on the situation you can tell me what's been happening to you since you grew up.'

Fran told him. He was surprisingly easy to talk to, despite the fact that he looked more like a typical city gent than the sort of person she normally consorted with. And older. She was used to younger people. Chrissie would approve of him, she thought. Chrissie had always hoped that she would suddenly morph herself into the blue rinse and Barbour jacket suitable for a putative grandmother and Charles matched that image.

'So.' They had ordered coffee and Charles sat back, stirring his thoughtfully. 'You've told me everything except the reason for these suffocating feelings. Presumably you're a – what, a psychic?'

Fran bridled. 'I'm nothing of the sort. I don't know what all that was about.' She took a deep breath. 'And it was very embarrassing, let me tell you.'

'Then how do you explain this suffocating

69

feeling? Or how you knew I was the genuine article when I called you?'

'Intuition?' She looked up. 'Instinct? I don't know. The children always called them "Mother's Moments".'

'So you've had them before?'

Fran shifted uncomfortably in her chair. 'Sort of. Just – you know – telling the children to be careful just before something happened. Or knowing who was on the phone before I answered it. Sort of thing that happens to everybody.'

'Hmm.' Charles was still stirring his coffee. 'And it was because of one of these "Moments" that you went hotfoot off to The Laurels.'

'Sounds silly, doesn't it?' Fran laughed, embarrassed. 'I expect it was guilt, like that Mrs Headlam said.'

'Nice woman, Marion Headlam.'

'Nice?' Fran frowned. 'I suppose she was all right. Terribly mercenary, I would have thought.'

'Oh, undoubtedly. But good at what she does. Attractive, as well.'

Fran hitched a shoulder. 'Do you think so?' she asked coolly.

'Oh, yes. Very well groomed.' Charles gazed up at the Peasants again.

Fran put her coffee cup down sharply and realised that he was staring at something distinctly Rabelaisian behind a haystack. He looked back at her and quirked an eyebrow. She blushed.

'Yes, well,' she said, clearing her throat. 'You'll see her again at the funeral. Apparently she attends all clients' funerals.'

'I suppose I'll have to sort that out, won't I?'

Charles looked worried. 'I think it's my job, isn't it? As executor?'

Fran stared. 'How would I know? I've never been one. I organised my mother's funeral, but that was simple. She was living with me when she died.'

'Perhaps I'd better go down there. Oh, God, I knew this wasn't going to be simple.' He scowled and called for the bill.

'When will you go?' Fran picked up her bag and dropped the complimentary mint chocolates inside.

'Tomorrow, I suppose.' Charles sighed and signed the cheque with a flourish.

'Could I come with you? I'd like to meet Barbara.'

Charles looked surprised. 'Why?'

'I don't know. We could ask about the bureau.'

'We?'

'Well, you could, then. Find the will.'

Charles laughed and stood up. 'Well, perhaps you can have one of your moments and find it for us. I never was shown the secret drawer.'

Fran beamed with anticipation. 'Goodness, a secret drawer. More storybook stuff. I can't wait!'

# Chapter Seven

I really must get an upstairs phone, thought Libby, as once again she struggled out of bed and tripped over Sidney to try and beat the answerphone to it.

'Charles is driving me down again this morning.'

Libby sat down on the bottom step and tried to unglue her eyelids.

'It's very early, Fran.' She pushed Sidney's nose out of her ear.

'Sorry, but we're leaving soon. He's got a meeting with Marion Headlam about the funeral. And we're going to see Barbara Denver.'

'Really? Will you be able to come by here on your way home and tell me all about it?'

'Charles will want to get back.'

'Well, I know *that*. Could you bring a bag with you? Then he could drop you off and you could stay down until the funeral.'

There was a pause. 'I suppose I could,' said Fran slowly. 'It's quite a good idea, isn't it? Are you sure you wouldn't mind?'

'Course I wouldn't. I've got Bel and Ad coming at some time in the next few weeks, but not imminently. And Sidney misses you.'

Fran laughed. 'OK. I'm sure Charles won't mind making the detour. He said he wanted to meet you, anyway.'

'Did he? What's he like?'

'Very city gent-ish. But nice. Lots of grey hair.'

'Like Ben's?'

'Not a bit like Ben's. More mane-like.'

Libby sighed. 'Lovely.'

'Libby, stop it. Now, do you want me to ring you when I know roughly what time we'll be arriving?'

'I suppose it would be as well. After all, you don't know what exciting things I might get up to, do you?'

After Fran had rung off, Libby hauled herself upright with the aid of the banister rail, tripped over Sidney and staggered through to the kitchen.

As she waited for the kettle to boil, her thoughts returned to Ben. What *had* gone wrong? The relationship had certainly got off to a dodgy start when they were rather thrown together during rehearsals for Peter's play, but she'd really thought they were on to a good thing eventually. But her own questioning of everyone's motives and basic insecurity had obviously pushed Ben away when she should have been there offering support. She sighed and poured water onto a tea-bag, wondering if there was anything she could do to retrieve the situation.

The smack of the cat flap signalled Sidney's departure on the business of the day, and Libby strolled into the conservatory to look at the latest view of Nethergate propped up on the easel. Guy Wolfe, she thought. Another one who seemed charmed by Fran. As Ben had been, she was sure. Ben had denied it, true, and proved quite conclusively that he was very attracted to Libby herself, but Libby remembered her insidious jealousy and hoped she wouldn't be dog-in-the-manger enough to resent Guy's attention to Fran. For Guy was her friend, and there had at one time been the suggestion there could be something more between them, but at the time Libby was still recovering from the break-up of her marriage and nervous of forming any sort of relationship with the opposite sex. Peter and Harry had helped her over that hurdle and Guy had retreated to the background of her life, emerging now and then to buy some more paintings and give her self-confidence a boost.

And what about Aunt Eleanor? Fran had had strange intuitions about the goings-on last spring, all of which had turned out to be correct, so was she right about this? Was there something "not right"? And if so, what was it? Surely not murder again.

A shopping trip to stock up the larder was obviously called for if she was going to have a house guest, and much as she preferred to use the village shops when possible, the occasional sortie to the supermarket was inevitable. Putting murder out of her mind, Libby went upstairs to dress.

Wandering round the aisles an hour later with only a newspaper and a bunch of flowers in her trolley, Libby became aware of the advisability of always putting on make-up no matter how trivial one's outing.

'Hello, Lib,' said Ben.

He was leaning on the end of a freezer cabinet

wearing jeans and a T-shirt, his short grey hair as neat as ever.

Libby felt dampness break out all along her hairline as her heart rate accelerated. She'd noticed these unfortunate teenagerish manifestations before when suddenly confronted with Ben, and they didn't get any easier.

'Hi,' she said.

'Haven't seen you for ages.' Ben looked at her intently.

'Well, you moved back to your flat, didn't you? You haven't been in the village much.'

'My mother had her hands full with my sister and Dad.'

'It's not been easy for any of you,' said Libby.

'Or you.' Ben gave a small forced smile. There was a short silence.

'I'm sorry–' They both spoke together, then stopped.

Libby laughed.

'Well, I *am* sorry,' she said. 'Your turn.'

'I'm sorry, too.' Ben stood away from the freezer and looked down in to her trolley. 'I got a bit emotionally unbalanced for a time.'

'Gee, thanks.' Libby felt her insides contract with mortification.

He looked up quickly. 'No, I didn't mean that, Lib. Oh, lord, I'm putting my foot in it again. I meant afterwards. The family kept coming first, and it was all so awful...'

'I know, but I was a bit – well – insensitive about it. I'm the one who put my foot in it.'

'How about we start again, then? Come to Harry's tonight with me.'

Libby's heart jumped. 'Oh, Ben, I'd love to, but I can't. Fran's coming down.'

'Oh.' Ben looked nonplussed. 'Well, couldn't she come, too?'

'She was down the night before last and we went there then.'

'Ah.' Ben nodded and looked down into the trolley again. 'How long's she staying?'

'Her aunt's just died and she'll stay until the funeral, I think.'

Ben raised his eyebrows. 'Did the aunt live near here?'

'In a home just outside Nethergate. I gather that part of the family came from round here originally.'

'Coincidence. She never mentioned it before, did she?'

'I don't think she knew before. It's all come as a bit of a shock to her.'

'Well, how about dinner on Friday, then? That Thai place we went to before? Or we could go to the pub. Their food's got a lot better, apparently.'

Libby smiled. 'OK, thanks. I'd like that. If Fran's here, I'm sure she won't mind.'

'The pub?'

'Yes, please. I think I'd prefer to be out of Pete and Harry's sight line, and it means you don't have to drive all the way out from Canterbury and back again with me. Or I could drive in and meet you, I suppose.'

'And not have a drink? Heavens above! Wouldn't think of it.' He grinned at her, the old teasing Ben once more. 'And I'll stay at the

Manor for the night so I can drink, too.'

Libby just stopped herself from saying 'You can stay with me.'

'See you about seven thirty on Friday, then?' He leaned forward and kissed her cheek. 'And lets hope nothing happens this time.'

'Like murder, you mean,' she said, and could have bitten her tongue out.

He smiled again, a little crookedly. 'Yes, like murder.'

Marion Headlam looked surprised as Charles and Fran walked in through the front door of The Laurels.

'Well, hello again,' she said. 'Mrs Castle, isn't it? I didn't expect to see you so soon.'

Fran tried not to look as sheepish as she felt. 'I just thought I'd keep Charles company,' she said weakly.

'And we're going on to see Mrs Denver,' added Charles. 'There are things to sort out.'

'Of course.' Marion Headlam nodded, not a hair on her perfectly groomed head dislodged by the movement. 'You'll want to sort out the funeral.'

'Exactly,' said Charles. 'Have any arrangements been made?'

'Oh, yes. Mrs Denver organised it.'

'Oh? I thought as the executor – and her power-of-attorney–' Charles was now looking exceedingly grumpy.

'I'm sorry, Mr Wade, but I dealt mostly with Mrs Denver, as you know.'

'I signed all your cheques.'

Marion Headlam smiled sweetly. 'Yes, Mr Wade, and, of course, I shall send you the final account.'

Charles and Fran both looked taken aback.

'Already?' said Charles.

'We are a business, Mr Wade. Naturally, we won't pressure you at this sad time, but we have a waiting list for that room.'

'I understood my cousin had cleared it of my aunt's possessions, so you could let it out right now, surely.'

'Not completely cleared, Mr Wade. There are some clothes left. Perhaps, as you're here, you and Mrs Castle could take care of that now?'

Charles opened his mouth, looking put out, and Fran rushed into the breach.

'That might be sensible,' she said. 'Of course. Come on, Charles.'

Marion Headlam left them alone in Aunt Eleanor's room.

'Bit of a cheek,' said Charles, as soon as the door had closed.

'No, it isn't Charles.' Fran went to the wardrobe, where she'd noticed the few clothes last time. 'You just said you were the executor. She's every right to ask you to take stuff away. And as there isn't much of it left and you live in London, best do it while you're here. It makes sense.'

Charles made a sound suspiciously like harrumph, and began to prowl round the room, picking things up and putting them down again. 'Barbara certainly did a thorough job,' he said eventually, as Fran continued to lay faded print dresses on the bed. 'But when did she do it? She left when I did, I'm certain of that, and she seemed too shocked to have come back the same day. And you were here the next day.'

'She must have come in the morning. I didn't get here until the afternoon.' Struck by a thought, she swung round to face him. 'And how come the funeral was arranged so quickly?'

'The efficient Barbara obviously did *that* the next morning, too. What I can't understand, is why she didn't phone me first. I was the one with power-of-attorney, and she knew I was the executor.'

'She probably thought she was doing you a favour. After all, she was the one visiting regularly, wasn't she? And her son?'

'I couldn't visit regularly. I live in London.'

'Exactly.' Fran began folding clothes. 'You're operating on a double standard, here, Charles. And what did you say to me last night? You didn't know what to do about the funeral. Well, here it is, all done for you, and you're still complaining.'

Charles looked away and went to stand by the french windows.

'You're right,' he said, 'I'm being stupid.' He swung back. 'I'm sorry I'm behaving badly in front of my long-lost cousin.'

Fran grinned. 'Oh, don't mind me. And I'm not exactly a cousin, anyway, am I?'

He grinned back. 'That's a relief.. Couldn't stand another Barbara.'

'What are we going to put these in? Shall I go and ask for a black bin bag?' Fran moved to the door.

'I'll go. I probably need to make my peace with Mrs Headlam,' said Charles, and went.

Fran went to the french windows and looked out at the neatly manicured grounds. Nothing was to be seen except fields in the distance, and a few brownish dots she took to be cows. She supposed the road ran somewhere behind the hedge in the middle distance, and, as if to prove her point, the roof of a car appeared skimming along the top of it.

Since they'd come in to the room, she'd been waiting for a repeat of the suffocating feeling, but nothing had happened. She told herself this meant she'd been imagining it before, but didn't really believe it. Something had happened, and possibly in this room. Which of course, it had. Aunt Eleanor had died here, and probably many other occupants, too.

Charles came back with a bin bag. 'She's most grateful,' he said.

'I bet she is,' said Fran, as she began to slide the garments in to the bag. 'Nothing else you can see, is there?'

Charles ran his hand along the sides of the wardrobe and inside the drawers. 'No. No suspicious bits of paper with cryptic messages. Your magic moment must have been wrong.'

'I was just thinking that. You see, I told you it wasn't reliable.'

They loaded the bin bag into the boot of Charles's car and said goodbye to Marion Headlam, who saw them go with a hint of relief showing on her professional face.

Blagstock House turned out to be a grey stone

building with ambitions to be a castle, set at the bottom of a gravel sweep depressingly bordered by laurels and other gloomy shrubs of Victorian taste. Plenty of room here to hide little old ladies in winceyette nighties.

Fran recognised Barbara Denver from Libby's description. Smallish, her fawn-coloured hair smooth against her head and in a neat pleat at the back, her clothes had the look seen at point-to-points and upmarket beauty counters. This was somebody who wouldn't take kindly to poverty. Fran tried to imagine her buying her linen skirt in a charity shop, and failed.

'Charles,' she said, with a slight smile, and offered her cheek to be kissed. 'And you must be our cousin Frances?'

'Please, just Fran.' Fran held out her hand. Looking vaguely surprised, Barbara shook it. 'And I was Uncle Frank's niece, really, not Aunt Eleanor's.'

'Oh, but we're still cousins.' Barbara ushered them into the hall, which could have been used as it stood for the set of a Victorian melodrama. The drawing room was slightly lighter, decorated mainly in shades of grey and eau-de-nil, which depressed Fran even further.

'Aunt's funeral,' began Charles, before he'd even sat down on the shiny silver sofa to which he'd been directed.

'Tea?' interrupted Barbara, indicating a tray set on a low stool. 'I'll just boil the kettle.'

Charles looked helplessly at Fran as she left the room. 'This isn't going to be easy.'

'No. And it's worse because I'm here. I

shouldn't be.'

'You wanted to be.'

Fran nodded and looked round the room. Even the weather had turned cloudy now, further increasing the depression factor. She tried to find some kind of intuitive reaction to it, but came to the conclusion that it was simply a dismal place altogether.

Barbara returned carrying a china teapot, placed it on the tray and sat down next to Charles on the sofa.

'You were saying?' she said.

'Mrs Headlam tells me you've arranged Aunt's funeral. You didn't tell me.'

'Oh, Charles, I'm sorry. But I saw Aunt regularly, so I assumed you would want me to do it.'

'Even so, you hadn't thought to inform me afterwards. 'How would I have known?'

'Paul was supposed to phone you from the office.'

Barbara had the grace to look a little discomfited. 'I'm sorry if he hasn't.'

'So what would you have done if I hadn't been there?'

Charles wasn't going to let this go, Fran saw.

'I – I – I don't know.' Barbara now looked worried. 'Goodness, how terrible.'

'Yes, isn't it. Perhaps you'd better check with young Paul that he's done anything else you asked him to do.'

'I will. I'll call him now.' She began to get up, but Charles put his hand on her arm.

'Leave it until after we've gone.' She sat down again.

'Now, the other thing is, her will. I know she kept it in her bureau, and you brought that away, didn't you?'

She looked even more downcast. 'Oh dear, was that wrong, too? I just thought Mrs Headlam would need the room cleared as soon as possible.'

'Barbara, I'm her executor, you know that.' Charles sounded exasperated. 'And I had power-of-attorney. None of this is strictly to do with you, you know. So fetch me the will and be done with it.'

She looked at him in silence for a moment. 'I can't,' she said. 'It wasn't there.'

'So you knew where it was kept, too?'

'Well, yes. She told everybody.'

Charles sighed and stood up. 'Let's have a look at the bureau, then.'

'I'm afraid you can't do that, either,' she said, now looking definitely uncomfortable. 'It's in Paul's office.'

'It's where?'

'Well, we didn't have room for it here. Some of her other stuff is there, too.'

'Barbara, you have no right to do any of this. You'd better organise young Paul to get that stuff taken up to Mountville Road as soon as possible.'

'You don't want any of it, surely,' she said, her eyes wide.

'That isn't the point,' he said. 'But I see that you might have done. Or Paul.'

'That's not a very nice thing to say.' Barbara was indignant.

'It wasn't a very nice thing to do, was it? Come on, Fran, we'll get off. What's the name of the funeral director?'

Fran could see Barbara didn't want to tell him, but knew she had no choice.

'Stallwood and Stallwood in Nethergate,' she said. 'They do all The Laurels funerals.'

'Nice for them,' said Charles. 'Right, Fran, next stop Stallwood and Stallwood.'

'We never had any tea,' said Fran as they set off in a spray of gravel to drive into Nethergate.

'What an irritating woman,' said Charles. 'Didn't want her bloody tea.'

'I could see that,' said Fran, mildly. 'So now we're going to the undertakers and then to Paul's office, are we?'

Charles looked briefly at her, a startled look on his face. 'Yes. How did you know?'

'It was obvious. You don't trust either of them, so you want to make sure the bureau is in his office and not hidden away somewhere else.'

'Well, yes.'

'Let's get on with it, then,' said Fran, and settled back comfortably in her seat.

# Chapter Eight

The comfortable and caring lady at the reception desk of Stallwood and Stallwood was most accommodating and sympathetic. Mrs Denver was going to produce the death certificate and other paperwork, she understood. Perhaps Mr Wade would be kind enough to clarify the position as soon as he could?

Cross, Charles set off down Nethergate High Street to find Paul Denver's office, Fran trailing in his wake.

'Death certificate,' he said, 'that means she represented herself as next-of-kin. That's – that's – I don't know, falsification or something, isn't it? Criminal?'

'No idea,' panted Fran. 'How do we find out?'

'From this little bastard,' muttered Charles, pushing at the glass door of Denver and Denver, Estate Agents. It remained firmly shut.

'Never open, 'e isn't, love.' A female head popped out of the newsagent's next door. 'Nothing to sell, anyway.'

A glance in the window confirmed this. A couple of flyblown old pictures of houses with no prices attached were all that indicated the nature of the business.

'You don't know where we could find him?' Fran asked.

The woman shrugged. 'No idea, love. I don't

move in his circles.'

'Now where?' said Charles. 'Back to dear Barbara?'

'I suppose so. We need to find out about this death certificate business. Don't you have to provide some sort of proof of identity, or something?'

'What happened when your mother died?'

'Oh, I don't know. The doctor gave me the medical certificate and I took it to the registrar. There wasn't any question about who I was or anything. Perhaps it doesn't matter who does it?'

Charles looked thoughtful. 'Perhaps that's the case. And after all, if an old biddy dies somewhere like The Laurels there might not be a next-of-kin handy.'

'I think what we really need is the medical certificate.'

'I never thought of that.' Charles stopped suddenly. 'Who signed it? We all left Mrs Headlam in charge. I suppose she got a doctor in.'

'They'll have a regular doctor there, I should think. Do they have to have a medical certificate before the body can be moved?'

'Oh, lord, I don't know. Let's ring her.'

Back in the car, Charles found The Laurels' phone number on his mobile. Fran listened to his end of the conversation.

'I'm sorry to trouble you again, Mrs Headlam, but who signed the death certificate for my aunt? Oh, really? Are they allowed to do that?'

He switched off and turned to Fran.

'It appears that if the doctor treating the deceased isn't available, the body can be removed by ambulance, and has to be reported to the coroner. Stallwood and Stallwood are probably expecting the certificate to be sent to Barbara to go and get the death certificate from the registrar.'

'So the funeral couldn't possibly go ahead yet?' said Fran, surprised.

'I don't think so. We need to find out from Barbara. Come on.'

A low-slung silver sports car sat on the drive of Blagstock House when they returned.

'Paul,' said Charles. 'Watch out for fireworks.'

It took a long time for Barbara to open the door, and when she did, she looked flushed and nervous.

'I didn't expect you back,' she said, although not expecting to be believed, if Fran was any judge.

A young man appeared behind her, smiling determinedly.

'Charles,' he said, 'and Cousin Fran. Good to see you.'

*Oh, yeah,* thought Fran.

'Paul.' Charles nodded. 'Barbara, we need to talk. I'm afraid you've led us up the garden path. May we come in?'

Paul took his mother by the shoulders and moved her aside. 'Of course,' he said. 'Do come in, both of you. I gather you didn't get any tea on your last visit? Shall we make some more?'

'No, thanks. We'd just like a chat.' Charles went straight past mother and son into the drawing room, where the abandoned tea tray still sat. Fran followed, getting a whiff of something sharp and expensive as she sidled past Paul.

87

'The funeral isn't booked, Barbara,' began Charles, standing in front of the empty fireplace like a Victorian squire. 'I thought you said it was.'

Barbara looked as though she might faint. Paul pushed her into a chair and turned to face Charles.

'She isn't *playing* at anything, Charles. I'm sure, if you've been to see Stallwood and Stallwood you know the position.'

'I gather Marion Headlam had the body removed and because Aunt Eleanor wasn't being attended by a doctor, the coroner had to be informed before a death certificate could be issued. So why not tell me this in the first place?'

*And that was the idea*, thought Fran. *They didn't want Charles to know anything about it.* Startled, she looked at Charles. He flicked a glance at her and looked back at Barbara. Her colour had returned, but her eyes were wide, and Fran could swear she could see her heart beating fast beneath her pale blue cardigan.

'Barbara, there must be an explanation for all this,' she said gently. 'You removed all Aunt Eleanor's things without permission and tried to keep the facts from Charles. And me, for that matter.'

'Fran, excuse me, but what's it got to do with you? You never visited her,' said Paul. His mother opened her mouth as if to say something, but Paul pressed her shoulder and she stopped, like a gasping cod.

'That's beside the point,' said Charles, irritated. 'You didn't tell me. I had Power of Attorney and I'm the executor of the will – which, you tell me, now can't be found.'

'That's hardly our fault, is it? And as to moving the belongings, Mrs Headlam wanted to clear the room as soon as possible. I would have thought,' said Paul, smiling sweetly, 'we were doing everybody a favour.'

'Well, if you don't mind, you can have everything packed up and moved to Mountville Road.'

'Why should we?' Paul's manner was beginning to turn belligerent.

'Because you removed it without permission. Now you put it back. All those items are covered by the will, and the will has to go to probate, or didn't you realise that?'

'Of course we did.' Barbara had obviously recovered. 'There was no intention of removing anything for ourselves. I told you, most of it's gone to the office – we haven't room for it here.'

'Plenty of room at the office, though,' said Charles, with a nasty little smile. 'Nothing much else there, is there?'

Paul looked uneasy and Barbara furious.

'Anyway, get a van and have it delivered to Mountville Road. Tell me when it's coming and I'll be there to receive it. You can send the bill to the solicitors and the estate will settle it.' Charles began to move towards the door.

'But we can't find the will, and we don't know who the solicitor is.' Barbara's voice was a harsh contrast to her previous cooing tones.

'As soon as I've found out, I'll let you know,' said Charles, 'and they'll have a copy of the will, so I shouldn't worry about it.' He continued to the door. 'Come on, Fran.'

Fran smiled nervously at the Denvers, who watched her leave with defiant expressions on their faces, and scurried out to Charles's car.

'Well!' she said, as, with another scattering of gravel, they pulled out of the drive of Blagstock House. 'I hope you can find the solicitor's letter. Otherwise, everybody's in a right old state.'

'I'll find it,' said Charles, grimly. 'Did you see their faces? They didn't expect me to know who the solicitor was. That was a shock to them.'

'They didn't want you to know anything. That was the whole point.'

'Are you having a Moment?' Charles darted a look at her from the corner of his eyes.

'I don't know. I just knew it.'

Charles sighed. 'But I'd have asked about the funeral eventually. If it hadn't happened, they could hardly say it had, and what excuse would they have had for not letting me know?'

'No idea.' Fran turned to look out of the window. 'What they did was perfectly reasonable, you know. Barbara and Paul visited regularly and, as Mrs Headlam said, she dealt mainly with Barbara, so what more normal than for her to clear the stuff? And sort out an undertaker. I expect the Headlam told her to use Stalker and Stalker.'

'Stallwood and Stallwood.'

'Whoever. But don't you see? It was all perfectly normal. The only thing they didn't do was let you know what was going on. And Barbara did say Paul was supposed to have phoned you.'

'So why didn't he?'

'Ah, well, that's the point. For some reason they

didn't want you to know. I'm certain of it. Where are we?'

'Going towards Steeple Martin. That's what you wanted, wasn't it?'

'Yes, but we're a bit earlier than I expected. I'd better make sure Libby's ready for me.'

Predictably, Libby's mobile was either switched off, or out of credit. The landline went straight to answerphone, so Fran left a message asking Libby to call her back.

'Where do you want to be dropped, then?' asked Charles. 'Do you want me to wait with you?'

'We could go to the pub,' suggested Fran, 'and I'll buy you a pint and a sandwich.'

'It hasn't changed much,' said Charles, as they walked from the car to the pub. 'Fancy being able to park almost in front of the pub.'

'Not at night, though,' said Fran. 'All the spaces are taken up by residents. There's a free car park down one of the side streets where the new houses are.'

'New houses? I didn't think they'd be allowed!'

'I don't know about that. I've only visited a couple of times.' Fran pushed open the door to the pub. The barman caught her eye and nodded, although she was sure he couldn't place her.

Charles was ordering drinks when Fran's mobile rang.

'Hi!' said Libby. 'Where are you? I was out stocking up for your visit when you rang. There was no signal inside the supermarket.'

'I'm in the pub with Charles. Do you want to come and join us?'

'Will he want that? Won't I be butting in?'

91

'No, of course not. He says he wants to meet you.'

'OK. See you in five.'

In fact it was nearer ten minutes when Libby erupted into the bar in a flowing of scarves. Charles looked startled.

Fran introduced them and gave Libby a succinct, edited version of the morning's events. Libby thoughtfully sipped her lager and regarded Charles over the edge of her glass.

'So, Charles, what are you going to do now?' she asked.

'I'm going back home to try and find the solicitor's letter. I can't have been mad enough to destroy it.'

'Home?' asked Fran. 'I've just realised I don't know where you live.'

'Why, Mountville Road, of course,' he said. 'I thought you knew.'

## Chapter Nine

'So there you are,' said Fran. 'Barbara and Paul were trying to keep the whole thing from Charles.'

Charles had dropped them at 17 Allhallow's Lane after refusing a sandwich. Libby had rifled through her recent supermarket purchases, and now carefully placed a tray with tea, bread and cheese on her unpredictable garden table.

'That's ridiculous,' she said, flopping down on

to one of the equally unpredictable chairs. 'They'd never have got away with it for a minute. The Headlam person would know about the coroner business, and Charles would have asked about the funeral anyway. I can't understand why he got into such a state about it.'

'He was a bit flaky about it all,' said Fran, thoughtfully. 'When we met for dinner he said he didn't know what happened about funerals, and was he supposed to arrange it.'

Libby snorted. 'He seems a bit up his own backside, doesn't he? Is he one of these people who expects everyone else to do all the dirty work?'

'I think he may be.' Fran chewed absent-mindedly on a piece of bread. 'I thought he was really attractive at first, but I'm not so sure, now.'

'Oh, he's attractive, all right. But if they're attractive and single at his age, it usually means there's something wrong with them.'

'Like Guy and Ben, you mean?' Fran looked sideways at her.

Libby sniffed. 'Well, they're both divorced. Not easy to live with. Ladies' men.'

'God, Libby, you're so suspicious.'

Libby stared at her for a moment, then dropped her gaze. 'I'm going out with Ben Friday night.'

'Fantastic! I'm so pleased, Lib. When did this happen?'

Libby told her about the meeting in the super-market. 'But what about you? I've just realised, no funeral booked, what are you going to do?'

'Oh!' Fran looked nonplussed. 'Oh. Well, go

home, I suppose.'

'Are you sure you want to? You're welcome to stay here.'

'You've got the kids coming soon, haven't you? And who knows how long I'd have to stay until the funeral? And I don't want to cramp your style with Ben.'

Libby felt the colour rising up her neck. 'He's staying with his Mum on Friday.'

'I didn't mean Friday, necessarily. I meant – well, anytime.'

Libby thought about it. 'Suppose you stay here tonight, at least, and think about it. You might hear from Charles, and there might be something you could do while you're here.'

'Thanks, Libby. I've got enough clothes for a few days. I might even go over and see Barbara Denver again.'

'What on earth for?' Libby sat upright. 'I seriously think Charles is making a fuss about nothing. I don't think there was any intention of concealing anything from him, it was just the natural thing to do. She shouldn't have removed the stuff without asking him, perhaps, but that's all.'

'That's the point. I want to know why she did it. Was it just to look for the will? Charles was concerned about the will, as well. And come to think of it, if he had power-of-attorney, how come he didn't know who her solicitors are?'

'You can do that without a solicitor,' said Libby. 'Peter's done it for Mad Millie.' Her eyes widened. 'Whoops. Mustn't call her that.'

Fran smiled. 'Is she still bonkers?'

'You heard what he said the other night. As well as can be expected. The companion's a bit dim, but just what Millie needs. An ex-nurse, apparently. Goodness knows how long they'll be able to afford her.'

'Will they sell Steeple Farm, do you think?'

Libby shrugged. 'I don't know. I can't see Peter and Harry living there, but if James gets married he might want to.'

'James? Already?'

'No,' Libby laughed. 'I meant if ever he gets up the courage to have another relationship.'

'Unlikely, I'd have thought, after Paula.'

They both fell silent, thinking of James's dead girlfriend.

'Then there's another thing,' said Libby, slowly.

'Mmm?'

'How come Charles is living in Mountville Road? And how come you didn't know?'

'He's Eleanor's nephew, and if it was her house, I expect he was offered the flat. After all, he must have needed somewhere to live after his divorce.'

'Eye to the main chance, if you ask me,' said Libby. 'If your old Auntie's estate is divided between him and Barbara.'

'What, you mean possession's nine points of the law?'

'He's in situ. They can't chuck him out.'

'But he'd have to buy them out if he wanted to stay there. And the will might state the house must be sold to divide the proceeds. Suppose that's all there is in the estate? They'd have to sell it then, to pay for the solicitor and everything.'

'Do you suppose they want to sell it anyway?' Libby leant back in her chair and looked up at branches of the cherry tree.

'It'll be worth a fortune, even if it does want doing up. No wonder they're concerned about the will. She could have left it to just one of them, couldn't she?'

'Well, whether I like him or not, if she has, I hope it's Charles. I'd hate that cow Barbara to get it.'

Fran frowned. 'She didn't seem that bad to me,' she said. 'A bit nervous and ineffectual, if anything.'

Libby raised her eyebrows. 'You must be joking! She's a bloody good actress, then. She's the one who holds the whip hand in that family. Most manipulative bitch I've ever known.'

Sidney appeared under the table, ecstatic at Fran's return. She bent down and lifted him on to her lap. 'I still don't know,' she said, stroking his head, 'what all this is about. Why I got all those unpleasant feelings. Nothing since.'

'It'll come to you,' said Libby, comfortably. 'Now, I've got loads of food for us tonight, and a choice of DVDs from the village shop, so stop worrying about it all, and lets talk about something else.'

But when Charles phoned in the morning, Fran started worrying about it all over again.

'The coroner's ordered a post mortem. Apparently it had already been ordered when we went galloping all over the area yesterday.'

'Why weren't we told?' Fran's suddenly shaky legs let her down on to Sidney's step.

'I'll give you three guesses.'

'Not Barbara. If she'd been told, she would have said, surely? And the undertakers didn't know. Perhaps it all happened after we'd gone?'

Charles sighed. 'Look, Fran, I'm really sorry I got you involved with this. It's nothing to do with you anyway.'

'I *was* her niece.'

'You hadn't seen her for years.'

'That wasn't my fault.'

'Oh, well, I'm sorry.'

'And did you find the solicitor's letter?'

'Oh, yes.' Charles sounded gloomy. 'It's not the right solicitor. We had to seek Power of Attorney when Auntie became unable to look after herself and we wanted to get her into a home. She'd consulted a solicitor about some neighbour trouble a couple of years before, and I went to him because I found the letter. I assumed he did the will, too, but he says no. As it happens, all he had to do for me was witness my signature, but anyone could have done that.'

'Yes, Libby's friend Peter did that for his Mum. She told me yesterday. So where do we go from here?'

'Look, Fran, I've already said, you don't have to go anywhere with it. It's not your problem.'

'Well, I'm staying down with Libby for a few days, so if I can do anything while I'm here, let me know. And let me know when the coroner's ready to release the – er – Aunt Eleanor.'

'Will do. And Fran,' added Charles, sounding slightly worried, 'don't go having any of your moments, will you?'

'Wimp,' said Libby, when Fran told her. 'I'd want you to have as many moments as possible – find out what's going on.'

'They don't come to order, you know,' said Fran, with a smile. 'Remember when I went down to the theatre to see if I could find anything out? Not a dickey bird.'

'I know, but you did know who the murderer was.'

'Who it wasn't, more like,' sighed Fran. 'And you know what? I've just remembered, Charles said he had a letter from the solicitor when he was made executor. Not the power-of-attorney solicitor. So he must have a letter from the proper solicitor somewhere.' She stood up. 'I'm going to ring him back.'

But Charles's land line went straight to answerphone, and his mobile to voice mail.


## Chapter Ten

Fran's phone rang while she was chopping vegetables for one of Libby's eclectic stir fries that evening. Wiping her hands on a tea cloth, she fumbled for the buttons.

'Fran, it's Charles.'

'Oh, Charles, I'm glad you rang,' she began, but he interrupted.

'Bad news, I'm afraid.'

'What? Did you find the other solicitor's letter? Because that's what I–'

'She was murdered, Fran.'

Fran's whole head tingled with the shock of it, and she found herself gasping for breath. Libby looked at her sharply.

'You can't mean it,' she said, although the memory of the black suffocation told her it was true. She had known all along.

'I don't know all the details,' said Charles, with the suspicion of a sigh, 'but apparently the evidence is conclusive. We're all being interviewed by the police.'

'All?' Fran's voice came out in a squeak.

'Barbara, Paul and I. And the staff at The Laurels, presumably.'

'What about me?'

'Why on earth should they interview you? You weren't there.'

'Marion Headlam will tell them about my visit. She wondered why I was there.' Fran knew as surely as if she'd heard Marion Headlam speak that this was what she would do.

'I can't see it myself,' said Charles, sounding faintly irritable. 'Anyway, it means there'll be an inquest, which will be adjourned for the police to make further enquiries. You certainly won't have to attend that. Oh, and if Mrs Headlam does contact you...'

'Why should she?'

'She called me, first of all on the pretext of discussing the murder, but really to find out about the will. Apparently she's expecting to be left something.'

'Well, she's not going to find out about it from me, is she?'

'I know, but don't say anything about all the shenanigans over the funeral yesterday, will you? I don't want her thinking we're all at each other's throats.'

'But you are.'

'Fran! Don't be difficult.'

'All right, all right. So are you coming back down here? Or will they interview you in London?'

'I've got to give evidence at the inquest. They've established I'm the next of kin, and I get a little leaflet about what to do and so on. The inquest's tomorrow.'

'Thursday! Inquest instead of a funeral. Do you want me to come with you?'

'You can come if you want, but I can't see why.'

'To keep you company, for God's sake! For support. I won't bother.'

'Sorry.' Charles was contrite.

'Let me know what happens.'

'Of course. Sorry, Fran. You were right about something being wrong, weren't you?'

'Do you think it was him?' asked Libby, after Fran had finished filling her in on Charles's side of the conversation.

'What, Charles as a murderer? Of course not. He's suave, when he wants to be, irritable and a bit insensitive. I don't think he's a murderer. Anyway, why would he have involved me, and gone round making a fuss yesterday? No, it's nothing to do with him.'

'And why do they think she was murdered?'

'Do you mean what was the evidence for it, or what was the motive? Because I don't know either.'

'I meant evidence. The coroner ordered an inquest, so something turned up in that. That's one reason for an inquest. The others are work related deaths, deaths in custody...'

'All right, Libby, I get the picture. And I haven't got a clue. Charles didn't say.'

Libby darted back out of the way of spitting olive oil as she poured chopped vegetables into the pan. 'Are we going then?' she asked.

'Eh?'

'To the inquest. Did he say when it was?'

'Why on earth do you want to come?'

'To find out, of course. Don't tell me you don't want to. Why did you go down to The Laurels after she was dead if you didn't think there was something wrong?'

Fran sat down at the kitchen table and picked up a fork. 'I don't know. I wish I hadn't.' She stabbed the fork viciously at the table.

'Hey, watch my valuable antique.' Libby poked her with a spatula. 'We're going, then. Now, can you feed Sidney?'

Libby, in an excess of zeal and nosiness, managed to find out where and at what time the inquest was to be held, and she and Fran turned up in plenty of time.

'Look! It's our pet policeman.' Libby pointed across the room.

Fran fumbled for her glasses. 'Which one?'

'The bald one with red hair.'

Fran looked at her. 'The bald one with red hair. Of course.'

'No, look. He's got red hair just round the back

101

of his head and over his ears. It's what 'is name –
DCI Murray. Donnie Murray.' She giggled.

'Donnie?'

'His wife brought him to see *The Hop Pickers*
and let it slip.'

'Is he nice?'

'I wouldn't know. I only saw his formal side.'
Libby looked round and nudged Fran. 'And
that's his sidekick – DS Cole.' A tall, thin man
with a thin moustache leaned nearer to DCI
Murray in whispered conversation. 'Flash Harry
from St Trinian's.'

'Libby!' admonished Fran. 'Look, over there.
Barbara and Paul are sitting with Charles.'

'Who's the other woman?'

'Marion Headlam. Looks as though she's trying to make up to Charles.'

'Hard faced cow, isn't she? Men are so super-
ficial.' Libby sniffed. 'Oh, here we go. On with the
Motley.'

The inquest provided no surprises. Barbara had
realised Eleanor was dead after sitting with her
for several minutes, Paul and Charles had arrived
within seconds of each other immediately after
the discovery. Little Nurse Warner was called and
said in a whisper that she had pushed her client
to the french windows so that she could look at
the gardens a few minutes before Mrs Denver
arrived. Nurse Redding said she had gone into
the room while Nurse Warner was there and left
again without delay. Both swore that Eleanor
Bridges was alive when they left her.

'There's something they aren't saying,' whispered Fran.

'How do you know?'

Fran shrugged. 'I just know.'

The pathologist gave her evidence of conjunctival petechial hemorrhages, fragments of white cotton around the mouth and traces under the fingernails. She reminded the coroner that the diagnosis of suffocation could be impossible to establish with certainty on the basis of the post-mortem examination alone, but that in this case, although not immediately obvious to the untrained eye, there were enough indications for her to be certain.

Emerging into the sunlight after the coroner had adjourned for the police to continue their enquiries, Libby came face to face with DCI Murray.

'Mrs – ah!' he said. 'Quite recovered, now, have we?'

'Yes, we have,' said Libby seriously, 'but there's still the trial to come, isn't there?'

'Certainly is,' said DCI Murray, 'so tell me, why are you here?'

'This is my friend Fran Castle,' said Libby, pulling Fran forward. 'You remember, she was the one who phoned you.'

'Ah. Yes.' He looked uncertain, but held out his hand. 'Pleased to meet you.'

'Well, Eleanor Bridges was her aunt.'

Libby heard the hiss of Fran's indrawn breath, and felt herself blushing. Damn. She'd got it wrong again.

'Really?' DCI Murray's eyes brightened. 'So, tell me, Miss Castle, did you not visit her on her birthday?'

'No, I went down the next day,' said Fran, reluctantly.

'The next day? Had no one told you she was dead?'

'Um, well, yes. I hadn't visited her before, so I wanted to see where she'd died.'

DCI Murray frowned. 'Bit morbid, wasn't it?'

Fran hesitated. 'Guilt, Inspector,' she said eventually. 'I was quite upset.'

'Hmm.' He peered at her. 'Wasn't your psychic stuff again, was it?'

Libby stood frozen. Fran wasn't going to like this.

'I told you, Inspector. I felt guilty. Mrs Headlam quite understood.' Fran took Libby's arm. 'I think I'd like to go now, Libby.'

'I may want to speak to you again, Miss Castle. Could you give me a phone number?'

'She's staying with me at the moment, Mr Murray,' said Libby firmly, 'so you can get in touch with her there. Come on Fran. Goodbye, Inspector.'

'Fran!' Charles appeared in front of them as they turned away. 'Why didn't you tell me you were coming?'

'You didn't want me to come, so why should I tell you?'

'It wasn't that.' Charles looked uncomfortable. 'I just don't want you to get involved.'

'Well, I am involved. The Inspector wants to talk to me, so I don't think you've a hope of keeping me out of it, do you?'

Charles sighed. 'Don't be angry with me, Fran. This is bad enough already. I've just had the

104

Denvers blaming me for the whole investigation.'

'That's ridiculous,' said Libby. 'Sorry for butting in, but you had nothing to do with the pathologist's report, had you? You didn't ask the coroner to call an inquest?'

'I know, but they seemed to think our poking about yesterday had something to do with it.'

'That's nonsense. We got Libby's friend Peter to look it up on the internet yesterday. If the deceased isn't currently being seen by a doctor and there isn't one to sign the death certificate, the coroner's officer has to be called, and the coroner will ask for a post mortem. Then if that turns something up, like this one did, there will be an inquest. You might find, though, that they'll now release the body for burial.'

'Will they?' Charles brightened. 'That would be a relief, wouldn't it?'

'There'd still be the investigation,' said Libby.

Charles looked at her with distaste.

'She's right, Charles.' Fran patted his arm. 'Don't worry about it. It hasn't got anything to do with you, you weren't even there when she died.'

'But I was straight afterwards. And as far as I can see, Barbara's the only one who could have done it. God,' he said, shaking his head, 'this is a nightmare. I don't like the woman, heaven knows, but to think of that. It's disgusting.'

Libby and Fran regarded him thoughtfully.

'How about lunch, Charles,' said Libby suddenly. 'Cheer you up.'

Fran gave her an incredulous look.

'If you're sure?' Charles looked from one to

another. 'I could use some friendly company.'

Libby smiled evilly. 'Then come along with me,' she said. 'I know just the place.'

## Chapter Eleven

'What do you think you're doing?' whispered Fran. 'Where are we going?'

'That pub where we first met. OK, Charles, cross here.' Libby took his arm and guided him across the crowded street. 'Just down here.'

The pub, in a side street where Libby and Fran had first been introduced, was still fairly quiet. The decorative barman didn't sparkle quite as much as he had done to Harry, but provided them with drinks fairly rapidly, and indicated the blackboard where simple lunches were chalked up.

'Well, surprise, surprise.' Ben stood up from the table in the window.

Fran looked suspiciously at Libby.

'Hi, Ben,' beamed Libby. 'This is Charles, Fran's cousin.'

Ben held out his hand. Charles took it tentatively and cleared his throat.

'Ben Wilde,' said Ben. 'Friend of Libby's, and I occasionally work with Fran.'

Charles looked surprised. 'I didn't know you worked,' he said to Fran.

'Didn't she tell you? She's a psychic investigator,' said Ben.

Convinced now that the meeting had been set up between Ben and Libby, although she didn't know how, Fran opened her mouth to refute the statement.

'Didn't you tell him, Fran? Naughty of you,' said Libby, settling herself more comfortably into the corner of the bench set. 'She's very good at it, Charles. She found a murderer a couple of months ago.'

Charles was looking pale. 'You said you had "moments",' he said faintly.

'I do,' said Fran, crossly. 'Honestly, you two. Don't make me out to be something I'm not.'

'But you are, Fran. You investigate properties for a major estate agent and you virtually saved Libby's life after *The Hop Pickers*.' Ben sounded reasonable.

'I wouldn't go that far,' said Fran. 'All I did was make a phone call. Libby wasn't in any danger.'

'What are we having to eat?' asked Libby. 'Charles?'

'I don't think I want anything, actually,' said Charles. 'I'll just finish my drink and get going. I've got to get back to London.'

'I thought you wanted company?' said Libby.

'Well, I've got it, haven't I?' Charles smiled weakly. 'But I really have got to get back to London. I've got to organise the transport of Aunt's furniture back to the house.'

'I thought you told Paul to do that?' said Fran.

'I can't trust him to do it. I'll do it and he won't have a choice.'

'Didn't Fran say it was at his office and he's never there? How can you trust him to be there

107

when the removals people arrive?' said Libby.

'He wouldn't dare,' said Charles, sounding more confident, 'it would be tantamount to theft, which it already is, technically.'

'About the will, Charles,' said Fran suddenly, leaning across the table. 'I forgot to say yesterday when you phoned, but you said you heard from the solicitor when you were made executor. And the letter you found was from the solicitor who did the Power of Attorney. So there must be another letter.'

Charles looked at her like a rabbit caught in headlights.

'Yes,' he said eventually, 'I don't know why I didn't think of that.'

'Well, I'd go home and have another jolly good look, if I were you,' said Libby, 'because if you don't find a will, probate will take ages and...' she stopped. 'Well, it'll be a right pain, anyway,' she finished.

Charles looked at his drink for a minute, picked it up and downed most of it.

'I'll be off, then,' he said, suppressing a belch and standing up. 'Thanks for coming, Fran.' He lifted a hand vaguely at Ben and Libby and went, bumping into several tables on the way.

'That was a put up job, wasn't it?' said Fran.

Libby nodded. 'I wanted to see what he'd say about the will, and find out why he's so fidgety. I thought Ben might help, so I called him while you were upstairs this morning.'

'Libby, I hate to say this, but it isn't any business of yours.' Fran sat back in her chair and picked up her drink.

Ben leant forward. 'Libby only wants to help, Fran. I know she goes about it like a bull in a china shop, but she means well.'

'Gee, thanks,' muttered Libby.

'And,' continued Ben, 'I know I don't know anything about it, but there does seem to be a lot of bother about this will, and the furniture, doesn't there?'

'The bureau,' said Fran absently, 'yes. I wonder why?'

'If it isn't found,' said Libby, forgetting to be offended, 'Charles, as next of kin, will cop the lot.'

'Bloody hell, yes.' Fran was startled. 'So why is he so concerned to find it?'

'To destroy it?' suggested Ben.

'But what about the original solicitor? Surely eventually he'll get to hear about it?' said Fran.

'Yes, don't they post lists of intestates somewhere?' said Libby. 'In a solicitors' newsletter, or something?'

Ben screwed up his face. 'Not sure, but I'll ask around. If you don't mind, Fran,' he added hastily.

'No,' sighed Fran, 'I suppose not. I don't know why I'm bothered, anyway. It's nothing to do with me, any more than it is with Libby.'

'She was your aunt. She might have left you something,' said Ben.

'Hardly likely, unless Uncle Frank left me anything, and I'd have heard by now.'

'Drink up, then. Do you want a sandwich or something?' asked Libby briskly.

'Not really. I think I'd rather go home. Or, rather,' said Fran going slightly pink, 'to your home. If you don't mind.'

Libby looked quickly at Ben. 'No, not at all. Come on, then.' She stood up.

'Sorry, am I breaking up a pleasant lunchtime?'

'No!' said Libby and Ben together, then both looked embarrassed.

'I am, aren't I? Oh, bother.'

'I've got to get back to the office, Fran,' said Ben gently, 'and Lib and I are having dinner at the pub tomorrow, so don't worry about it.'

Fran looked doubtful, but Libby patted her arm and began to move towards the door. Ben gave them both a kiss on the cheek, and disappeared in the direction of his office.

'He's gone back to work, then?' said Fran, watching his trim figure walk away.

'Oh, yes, but I don't think he does much, now. But you'd know, surely?'

'I haven't worked with him for ages,' said Fran. 'In fact, I haven't had much work at all for ages.' She sighed. 'I'm beginning to think I'd better try and get a shelf stacking job.'

'You don't own your flat, do you?'

'Chance would be a fine thing. When my mother died, after the mortgage had been paid there was hardly anything left, so I ended up renting my little hovel. Which is exorbitant, being London.'

'Couldn't you move – down here, for instance? Wouldn't it be cheaper?'

Fran looked at her in surprise. 'I'd never even thought about it. But where would I find a flat in Steeple Martin? Or do you mean Canterbury? Or Nethergate?'

'Nethergate's all holiday lets. There are a few

places in Steeple Martin, and quite a lot in Canterbury, because of it being a University town. Why don't you think about it?'

'Yes,' said Fran slowly, 'it's worth a thought. I wonder what the children would say?'

'How often do you see them?'

'Hardly at all. Chrissie lives in Sussex and Jeremy's in America. Lucy still lives in London, but I don't see her much. I suspect, if I lived in the country I'd see a lot more of her and the grandchildren.'

'Wow!' said Libby. 'I didn't realise you had grandchildren.'

'Rachel and Tom,' said Fran. 'Nice kids, but I'm not much of a granny.'

'Don't think I will be, either,' said Libby, 'although I don't think there's much chance of it with my three.' They'd reached the car and climbed in before Libby said diffidently, 'Of course, there's the empty flat over the Pink Geranium. You could always borrow that while you were looking – or making your mind up.'

'And what would Peter and Harry say about you offering it to me?' Fran grinned across at her.

'Just a suggestion. I thought I might ask them later on. Now,' said Libby, without a break, 'what are we going to do about Charles and this will?'

When they got back to 17 Allhallow's Lane, there was a message on the answerphone for Fran from DCI Murray asking her to call him back.

'Don't let him haul you back into Canterbury,' said Libby, pushing Sidney off the draining board while she filled the kettle. 'If he wants to talk to you, make him come here.'

'Didn't you say that they talked to you here, *and* made you go into Canterbury when Paula died?'

'That was different. You're hardly involved in this, are you?'

'Murray thinks I am, obviously.' Fran sighed and took out her mobile.

'No, don't use that, Fran. He'll be able to get your number and you won't have any peace. Use the land line.'

'What about your peace?'

'I can say you're not here any more, can't I?' Libby took two mugs from the draining board and blew Sidney's fur off them. 'Bloody cat.'

Fran was finally put through to DCI Murray.

'I'm afraid it's rather difficult for me to get in to Canterbury,' she said. 'If you want to talk to me, would you mind coming here? Mrs Sarjeant says she doesn't mind. But it will have to be soon, as I'm planning on going home in a day or so.'

There was a short silence. 'That will be quite in order, Miss Castle,' said Murray at last.

'And actually, it's *Mrs* Castle,' said Fran.

Another silence. 'I'm very sorry, *Mrs* Castle. Perhaps we could pop round and see you tomorrow morning? About ten?'

'Ten tomorrow?' repeated Fran, looking over at Libby. 'Yes, that will be fine.'

'And it's 17 Allhallow's Lane, I believe.'

'Certainly is. I'll see you tomorrow, then.'

Libby brought over a mug of tea. 'I wonder what it's all about?'

'Background, I should think. After all, they know exactly when Aunt Eleanor died, and there's no way it could have been me.'

'It could, you know,' said Libby sitting on the cane sofa gingerly to avoid the creak.

'Eh? What do you mean?' Fran looked offended.

'As soon as they find out that you knew the others were going down that day, and they will when they talk to Charles, they'll think you could have sneaked down without telling anyone and got there before all the others did.'

'Those two nurses saw her just before she died, just before Barbara arrived. How could I have got in?'

'French windows? They mentioned french windows at the inquest.'

'How would I have known which room was hers? And how would I have got round the back, anyway? I'd have been seen.'

Libby looked thoughtful. 'I bet there's a way. And I bet that's what they'll think. Maybe not seriously, but as a relative, and with no will in sight...'

'Oh, that bloody will. If it wasn't for that, this would all be perfectly simple.' Fran moved her mug out of reach as Sidney inserted himself on to her lap.

'I wouldn't say that, exactly,' said Libby. 'Murder's never simple. Look at...'

'I know, look at Paula. But this is different, Libby. This isn't a *crime passionel*, or whatever you call it. It's a ... well, it's a...'

'Murder for money?' said Libby, looking at her over the rim of her mug. 'Because that's what it is, Fran. Why else would the old lady be bumped off? Therefore, it has to be a relative. There's no one else in the frame, is there?'

'There might be.' Fran bridled. 'There's the Headlam for a start. She thinks she was left something in the will. Perhaps The Laurels is in debt. Then there could be all sorts of people I don't know about from her London days; other relatives, Charles's daughter, Kate, for instance.'

'All of whom might think they'd got something in the will?'

'Yes. It's not that far fetched, is it?'

'No, and I'm sure our Mr Murray will have started looking in to all that. But meanwhile, he's got the people here on the ground, as you might say. You, Charles, Barbara and Paul. And the Headlam. We ought to start with them.'

'What do you mean, we ought to start with them?'

'Investigating, of course. After all, it's in your interests, isn't it?'


## Chapter Twelve

Libby was saved from phoning Peter to ask about the flat when he and Harry turned up a little later to ask how the inquest had gone.

'What a trial, dear heart,' said Harry, squeezing himself in beside Libby on the sofa, while Peter sat on the floor in front of the empty hearth. 'Don't know how you stood it. We didn't have

114

one of those, did we, Lib?'

'I don't know whether we did or not,' said Libby, 'but this one was very short. No problems, were there, Fran?'

'No, I suppose not,' said Fran.

'But we're going to have to find out a bit more...' began Libby, before being howled down by Peter and Harry.

'Remember last time,' said Peter.

'Yes, but Fran's being interviewed by the police tomorrow. By one of our friends.'

'Mr Plod? Or the little Ploddette?' said Harry, interested.

'No, dear Donnie Murray himself. He's coming here in the morning.'

'So you're not going back up to London, yet?' said Peter.

'No,' began Fran.

'That's what I was wondering, you see,' broke in Libby. 'I mean, she could stay here, but she's actually thinking she might move down, and so while she was thinking about it, and while she's got to be here anyway, because of this murder...'

'Slow down, you old trout,' said Peter, patting her knee. 'Of course she can borrow the flat. You only had to ask.'

Libby beamed, first at Peter, then at Fran and finally at Harry. 'You don't mind, do you, Hal?'

'Course not.' He grinned over at Fran. 'Might even get a bit of part time help out of it.'

'Is there a separate entrance?' asked Fran. 'I don't want to be disturbing you all the time.'

'Yes, at the side,' said Peter. 'And a fire escape into the back yard at the back. We do keep some stock up there, but we can put it all in the little bedroom.'

'Is it still furnished?' asked Libby.

'Bit sparse, but yes. Bits of both of ours before we shacked up. Mine's the tasteless stuff,' said Harry.

'And now we've sorted that out,' said Peter, 'tell us what happened at the inquest.'

After Fran and Libby had told them the essential details and Libby's inessential thoughts, Harry stood up, saying he had to get to the caff to open up for Donna.

'Let us know when you want to move in,' said Peter, when they left. 'You'll need to go back to London to get some more bits, won't you?'

'I suppose so. I wish I had a car.'

'You can borrow the Renault,' said Libby. 'It's a bit of a wreck, but it goes.'

'You'll take your life in your hands,' said Harry.

As Libby got plates out for their supper, she said: 'You could go up tomorrow afternoon and come back on Saturday, couldn't you? Give you plenty of time to sort out what you need and let people know. That kind of thing.'

Fran laughed. 'And leave you a free house for tomorrow night's date?'

Libby coloured. 'Well, there is that, yes. But I hadn't actually thought of it...'

'Actually, Lib, it's a good idea. I'll have to try and see Lucy, and I could go via her place on the way home with a car. It's really kind of you to lend it to me. And to sort out the flat.' Fran gave her an impulsive hug. 'You're a really good friend.'

Libby's colour got even brighter. 'Um. Thanks,'

she said, and hurriedly turned to the Rayburn to rescue the potatoes.

The following morning, Libby tactfully retired to the kitchen when DCI Murray arrived, after letting him and the schoolboy DC Bulstrode in.

'Ah, I remember this gentleman,' said Murray, as Sidney glared at him from the stairs. 'Quite saved the day, as I remember.'

'Yes, he's very good at tripping people up,' said Libby.

Fran sat in her usual armchair, leaving the cane sofa for DCI Murray, while Bulstrode perched uncomfortably on an upright chair and tried to manipulate his notebook.

'So, Mrs Castle. Could I have your full name and address?'

Fran gave it.

'And you were Mrs Bridges' niece?'

'No, I was her husband's niece. Frank Bridges. His brother Herbert was my father.'

'And did you visit her regularly?'

'No, there was a family dispute, and I hadn't seen or heard from her in over thirty years.'

'Oh.' Murray looked confused. 'Then, why...?'

'Why did I go this year? Because my cousin – or rather – her nephew, Charles, thought we should mend the rift, and traced me. He invited me to go down for the birthday. I couldn't as it happened, but decided to go the next day.'

'And you said you went even though you knew by then she was dead. Guilt, I think you said.'

'Yes,' said Fran, feeling the colour rising up her neck.

'And this was nothing to do with any – er –

117

psychic revelations?' Murray looked slightly embarrassed at this.

Fran was silent.

'Well, Mrs Castle? Or do you think I won't believe you?'

'There is that,' said Fran.

'Well, I can't say it doesn't go against the grain, but I'd sooner believe that than your feeling of guilt. Especially,' he said heavily, 'after your – er – phone call. After Miss Wentworth's – er – death.'

'There could have been any number of explanations for that,' said Fran, her colour still alarmingly heightened.

'I know, and I looked in to them,' said Murray, surprisingly. 'Let's just say, if you felt anything was wrong about Mrs Bridges' death, I'd be obliged if you'd tell me.'

Fran cast a quick glance at DC Bulstrode, who was watching his superior with his mouth open. Bet they'll love this at the station, she thought.

'All right then, yes. I did feel that something was wrong. When Charles – Mr Wade – phoned me to tell me she was dead. And again, when I went in to her room at The Laurels.' She didn't mention the suffocating feeling. That might be over-icing the cake.

'Right.' Murray was watching her carefully. 'And is that all?'

'If you mean did I get any ideas about who might have suffocated her, no, I didn't. Nor do I have any ideas about why.'

'Mrs Headlam says there was some trouble about a will.'

118

'I believe it can't be found,' said Fran, 'but it's nothing to do with me. I wouldn't be in it.'

'So you don't have any – *ah* – feelings about where it might be?'

Fran glanced at DC Bulstrode, who was looking quite gobsmacked at this further evidence of lunacy. 'No,' she said. *And I wouldn't tell you if I had*, she thought.

'You say Mr Wade traced you. Hadn't you seen him recently, either?'

'Not since Eleanor married my uncle. I was twelve.'

'And Mrs Denver?'

'I didn't know her at all. I didn't even know she existed until a couple of days ago. Or her son.'

DCI Murray sighed. 'All right, Mrs Castle. That's about all, then.' He stood up. 'We might want to talk to you again. And if you think of anything else – well, perhaps you'd give me a ring.'

'Even if it's a feeling?' asked Fran wickedly.

He smiled slightly, looking as though it hurt. 'If you think it's worth it, Mrs Castle.' He looked through to the kitchen where Libby had been unashamedly listening. 'Bye, Mrs Sarjeant.'

'Well,' said Libby, 'that was interesting.'

Fran watched the unmarked police car reverse down Allhallow's Lane. 'It was odd,' she said. 'You don't think he really believes my funny moments, do you?'

'Why not? I bet he looked in to your background last time. If a prestigious estate agency like Goodall and Smythe believe you, why shouldn't he?' Libby brought her a steaming mug.

'The police aren't exactly known for their unquestioning beliefs, are they?' Fran turned away from the window. 'Not the most trusting of souls.'

'He certainly seemed to be placing trust in your feelings this time,' said Libby, flopping into the sofa and forgetting the creak.

'That's going to collapse one of these days,' said Fran, returning to her chair.

'I know,' said Libby gloomily, 'and I don't suppose I shall be able to replace it. 'Anyway, what are we going to do next? Will you go and see the bureau when Charles gets it back? See if you can pick up anything from it?'

'Like where the will is?' Fran raised her eyebrows. 'I don't suppose I could. In fact, I don't suppose Charles really wants me poking my nose into things now. I bet he wishes he hadn't got in touch with me in the first place.'

'I rather thought he fancied you,' said Libby.

'So did I, at first. Heaven knows why. I'm hardly fanciable material any more, am I?'

'We've had this conversation before,' said Libby, 'and it doesn't get us anywhere. Anyway, there's still Guy Wolfe. He fancies you, and he's unattached.'

'We weren't talking about unattached men, Libby. We were talking about Charles and wills.'

'Well, are you going to do anything about it? Charles can hardly complain if you drop in to see him, can he? You used to live there, after all, and it's only natural that you should be interested in what's happening. He got you in to it in the first place.'

Fran sighed. 'I suppose so. Perhaps I'll give him a ring when I get back to the flat later on. If you're still sure I can borrow the car?'

'Of course. When do you want to go?'

'I'll go and pack, then I'll make a move, if that's OK.'

'Stay and have some lunch before you go,' said Libby, 'and is there anything you'd like me to do at the flat?'

'Just make sure Peter and Harry really don't mind. And if we're going to have some lunch before I go, I'll go and buy it.' Fran stood up.

'You don't have to,' said Libby.

'I know I don't, but you've been so good to me. At least let me treat you to some pâté or something.'

Fran called in to see Harry in The Pink Geranium after buying lunch at the eight-til-late.

'Come to view the premises?' he asked. 'Come on, I'll take you up. We're not open at lunchtime today.'

Fran admired the flat and thanked Harry profusely, delicately mentioning the subject of rent.

'Oh, I shouldn't think Pete wants to bother with rent,' he said, 'although perhaps you could take a share of the bills and stuff? It's not separate from the caff, you see.'

'That's fine,' said Fran, 'and I don't expect I'll be here for long. Libby thinks I should move down here permanently, so I'd have to look for a long term let.'

'Do you want to move?'

'Yes, now she's put the idea in my head. I don't know why I didn't think of it before, except that

121

I wouldn't have known where to move to.'

'Well, you've got us, now, ducky,' said Harry, draping a friendly arm round her shoulders. 'Good place to move to.'

'Thanks, Harry,' said Fran, going pink.

After a lunch of pâté, bread and cheese, Fran left, jerking down the lane in the unfamiliar car, early enough to beat the worst of the Friday rush hour. 'Although you'll be going against the traffic most of the way,' said Libby, as she waved her off. 'Until you get to the M25, anyway.'

Returning to the conservatory, Libby propped her latest views of Nethergate against the wall and surveyed them critically. She knew they were of no great artistic merit, but, as Guy Wolfe said, they sold to the visitors who had discovered the retro charms of Nethergate. People who, like her, had fond memories of seaside holidays in the fifties and sixties and were surprised to find that somewhere like this still existed.

There was one, at the end, of the view through the cottage window that Guy had said was a favourite. She had told him that she'd been to see it when house-hunting, but that wasn't the only reason she loved it. When she was a child, she'd had a picture on her bedroom wall exactly like it. She couldn't remember where it had come from, but it reminded her of holidays spent with her family in a boarding house just round the corner from The Swan. Perhaps her parents had bought it for her as a holiday present, and just perhaps it was that self same cottage. She still felt drawn to it, and had been quite devastated to realise she couldn't afford to buy it. One day, she said to herself, and then wondered how. Her "pretty peeps", as Agatha Troy would have called them, were hardly likely to earn her a fortune, and at her age she was unlikely to fall in to any kind of lucrative career, unless...

At that point, the rather startling thought popped in to her mind of re-marriage. To Ben. 'No,' she said out loud, and shook her head to dislodge the thought, which seemed to be making her scalp crawl. She must *not* think like that. She was perfectly happy on her own with Sidney, she had her own friends and no longer had to wash anyone's socks, or apologise to them for being late. And her relationship, if it could be called that, with Ben was hardly such that any sort of shared life would be on the cards.

'Think about something else,' she said to Sidney, going back into the kitchen. 'Think about Fran's Aunt Eleanor.'

She made herself a cup of tea and took it in to the garden under the cherry tree. Sidney accompanied her and sat on Fran's chair, no doubt intending to inform her that she was an inferior lap.

'So,' she told him, 'Auntie's murdered, either by Barbara Denver while she's alone in the room with her, or by someone else, between the time the two nurses saw her and Barbara arriving. Or could one of the nurses have gone back? Or someone come in through the french windows?'

Sidney made no answer, but gazed at her through slitted eyes.

'Oh, you're no use,' she said.

'Who isn't?' said a voice.

Libby spilt her tea.

'How did you get here?' she said.

'Down the path from the top of the lane,' said Ben. 'Didn't you realise there was one?'

'No, I certainly didn't,' said Libby. 'I shall never feel safe again.'

'Whether there's a path or not, anyone could have got over your back fence from the field, couldn't they? I just have.' Ben grinned and, picking up Sidney, sat down on the other chair.

'I didn't even hear you,' said Libby indignantly.

'No, because you were talking to Sidney, very seriously.'

Libby blushed. 'Yes, well, I'm on my own a lot.'

'More, perhaps, than you need be,' said Ben.

'Would you like tea?' asked Libby, standing up hurriedly. 'I spilt mine.'

'That would be nice. Actually, I came to find out whether you still wanted to go to the pub tonight. I'm quite happy to go further afield.'

'I thought we'd decided on the pub because of driving?' said Libby.

'We did, but I just thought it would be nicer to get out of the village for a change. We could go down to Nethergate, if you like.'

'Why Nethergate?'

'It's come up rather a lot recently, hasn't it? And I haven't been over there for ages. We could go to The Swan, if you like.'

Libby shook her head. 'Not The Swan,' she said, 'but if you'd like to go over there, I'm quite happy. There's that nice little flint pub on the harbour wall, isn't there? That's got a restaurant.'

'The Sloop? I'll give them a ring. Do you want

to look up their number while you put the kettle on?' Ben fished in his pocket and retrieved his mobile.

Libby nodded and went back in to the house. What was it about Nethergate? First of all Fran's relations, then the cottage on the sea wall, now Ben wanted to go there. As she moved the heavy kettle back on to the Rayburn she tried to push the thought that these coincidences were omens to the back of her mind. Omens they might be, but good, or bad?

She looked up The Sloop's telephone number while the kettle boiled, and shouted it out to Ben. By the time she took two fresh mugs of tea outside, he was idly stroking Sidney and gazing up through the branches of the cherry tree.

'It's nice here,' he said, accepting his mug. 'It's a proper garden, not like the one at the Manor. That feels like a municipal park.'

Libby was shocked. 'It's a beautiful garden,' she said.

'For a park.' He grinned up at her. 'The Sloop has a table for us at eight o'clock. Shall we go early? We can have a walk along the front.'

Libby looked up at the sky. 'If the weather holds.'

'Pessimist. Can you be ready by six thirty?'

Libby nodded. 'Lovely,' she said.

Later, climbing out of the shower, she wondered why Ben had bothered to walk all the way down to see her this afternoon. He could easily have phoned. A treacherous thought suggested he might have wanted to see Fran, not knowing she was going home, but he hadn't even mentioned Fran, and Libby hadn't told him about the planned move to the flat over the Pink Geranium. No, she mustn't think like that. Just be glad he wanted to see her, and stop all this nonsense about people's motives. Face value, that was how you should take people. Stop all this analysing.

Finally arrayed in a long floaty skirt that had recently returned to fashion and a tunic that, as far as Libby was concerned, had never been away, she fed Sidney and locked the back door, just as she heard Ben's car in the lane.

The sun still shone as they drove down the hill in to Nethergate, between flint cottages and ship-lap houses. They turned left at the bottom along Harbour Street, past Guy Wolfe's gallery and up to where The Sloop Inn overlooked the tiny harbour and the Harbour Master's Office. Getting out, Libby breathed in seaweed and fish and smiled happily.

'Like it here, then?' said Ben, coming round the car to join her.

'Love it. See along there?' Libby pointed. 'That's the cottage I wanted to buy before I bought number 17.'

'Why didn't you?' Ben turned to look at it.

'Too expensive. Sea views at the front and tree covered hills at the back are out of my price range.' Libby sighed. 'It was gorgeous, though.'

Ben took her arm and they began to walk along the harbour wall towards the cottage.

'Is it the one you paint? The view from the window?'

'Yes.' Libby looked at him in surprise. 'How did

126

you know?'

'Because you've done several pictures of the same subject. I bought a winter one from Guy.'

'You didn't!' gasped Libby.

'I did.' He grinned at her. 'I liked it. Still like it. It hangs in my flat, although if I come back to the village permanently it might have to go into storage unless I can persuade Mum to hang it on her wall. More of a Green Lady person, my Mum.'

'Are you thinking of coming back permanently, then?'

'Well, now I'm semi-retired and Mum's struggling with the upkeep of the Manor I thought I might. Susan's going back home, did you know?'

Susan had been staying with their mother since the death of her husband, and Libby was pleased that she might be getting back on her feet.

'That's good,' she said. 'Do you think I should visit her?'

'I'd leave it a bit,' said Ben, 'and I'll have a word with her. She's very sensitive, you know.'

Libby personally disputed this, remembering Susan's stoic and unimaginative demeanour, but said nothing. Ben paused outside the cottage. The window that was the subject of Libby's paintings stood open, a yellow patterned curtain blowing gently beyond the deep window shelf.

'Lovely,' murmured Ben, almost to himself.

'Yes.' Libby turned to look at the view. 'Lovely.'

They walked to the end of Harbour Street and sat outside The Swan with a drink before walking back to The Sloop for dinner, where they sat at a table overlooking the harbour, with a small red-shaded lamp between them. They chatted in a desultory fashion through the starters, the main course and Ben's dessert, but when the coffee was served, he put his elbows on the table, rested his chin on his hands, and said, 'So what's all this about Fran moving into the caff?'

Startled, Libby sat back in her chair. 'Did Peter tell you?'

'Of course. Was it a secret?'

'No, but you hadn't mentioned it.'

'If I had, you would have thought I was interested in Fran, wouldn't you?' He gave her a sly grin. 'You still do.'

Libby felt the familiar colour rising up her neck. 'No, of course not,' she said hastily.

'Yes, you do. You thought so when I first introduced you, and you've never quite got rid of the suspicion, have you?'

Libby stared into his eyes as though mesmerised. She shook her head.

He reached across the table and took her hand. 'Well, you can get rid of it right now. Fran and I worked together on a couple of projects, but that's all. I felt sorry for her living in London, so I used to get her down here whenever I could. I never fancied her. Honest.'

Libby nodded. 'Sorry I was so transparent. And so childish.'

'No you weren't. Don't forget I've had the benefit of your views on men and marriage. You're hardly likely to take me on trust. Especially after I behaved so badly during the – well, after the...'

'I know. But I think we were all in a state then. Better to start again and put it all behind us.'

He squeezed her hand. 'I always knew you were a sensible woman,' he said, smiling.

'I don't think I've ever been called sensible before,' mused Libby. 'I'm not sure I like it.'

## Chapter Thirteen

Fran drove carefully in Libby's Renault, got stuck in traffic and watched worriedly as the engine began to overheat. Luckily, the jam broke before the engine and Fran limped home with relieved sweat on her brow.

The Betjeman flat looked even more depressing after the cosiness of Libby's cottage and the bright cleanliness of The Pink Geranium flat. Fran sighed, filled the kettle and decided to phone Charles. This time, he answered.

'The police interviewed me this morning, Charles. Have they been to you, yet?'

'Yesterday, when I got home. What did they ask you?' He sounded tired.

'Not a lot. How long was it since I'd seen you and Aunt Eleanor, whether I'd met Barbara and Paul before, how much I knew about the situation. That's all, really. What about you?'

'What you'd expect. Had I actually arrived before I'd said and shoved a pillow over Auntie's face. What about the will. Where was it, and why didn't I know.'

'It does sound odd, you must admit.' Fran moved over to the kettle and poured boiling water on to a teabag in her favourite cat mug. 'As executor, you'd expect to know where it was, who the solicitor is and what was in it, wouldn't you?'

'All right, Fran, I know.' He sounded irritated. 'I'm hopeless. You must wonder how on earth I got this far in life. Well, you'd be right. I'm still living in a flat in my dead Aunt's house, I've got no money to speak of and a failing career. There, now you know the worst.'

Fran was silent for a long moment. 'Well, that makes two of us, doesn't it, Charles?' she said at length. 'I'm just about to move in to the flat over The Pink Geranium–'

'The what?'

'Peter and Harry's restaurant. Libby's friends, you know?'

'Oh, right. So, a charitable gesture, is it?'

'Exactly. So you see, we're exactly the same. Failing career, charity homes, no money.'

'You mean your – er – investigation career?'

'I don't get much work that way, you know. When Goodall and Smythe first started using me it was quite a selling point, but it's become passé now, I suppose.'

'So,' said Charles slowly, 'you're moving down to Steeple Martin. Is this because of the – er, well, Aunt Eleanor?'

'No, Charles.' Fran fished out the teabag and added milk to the mug. 'It's because Libby suggested it. I've got nothing to keep me in London, and if I do get any work I can travel from Kent just as easily as from here.'

'But you'll be down there. You could keep an

eye...' he tailed off.

'The day before yesterday you didn't want me to get involved.'

'Well.' He hesitated. 'I suppose you've made me feel better about my circumstances, now.'

Privately Fran still felt that Charles was a bit of a failure, and a wimp, as Libby had said, but now he had admitted it she felt slightly more charitable towards him.

'I'm certainly interested, especially now DCI Murray himself has been to see me. If I hear any more, I'll let you know.'

'Yes, keep in touch. I expect I'll need to come down again, so I'll give you a ring, shall I?'

'Yes, do,' said Fran, 'But I was actually going to ask if I could pop round and see the old house while I'm up here. Would you mind?'

'Of course not,' said Charles, sounding surprised. 'When did you want to come?'

'I thought on my way back to Kent tomorrow, would that be OK?'

'Give me a ring when you're leaving, then,' said Charles. 'Are you sure you know how to get here?'

'Unless they've dug up the roads, or turned them all one way I should be all right. I'll ring you in the morning,' said Fran, 'see you then.'

Next, she rang her daughter Lucy, and after the required conversations with her grandchildren explained what she was about to do. Lucy wasn't entirely pleased that her mother was leaving London and depriving her of an occasional babysitter, but brightened up when she was told that the move wasn't necessarily permanent, and anyway, she and the children could come down for a holiday in the country.

Next, she rang Chrissie, the youngest of her children. She and her husband Bruce thoroughly disapproved of Fran and her lifestyle, so the information that she was moving to the country, however temporarily, came as a pleasant surprise. She sent a text to son Jeremy in America, and wondered if there was anyone else she should tell. Depressingly, there wasn't.

The following morning, Fran was ready to go. She rang Charles, and set off across London. She found Mountville Road without mishap, and pulled in to the first parking place that she could find, stood on the pavement underneath the lime tree and looked up at the house. It hadn't changed much. No one had replaced the original sash windows with aluminium or white plastic and the patterned tiled path to the front door remained the same. The other houses in the street had all been smartened up, but this one had always been a family home and sat unchanging, like an elderly relation in the midst of its newly grown family. There were sleeping policemen in the road, too, to prevent the boy racers who met on the common at one end of the road from launching themselves and their vehicles towards the hospital at the other, where they frequently ended up anyway.

The leaves of the lime tree whispered above her head and she took a step forward. She put a hand tentatively against the stained glass and pushed. Ahead of her was the passage that she remembered and the flight of stairs to the upstairs flat where Frank and Eleanor had lived. The door at the top of the stairs was open, too, and light spilled out illuminating the worn stair carpet.

At the top of the stairs, just as she remembered, a corridor ran both ways with the door ahead open on to a large bright room that she thought had been the kitchen. It still was. A rather tatty looking blue formica topped table stood just to the right of the window, which looked, just as she remembered, over the large garden with more lime trees at the bottom. On the right hand wall was a cream painted fireplace with a gas fire and a sagging armchair at the side and to the left a deep, cracked butler sink and a free standing cooker with an eye level grill. Fran frowned. It looked almost exactly as it had forty years ago when she had last sat here. She looked over her shoulder and the built in dresser was still there, but no radio stood on the end and the china inside was different.

'Sorry, I was putting out the rubbish.'

Fran jumped and turned round to find Charles smiling at her, and looking far more relaxed than he had for the last week.

'I shouldn't have barged in, I'm sorry,' she said, 'but the door was open, and I just couldn't resist it. It's hardly changed.'

'No, I don't think Aunt liked change, much. My flat's a bit different.'

'Oh! This is isn't yours?'

'No. I've got the one downstairs. They used to rent it out.'

'They did *what?*' Fran was aghast. 'Do you mean they turned my family out when they

133

didn't actually *need* it?'

Charles turned faintly pink. 'I don't think it was quite like that,' he said. 'Although I don't know any of the details, of course.'

'Well, I wish I could find out. That makes me really cross. When I think of what my mother went through, and having my father die so young, too. I can't believe his own brother would be so cruel. It must have been your Aunt Eleanor's fault.' Fran glared at Charles, who turned even pinker.

'Honestly, I don't know what happened, Fran,' he said. 'If I could find the will there might be some explanation. Or papers.'

Fran looked round. 'Aren't there any here? Have you looked?'

'Not really.' He looked worried. 'Do you think I should?'

'Oh, Charles!' Fran was exasperated. 'I don't believe you. Do you really mean to tell me you haven't looked up here – in her old home?'

'She kept all her important papers in the bureau,' said Charles, rallying. 'I told you that.'

'I bet you'll find she didn't. I remember my mother hiding all sorts of things in different places. She always told me what she'd done, but sometimes she'd forget. When she died I had to hunt round everywhere to find her building society book.'

'I suppose it's all right if I look, then.' Charles looked round the kitchen. 'Do you want to give me a hand?'

It was odd for Fran to hunt through the kitchen dresser and cupboards she had known as a child.

Part of her wished it had all been changed, especially as it would all belong to someone else very soon. The wiring had been attended to, which was a relief, she thought, remembering the fabric covered wires and wobbly plugs.

Nothing was found in the kitchen, except a few old wartime recipe leaflets tucked into the back of a shelf. Guessing they had belonged to her mother, Fran carefully wrapped them in tissues and slid them in to her handbag.

The large sitting room overlooking the street was sparsely furnished, but still contained an old television with a sliding door. Fran slid it aside until it stuck and pressed the switch, but, perhaps unsurprisingly, nothing happened. Charles went round the edges of the rug, peering underneath, and Fran looked behind all the remaining pictures on the wall. There was very little to search.

The bedroom, however, was a different matter. Aunt Eleanor had had a very smart inlaid walnut bedroom suite, ladies and gents wardrobes, tallboy, dressing table, chest of drawers, bedside cabinets and a splendid bed.

'These'll take some searching,' said Charles gloomily. 'Shall I make some tea?'

'That'd be nice,' said Fran, brushing dust off her nose. 'I'll make a start on the wardrobes.'

Aunt Eleanor's wardrobe smelt like an old fashioned fur depository, and Fran was suddenly reminded of one of her favourite books, where two girls go to collect their Aunt's legacy, only to find it comprising several old fur coats. Smiling to herself, she began to go through the pockets.

The contents were interesting, but unenlightening.

Charles brought in two mugs of tea, apologising for taking such a long time, but explaining that he'd had to go downstairs to make it. The faint suggestion of complaint in his voice made Fran grit her teeth.

They set to again, and after about half an hour, Charles gave a surprised grunt.

'What?' said Fran.

'Something stuck here,' said Charles, struggling with a drawer in the tallboy. 'Can you give me a hand?'

'What do you think it is?' Fran came over and knelt beside him. 'Could it be the will?'

'How do I know? It just feels as though something's jammed and I can't pull the drawer right out.'

Fran felt as far as she could along the side of the drawer. 'I can feel paper. Perhaps it's just a newspaper that's got stuck.'

'What would a newspaper be doing in a drawer?' asked Charles.

'Lining it. My mum lined drawers with newspapers.' Fran withdrew her hand and pulled out the drawer above. 'There, now we can see down in to it.'

Poking up above the left hand side of the drawer was what looked like a brown envelope. Fran carefully began to ease it out, while Charles made unhelpful suggestions from the sidelines. Eventually, it was free, and proved to be something like an old ration book.

'Damn,' said Charles, sitting back on his heels

and reaching for his mug. 'I thought we'd got it, then.'

Fran looked at him thoughtfully. 'I think we might be on to something here,' she said. 'If that's one hiding place, I bet she used a similar one for other documents.' She stood up. 'Let's check all the other drawers.'

However, there was nothing in any of the drawers in the bedroom, and they returned disheartened to the living room.

'No drawers in here,' said Charles. 'Shall we try the small bedroom next?'

'Yes, but hang on.' Fran went over to the television. 'This stuck, didn't it?'

She knelt down and began to push back the sliding door, which refused to move. Inserting two fingers between the door and the screen, sure enough she felt more paper. This was slightly easier to remove than the ration book in the bedroom, and was revealed as a long white envelope labelled 'The Last Will and Testament of Eleanor Ann Bridges'.

## Chapter Fourteen

The colour bled from Charles's face. Fran raised her eyebrows at him and held out the envelope.

'You open it,' he said in a shaking voice.

'I can't,' said Fran, 'I expect it's against the law or something.'

'If I'm the executor I can ask you to open it,

137

can't I?'

'I suppose so,' said Fran, doubtfully.

'Is the solicitor's name on the front?' Charles edged a little nearer.

'Yes.' Fran turned the envelope over. 'It could be a different will, couldn't it? Not the one you know about.'

'Oh, for God's sake, just open it and let's find out.' Charles sat down suddenly on the edge of a chair.

Fran opened the flap and withdrew the folded document. 'Dated ten years ago,' she said, and read a little further. 'Naming you as the executor.' She held it out. 'Here. I mustn't read any further.'

Reluctantly, he took it. 'I suppose I'd better phone the solicitor,' he said, turning it over in his hands.

'For someone who was so concerned to find it, you don't seem very keen,' said Fran.

Charles smiled weakly. 'It's just – I don't know – after all the worry, it's a bit of a shock.'

'Well, why don't we go downstairs and you can ring the solicitor.' Fran got up and went towards the bedroom. 'I'll collect the mugs.'

'I can't ring the solicitor, it's Saturday.'

'Oh, so it is. What a lot's happened in a week, hasn't it?'

'I met you, for a start,' said Charles, brightening.

*Oh, Lord,* thought Fran.

'Get the mugs,' said Charles, standing up, 'and I'll show you the flat downstairs. It's really rather nice.'

The flat downstairs had been substantially modernised, unlike the one on the first floor. The layout was the same as Fran remembered, a big living room and main bedroom at the front, and a bathroom and bedroom at the back, but the tiny kitchen had been knocked through into the second bedroom to make a good sized kitchen with a dining table in the window.

'Very nice,' she said. 'And the garden looks good, too.'

'I've tried to keep it up,' said Charles, moving to stand beside her, 'but I'm not a very good gardener.'

'Neither am I,' said Fran, 'but I loved the hollyhocks and the tea roses. They ought to be kept.'

'They are,' said Charles, pointing, 'but they're a bit out of control. So is that lilac.'

'Well, when the will is proved, perhaps you'll be able to afford a gardener,' said Fran, turning away from the window, unexpectedly moved by the sight of the garden.

'Yes,' said Charles, looking down at the will, which he still held as though it was about to go off in his hands.

'Why don't you see what it says?'

Charles sighed. 'I suppose so.' He perched on the edge of the table, spread the will out in front of him and began to read.

'Much as we expected really,' he said at last. 'The estate to be split down the middle, half to me and half to Barbara and Paul between them.'

'Well, that's excellent. You could buy out Barbara and Paul and keep the house.'

'I told you, I haven't any money.'

'But you have half the estate, not just half the house,' said Fran. 'Couldn't you use that?'

'I don't know that there's any money left,' said Charles, still staring down at the will.

'Well, you ought to know, you had Power of Attorney,' said Fran.

'Yes, but the fees at The Laurels were very high. And what with the bills here, and the rates, we'd almost gone through her capital.'

'Didn't she have a pension?'

'Only a state one, and it was based on Uncle Frank's. She'd never worked.'

'Didn't he have a proper pension plan?'

'I don't know.' Charles looked up. 'I didn't know anything about his affairs. I assume she sorted it all out.'

'Well, her solicitor will know,' said Fran. 'Let me know what happens.'

'I suppose I'd better let the police know, too,' said Charles, standing up and sighing again. 'This definitely gives me a motive, doesn't it?'

'Yes, but you knew that, didn't you? So did they. It doesn't really change anything.'

'No.' Charles put the will back in its envelope. 'I'll ring the police station now. Should I ask for – what's-his-name – the Chief Inspector?'

'DCI Murray. Didn't he give you a card when he interviewed you?'

'It wasn't him.' Charles went to a drawer in a kitchen cupboard. 'Here. DS Cole. He was at the inquest.'

'Well, they can't be very worried about you, then. I got the DCI.' Fran grinned at him. 'Stop worrying, Charles. It wasn't you, was it? So they'll catch whoever did it, and everything will be all right. Now,' she said, 'I must be off. Libby's old car isn't the most reliable at high speeds.'

Charles showed her to the door, and she took a last look at the majestic frontage.

'I loved it here, you know,' she said wistfully.

'Well, you can always come and visit while I'm here,' said Charles, leaning forward to kiss her cheek. 'Don't know how long that will be, of course.' He looked up at the house next door. 'Both that one and the one the other side have been bought by developers.'

'What!' gasped Fran. 'They aren't going to knock them down? They can't.'

'No, they're going to turn them into luxury flats, apparently. They wanted to buy this one, too, so that they could have communal gardens and convert the attics across all three to make a penthouse, but Aunt Eleanor refused. I bet she would have made a bundle.' He looked regretful for a moment. 'Still, they might want it even now.'

'They might. Shame you have to sell, though.'

'Wouldn't you, if it was yours? Much too big for just me.'

'You could always let out the other flat, like Aunt Eleanor did.'

'I'd have to do it up, first. There are regulations about letting property, you know.'

It was Fran's turn to sigh. 'I wish someone would tell my landlord that.'

'How much does he charge you?'

'Not much, so I suppose if he complied with all the regulations I wouldn't be able to afford it.

Anyway, I shall start looking for something down near Steeple Martin, then I won't have to stay there any longer.' She gave him a return peck on the cheek and turned to unlock the car. 'Keep in touch, Charles. Let me know what the police and the solicitor say.'

The drive down to Steeple Martin was much easier than the drive up. Fran drove into the village in the dusty heat of an August afternoon, and managed to park very close to The Pink Geranium. Harry was sitting at the old pine table in the window reading a newspaper.

'So, there you are! Have a good time in the fleshpots?'

'Hectic, naturally. I've brought as much as I thought I would need. Can I unload it now?'

'I'll take you up,' said Harry. 'Hang on while I get the keys.'

After he'd helped Fran take her bags and boxes in to the flat, he rang Libby.

'Thought you might want to celebrate with your mate,' he said. 'Your car's outside, too.'

'I'm driving that back,' said Fran loudly, so that Libby could hear. 'I'll come now.'

Harry shook his head. 'No, she says she's coming over with a bottle. You just potter about and wait for her. I'll probably come up and cadge a glass when she arrives.' He looked round the flat with an approving nod. 'Going to be good having someone up here.'

Libby arrived ten minutes later and puffed up the stairs flourishing a bottle of champagne.

'Golly, it's real,' said Fran, who seemed to have caught Libby's habit of schoolgirl exclamations.

'It's been kicking around since – well, since *The Hop Pickers,*' said Libby. 'I couldn't seem to find a time to break it out. Harry's coming up with glasses in case you didn't bring any.'

'Damn, I didn't. I didn't bring any crockery or pots either.'

'Never mind, I expect most of that's here, or Harry can find you some. Come on, tell me all about your visit to the big smoke. Did you go and see Charles?'

Fran told her all about the search for Aunt Eleanor's will, interrupted half way through by Harry with the glasses, who opened the bottle with panache and listened avidly to the rest of the story.

'Very suspicious,' he said, after toasting Fran and the flat. 'Do you reckon he's been pocketing the funds and needs to sell the house?'

'What funds?' said Libby.

'Auntie's, of course,' said Harry.

'There aren't any, according to Charles,' said Fran. 'The nursing home fees and running the house took everything she had.'

'Oh, well, nice idea,' said Harry.

Soon after that, Harry left to get on, he told them, with prepping up for the evening. Fran topped up Libby's glass and sat back in her chair.

'So what happened to you last night?' she asked.

'Not a lot.' Libby looked out of the window. 'We went to Nethergate.'

'I thought you were going to the pub here?'

'No, Ben wanted to get away from the village. So we went to The Sloop. It's opposite the Harbour. Just along from Guy's gallery.'

'And?'

'And nothing, really. We had a very nice meal, then he drove me home and came in for a coffee.'

'A coffee? A euphemistic coffee?'

Libby blushed. 'No. A real coffee. And a whisky. He parked his car right up the lane on their land and walked home that way.'

'I'm not prying, but was any progress made?'

'You are prying, and yes it was. Not physically–' Libby felt the colour come back in to her cheeks '–but we decided we should take it slowly and see how we go.'

Fran sniffed. 'Doesn't sound as though he's very keen,' she said.

'It was me, really,' said Libby. 'I'm even more wary than I was before.'

'Wary about Ben?'

'About the whole thing. Sex and everything.'

'I thought you and he – well, you said...'

'Yes, we did, but as I think I said to you, it was a life affirming thing, I'm sure. You know, like after a funeral.'

'No.' Fran looked surprised. 'What about funerals?'

'Apparently there are more frantic couplings after a funeral than any other event. It's supposed to be a need to make sure you're alive. Even if it's with an unsuitable partner.' Libby took a huge swig of champagne and coughed.

'Sounds interesting,' said Fran. 'Trouble is, the only funerals I've been to have had very old people as guests.'

'Perhaps Aunt Eleanor's will change all that.' Libby topped up Fran's glass and then drained the bottle in to her own. 'So tell me what you're going to do next?'

'About Aunt Eleanor? Nothing. It's nothing to do with me. And now Charles has found the will there's no need to go badgering the Denvers, is there?'

'Nooo...' Libby looked thoughtful. 'But I'm still not sure about them. Very suspicious, if you ask me.'

'Well, if they took the bureau to conceal the will it's just too bad, because we've got it, now, haven't we?'

'Yes, but didn't you say something about the Headlam and a legacy? Suppose there's a later will?'

Fran looked at Libby, open-mouthed in horror. 'Oh, my God, of course! That's what all the fuss is about.'

'Is it?'

'Of course it is. I don't know why. But you're absolutely right, Libby. There is a later will.'

## Chapter Fifteen

Libby helped Fran unpack, and discovered that the flat was, in fact, equipped with all the basic necessities, other than champagne glasses.

'I can cook something for myself this evening, then,' said Fran happily. 'Would you like to join me? Or are you busy?'

'No, I'd love to. But I'll take Romeo home first.'

'Romeo?'

'Romeo the Renault. Sorry. I don't usually do silly things like naming cars, but it just seemed appropriate.'

Fran raised her eyebrows. 'I won't ask why,' she said.

Libby drove the Renault home despite the two and a bit glasses of champagne, and parked thankfully on the edge of the so-called green opposite number 17. Sidney greeted her from the front door step, demanding to be let in and fed.

'Come on, then, horrible,' she said. 'Then I'll go and have a shower and change. I'm dining out – again!'

By now, it was late afternoon and the brassy August sky had clouded over. Libby fed Sidney on his favourite chipped Victorian saucer and stood outside the conservatory gazing out at the fields. What a weird week it had been. First, Fran's surprise visit and the news about her dead Aunt, then meeting with Ben, finding out about the murder and the inquest, then the date with Ben and finally, Fran moving into The Pink Geranium. Libby wondered what her horoscope had to say about all this. 'You are entering an exciting new phase in your life,' perhaps.

She went back inside and rummaged for a bottle of wine to take with her. There were none, so that meant dropping in to the eight-til-late on the way to Fran's. Luckily, they kept a few decent bottles, so that shouldn't be a problem. She went upstairs to shower and think about Ben.

Last night he had kissed her. Once when they arrived at number 17, and again when he left. He had understood instinctively that this was as far as she could go, despite their recent brief relationship, but it didn't stop her wishing it had gone further. She held her face up to the grumbling, sporadic water and sighed. Here she went again, all confused about middle aged relationships. If Ben had any sense, he'd fend her off with a barge pole, and if she carried on being so erratic, he would. The trouble was, she thought, as she flung a towel round her shoulders and dripped in to the bedroom, when he got close to her, she went all breathless, and something happened to her solar plexus, whereas when she actually *thought* about it, she started wondering if all he wanted was one thing (which he'd already had), whether she was stigmatised as *easy*, as her mother would have said, and whether she was going to be abandoned for a younger model as soon as one happened along. She sighed. It was very difficult being faded, fat and over fifty.

Harry waved to her as she waited outside the door to the flat. Fat raindrops plopped on to her head from the darkening sky and she hunched her shoulders into her cape.

'You look cheerful,' said Fran, as she opened the door.

'It's the weather,' said Libby going past her and beginning to haul herself up the stairs. 'And being fat and over fifty.'

'Never mind,' said Fran, following her up and into the pleasant living room which looked out over the village street. 'Now I'm here, we can go out on the pull. Do they have any geriatric night clubs in Canterbury?'

Libby laughed, handing over the wine. 'There's the Over Sixties – but we'd be far too young for them. That would be nice, wouldn't it? Being the flighty young things.'

Fran, looking more casual than Libby had ever seen her, in jeans and a loose shirt, took the bottle in to the kitchen to open it. 'Is this something to do with going out with Ben last night? Introspection and all that?'

'Part of it. I can't seem to relax and let it happen, if you know what I mean. I suppose I'm expecting him to do a Derek.'

'And go off with a floosie?' Fran handed Libby a glass of wine. 'I'm sure he wouldn't.'

'Oh, well, anyway, let's talk about the murder instead.' Libby sat down in a chair by the window. 'Far more interesting.'

'Charles phoned.' Fran sat down opposite. 'He told DCI Murray about the will, and they want to see him again. Apparently, he said he couldn't come down – business commitments, or something – so someone's going up to see him tomorrow.'

'Will they want to take the will as evidence, or something?'

'I expect so. Oh, dear, that's awkward, isn't it?'

'I don't think he should let them have it. Couldn't he go out and find somewhere to make a photocopy of it?'

'I'll suggest it. But as he's now got the name and address of the solicitors it doesn't really matter, does it? They'll have a copy.'

'And what does it matter anyway,' said Libby, leaning forward conspiratorially, 'if there's another will?'

'But we don't know that for a fact,' said Fran uneasily.

'You do. And you're always right.' Libby sat back with an air of having proved her point. 'All we have to do is find it.'

'Oh, great. Here we go again.' Fran stood up and went towards the kitchen. 'Come and help me with the dishes.'

Later, as they sat over the rather nice cheese supplied by the eight-til-late, Libby returned to the subject.

'If Marion Headlam is so sure she – or The Laurels – was left something in the will, perhaps she witnessed it?'

'No.' Fran shook her head. 'You can't witness a will if you're a beneficiary. You can be an executor, but not a witness.'

'How about the nurses? Those two who were at the inquest?'

'That's a thought,' said Fran, putting down her wine glass. 'I wonder if anyone's asked them?'

'I bet Barbara has, if she was so concerned to find the will in the first place. By the way, has Paul organised the transport of the furniture yet?'

'I didn't ask, but I suppose it isn't as crucial now, is it?'

Libby thought for a moment, then stood up. 'I hope you've noticed how little I've been smoking over the last few days,' she said, 'but now I need one. Can I go and stand on your fire escape in the rain?'

Fran laughed. 'The rain's stopped,' she said, 'and we can go down into Harry's little garden if

149

you like. There's a table and chairs out there.'

Ensconced at the table, having shouted to Harry in his kitchen, Libby lit her cigarette and blew out smoke with relish.

'So, how about I make friends with one of those nurses and find out?' she said.

'And just how do you propose to do that?' asked Fran. 'Go up and say "Please can I be your friend? And did you witness a will recently?"'

'I'm sure I could find a way,' said Libby. 'I wonder where they live?'

'Not far from The Laurels, I would have thought. But I still don't see how you can do it.'

'No, neither do I,' said Libby, 'but I sure as hell intend to try.'

'What do you suppose Charles will say?' Fran topped up their glasses from a new bottle. 'It's nothing to do with you, after all.'

'I'm only doing it to help,' said Libby, affronted. 'Anyway, why would it have anything to do with him? Me making friends, I mean.'

Fran shook her head. 'It'll end in tears,' she said.

'What will?' Peter appeared from the kitchen door, carrying a glass.

'Libby investigating,' said Fran.

'Not again,' said Peter, sitting down between them. 'You know what it does to friendships, Lib. Can't you leave it alone?'

'This doesn't affect any friends, Pete. This is academic.'

'Nosey, more likely. And what investigating are you going to be doing, anyway? Is it going to put you in danger like last time?'

'Of course not.' Libby looked away uncomfortably. There were certain things she didn't want to be reminded of.

'She's going to make friends with a couple of murder suspects,' said Fran, grinning.

'They aren't suspects, are they? I thought we said witnesses to the will.'

'*We* didn't say anything. And either of them could have done it, couldn't they? Before Barbara got there?'

'Oh, well, if they were witnesses to the will they can't have done it for money, and what other reason could they possibly have had?'

'Libby, we don't know they were witnesses to the will!' said Fran, exasperated. 'For goodness' sake.'

Peter patted her on the arm. 'See what she's like? Bull in a china shop. Aren't you sorry you moved down, now?'

'It's not permanent,' said Fran hastily. 'At least not in your lovely flat.' She stopped. 'That sounded rubbish, didn't it? I mean, I'd love to be able to stay in your flat, but I must find somewhere permanent. And I don't regret it, not a bit. I don't know why I didn't think of it sooner.'

'Well, that's good, then,' said Peter. 'Do you want a nightcap? Harry can come and relax for five minutes before he starts the washing up.'

'Washing up? He doesn't have to do it, does he?' Fran was shocked.

'Who else? Him and Donna, and me, occasionally, we do everything.'

'But he's left Donna on her own sometimes, I know he has,' said Libby.

151

'Ah, well, we've got the boy.' Peter tapped the side of his nose and stood up. 'Mind you, the "boy" does change from time to time, depending on who we can get hold of. I'll go and fetch chef.'

Much later, Libby wandered home along the damp high street, replete with red wine and Harry's brandy. All three of them, Fran, Peter and Harry, had tried to dissuade her from investigating anything to do with Aunt Eleanor's murder, and though she knew they were right and sensible, she also knew she would carry on regardless. If, she thought, as she turned in to Allhallow's Lane and stepped in a puddle, she could find a way to do it.

The red light on the answerphone winked at her when she came in. Ignoring Sidney's importuning, she pressed the button and felt her stomach go into its little routine as she heard Ben's voice.

'Hi, Lib, sorry I didn't ring earlier, but Dad had a bit of a turn this morning and Mum and I ended up in hospital all day. He's fine now, but they're keeping him in overnight. I'm going to stay at The Manor for the time being, as now Susan's gone back home Mum's going to find it difficult to cope on her own. Anyway,' she heard him take a breath, 'you'll never guess who I saw at the hospital? One of the nurses from that nursing home. And I bet you're wondering how I knew, aren't you? Well, give me a ring, and I'll tell you. Speak soon. Bye.'

There was a pause, then she heard the hum of the dialling tone.

'Too late now,' she told Sidney, as she went

towards the kitchen, shedding cape and basket as she went, 'I'll have to ring him in the morning.' She found she was grinning. 'And he wants me to.'

It was well after breakfast time when she finally plucked up courage to ring The Manor, only to be told by Hetty that Ben had gone to pick his father up from hospital. Deciding he wouldn't be able to answer his mobile on such a delicate errand, Libby left a message with Hetty, and went into the conservatory to pretend to work. The rain had eased off over night, but the blazingly hot days of earlier in the summer seemed to have come to an end. Autumn was obviously on its way. She decided on a new painting from "her" window, with a jar of red leaves on the sill, a rough sea and ominous sky.

For once, she was so absorbed in her work, it took her several minutes to realise that someone was knocking quite hard on the front door. Even Sidney, curled up on top of the unlit Calor gas heater, raised his head and glared at her reprovingly. Wiping blue paint-stained fingers on her painting shirt, she went to open the door.

'Ben!'

He was leaning against the doorjamb, arms folded, legs crossed at the ankles, looking for all the world, she thought, like a model for the older man. *What could he possibly see in me?* she wondered.

'You've been working.' He stood upright and nodded at the shirt.

'Makes a change, doesn't it?' She stood aside. 'Coming in?'

153

'I wouldn't want to disturb you.'

'Don't be silly. It's time for a cup of tea, anyway.'

He followed her into the kitchen and perched on the edge of the table while she lifted the kettle on to the Rayburn.

'So,' she said turning round to face him. 'What's all this about a nurse?'

'Well,' he said, settling himself more comfortably, 'when Mum and I took Dad in to hospital yesterday, I went along to the Friends' coffee shop to get us a drink and a biscuit. You know where it is?'

Libby nodded. With three children she had frequented the hospital more than she might have liked.

'Anyway, while I was waiting to be served, I caught a bit of conversation. So I had to listen.'

'What conversation? What made you listen?'

'This woman was talking about The Laurels and the murder. And she said she'd been questioned.'

'Who was it?' Libby was excited. 'What did she look like? Perhaps it wasn't a nurse. Perhaps it was Marion Headlam, the owner.'

'No,' said Ben, 'because she said she'd been looking after the victim. I didn't get a good look, because I could hardly turn round and stare, so I had a quick glance when I left. She was sitting at a table with a woman in nurse's uniform, but she wasn't.'

'Wasn't what?'

'In uniform. She was wearing a sort of zip-up jacket. Dark hair and no make-up.'

'Ah. Nurse Redding. Did she have a moustache?'

Ben looked startled. 'I didn't notice.'

'Well, she's got one.' Libby turned round and poured water into two mugs. 'So what was she saying?'

'As far as I could make out, she was highly indignant about being questioned, and seemed to think it was all someone else's fault. She kept saying she could tell them a thing or two.'

'About what?' Libby pushed a mug across to him and sat at the table.

'How do I know? That's what she said: "I could tell them a thing or two." Then her friend said "I bet you could," in a gossiping sort of way, you know?'

Libby nodded. 'I wonder what she meant? Do you think she meant about the murder, or about something going on at The Laurels?'

'Could be nothing,' said Ben, blowing on his tea. 'Could be something like the owner not letting them have time off, or not being nice to the inmates. Something really simple.'

'Or it could be something she saw around the time of the murder. She and Nurse Warner were both in the room just before Barbara Denver arrived.'

'Surely she'd have told the police, then?'

Libby was getting excited again. 'No, because perhaps she decided to blackmail whoever it was she saw!'

Ben reached over and patted her hand. 'Don't get carried away, Lib. You don't want to be Miss Marple, remember?'

155

'Sorry.' Libby grinned at him. 'But listen, you haven't heard the latest from Fran. All sorts of excitement.'

She told him the recent developments about the will, and that Fran was certain there was a later version.

'So I wondered if either of the nurses witnessed a new version. I want to find out, but Fran, Pete and Harry told me not to,' she concluded.

'But you're going to anyway,' said Ben.

'I don't see how, but yes.'

'It really isn't any of your business, you know, Lib. But everyone will have told you that already.' He sighed. 'At least you were more-or-less legitimately involved in the last business. This time you aren't.'

'But you still tried to stop me last time.'

He looked uncomfortable. 'Lib, we've been over this. Don't rake it up again.'

'No, all right. Sorry.' She looked down at the table. 'I know I shouldn't be prying, but it's so intriguing. Especially as Fran sort of knew about it right from the start.'

'And she's certain about the will?'

Libby nodded. 'Absolutely. And from what I've seen of her magic moments, I'm sure she's right. What do you think? I mean, when she's done some investigating for you, has she always been right?'

'Well, she hasn't always found anything, if that's what you mean, which isn't to say there isn't something to find, just that she hasn't picked up on it. But when she's found something and we've checked into it, she's always been right. Goodall

156

and Smythe would never have employed her otherwise.'

'What kind of things did she find?' asked Libby. 'She's never told me.'

'Well, we told you about the thing that started it all off, didn't we? When she was showing someone round a house and started telling them about a murder that had happened?'

'Yes, that was when she worked for an ordinary estate agent, and they lost the sale and sacked her.'

'That's right, and when the clients went to Goodall and Smythe and told them all about her, she was offered the job. After that, she found out about hidden water courses, lost children, deaths, that sort of thing. She picked up on a couple of murders, too.'

'Did the police get involved?' Libby was wide eyed now.

'No, because they were murders that had been solved years ago. Quite naturally, when the houses came to be sold, no one was told about them. People don't want to live in houses where people have been murdered.'

'So,' said Libby, sitting back in her chair, 'you'd believe her if she had a feeling about something.'

'I'd certainly be willing to listen,' said Ben.

'So what do you think I should do?'

'About Fran? Or about investigating?'

'Both.'

'If Fran doesn't want you to, I don't think you should. Remember last time.'

'That's what Pete said last night. But I don't think it's that Fran doesn't want me to, it's just that she's more nervous than me.'

'Most people are,' said Ben. 'You just … well…'

'Blunder in like a bull in a china shop,' Libby finished for him. 'Pete said that last night, too. Ah, well. I'll have to think about it.'

'While you're thinking, what are you doing tonight?' Ben caught her hand again and her stomach turned over.

'Er – nothing.'

'Come for a drink? We can always ask the others if they want to join us.'

'Yes,' said Libby, mentally consigning "the others" to the farthest reaches of the county.

'Yes what? You'll come for a drink, or we can ask the others?'

'Well, either. Or both.' Libby felt the familiar colour creeping into her cheeks.

Ben stood up, went round the table and pulled her to her feet.

'We can always leave and come back here,' he said, putting his arms round her.

'Er – yes.' Libby cleared her throat. 'But then they'll … sort of…'

'Know we want to be together? So what's wrong with that? They knew before.'

And I was embarrassed before, Libby wanted to say.

'What is it that keeps worrying you?' Ben pressed cool lips to her forehead.

'Nothing,' muttered Libby into his chest.

He pulled back and smiled down at her. 'All right. I won't push. Not now, anyway.' He let her go. 'So, are we on for tonight?'

Libby nodded.

'I'll pick you up about eight, then, OK?' He leaned forward and kissed her again. 'See you then.'

## Chapter Sixteen

Despite Libby's best efforts, when Fran, Peter and Harry joined her and Ben in the pub later that evening, the subject of "Libby's investigation" came up yet again. Fran seemed more amused by it than anything else, and in the end, Ben gave up and insisted on calling her Miss Marple all evening. When he walked her home, he slung a casual arm round her shoulder, and called attention to it by calling good night to everyone they passed.

'So now,' he said, as they settled down in the living room, 'tell me what's worrying you about me.'

'It's very silly,' said Libby, not looking at him.

'Is it to do with me or what happened before?'

'No, it's me.' Libby took a deep breath. 'I've been alone a long time, and out of the dating game for donkey's years. I hate the thought of people talking about me behind my back and saying...' she stopped.

'Saying what? Isn't it nice for Libby and Ben that they've got together?'

'But is that what they'll say? Won't they think I'm being a sad old woman and you could do much better for yourself?'

'Is that really what you think?' Ben said.

'Well, sort of.'

There was a pause, while Libby stared into the empty grate and wished she'd never said anything.

'I think,' said Ben carefully, 'you're afraid I'll do a runner like your ex. And you think you'll be left looking foolish.'

Libby looked up. 'Yes.'

'Well, I can't say we're going to be together for ever, can I? It's far too soon to say anything like that.'

'I know, but we've already had one – er – upset.'

'Because of the exceptional circumstances. I don't suppose anyone thought you were foolish then.'

'I did.' Libby looked back at the fireplace.

'Oh, come here,' said Ben, standing up and pulling her into his arms. 'I don't think you're foolish, and I *don*'t think I could do any better for myself.'

'Thanks.'

'In fact, I think it's completely the other way round. What about Guy Wolfe? He fancied you rotten.'

'Guy? No, he didn't. Anyway, I think he's taken a fancy to Fran, now.'

'Has he, now? Good job, too. When did he meet her?'

'In The Swan when I went to pick her up last week. Gosh, what a long time ago it seems.'

'Well, a lot's happened.' He nuzzled her neck and she shivered. 'So what happens next?'

'Next?' asked Libby in a strangled voice.

'Now,' he whispered.

Fran had spent two very comfortable nights in the flat over The Pink Geranium. Sunday she pottered around unpacking and refused Harry's offer of Sunday lunch downstairs.

'I'll start relying on you too much, and then I'll stop cooking entirely,' she said. 'Besides, I still have a hankering for an old fashioned English roast.'

She had her roast, a lamb chop from the eight-til-late and slightly underdone roast potatoes, and, much to her surprise, dozed in the chair by the window in the afternoon. In the evening, after Ben phoned, she joined the others in the pub, and felt pleasingly like part of the community.

'I don't ever want to go back to London,' was her last thought before she fell asleep.

Monday morning she phoned Charles.

'I thought you were going to tell me what the police said yesterday,' she said when he answered.

'Not much. They didn't take the will away, but read the contents and took the name of the solicitors. I've just rung them, and someone's going to ring me back.'

'Charles, since I saw you on Saturday I've had a thought.' Fran sat in her window chair and looked down on the high street. 'I think there's a later will.'

'What are you talking about?' Charles sounded impatient. 'Why would there be?'

'Perhaps that's why Barbara and Paul were so keen to find it. And remember Marion Headlam thinks she's been left something? Well, there

161

couldn't possibly be anything in the old will, could there? Auntie was still living at Mountville Road when she made that. Where were you, then?'

'I was still married and living in Surrey.'

'So it's an old will. See what I mean?'

'Yes,' said Charles slowly. 'And possibly in the new one I'm not executor.'

'Well, I wouldn't worry too much about that. But I think you ought to tell the police.'

'Tell them what, exactly? That my cousin *thinks* there might be a new will? On no evidence other than a feeling?'

Fran thought for a moment. 'If you ask for DCI Murray and tell him exactly that, and that it's me who had the feeling, you may find he'll listen.'

'Oh? Knows about you, does he?'

'Yes. I told you, he came to interview me on Friday morning.'

'Well, I'll try,' said Charles, not sounding too hopeful, 'but I don't know what they can do.'

'They can insist on having a look at the stuff Barbara and Paul removed from The Laurels. Or have they sent it up to you already?'

'You must be joking. I phoned Barbara yesterday to tell her about the will and asked if they'd made any arrangements yet and she said Paul was going to do it today.'

'Was she relieved about the will?'

'Very. Said she wanted to talk to me about the house.'

'Oh, yes?' Fran's mind went into overdrive. 'They want to buy you out, I suppose?'

Charles was surprised. 'Yes, I think that's what

she wants. Not sure I can be bothered to argue.'

'Don't do anything yet,' said Fran. 'Not that you can anyway, until probate's sorted out.'

'I know. Are you coming up to London again soon?'

'I don't think so,' said Fran, 'but I think Libby's right. I think we need to find out about the new will. Or if there was one.'

'Look, I don't know what you and your friend Libby have cooked up, but don't you think it could just be Marion Headlam hoping there was something? Perhaps Aunt Eleanor told her she could expect something in the will, but never actually did anything about it.'

'It could be, but I don't think so. We'll find out, don't worry.'

'I thought you said the police would?'

'OK, the police or me. We'll find out between us.'

Fran wasn't surprised to receive a phone call from DCI Murray a little later.

'You're sure about this other will, then, Mrs Castle? Mr Wade seems a little sceptical.'

'He hasn't seen me in action, Mr Murray,' said Fran, amused.

'And he seems concerned about a bureau that was in Mrs Bridges' room at The Laurels.'

'Which is now in Mr Denver's office in Nethergate, yes.'

She heard a deep sigh. 'Well, I suppose we'd better go and take a look. And I'll be asking Mrs Headlam about it, too.'

*So will I*, thought Fran and dialled Libby's number.

'You sound cheerful,' she said, when Libby answered.

'I am.'

'Oh? Anything to do with you leaving with Ben last night?'

Libby giggled. 'Could be.'

'Right. I'm very pleased to hear it. I just thought I'd let you know the latest developments.'

'Well, I think our best bet is to talk to the nurses,' said Libby, when she'd been brought up to date. 'I'm sure they must have witnessed it.'

'I don't think either of them would talk to me. That little Nurse Warner was terrified.'

'I'll do it. I'll go and wait outside The Laurels and then trail them home. Bet I can do it.'

'Oh, Libby, you can't! You'll be a stalker. That's against the law.'

'Ah. You may be right. I know! I'll look them up in the phone book.'

'How would you know if you'd got the right one?'

'Well, what's-her-name, Redding, the one Ben saw at the hospital – we told you last night – that's an unusual name, isn't it?'

'Look, Lib, I think the best bet is for me to go and ask Marion Headlam. You can come with me if you like, but I don't think you ought to do anything on your own.'

'Oh, all right. I'd like to get a look inside that place, anyway. Can we go today?'

'All right. This afternoon. Will you drive?'

'Of course. I'll pick you up at about two, shall I?'

Despite Fran's misgivings, Libby decided to

164

look for Nurse Redding in the phone book, guessing that she couldn't live far away if she worked near Nethergate and had friends at the hospital in Canterbury. Sure enough, there were only a handful of Reddings in the phone book, and after ringing them all, she was left with the choice of two who hadn't answered. One was in a village near Deal, the other in Canterbury.

There were far too many Warners to contemplate doing the same thing with them, so Libby, still in a post romantic glow, confined herself to staring at her autumn painting and remembering the night before.

At two o'clock, Romeo the Renault hooted loudly outside The Pink Geranium. Fran came out immediately, looking solemn.

'What's happened?' asked Libby, as she got into the car.

'Apparently, Barbara Denver told the police that Charles is the obvious suspect as he's in a bad way financially, and now they've seen the will, they've hauled him down here for interrogation.'

Libby gaped. 'But how? He didn't get to The Laurels until after them, did he? And what a cow! I told you.'

'He could have got there before them and doubled back. He said so himself.'

'He'd have been seen,' said Libby, putting the car in gear and pulling away from the kerb.

'By Redding and Warner. Yes, I thought of that. I'm sure those two are hiding something.'

'In cahoots?'

'I wouldn't have thought so. They didn't seem as though they liked one another at all. In fact,

Warner seemed scared of Redding. Mind you, she seemed scared of her own shadow. Pretty, but ineffectual.'

'So, not a murderer, then?' Libby grinned at the road ahead.

'I don't know, do I?'

'You should. Haven't you got a feeling about any of them?'

'No,' said Fran, exasperated. 'I can't turn it on and off like a tap, Libby, I told you.'

'OK, OK. Did I tell you I found out where Redding lives?'

'Libby, how? I told you not to.' Fran turned to look at her.

'Oh, I'm supposed to do what you tell me, now, am I? Sucks to that. No, I looked in the phone book, like I said. I've narrowed her down to an address in Canterbury.'

Fran looked dubious. 'I still don't see what good it'll do us.'

'She's a suspect, isn't she? Best to know where she lives.'

Fran sighed.

The Laurels looked slightly better than when Fran had first seen it a week ago. Since then, there'd been rain to perk up the few plants and the grass looked much greener. Marion Headlam, on the other hand, looked slightly worse.

'Mrs Castle,' she said, with an effort. 'What can I do for you?'

'It's about the will, Mrs Headlam,' began Fran.

'Have you found it?' Marion Headlam broke in eagerly.

'Well, yes, but I'm afraid it's an old one, made

before she came here. It doesn't mention The Laurels at all.' Fran glanced awkwardly at Libby. 'I'm sorry.'

Marion Headlam looked from one to the other. 'Is this your solicitor?' she asked.

'No, this is my – er – colleague, Libby Sarjeant,' said Fran.

'With a J,' said Libby helpfully.

'Well, I can assure you there is another will, Mrs Castle. Or at least, a codicil. I saw it. And I saw it witnessed.'

Libby found she was holding her breath.

'Did the nurses witness it?' asked Fran, after a pause.

'Good Lord, no, that wouldn't have been right. Or ethical.'

Marion Headlam looked doubtful for a moment, as if she wasn't sure if it was ethical or not, then went on. 'No, we had a delivery that day, and the driver and his mate witnessed it.' She brightened up. 'You can check if you like. I've got their addresses. Mrs Bridges wanted to send them each something for their trouble.'

'Did she? That was nice of her,' said Libby.

'Have the police asked you about this, Mrs Headlam?' said Fran.

'No. They've talked to all us several times, but not about the will.'

'They will,' promised Fran. 'And now, perhaps I could have those addresses?'

'She didn't ask why you wanted them,' said Libby, as they got back into the car.

'She didn't have to. She offered them as a means to check what she said was true.' Fran

167

fastened her seat belt. 'It's got even more complicated now, hasn't it?'

'I know,' said Libby as they drove down the
drive more sedately than Charles had, 'let's go
and see Guy.'

'Why?' asked Fran. 'He's got nothing to do with
all this.'

'No, but he'd like to see you, and he'll probably
know where Nurse Redding lives.'

'What *are* you on about?'

'I've got the address, but I don't know where it
is. I bet Guy does.'

'Look, Libby, it doesn't matter if he does. We
know now that the nurses didn't witness the will.'

'But they're hiding something. So we need to
find out what.'

'Probably nothing,' said Fran, unconsciously
echoing Ben. 'Some corner they cut, minor theft
... I don't know. Could be anything.'

'Suit yourself.' Libby shrugged.

Libby parked in The Swan car park and showed
Fran where she and Ben had eaten on Friday.
Guy was delighted to see them.

'So, to what do I owe the honour?' Guy's dark
brown eyes twinkled at Fran and brought her out
in a nervous glow.

'We thought you might give us tea,' said Libby,
sitting on one of the brown leather armchairs provided for Guy's wealthier clients, 'hello, Sophie.'

'Hi.' Sophie waved a languid hand. 'Shall I
make the tea, Dad?'

'Thanks, darling.' He sat on the edge of his
desk. 'So, is tea the only thing you want?'

'No.' Libby fished in her basket. 'Do you know

where this address is?'

Guy wrinkled his brow as he took the piece of paper. 'Up at the back of the town, somewhere, I think. Near the cricket ground? Why do you want to know?'

'One of the nurses at the home where Fran's aunt died lives there,' said Libby.

'Libby, please. Everyone doesn't need to know,' said Fran.

'Oh, of course!' Guy looked at Fran curiously. 'I didn't put two and two together. It was your aunt who was murdered, was it?'

'I'm afraid so,' said Fran, trying to look discouraging.

He put his head on one side, looking a little like an inquisitive, middle aged faun. Fran couldn't see the chimp likeness at all.

'We're looking into it,' said Libby, importantly, and Fran sighed.

'Oh, dear.' Guy smiled at her. 'Worrying for you.'

'Why does everybody seem to think I'm some kind of ... of ... clumsy...'

'Bull in a china shop,' Fran finished for her. 'I don't know, Lib, but as it seems to be the general consensus of opinion, I'm inclined to believe it.'

Sophie emerged from the back of the gallery with four mugs on a tray.

'I put milk in all of them, if that's all right,' she said. 'I'll go and get the sugar.'

'Pretty girl,' said Fran, watching her go.

'Thank you. One of my better efforts,' said Guy.

'So you're related to the Denvers, then?' he said

later, when they were all sitting round the coffee table with their mugs.

Fran looked up, surprised. 'Not really,' she said. 'I was a niece by marriage, they're blood relatives – I think. How did you know?'

'Barbara came in to order a piece of sculpture as a headstone. Didn't she, Soph?'

Sophie peered up from between curtains of pale lemon hair. 'One of Philip's.'

'Philip Massey?' Libby's face was a picture. 'My God, how much will that have cost her?'

'Who?' asked Fran.

'Famous sculptor and neighbour. Lives up the back. I think he'll be doing a cut-price number for our Barbara, won't he, Sophie?'

'That's all very well, but it's not her job to do that, is it? I assume it's for our mutual aunt?'

'So she said. Not mentioning you, of course.'

'Bit of a cheek, though,' said Libby, 'much like all the other stuff.'

'I'll have to tell Charles,' said Fran.

'Not till he comes out of durance vile,' said Libby.

'Libby!' Fran sent her a reproving glare.

'Don't mind me,' said Guy, looking amused.

'Anyway,' said Libby, oblivious, 'now we know roughly where Nurse Redding lives.'

Fran shook her head and cast her eyes up to Guy's pretty coving.

He laughed. 'How about you two staying down here for dinner? My treat?'

Fran noticed Libby's colour surge up her neck. 'I've got to get back,' she said, 'but thanks for the thought. But–' she sat up straight in her chair –

170

'how about you coming to dinner with us? Fran? Is that all right with you?'

'When you say us...?'

'I mean, I'll cook. Ben's coming over, and you could come, and Guy. How about it?'

Fran looked at Guy.

'I'd like that if it's not too short notice,' he said. 'And Ben's back on the scene, is he? Why, only last week...'

'Yes, yes, all right,' said Libby hastily, and stood up. 'Now, Fran, all we've got to do is find out where Nurse Warner lives.'

Sophie looked up. 'Do you mean Sue Warner who works at The Laurels? Oh, I know her.'


## Chapter Seventeen

'Do you?' It was left to Guy to ask, as Libby and Fran seemed deprived of speech.

'We were at school together. She lives in Canterbury somewhere, I think.'

'Could you find out?' asked Libby.

'I suppose, I could. Is it important?'

'No, don't bother, Sophie,' said Fran, 'but it's very kind of you.'

'But–' began Libby.

'No, Libby. It's nothing to do with us.' Fran stood up. 'Come on, if you've got to cook dinner for us all.'

'Oh, all right.' Libby got to her feet. 'Do you want to come back with us, Guy?'

'How would I get home?' He patted her shoulder. 'No, it's all right. I'll drive over and possibly beg a bed from Ben.'

Libby reddened and opened her mouth, then thought better of it.

'Bye, Sophie,' said Fran. 'Nice to meet you.'

Guy ushered them out of the gallery. 'See you about eight, then?' he said.

'We do seem to do a lot of eating, don't we?' said Libby, as they walked back down Harbour Street.

'Most people do,' said Fran.

'Yes, but we always seem to have our important chats over food and drink.'

'Well, you don't suggest meeting friends to watch television, do you? Eating and drinking are social pastimes.'

'I enjoy them, anyway,' said Libby. 'Hop in.'

'Why did you invite Guy over?' asked Fran, as they bowled along a tree shaded country road. 'Wasn't it a bit sudden?'

'He invited us to dinner in Nethergate, didn't he? And as I'd already made arrangements with Ben, I couldn't go, but I didn't want to put him off.'

'He would have understood.'

'Yes, but you have to strike while the iron's hot,' said Libby obscurely.

'You want him to help us?' Fran frowned.

'No! He's interested in you. I didn't want him put off.'

'Oh, Libby, really. Surely, it's up to him? Or me, come to that.'

'Well, yes, but a little helping hand now and

172

then never did anyone any harm.'

'Did it occur to you that my life might be my own?'

'Fran!' Libby turned to look at her. Fran squealed and Libby hauled the car back onto the road. 'Am I interfering?'

'Yes, Libby,' said Fran firmly. 'Not only with Guy, whom I don't know at all, but with this business of Aunt Eleanor. I told you, it's nothing really to do with me, so it's certainly nothing to do with you.'

'It was you who said we should find out about the other will,' said Libby huffily. 'Make your mind up.'

'I know,' sighed Fran, 'I'm being inconsistent. I feel I've got to find out about it, yet I know I shouldn't.' She sighed again. 'It's all very muddling.'

'Well, look on it as me helping sort out the muddle,' said Libby, cheering up. 'I'll let you sort yourself out over Guy.'

'Gee, thanks,' said Fran, 'but I don't think there's anything to sort out.'

'He fancies you,' said Libby firmly. 'Definitely.'

'Well, aren't we lucky? Two middle aged, over-the-hill women, and according to you, we've both got suitors.'

'Suitors. What a lovely word.' Libby swung onto the main road. 'Or possibly swains. Middle aged swains. Or should it be swain?'

'I've no idea, but whatever it is, you're cooking for it, so hadn't we better get a move on?'

Back at number 17, Libby left a message for Ben telling him that their dinner à deux had been

173

expanded and surveyed the contents of the larder and fridge.

'Keep it simple,' she muttered to herself, and wondered if she was doing the right thing.

Wouldn't the conversation automatically turn to Aunt Eleanor? And even, possibly, to Fran's moments, which she hated being discussed? Libby sighed. Bull in a china shop, she told herself. They're right.

Ben, amiably accepting the ruination of his tête-à-tête, arrived early and helped set the kitchen table. Sidney, indignant at being turned off both Rayburn *and* table, was shut protesting inside the conservatory.

'Bit of a squash, really,' said Libby, squeezing between the table and the sink. 'Once we sit down we won't be able to get up.'

'What do you do when the children are here for Christmas?' asked Ben.

'Clear the conservatory and put the table in there.'

'Couldn't we do that now?'

'Too much effort. I have to start thinking about it days in advance. Besides, I've got a painting half finished.'

'Oh, the autumn cottage window. You can show Guy this evening.'

Libby stopped and pushed her hair off her face. 'Am I being an interfering old matchmaker?' she said.

'Yes,' said Ben, 'but you're *my* interfering old matchmaker, so that's all right.'

Libby, well pleased with this statement, allowed herself to be kissed.

Despite the cramped conditions, the impromptu supper party was successful. Libby's simple menu went down well, and Ben and Guy's wine contributions even better. Guy had sensibly thought to ring Ben before he set out regarding a bed for the night, and Ben had coerced Peter and Harry into giving him their spare room. Ben had heard Harry loudly protesting in the background about being left out of the party.

'Coffee in the sitting room?' suggested Libby. 'I've even got some brandy, I think.'

'Before we go in, can I see what you're up to in the conservatory?' asked Guy. 'I've been trying to see what's on that easel all through dinner.'

'Come on, then,' said Libby. As she opened the door, Sidney shot out like a champagne cork.

They all crowded into the conservatory, and Guy turned the easel towards the light. 'Hmm,' he said.

'What's up, Fran?' Libby turned as she heard a tiny sound from her friend, and wasn't surprised to see her with a rather startled look on her face.

'Nothing.' Fran kept her eyes fixed on the painting. Libby saw that Ben was watching her.

'It's a favourite subject, Fran,' he said. 'Haven't you seen any before?'

'No.' Fran turned to Libby. 'I haven't, have I?'

'I don't think so. You've been past the cottage, though.'

Guy turned from the easel. 'It's actually right down near the harbour,' he said. 'Don't you like it?'

Fran smiled brightly. 'It's lovely,' she said. 'Have you got any more here, Libby?'

'Several,' said Libby. 'I'll show you tomorrow.'

'If you've got several,' said Guy, 'why haven't I been given them to sell?'

'They're not really up to scratch,' muttered Libby, turning the easel away from them.

'I'll be the judge of that,' said Guy. 'Come on, let's have a look.'

'We're supposed to be having coffee,' sighed Libby.

'And brandy,' said Ben, taking her arm. 'Come on, Lib. We'll leave them here to ferret and we'll go and sit in comfort.'

'Fran saw something in that picture, didn't she?' said Libby, once they were settled in the sitting room.

Ben nodded. 'She'll tell us eventually. Odd, though, because you painted it.'

'You think it could be something to do with me rather than the picture?'

Ben shrugged. 'Who knows? I wonder if she's telling Guy all about it right now?'

'I doubt it.' Libby sipped her brandy. 'Good if Guy does take some of those pictures, though. I could do with the money.'

When Fran and Guy came into the sitting room, Guy was carrying several paintings and Fran was looking thoughtful.

'When I go home tomorrow, I'm taking Fran back with me so she can see your cottage,' said Guy, sitting on the floor and accepting a brandy. He sent her a puzzled look, but didn't say anything more.

'I was wondering if it was available to rent,' said Fran. 'It looks very pretty.'

'You can only see the window frame in the paintings,' said Libby dubiously. 'How can you tell if it's pretty?'

'The view's pretty,' said Fran with finality, and changed the subject.

Later, Guy gallantly offered to walk home with Fran, although, as Ben said, he would go past her door on his way to Peter and Harry's anyway, and left Libby alone with Ben.

'Washing up,' she said, suddenly shy.

'In the morning,' he said.

'Aha! You'll be gone by then,' said Libby, hoping he couldn't see her heart hammering away like a pneumatic drill underneath her top.

'Who said?' asked Ben, bending to touch his lips to her neck. Libby shivered, as all the bits brought to life last night leapt once again to attention.

'Sidney,' she said faintly.

'Go and feed him, then,' said Ben, giving her a little push, 'and then come back to me.'

As Sidney was discovered hoovering up the remains of dinner, Libby decided he'd eaten enough, and shut him in the conservatory. His habit of acting as doorkeeper to her bedroom was, she felt, superfluous tonight.

The following morning, she discovered Ben had done most of the washing up and fed Sidney before she was even awake.

'It seemed a pity to wake you,' he said with a grin, fetching her a mug of tea. 'Couldn't remember if you preferred tea or coffee in the morning.'

'Tea,' said Libby, wrapping her hands round her mug. 'I thought you'd be gone by now.'

'A very cavalier attitude, I must say!' He sat down beside her on the creaking sofa. 'I wouldn't sneak out into the dawn, leaving not a wrack behind.'

'What is a wrack?' said Libby. 'I've often wondered.'

'Wreckage,' said Ben, 'like what I feel at the moment.'

'Oh, dear.' Libby looked at him with interest. 'You don't look as if you've got a hangover.'

'I haven't,' said Ben, tracing a finger down her neck, dangerously close to her dressing gown. 'But I'm not as young as I was.'

'Oh,' said Libby, blushing.

'I will go now, however,' he said, standing up. 'You'll want to ring Fran to find out about last night...'

'I wouldn't be so nosey!'

'No, I meant about her reaction to the paintings.'

'Oh.' Libby thought for a moment. 'Yes, I'd better, before she goes off with Guy.'

He bent to kiss her. 'I'll see you later, then,' he said. 'Got some estate work to do for Dad, then Mum wants to go into Canterbury.'

'OK.' Libby nodded and watched him leave before getting to her feet and going to the window to see if she could still see him walking up the lane. *How pathetic*, she thought, craning sideways to catch the last glimpse. *How old am I?* Sighing, she turned from the window and went to call Fran.

'No, he didn't come in,' said Fran, 'before you even ask.'

'I wasn't going to,' said Libby indignantly. 'I was merely going to ask about the picture.'

'Oh, that,' said Fran in a weary voice. 'I really don't know.'

'What do you mean, you don't know?'

'It hasn't any relevance to Aunt Eleanor. It's just – I keep feeling I've been there before. As a child. I keep seeing a child. And a bedroom, although it isn't mine.'

'I suppose it couldn't be mine?' asked Libby slowly.

'Yours? Why?'

Libby told her story about the picture on her bedroom wall. 'That's why I keep painting it. I have no idea if it's that cottage, but when I went to view it, it felt right.'

'So it was for sale?'

'Oh, yes, but too expensive for me. Sea front, you see. Prime position.'

'Do you remember who the agent was?'

'No. Fran, you couldn't afford it! Don't be silly.'

'If they haven't sold it, they might be willing to rent it out,' said Fran, sounding stubborn.

'It's bound to have been sold. Very desirable property, that.'

'I'll have a look, anyway. I need to find out about it.'

'Well, let me know,' said Libby. 'How will you get back?'

'Oh, I'll think of something,' said Fran vaguely. 'I'll ring you.'

Libby rang off, thought for a moment, then dialled again.

'Sophie? Hi, it's Libby Sarjeant...You remember

179

yesterday you said you thought you could find out where young Nurse Warner lives? Well, could you?... Yes, I know what Fran said, but I think we need to know... No, I think he's on his way back now ... yes, right... OK. Thanks very much.'

Right,' she said to Sidney, who had appeared deciding it was lunchtime already, 'now to find where Nurse Redding lives.'

But before she could do anything about either of the nurses, the phone rang again. This time it was Marion Headlam asking if Fran had another contact number.

'I'm afraid not,' said Libby, 'only her mobile number. Is there a problem?'

'I just wondered if there was any news.' Marion Headlam sounded nervous. 'It's all been rather unsettling.'

'About the will, you mean?' asked Libby, trying to inject warmth and sympathy into her voice. 'I'm sure it is, if Mrs Bridges said she was going to leave you something.'

'Oh, well,' said Mrs Headlam with a shaky laugh, 'not me, of course, only the home. And I wouldn't want to appear greedy. I do so hate it when that sort of thing happens with relatives, don't you?'

'Er – yes,' said Libby, who had no experience of it.

'Well, never mind.' There was an effort to sound normal and light hearted. 'Such a pity we can't bury the poor lady, then we could all get on with our lives, couldn't we?'

Libby wondered whether Marion Headlam felt the same about all her clients, who, after all, probably left her in this state quite regularly.

'Before you go, Mrs Headlam,' she said, thinking rapidly, if not sensibly, 'I was wondering if you could put me in touch with Nurse – er – Redding?'

'Nurse Redding?' Marion Headlam sounded surprised. 'Well, we don't give out details of staff, you know.'

'Oh, no, of course not,' said Libby, improvising frantically, 'but my – er – friend saw her at the Kent and Canterbury Hospital the other day and wanted to return her–' *think, Libby, think* '–her book. She left it in the Friends coffee shop.'

'Did she?' There was no doubt about the surprise now. 'I didn't know she read much. Oh, well, you can always drop it in here next time you're passing. Or perhaps give it to Mrs Castle?'

'Yes, we'll do that,' said Libby, wondering what Nurse Redding would say when she learned that a strange man was returning her non-existent book. 'Thank you, Mrs Headlam. I'll tell Mrs Castle you called.'

That was all very odd, thought Libby, as she got under the reluctant shower. Why was that woman so concerned about the will? She must be expecting quite a legacy. Obviously, she needed it to be found. But why so nervous? Unless...

Libby stepped out of the shower and shook her head. Unless Marion Headlam felt that she had done something for nothing? If the will wasn't found? Could she have killed Aunt Eleanor? Libby wrapped a towel round her, went downstairs, found paper and a ball point pen and began to work it out.

If The Laurels was in a financially parlous state, perhaps Marion Headlam had persuaded Aunt Eleanor to leave her enough money to keep it going. Perhaps she'd asked her first for a loan? Libby realised she had no idea of Aunt Eleanor's mental state before she died. Fran had told her that she could no longer look after herself, but that could mean anything. Anyway, if there was a codicil, or a new will, as Libby now firmly believed, in order to collect the money, Aunt Eleanor would have to die. So could Marion Headlam have got into that room between the nurses leaving it and Barbara Denver entering?

Yes, thought Libby, she could. Who would question her presence anywhere in the building. And if she heard someone coming – of course! Out through the french windows.

Libby put down her pen and went back upstairs to dress. What she really needed to do now was to talk to those nurses and find out exactly what they knew.

## Chapter Eighteen

Fran found the drive to Nethergate with Guy far more restful than with Libby. For a start, the car was a considerable improvement.

'So, you're thinking of moving down here permanently, then?' Guy slid a glance sideways.

'Yes. There's nothing to keep me in London any more.' Fran looked out of the window at the

182

hedgerows. 'This is much more pleasant.'

'What about work?'

'Oh, I can probably do that down here as well as up there.' She turned towards him. 'So you know nothing about this cottage, then?'

'Changing the subject, Fran?'

'Just wanted to know, that's all.' She turned back to the window. 'It's very kind of you to drive me to see it.'

'I wish I knew why you really wanted to go.'

*So do I*, thought Fran. 'It just seemed familiar, that's all,' she hedged. 'I expect I've seen a picture, like Libby.'

Guy drove down the service road at the back of Harbour Street and parked behind the gallery.

'Shall I show you which one it is?' he asked, as he ushered her inside.

'Isn't it easy to spot?' asked Fran, privately convinced she would know.

'Well, Lib's paintings are a view from inside. You might not recognise it.'

'All right, thank you.' Fran gave him a small smile.

Guy sighed gustily and shook his head at her. *How attractive he is*, she thought. *Why is he paying attention to me?*

Sophie appeared from the kitchen.

'Hi, Dad. Good evening?' She raised her eyebrows slightly at Fran.

'Excellent, thanks, Soph. Any business this morning?'

'Oh, yes,' Sophie rummaged among pieces of paper on the desk top, 'Mrs Denver called again about that sculpture.'

'Really?' Guy looked at Fran. 'Saying what?'

'Did we know any more about it.' Sophie looked from one to the other. 'Do we?'

'I'm putting it on hold for the moment, so just say we can't get in touch with Phil if she calls again.' He put his head on one side and looked at Fran. 'Is that all right with madam?'

'Don't blame me,' said Fran, alarmed.

'But you said yesterday...'

'Yes, I know.' Fran frowned. 'Thank you. I must let Charles know.'

'Ah, yes, Charles. Your cousin.'

'Only by marriage. I hardly know him.'

'Hmm,' said Guy. 'Come along then. I'll show you your cottage.'

'Libby's cottage,' corrected Fran, as they went out into the sunshine.

As she had thought, Fran knew the cottage before Guy pointed it out. Perching on the sea wall opposite, she focussed her mind.

'How do we find out about it, do you think?' said Guy, leaning on the wall beside her.

'Don't you know? After all, you're almost neighbours.'

'Of course I don't. I know some of the shop-keepers. Maybe they'll know.'

'I can't just go in and ask!' Fran felt herself going pink at the thought.

'Oh, come on, then.' Guy took her arm and hauled her upright, before marching them both into the nearest shop, a tiny frontage selling local ice-cream.

'Hi, Lizzie, how's business?' he asked the cheerful looking blonde behind the counter.

'Better for me than you, I expect, Guy,' she chuckled. 'What can I get you?'

'I'd like a vanilla double,' he said. 'Fran?'

'Oh–' Fran was taken aback, 'strawberry, please.'

'And do you know anything about Coastguard Cottage, Lizzie? Is it a holiday let?'

Lizzie handed over Fran's strawberry cone and wiped her hands on her apron. 'I think it is, or at least someone's holiday home. Bloody week-enders.'

'You don't know who owns it, then?' said Fran.

'No idea.' Lizzie handed Guy's ice cream and change. 'Tell you who'd know, though. Old Sheila. She cleans it, I've seen her coming out. Know who I mean?'

'Of course I do, she does for me, too.' He beamed. 'Thanks, Lizzie.'

'Was you thinking of renting it, then?' she said, giving Fran an interested inspection.

'Possibly.' Fran gave a vague smile and followed Guy out.

'There you are then. I'll ask old Sheila. Want me to do it now?'

'Oh, I don't want to put you to any more trouble. It can wait until you next see her,' said Fran. 'Thanks for the ice-cream. It's lovely.'

He looked at her doubtfully. 'If you're sure. What are you going to do now. Go and have another look?'

'I thought I would,' said Fran diffidently. 'There must be access round the back, isn't there?'

'Not from this end, but from The Sloop end, yes, there's a drive that goes right along the back.

Don't go trespassing.'

'No, I won't,' said Fran. 'I'll come and let you know what I find out.'

Savouring the last of her strawberry cone, Fran retraced her steps right down to The Sloop, and then out on to the little jetty. From here she looked back on to Harbour Street, and picked out Coastguard Cottage. There was definitely something about it. But the bedroom she'd seen in her head didn't seem to match. Perhaps Libby was right, it was hers, and somehow she'd imbued her paintings with her childhood memories. It was all very confusing.

She strolled back down the jetty and made her way round to the drive at the back of the cottages. High garden fences stood on one side and on the other the beginning of the green covered chalk cliffs. Picking her way along the track, she counted roof tops and garden gates until she was pretty sure she stood outside Coastguard Cottage. A high fence with a sturdy looking gate protected it from view, and, greatly daring, Fran tried the handle. Naturally enough, it was locked. Glad she was wearing jeans, she scrambled a little way up the cliff on the other side of the track and found herself in a position to look down into the garden.

It wasn't very big, and had been turned into a Mediterranean style patio, with colourful pots and spiky leaved plants. The back door was open, and washing hung on a line strung from fence to fence. Fran stared, and now something was coming through. Something not very pleasant.

This time, there was no choking blackness, but

Eleanor's face was there again. And her own mother's. Was it her mother? This dark haired, frantic faced woman, who was screaming? Fran's heart lurched, and she found she was trembling. She forced herself to continue looking at the back of the cottage, but nothing else came to her, and she was just looking at a sunny back yard in a seaside town.

Someone came into the little garden and Fran half slid, half scrambled down to the track, not wanting to be seen. She found she was near an alleyway on to Harbour Street, and slipped through, brushing herself down. Calmly, she walked back to the gallery and went in.

Guy was with a customer and Sophie smiled at her from behind the desk.

'Did you get a look at it?' she asked. Fran wondered what Guy had told her.

'Yes, I went round the back and saw the back yard. There are people in it at the moment – holiday-makers, by the look of them – you know, wellies and buckets by the back door. It doesn't look like a long term let.'

'Right.' Sophie nodded, then looked up to take a credit card from Guy's customer.

Fran repeated what she'd said to him.

'I phoned old Sheila while you were gone. She said the lettings are handled by a company who pay her, so she doesn't know anything either.'

'I'm not sure I'd want to live there, anyway,' admitted Fran. 'There's something uncomfortable about it.'

Guy screwed up his face. 'How do you mean, uncomfortable? How could you tell, if you didn't go inside?'

'Oh, you know,' said Fran, trying to brush it aside, 'when you get a good feeling about a house. Estate agents rely on it.' And she should know, she thought.

Guy nodded, looking unconvinced. 'Do you fancy lunch?' he said, 'or are you anxious to get back?'

'I've got to check on buses. Libby said there aren't any from here to Steeple Martin.'

'No, but you could get a train to Canterbury and a bus home from there. I'd take you myself, but I'd better not leave Sophie too often.' He smiled over at his daughter, who, having wrapped the customer's purchase, gave him a beautiful smile, and then pulled a face at her father.

'I'll find out the times of the trains, then,' said Fran.

'Ten past and twenty to each hour,' said Guy, 'so if we go and have a quick early lunch now, you could catch the ten past one.'

'That's very kind of you,' said Fran, 'if Sophie doesn't mind.'

'I don't mind,' said Sophie, 'I shall just take most of the afternoon off.'

'See what I have to put up with,' sighed Guy in mock exasperation.

'So tell me why you really wanted to see the cottage,' he said, as they strolled back along Harbour Street.

Fran looked at him sharply. 'What do you mean?'

'You don't want to rent it. Libby keeps painting it. What is it?'

Fran sighed. 'I don't know why Libby keeps painting it. And it attracted me. I did think I could possibly rent it.'

Guy looked sceptical. 'Why don't I believe you?'

'No idea.' Fran looked out across the sea. 'But thank you for bringing me, anyway.'

The train to Canterbury and the meandering bus back to Steeple Martin gave Fran a long time to think about the morning's events. Guy had flirted gently with her all through lunch, and given her a slightly lingering kiss on the cheek as he said goodbye at the station. This was gratifying, but unnerving, as Fran, like Libby, had had no experience of new relationships for a good many years. Like Libby, too, she had an abundance of insecurities, and very little sense of self worth. *Perhaps we should start a society*, she thought, brooding over the dry August countryside.

But exercising her far more were the disturbing images provoked by the sight of the cottage. She had been pretty sure last night that she either knew it personally, or it had some relevance. Now she knew it did, but what was a mystery. And why had she seen her mother's face?

The flat over The Pink Geranium had been shut up all morning and was hot and airless. Fran opened the sash windows onto the high street, made a cup of tea and took it out into Harry's little garden. After staring at the whitewashed walls and the single climbing rose that had survived Harry's ministrations for a good twenty minutes, she decided she need to talk to someone. Not just someone, but Libby. Over-enthusiastic she might be, and liable to fly off in all directions, but at least she understood more about Fran than anyone else at the moment.

This, she reflected, as she climbed the stairs back up to the flat to fetch her mobile, was rather lowering. You would expect to have someone in your life who had been there for years, who understood from hay to nuts. Not someone who breezed in a few months ago and took you over.

'So there you are. What do you think?' Fran sat in the armchair by the window and stared down at a few desultory shoppers.

'You must have been there as a child.'

'I'm sure I haven't. I don't remember ever having had a holiday after my father died.'

'What about your mother?'

'I suppose she might have gone there, but why? It had no connection with our family. It's all Charles and Eleanor's side. Frank lived in the upstairs flat at Mountville Road, we lived in the downstairs one, until after he married Eleanor. Even then, we knew nothing about the connection with Kent.'

'And the bedroom?'

'Doesn't seem to fit in at all.' Fran shook her head at herself. 'I'm losing it.'

'Don't be daft. It's got to mean something if it was that overwhelming.' There was a pause. 'Look, Barbara Denver lived here all her life. That means Aunt Eleanor might have done.'

'Charles lived in Steeple Mount and went to school in Nethergate. Didn't I tell you?'

'Oh, good Lord, well, there you are then. You're seeing something from the past. Do you think they could have lived in the cottage?'

'No, Charles would have mentioned it.'

'Not necessarily. He might have said he lived in Nethergate.'

'He didn't. He went to *school* in Nethergate.'

'Well, there's a family connection, anyway. Where your Mum comes into it, I've no idea, but I think you should try and find out.'

'I don't know how I'm going to do that. I can hardly ask the Denvers, and Charles is incommunicado at present.'

'Still? Have you tried to get hold of him?'

'No, come to think of it I haven't. I'll give him a ring.'

'Do that,' said Libby, 'and let me know what he says.'


## Chapter Nineteen

But all questions about the cottage in Nethergate flew out of Fran's mind when she spoke to Charles.

'It looks as though I'm in trouble, Fran,' he said heavily.

'Why? You didn't kill her,' said Fran, aware that her heart was beating so hard she could hardly breathe.

'No, but...it's her money.'

'What about it.'

There was a silence.

'Come on, Charles, what's the problem?'

191

'I'm afraid I used rather a lot of her money,' he said baldly.

'Charles!' Fran took a moment to assimilate this. 'As Power of Attorney, I suppose.'

'Yes.'

'And the police have found out?'

'Yes.'

'Well, they would, wouldn't they. They can get access to bank accounts and all sorts. What made you do it?'

'I was broke, I told you. I always intended to put it back.'

'They always say that, don't they?'

'Who do?'

'Embezzlers,' said Fran. 'That's what it is, Charles. Make no mistake. What are they going to do to you?'

'I've no idea at the moment. They've let me go home – no bail or anything.'

'Well, you're off the hook for the murder, then.'

'How do know that?' asked Charles, sounding surprised.

'It would be in your interest to keep her alive until you'd sorted out the money, wouldn't it? If she died it would all come to light as it has done. Barbara and Paul would have found out, and all hell would have broken out. Which it will do now.'

'Oh, God,' groaned Charles. 'I can't take any more.'

'You shouldn't have taken it in the first place,' said Fran, with an ill-placed attempt at humour. 'Hadn't you better see a solicitor?'

'I suppose so. The one I saw before, do you think?'

'If he knows you. And he certainly knew about the Power of Attorney, didn't he. He'd be best.' Fran thought for a moment. 'Perhaps you could have used the money for essential repairs to her property.'

'I'd have to produce bills and receipts and things, wouldn't I?'

'Yes, you would.' Fran sighed. 'Oh, well. It was a thought.'

'You're not too shocked?' said Charles.

'No, I'm not. I suspect a lot of us would do the same in your circumstances,' said Fran. 'But before you go, Charles, you told me you grew up in Steeple Mount. Did the whole family come from here?'

'Yes, I thought I told you. Barbara's always lived around here as well.'

'Any of you in Nethergate?'

'Barbara and her family did. I went to school there.'

'Did anyone have a cottage on the sea wall?'

'Harbour Street? Good Lord, no. When I was a child they were ramshackle old places, and after I grew up they were beyond my reach. Why?'

'I thought I recognised one, that's all,' said Fran evasively.

'A magic moment, was it?' For the first time in the conversation Charles's tone lightened. 'Well, you couldn't have done. I don't think you ever came here after Uncle Frank and Aunt Eleanor married.'

'No, it does seem unlikely,' said Fran slowly. 'It wasn't long after their marriage that we left Mountville Road.'

193

'Must be leading you astray, then,' said Charles.

'Yes, it must be. Well, Charles, let me know how things go, and if you're coming down this way again, soon.'

'I will, Fran, and thanks for being so understanding,' said Charles, his voice as warm and friendly as it had been when they first met and before the layers of his personality had been stripped off. How attractive he had seemed at first, when they met in La Poule Au Pot. Fran took herself to task for not having seen below the surface at that first meeting, and phoned Libby to tell her what Charles had said.

'I said I didn't like him, didn't I?' said Libby.

'I don't remember you saying that,' said Fran. 'You did call him a wimp, though.'

'There you are then,' said Libby. 'So, what are you going to do now?'

'Nothing. What should I be doing?'

'Finding out what your – your – *experience* meant. Is it to do with Auntie's murder?'

'Of course it isn't. My mother's been dead for years, and we never had much to do with Eleanor when Frank married her anyway.'

'Just a thought. She could have been jealous of your Mum.'

'What *are* you on about? How could she be?'

Fran could almost hear Libby's shrug. 'I can think of reasons. Anyway. What about the nurses?'

'The nurses?' Fran was bewildered by Libby's change of direction.

'Redding and Warner. I still want to get to the bottom of them. Don't you?'

'I told you, no. I can't see what they've got to

do with anything.'

Libby let out an exasperated sigh. 'Don't you care about your Aunt's murder?'

'Of course I care. But it's nothing whatsoever to do with me, I hardly knew her, I'm not a suspect, and I don't gain anything from her death. So why don't you let it alone?'

Silence.

'Well, Lib?'

'Because I want to know,' said Libby in a small voice.

'Because you're bloody nosey.'

'Yes, there is that.'

'Well, just don't tread on anybody's toes, that's all.'

'Yes, Fran.'

After ringing off, Libby stood and looked at the telephone. Fran was quite right. She shouldn't interfere. Ever since the business over *The Hop Pickers*, people had been telling her not to interfere, and she was still uncomfortable about maybe having precipitated someone's death during that investigation. Was she likely to do that in this case?

She moved slowly back towards the conservatory, where the autumn painting was almost finished. She couldn't see how asking a few questions of the nurses at The Laurels would precipitate anything, except her own vilification as a nosey parker. But, you had to accept that not only could *they* have murdered the old lady, so could Marion Headlam. She, at least, had a motive, or thought she had. And that reminded Libby, what about those two witnesses to the will? Had the police found them?

She retrieved her basket from under Sidney, and rooted about until she found the old envelope on which she had copied the names down after Mrs Headlam had given them to Fran. She wasn't sure Fran had approved of this, but it was always better to have a back up, wasn't it?

Fran would definitely class this as both interfering and bull-in-a-china-shopping, but Libby still dialled the first number on the envelope.

'Oh, I'm so sorry to bother you,' she said, when a woman's hesitant voice answered, 'but I was hoping to speak to Mr Edwards.'

'Which Mr Edwards?' asked the voice.

'Mr Len Edwards?'

'I'm afraid my husband died six weeks ago,' said the voice.

'Oh!' Libby couldn't think what to say. 'I'm sorry. I didn't know.'

'Obviously,' said the voice. 'Could you tell me what it was about?'

'I believe he witnessed a will, or a codicil to a will, a little while ago,' said Libby.

'Oh, yes, he did. The old woman wrote to him – sent him a couple of quid for his trouble.'

'Can you remember her name?' asked Libby, almost holding her breath.

'Afraid not, love, but she was in a home over to Nethergate in Kent. Is that any help?'

'Oh, yes, very much so,' said Libby, although she wasn't sure it was any help at all, merely confirmation of Marion Headlam's conviction that there was a new, or updated, will. 'Thank you so much, and I'm sorry to have bothered you.'

Libby heard a sigh. 'No trouble, love.'

Well, what did you expect, she asked herself as she went to put the kettle on. Witnesses to wills were hardly likely to know what it was they'd witnessed, were they? At least they knew there was one.

Deciding that what Fran didn't know wouldn't hurt her, Libby sat down on the sofa with her tea and found her mobile. The phone book was still out from when she tried to trace Nurses Warner and Redding, and, settling back, she dialled one of the two remaining numbers for Reddings. Rather to her surprise, the second one was answered.

'Could I speak to Nurse Redding?' she asked, after clearing her throat.

'Speaking,' said a surprised voice.

Libby realised she had no idea how she was going to continue.

'I believe you were in the Kent and Canterbury hospital the other day,' she said eventually, falling back on the book.

'Visiting only. I don't work there any more.'

'No, no, my friend saw you in the Friends' Café,' said Libby.

'Oh, yes. I was there last week.'

'Well,' Libby cleared her throat again, 'my friend thought you left a book behind and wanted to return it.'

There was silence for a moment. 'I don't think I had a book with me,' said Nurse Redding, 'and anyway, how did he know who I was if I don't know him?'

Libby felt as if she were going down in a lift.

Bugger. Why hadn't she thought this through?

'I'm afraid,' she said slowly, thinking on the hoof, 'he overheard something about someone dying and the police. As we know someone who's recently died and the police are involved, he rather put two and two together.' And that's the truth, thought Libby. He did.

'Oh, really? And how do I know who you really are and what you want? You know I didn't have a book.' Nurse Redding sounded definitely suspicious now.

Feeling perspiration break out on her brow, Libby took a deep breath and decided to lay her cards on the table. With an ace up the sleeve, of course. Although it felt more like a joker.

'Actually, we're a bit worried about it all,' she said. 'I'm sure if I could have a word with you, and perhaps the other little nurse, it would help enormously.'

'Are you the papers?'

'No, no,' said Libby, wondering if perhaps she should have said yes. Nurse Redding didn't sound as though she would have minded seeing her name in print. 'I'm a friend of the family.'

'You don't need to talk to anyone else. I can tell you what you want to know.'

Libby felt her heart leap with excitement. A breakthrough!

'Really? That would be so kind. Could I meet you? Buy you tea?'

'Not here. Not in Nethergate.'

'No, no, of course not. How about – Steeple Martin? There's a very nice café where they do a good tea.' Libby crossed her fingers and hoped

Harry wouldn't mind. 'When would be convenient?'

'I'm on earlies this week, so tomorrow afternoon.'

'About this time?'

'All right. Where is this café?'

'In the high street. It's called The Pink Geranium,' said Libby. 'I'll sit at the table in the window. My name's Sarjeant. Libby Sarjeant, with a J.'

'All right,' said Nurse Redding again. 'I'll see you tomorrow. Oh, and how did you get my number? They wouldn't have given it to you at The Laurels.'

'Oh, I looked it up,' said Libby hastily. 'Goodbye. See you tomorrow.'

And before Nurse Redding could say another word, she switched off the phone. Now all she had to do was to convince Harry to open up for her tomorrow afternoon, and hope Fran didn't barge in on the tête-à-tête.

## Chapter Twenty

Deciding that the face to face approach was preferable, Libby strolled down to beard Harry in his den later that evening. She wasn't sure about disturbing him on his evening off, but trusted in his innate curiosity – almost as bad as her own – to carry her through.

'Hello, ducks,' he said, opening the door. 'To what do we owe this doubtful pleasure?'

'Aren't you pleased to see me then?' said Libby, sidling past him into the living room, where Peter sat at the scuffed old oak table, sheets of paper strewn around him.

'If it's an excuse for a drink, yes,' said Peter, pushing a hand through his limp blond hair, 'if you want something, no.'

'Sit down, petal.' Harry put a hand on Peter's shoulder. 'Wine? Whisky? Beer?'

When all three of them were supplied with their particular tipple, Libby began.

'Actually, Pete, it is a favour.'

'I knew it.' Peter threw up his hands. 'This bloody investigation of yours and Fran's, I suppose?'

'Fran's not exactly investigating,' said Libby.

'No, she's got more sense,' said Peter. 'Well, get on with it. What do you want?'

'I just wondered if Harry would open up the caff for me tomorrow afternoon?' She smiled in what she hoped was a winning manner. 'Would you, Hal?'

'If you stop glaring at me like some demented Cheshire Cat, I might,' said Harry. 'Who are you going to interrogate?'

'How do you know I'm interrogating anyone?'

'Why else would you want the caff? Unless you're pretending to be a gourmet chef or something.'

'Actually, I'm going to talk to one of Fran's nurses.'

'Fran's nurses?' echoed Peter.

'Who looked after her old Auntie in the home.'

'Oh, I see. You think she might have bumped

her off for her money.'

'Well, no,' said Libby. 'As far as we know, the nurses weren't mentioned in her will, although the home was.'

'So, why do you want to talk to her?'

'Because Fran thought they were hiding something.'

'They?' said Peter and Harry together.

'The two nurses. One of them seemed frightened, Fran said.'

'And this is the one you want to talk to?' asked Harry, beginning to look interested.

'No, the other one. You'll see if I can meet her in the caff tomorrow.'

'Oh, all right. I can be prepping up. What time?'

'I'd better be there about three thirty, just in case. Is that OK?'

'What about Fran?' asked Peter. 'Is she in on this?'

'Er – no. She's not as, um, interested as me.'

'Bloody nosy, you mean,' said Peter.

'That's exactly what she said.' Libby nodded thoughtfully.

'Great minds, ducks. Drink up, and I'll get you a refill. You can give Pete a hand now.'

'A hand with what?' asked Libby, handing over her glass.

'I'm planning the panto.' Peter cleared a space for her beside him.

'Have you finished writing it?' Libby picked up a brightly covered drawing. 'This looks like a child's picture book.'

'That's just what I want for the sets. Almost Disney. Pity we haven't still got Steve.'

They were all quiet for a moment, considering the unfortunate Steve.

'What about Guy?' suggested Libby. 'He's an artist.'

'So are you, you old trout, and I don't see you volunteering to do our sets.'

'I couldn't do big stuff, but he can. He used to do murals. And he restored some old wall paintings.'

Peter looked dubious. 'Panto sets are hardly in the same league, are they?'

'Can but ask. He might advise. When's the audition?'

'In a couple of weeks. I've got all the rest of the backstage team in place.'

'Are you directing?'

Peter looked surprised. 'No, I thought you were.'

'Me?' Libby gasped. 'You never asked me. I want to be in it, not direct it!'

Peter looked down his patrician nose. 'I didn't think I needed to. I assumed we were the Oast Theatre's permanent team.'

'Well, in a way, we are. I just didn't know I was official director.'

'Do it between you, then she can be in it,' said Harry, placing replenished glasses on the table. 'Stop squabbling, children.'

As she walked home a little later, Libby looked up at Fran's lighted window above The Pink Geranium, and wondered whether to tell her about tomorrow's meeting. If she kept quiet, Fran might see them if she came downstairs and would not only be annoyed, but would ruin the whole thing, then again, if Libby warned her, she would still be annoyed and might still ruin the whole thing.

When Ben called just after she arrived home, she asked his advice.

'If the nurse said she could tell you something, it's worth seeing her, isn't it?' he said.

'Yes, but I keep remembering your Uncle Lenny saying he could tell me a thing or two, when he couldn't. Well, he could, but not the right thing.'

'Well, maybe what she tells you won't be the right thing, but might help anyway. What you really want to know is whether you should tell Fran, isn't it?'

'Yes.' Libby sighed. 'I know she'll say I should mind my own business, but she really wants to know herself. Otherwise she wouldn't have come down in the first place, and she certainly wouldn't have come down the second time with Charles, or gone looking for the will. She's just confused.'

'Tell her, then. Say what you've just said to me. She might want to sit in.'

'Oh, no. I don't want that. Nurse Redding might clam up.'

'Play it by ear, then,' said Ben, 'and now let's change the subject. I didn't phone you to talk about murderous nurses.'

By the time Libby switched off the phone, she decided it was too late to call Fran, and feeling happier, fed Sidney and went to bed.

When she summoned up the courage to confess all the following morning, however, Fran's mobile was switched off. Frustrated, Libby called

Harry and asked him to see if Fran was in when he went to the caff for the lunchtime session. He called back just before midday to say that Fran wasn't in, and had been seen by Ali from the eight-til-late getting on a bus before nine o'clock. Puzzled, Libby tried Fran's phone again, and this time went straight to voicemail. She left a message asking Fran to call her back, but took the precaution of turning her own mobile off before setting out to meet Nurse Redding.

Harry had stayed on after lunch and was sitting at the favourite corner table with newspapers spread in front of him.

'I've made a carrot cake and some banana bread,' he announced, as Libby sat down in front of him. 'You'd better eat it.'

'Of course I will. Not all of it, though.'

'I'll take the rest home for Pete, unless I get any other customers. I just hope it won't set a precedent.'

'People might expect an afternoon cuppa, you mean?' Libby grinned at him. 'You'll have to invest in some doilies.'

'Doily yourself.' Harry stood up. 'What time's Miss Nightingale coming?'

'Any time in the next hour, I should think. If she turns up,' said Libby.

However, within ten minutes, Nurse Redding pushed open the door, looking vaguely surprised that Libby was the sole customer.

'How nice of you to come,' said Libby, standing up and pulling out a chair. 'I'll order tea, shall I? Or would you prefer coffee?'

'Tea'll be fine.' Nurse Redding, in an unsuitable tweedy skirt under the anorak Ben had described, or its twin, unhooked a large capable handbag from her shoulder and dumped it on Libby's chair.

Harry appeared from the kitchen and raised his eyebrows. 'Goodness, what strange friends you have, Miss Marple.'

'Shut up,' hissed Libby, then, raising her voice, 'Pot of tea for two, please, and have you any cakes?'

'Carrot and banana,' grinned Harry.

'Lovely.'

'So, what was it you wanted to know?' asked Nurse Redding without preamble.

'Er–' said Libby, taken aback.

'You said you were a friend of the family.' Nurse Redding sniffed. 'Can't say I took to the family much.'

'I'm actually a friend of Mrs Castle,' said Libby.

'Who? Oh, she came the day after the old woman died, that who you mean? Funny thing to do, if you ask me.' Nurse Redding unzipped her anorak and pursed her lips.

Harry appeared with a tray, which he unloaded as slowly as was humanly possible, with much fluttering of eyelashes at Nurse Redding. Libby felt a bubble of hysterical laughter rising and tried desperately to stifle it.

Nurse Redding leant across the table when Harry returned to the kitchen.

'Here. Is he queer?'

Libby opened her eyes very wide and took a deep breath. 'I think so. It doesn't bother you, does it?'

Nurse Redding shrugged. 'Doesn't bother me either way. Long as people get what they want. That's all that matters.'

Silenced by this startling announcement, Libby could only stare. Nurse Redding picked up the teapot and helped herself to tea, then cut a generous slice of both carrot cake and banana bread.

'Anyway, what was it you wanted to know?'

Libby pulled herself together. 'Well, you see, my friend, Mrs Castle doesn't really know the rest of the family, and seeing that the old lady was killed when they were all there, she thinks it must have been one of them. You saw Mrs Bridges just before she died, so you might have seen something.'

Nurse Redding chewed silently for a moment.

'Well, I did and I didn't,' she said. 'That Sue Warner was in the room when I went in. She followed me out. Then Marion Headlam came along the corridor, but didn't go in. Just asked Warner if the birthday cake was ready.'

'Birthday cake?'

'All the residents have a cake on their birthday, even if they don't know what's going on. The relations like it.' Nurse Redding looked as though she thought the relations were a bit dim-witted.

'So what happened next?'

Nurse Redding shrugged again and took a huge bite of banana bread. 'Mrs Denver arrived. The buzzer went. Mrs Headlam sent me.'

'And when you came back?'

'I opened the door and let her go in, then I closed the door behind her.'

'You didn't go in?'

There was that shrug again. 'No need to. I could see the old lady in the chair near the windows.'

'Alive?'

'I don't know, do I? I couldn't see her face. She looked like she did–' Nurse Redding stopped suddenly.

'Like she did when? When you came in the last time?'

'No,' said Nurse Redding slowly.

'What was different?' asked Libby, after a moment.

'I could see her face,' said Nurse Redding, staring at the carrot cake. 'I couldn't before.'

'So she'd moved?'

Nurse Redding looked up. 'Yes.'

'And that was between you leaving and Mrs Denver entering?'

'I told you, yes. After that I don't know what happened. That Mr Charles arrived.'

'And Paul Denver?'

Libby was surprised, and a little entertained, to see faint colour stain Nurse Redding's swarthy cheeks.

'Yes,' she said shortly.

'Did they arrive together?'

'More or less. I didn't see them come in. There was a hoo-ha going on.'

Libby watched the woman eating her way through the carrot cake for a few moments.

'Was that all you wanted to tell me? You said you could tell me everything.'

'I have.' Nurse Redding emptied her mouth. 'But watch that Warner. She's sly. And she was in the room with the old woman.'

'Yes, but you said she left with you. You'd have seen if anything had been wrong, wouldn't you?'

Nurse Redding stared defiantly at the banana bread. 'I know what I know,' she said.

'Well, what?' said Libby, exasperated. 'Something about the Denvers? You said you didn't take to them.'

'Untrustworthy,' said Nurse Redding, 'both of them.'

'Not Mr Wade?'

'He didn't come as often as them. Didn't try anything on.'

'What?' gasped Libby, appalling images invading in her mind.

'Borrowing money.' Nurse Redding spared her a glance. *'They* was always trying it on.'

'Ah,' said Libby, wondering if she dared ask about Marion Headlam.

'Wouldn't have got any. She was going to leave it to us.'

'Us?'

'The home. Mrs Headlam said. When she got those men to witness the will.'

'Right. Yes, we knew about that,' Libby nodded.

'Serve them right.'

'What?' Libby wasn't quite sure where she was in this conversation. Nurse Redding seemed to be in charge and Libby didn't know the lines.

'Got their comeuppance, didn't they?'

'I'm not sure what you mean.'

Nurse Redding showed Libby a sly smile. 'Wages of sin,' she said, and laughed.

Libby was so perplexed she couldn't answer.

Instead, she picked up the teapot. 'More tea?' she said.

Nurse Redding pushed her cup forward. 'Course,' she said, 'they wouldn't know.'

'Know? About what?'

'Sin.' The woman leaned forward and Libby saw a thin trickle of saliva at the corner of her mouth. 'It isn't always what it seems. Unless you know.'

Thoroughly confused, and by now alarmed, Libby put down the teapot with a thump. 'I'm still not sure–' she began.

'Thought you had a look about you,' said Nurse Redding, leaning back and picking up her cup. 'What do they call it – New Age.'

'New Age?' repeated Libby faintly.

'Crystals and all that. Those shops. Course, they're useful, but what a lot of crap.'

'I'm sure,' said Libby, faint but pursuing. 'Useful?'

But Nurse Redding had a crafty look on her face. 'Not to me,' she said. 'Anything else you want to know?'

'Er – no. No, thanks.' Libby swallowed her remaining tea. 'As long as you're sure none of the family could have got to Aunt Eleanor – I mean, Mrs Bridges.'

'You want to find out about those two men. Ask Marion Headlam.' Nurse Redding stood up. 'Thanks for the tea.' She made for the door, then turned round. 'If you do want to know any more about sin, give me a ring.' She winked and walked out, slamming the door behind her.

'Well!' Harry came out from behind the kitchen

door. 'What a performance.'

'Can I have another cup of tea?' asked Libby. 'I need it.'

'I should think so, petal.' Harry took her cup. 'Is she for real?'

'Sexual repression and sinful urges, do you reckon? All that about sin and stuff?'

Harry looked thoughtful as he poured boiling water on to a teabag. 'Yeah, but a bit more than that. What she was saying about New Age shops and so on.'

'I didn't understand a word of it.' Libby took the cup. 'I thought she'd gone off her head.'

Harry sat astride the chair vacated by Nurse Redding and leaned on the back. 'Think about it. Sin, New Age, useful. What she said about those men. Who were they, anyway?'

'Lorry drivers who witnessed the codicil to Auntie's will. One of them's dead.'

'Aha!' Harry looked triumphant. 'See!'

'No, I don't,' said Libby fretfully. 'I think you're as mad as she is.'

'Well, I'll have to sit down with a bit of paper and a pencil and work it out, but I reckon,' said Harry, taking a deep breath, 'that she's a witch.'

## Chapter Twenty-one

Fran's interview with the lettings agency had been difficult. The twelve year old behind the desk had been deeply suspicious, and did a lot of hair flicking, treating Fran to glimpses of deliberately dark roots. Eventually, she retreated into some inner sanctum and when she emerged, grudgingly revealed that the owners were in residence at present, as was their wont during August.

The lettings agency was within walking distance of Harbour Street. Fran stopped for a coffee in a strangely nostalgic 1950s style ice cream parlour, which, she decided, wasn't a revamp, but a lovingly preserved original. Stirring her coffee, she stared thoughtfully down the high street to the sea, deciding that, as the weather was continuing hot and sunny, the owners were likely to be out and about. A letter was required.

A card bought in a gift shop next door provided the means, and Fran walked down to a bench near The Swan and wrote a brief note. Wanting to avoid Guy, she made her way to the lane at the back and cut through the alley she had used the day before.

The sight of the green painted front door standing open left her standing irresolute with the card in her hand. Suddenly the idea of questioning the current owners didn't seem like such a good idea.

'Can I help you?'

Fran turned to see a young woman in obvious beach clothes behind her. Two children trailed along the pavement in her wake.

'I don't know,' said Fran. 'I feel rather embarrassed, now. Are you the owner?'

The woman looked amused. 'Yes, my husband and I own the cottage. If it's Coastguard Cottage you mean.'

Fran looked and noticed for the first time the discreet slate plaque beside the door. 'Yes,' she said.

'I'm afraid we have the cottage for the whole of the summer holidays, and the other lettings are done through an agency,' said the woman, waving the children inside the door. Reluctantly, staring at Fran, they went.

'Yes, I know about the agency,' said Fran. 'Actually, I wanted to find out whether you knew anything about the previous owners.'

The woman's eyebrows rose. 'Oh?'

Fran began to feel uncomfortable. 'My family came from here, you see,' she said, bending the truth a little, 'and I stayed in this cottage.' All at once, she was certain that she had.

'Oh, I see.' The woman bent to remove sandy beach shoes. 'Why don't you come in for a moment. I must check on the kids.'

Fran followed her into the dark, cool interior, where her eyes were drawn immediately to Libby's window, and she felt a jolt of recognition. The woman watched her curiously.

'Lovely view, isn't it?' she said.

'Yes, it is,' said Fran, smiling. 'My friend paints it all the time.'

'Your friend stayed here as well?'

'Yes,' said Fran, deciding that the full explanation would be just too long.

'Right, well, we bought it from a speculative builder,' said the woman, shuffling through a pile of papers on a side table. 'Here we are. He hadn't done much to it when we saw it, luckily, so we were able to stop the worst excesses.' She handed Fran a card. 'Would you like to look round?'

'No, no thanks.' Fran was scared she might disgrace herself as she had on that first visit to The Laurels. It seemed only too likely. 'I'll give this person a ring and see who he bought it from. It seems to have passed out of the family without anyone noticing.' *Now, how did I know that,* she wondered.

The woman frowned. 'I hope there was nothing wrong with the title,' she said. 'I'm sure our solicitor checked everything.'

'No, it was sold. I'd just like to know when. And it was lovely to see it again.' Fran smiled as reassuringly as she could. 'Thank you so much, and I'm sorry to have disturbed you.'

Fran could imagine the woman shrugging to herself and shaking her head as she shut the door. It all must have sounded a bit odd, to say the least. Throwing the now redundant card into a litter bin, Fran sat down on the bench and took out her mobile phone. Certain now that she *had* been to the cottage and that it had some relevance to her family, she wanted desperately to have this confirmed. Somehow, she had to find out why her mother had been so terrified.

The builder wasn't answering his phone. There

wasn't an address on the card, so Fran steeled herself to go into Guy's gallery and ask to borrow a telephone directory. She needn't have worried. Guy wasn't in.

'He's gone to see Philip about that sculpture,' said Sophie, handing over the directory, 'you know, the one for your relations.'

'Has Mrs Denver been on to you again, then?' asked Fran.

'No, he's just asking him to delay things a bit. After what you were saying yesterday. What were you looking for?'

'Oh, just a builder.' Fran leafed through the directory.

'Oh?' Sophie's raised eyebrow invited further explanation.

'Nothing important,' said Fran, smiling at her. 'Here it is.' She made a note of the address and handed the book back to Sophie. 'Thanks for that. I'd better rush off to catch the train now. Give my best to Guy.'

Walking back up the hill to the station, she congratulated herself on avoiding the questions Sophie was obviously bursting to ask. No need to tell anyone else what she was doing.

When she arrived back at The Pink Geranium, it was to see Libby and Harry sitting at the table in the corner deep in conversation. Assailed by a premonition of conspiracy, she pushed open the door and went in. Libby looked up.

'Hello, Fran,' she said brightly. Fran's suspicions were confirmed.

'What are you two up to?' she asked.

Libby and Harry exchanged looks.

214

'Er–' said Libby.

'I'll leave you to it,' said Harry, standing up. 'Tea, Fran? I'll make some fresh.'

'Coward,' said Libby.

'I'd love tea, thanks, Harry,' said Fran, sitting on his vacated chair. 'Come on, Libby. What have you been doing?'

'Promise you won't be angry?' said Libby, fishing for cigarettes in her basket.

'No, I don't. I expect I will be angry.'

Libby sighed and lit her cigarette. 'I've got down to less than ten a day, now,' she said. 'Except when I'm stressed.'

'Or nervous,' said Fran.

'OK, and nervous.' Libby took a deep breath. 'Well, it was like this. You know I thought we ought to ask Nurse Redding about – well, about everything?'

'And I said we ought to leave it. But you have, haven't you?'

'Yes.' Libby looked a little shamefaced. 'I rang her and she came here to have tea with me this afternoon.'

'How on earth did you manage that?'

Libby told her.

'And now Harry says he thinks she's a witch,' she finished. 'What do you think?'

Fran thought for a moment. 'I can sort of see why. It sounds as though she might possibly be a member of a kind of Satanist group, doesn't it?'

'That's what Harry says, although I'm not sure how he arrived at that,' said Libby, as Harry entered with a teapot and mugs. 'Fran agrees with you, Harry.'

'And isn't she mad?' Harry put the tea things on the table. 'Why aren't you mad, Fran?'

Fran sighed. 'It doesn't seem to have any point being mad with Libby. She goes ahead anyway. And it has thrown up a couple of useful things.'

'Like what?' asked Libby.

'The dead driver. Redding seems to think there's something more to that, doesn't she?'

'Isn't that just her seeing little nasties in everything?' said Harry, pouring tea.

'You said Marion Headlam seemed distressed when she rang you up, Libby.'

'Yes, but she supplied the names of the drivers, didn't she?'

'But perhaps she coerced them in some way. Perhaps the codicil wasn't genuine.'

'Well, they wouldn't have split on her, would they? They could be open to prosecution, too. If they'd signed as witnesses without seeing Auntie sign, or something like that. So she wouldn't have knocked one of them off, would she? She'd want them to confirm it for her.'

'Oh, I don't know. It's all so confusing.' Fran sipped her tea. 'Perhaps we ought to try and get in touch with the other driver.'

Harry raised his eyebrows. 'Well, there's a turn up,' he said. 'Want to get to the bottom of it, now, do you?'

'I always have, in a way. I ought to just walk away, really. It's nothing to do with me.'

'Bollocks,' said Libby. 'Of course it is. And where have you been, anyway? Your mobile's been switched off all day.'

Fran looked out of the window. 'I went to Nethergate.'

'Again? Is this a flourishing relationship with our Guy?'

Fran blushed faintly. 'No, nothing like that.' She looked at both of them. 'I didn't want to say anything, especially as Libby's bound to jump to all sorts of wild conclusions, but I need to get it into perspective. I don't think it's anything to do with Aunt Eleanor's death, but it's odd.'

Libby and Harry sat, spellbound, while Fran told them everything from the dinner party and Libby's paintings to this morning's visit to the cottage.

'So I've got the address of this builder, and I'm going to ask him who he bought the cottage from,' she concluded.

'Gosh,' said Libby.

Harry frowned. 'How sure are you about this, Fran? Could it be just – well – wishful thinking?'

'Harry!' Libby turned a shocked face to him.

'No, Lib, he's right. It could be. But I got all sorts of feelings about it, and now I'm sure I stayed there, and I'm also sure my mother had some connection with it. What I can't understand is why she was frightened, and why Eleanor's face came up.'

'So how will finding out who the builder bought it from help?' asked Harry.

'I want to try and find out who owned it when I was a child, and if it belonged to my family.'

'Or Eleanor's?' said Libby. 'But I still don't see that it will get you anywhere. Even if it was in your family, or hers, she and your mother are dead, so

217

no one will be able to tell you what happened.'

Fran sighed again. 'I know. It's so frustrating.'

'Couldn't the dodgy Denvers help?' asked Harry. 'Aren't they Auntie's relatives rather than yours?'

'I couldn't ask them. Not under the circumstances. Anyway, I don't expect they'd know.'

'Why not?' said Libby. 'Barbara's much the same age as we are, so she'd know if her family owned it. She lived in Nethergate herself, after all.'

'I couldn't ask, anyway,' said Fran firmly. 'Let's change the subject. Who are you going to interrogate next?'

'I don't know,' said Libby, eyeing her cautiously. 'Does this mean you want to be in my gang, now?'

'Well, I've already done my bit by helping Charles find the original will, haven't I? And I've talked to Inspector Murray. So I suppose I do want to be in your gang.' She looked at Harry. 'Are you in it, too?'

'Tea boy only, dear heart,' he said, 'and my best beloved will tell me off about that, I shouldn't wonder.' He stood up. 'And now I've got to get ready for this evening, so push off, both of you.'

'OK, Harry, we're going. Ring me if you have any ideas,' said Libby.

'Especially about witches,' added Fran mischievously.

'Are you seeing Ben tonight?' she asked when they got outside.

'I don't know,' said Libby. 'To tell you the truth, I'm still not sure where I stand with him.'

'I thought lying down would be a better description,' said Fran.

'Fran, I'm shocked.' Libby grinned at her. 'No, it's just that when I was a gel, if you were courting, you actually said when you were going to see each other, you didn't leave it until five minutes before and then say "are you in?", did you?'

'Oh, I suppose not, but our courting days were thirty years ago. Nowadays they do it all by text anyway, don't they? And sleep together on the first date.' Fran pulled a face. 'I know I sound old fashioned, but I still can't get used to it.'

'It's difficult, isn't it? I can't get used to feeling like I'm still sixteen, when I should be mature and responsible and know exactly what I'm doing.' Libby sighed. 'First I wonder if Ben's just using me, then I think he can't be, because he could find someone much younger and better looking, then I wonder if I should go to bed with him, or should I hold off. And of course, I can't bear the thought that he can see my appalling body.'

Fran nodded gloomily. 'It's enough to boost recruitment for a nunnery.'

'Anyway, why?'

'Why what?'

'Why did you want to know whether I was seeing Ben? What did you want to do?'

'Borrow Peter's computer again.'

'What for?'

'To look up witches. And Satanism.'

'And local covens,' grinned Libby. 'Oh, yes! I like it!'

# Chapter Twenty-two

'This is no use.' Disgusted, Libby pushed the mouse away from her.

'It's a very nice computer, thank you,' said Peter, looking up from his book.

'I didn't mean that.' Libby reached across and filched a cigarette out of the packet on the desk.

'She means all we can find is nice white witch, pagan and wiccan links. No nasty satanic ones.' Fran leaned over Libby's shoulder.

'Well, I don't suppose they want to advertise themselves, do you?' Peter closed his book. 'If it's one of those dancing naked around the fire jobs.'

Libby looked doubtful. 'Maybe. I'm still not sure why Harry latched on to it. We could be barking up the wrong forest, let alone tree.'

'And I don't know that it's got anything to do with Eleanor's death, anyway,' said Fran, collapsing into the sofa.

'It was your idea to look it up,' said Libby.

'I know,' Fran sighed, 'it was her saying something about those delivery drivers and the wages of sin. I thought she might know something.'

'Well, yes, she might,' said Libby, 'but what it's got to do with witchcraft, I don't know.'

'What I think is that you ought to buy your own computer,' said Peter, returning to his book. Fran and Libby stared at him, affronted.

'Well, we know where we're not wanted, don't we, Fran?' Libby stood up.

'Don't be stupid, you old trout,' said Peter, without looking up. 'Sit down and look up that delivery driver's name. I meant that you probably need a computer if you're going to carry on investigating things.'

'Of course I'm not! This is only because it's Fran's auntie,' Libby said indignantly.

Peter looked up under his brows. 'Oh, yeah?' he said.

'Why look up the delivery driver?' asked Fran.

'Type his name into the search engine and see if anything comes up. Then, if you've got it, do the same for the other one.'

Libby and Fran looked at each other, then Fran took Libby's seat at the computer. Libby dug out the scrap of paper with the names, and Fran typed the first one in.

'Gosh! Look at that!' gasped Libby, as the search engine provided thousands of results.

Peter got up to look. 'Most of those won't be relevant,' he said, 'but these first few are, look.' He pointed. 'See? They're news reports. That means he probably didn't die in bed.'

Fran and Libby looked at him. 'How do you know?' asked Libby.

Peter shook his head at her and patted her shoulder. 'How long have you known me, Lib? What is it I do for a living, exactly?'

'Ah.' Libby felt herself turning pink. 'He's a journalist,' she said to Fran. 'I forgot.'

'I know,' said Fran, and clicked on the first result.

After trawling through the first five entries, they knew what they were looking at. Len Edwards had been knocked down by a hit and run driver when he was inexplicably out of his car on a lonely road some miles from his home. No further information was available. The police were keeping the case open and still asking for witnesses.

'Now put in the other one,' said Peter, by now perching on the side of the desk.

Little to their collective surprise, Kyle Watson turned out to have been found dead in his car which appeared to have been involved in a crash on a remote road not far from his home. 'This incident is consistent with a vehicle being run off the road' a police spokesman was quoted as saying.

They looked at each other. Peter gave a small smile and returned to his seat and his book.

'That does it.' Libby lit another cigarette. 'They were murdered.'

'But who by?' said Fran.

'I think you ought to put your talents to work on this,' said Peter. 'Classic case for remote viewing, if you ask me.'

'Look,' said Fran, a little desperately, 'I've told you all before, I can't do it to order.'

'You used to for Ben,' said Libby, in a faintly accusing manner.

'I walked round buildings and sites. I was in places where, if something had happened, it was going to pop up at me. Like the cottage in Nethergate.'

'Cottage in Nethergate?' asked Peter.

Libby explained.

'You do see life, you two,' said Peter admiringly, and returned once more to his book.

'In that case,' said Libby, 'we'll have to go and find these places, won't we? And let you walk round them.'

Fran looked troubled. 'Is it going to help? Shouldn't we just tell the police?'

'Tell them what? They should have found this out for themselves, shouldn't they? Donnie Murray was looking into the will, wasn't he? He pulled Charles in for questioning, so he must have been.'

Fran sighed. 'I suppose so. When do you want to go?'

'Tomorrow? How far is it?'

'They're both in Sussex,' said Peter, looking up. 'What puzzles me slightly is that the police looking into their two cases haven't twigged.'

'Perhaps they have,' said Libby. 'We haven't got the full case history here, have we? There might have been further reports later on that we just haven't got to yet.'

'Well, I don't want to take up any more of Peter's time trawling through the internet,' said Fran. 'I'm going home.'

'OK.' Libby stood up and, slinging her basket over her shoulder, bent to kiss Peter's cheek. 'Thanks, Pete. We'll let you know what happens.'

'Ring me when you get back,' he said, 'and mind you don't get my Hal involved in anything else.'

'Where have we got to, then?' asked Libby, as she and Fran strolled down the high street towards The Pink Geranium.

'There's something wrong with the codicil, we can't find it anyway, we think the deaths of the drivers might have something to do with it, and we think Nurse Redding knows something.'

'Fair enough.' Libby hoisted her basket more firmly on to her shoulder. 'What about your cousins?'

'They aren't my cousins. But I really don't think they've got anything to do with it all, do you? Any of them. Paul and Barbara are far too anxious to find that will.' Fran stopped by her front door. 'And it still hasn't got anything to do with me, either.'

'I thought we'd dealt with that?'

'Curiosity killed the cat,' sighed Fran. 'Do you want a coffee or anything?'

'No, I'll get back if we're going out in the morning,' said Libby.

'And Ben might call, mightn't he?' grinned Fran. 'OK. I'll see you in the morning. What time?'

Ben did call. In fact, he called in person, and Libby forgot all about being too old, used or even investigating a murder. Until the morning.

# Chapter Twenty-three

'I don't know about a computer, I think I should have a satnav,' said Libby, pulling in yet again to the side of a high banked lane. 'Let's have another look at that map.'

Fran sighed. 'I told you, it just doesn't show the road number on this map. It's not detailed enough.'

'What did that report say? Near Applestone? Was that on the last signpost?'

Fran gave her the print out of one of the reports from Peter's computer. 'This is the one from the BBC website. I think it came from the local news service.'

Libby peered at it and shrugged. 'Oh, well, I suppose I just go on until I hit another main road and start again,' she said, and let off the handbrake.

'Look!' Fran yelped after they'd gone another ten yards.

'What?' Libby stood on the brakes.

'I can see some police tape over there.' Fran pointed to her left. 'There must be a turning. Do you suppose that's it?'

Libby inched the car forward. 'Could be. Bit unlikely, though. It looks as if it's in the middle of a field.'

But a turning there was, and it led to a slightly wider lane, at the side of which blue and white police tape fluttered, tied to two trees. Libby pulled up opposite, and Fran got out.

'Shall I come too?' Libby wound down her window.

'No, I'll poke around on my own, thanks.' Fran crossed the road and stood with her hands in her pockets. Libby lit a cigarette and waited. Finally, Fran turned and came back across the road.

'Well?' said Libby, as she got into the car.

Fran shook her head. 'I don't know. I did see someone's face, I think, but it looked dead.'

Libby grimaced. 'Len Edwards, then.'

'I suppose so.' Fran looked out of the window. 'There's something, though...'

Libby waited.

'Red. A red car?'

'A bus?'

Fran looked doubtful. 'Could be, but I don't think so. I couldn't see it properly. And I didn't get the automatic knowledge thing like I used to sometimes. Or at Nethergate.'

Libby sighed. 'Oh, well. Let's see if we can find the other one.'

'We'd better work out where we are first. But it's not far,' said Fran, 'only a few miles down this road.'

Libby looked at her. 'How do you know?'

Fran looked surprised. 'Because...' She stopped. 'I just know. There, see. I really knew that. Perhaps that means something.'

'Like it was murder, and the same murderer?' Libby was getting excited.

'Maybe, but I thought we'd already assumed it was.'

'Yes, but we came out here to find proof, didn't we? This could be it.' Libby let out the clutch and swerved sharply into the middle of the road. 'On this road?'

'I think so,' said Fran.

Ten minutes later, they had all the proof they needed. Standing by the side of the road in front of more blue and white tape, and surrounded by white-overalled scenes of crime officers, stood Detective Chief Inspector Murray.

'Shit,' said Libby, and tried to drive past, but a uniformed sergeant flagged her down, as DCI Murray approached.

Libby sighed and wound down her window.

'Mrs Sarjeant and Mrs Castle. Well, well, well,' he said.

'Hello,' said Libby and Fran together.

'Would you like to pull over there so we can have a little chat?' he said. Libby steered the car to the edge of the road and got out.

'Would I be right in thinking your appearance here is something to do with Mrs Bridges' death?' DCI Murray leaned against the bonnet and folded his arms.

Libby and Fran looked at one another.

'Yes,' said Fran.

'And can you tell me why?'

'You've obviously worked it out yourself,' said Libby.

'We're not as dumb as we look, you know,' said Murray, with the suggestion of a smile.

'We found out from Mrs Headlam at the home that two delivery drivers witnessed the codicil to the will,' said Fran. 'We thought we'd try and see if they knew what was in it, and then discovered they were both dead.'

'And it didn't occur to you that you might be interfering in an investigation?'

'Well, no,' said Libby, trying to look ingenuous. 'We just thought Fran might–' She came to a stop.

'And have you, Mrs Castle? I did ask you to let me know, didn't I?'

'Yes.' Fran looked uncomfortable. 'But I don't really know anything.'

'You must have spoken to someone to find all this out,' said Murray, his pale eyes darting from one to another. 'That could have been danger-ous.'

'Only Mrs Headlam,' said Fran, 'and *she* got in touch with *us*, because she was anxious about the legacy she's expecting.'

'And she gave you the names of the delivery drivers? Why?'

'She did that before, because she wanted to give us proof that there really was a legacy for The Laurels.'

DCI Murray looked sceptical.

'She must have told you, too,' said Libby, a little desperately, 'or you wouldn't be here.'

'Quite right, Mrs Sarjeant,' said Murray, running a hand over the remaining bristly red hair. 'With our colleagues from the Sussex force, we're looking at both accident sites. No reason to make a link before.'

'And it's murder, is it?' Libby persisted.

'We're investigating, Mrs Sarjeant. I'm sure Mrs Castle will be informed if there are any developments which concern her.'

'Which means we won't,' muttered Libby.

'And now, ladies, if you'd kindly move on. It's a longish drive back to Kent, and you don't want to hit the rush hour traffic.' Murray straightened up, nodded, and went back to his SOCOs.

'What rush hour traffic? A couple of tractors and a herd of cows?' Libby trod on the accelerator viciously.

'We'll be going round Tunbridge Wells,' said Fran, 'and it gets really jammed up round there.'

Libby drove in silence for the next fifteen minutes.

'Well, at least we were on the right track,' said Fran eventually. 'What do we do now?'

'Have another go at Redding?' suggested Libby.

'You'd better do that,' said Fran. 'I think I'd like to carry on with finding out about the cottage.'

'Do you think it has anything do with all this?'

'I told you, I'm not sure. But Aunt Eleanor's in there somewhere. It might be relevant.'

'I tell you what,' said Libby after a moment, 'this isn't half so straightforward as our other murder.'

Fran laughed. 'I thought you didn't want to be a Miss Marple?'

'I don't. Trouble is, this murder doesn't seem to be so close.' Libby looked sideways. 'Sorry, I know she was your Auntie.'

'I know what you mean. You were a bit ambivalent about the *Hop Pickers* murder because it involved you and your friends, I'm ambivalent about this one because it does actually involve my family.' Fran sighed again. 'Even if I don't like them much.'

'You liked your Uncle Frank.'

'Yes, I loved him. Up until I was twelve my childhood had been happy, even though my dad died. Uncle Frank did his best to take Dad's place, even took us on holiday–' she stopped suddenly.

'To Nethergate,' Libby finished for her.

'Yes.' Fran turned an astonished face to her friend. 'Good lord, how could I have forgotten?'

'I don't know,' said Libby. 'You remember things you've never even known. Must have been a trauma, or something.'

'Well, there was that picture of my mother screaming,' said Fran, 'perhaps that was something to do with it. But I really don't remember anything about those holidays, except that we went.'

'More than one?'

'Eh?'

'You said – holidays, plural.'

'Oh!' Fran looked startled. 'Yes. I shall have to think about it.'

'Haven't you got any photographs from when you were a kid?'

'I haven't, but my mother had.' Fran was silent for a moment. 'I'll see if I've got any next time I go up to London. I've got some boxes stashed away somewhere.'

'Well, that's no good, is it? You need them now.'

'I can't keep dashing backwards and forwards from London, Libby.'

'Why not? You dashed up and down several times last week.'

'But the whole point of living in the flat was to stop that,' argued Fran.

'Oh, all right. But if it has something to do with Aunt Eleanor, don't you think you really ought to look in to it?'

'What I think is that we need to ask Charles if he or the police have heard from that solicitor yet,' said Fran firmly. 'That's what I think.'

'OK,' said Libby, with a grin. 'We could have asked our Mr Murray back there, couldn't we?'

'I think he'd have arrested us,' laughed Fran.

'Well, go on then, phone Charles. See if he's heard.'

Fran paused. 'I haven't got my mobile with me,' she said.

'Oh, you're as bad as I am,' said Libby. 'Never mind, you can navigate us back to the M25 instead. I can't work out where we are, now.'

By the time Romeo the Renault breathed a sigh of relief outside The Pink Geranium, Harry was already open for the evening. He came to the door and surveyed them critically.

'Drinkipoos, girls?' he asked. 'You look as though you could do with it.'

'You're a bad influence, young Hal,' said Libby, climbing stiffly from the driver's seat. 'But yes, please. Love one.'

'I'll nip up and get my phone first,' said Fran.

'So, what did you get up to?' asked Harry, settling Libby on the sofa in the window.

Libby told him, while he opened a bottle of his best Sancerre and poured three glasses. Fran reappeared and collapsed beside Libby.

'So, what next?' Harry got up to get Libby an

ashtray. 'Got to stop this, you know, you old trout. I'm not allowed to have smokers in here when the punters are in any more.'

'No, I know, Harry,' sighed Libby. 'I'm feeling more and more persecuted by the day. And you haven't given up.'

'No, and I don't intend to,' said Harry, taking one of Libby's cigarettes. 'I get bolshie when the government start telling me what I can and can't do with my own life.'

'Even when it's for your own good?' said Fran.

'The worst of the nanny state,' said Harry, swinging a leather clad leg over the back of his chair. 'Now, come on. What are you two sleuths going to do next?'

'Fran's going to find a builder and I'm going to resume my interesting relationship with Nurse Redding,' said Libby.

'A builder?' Harry's eyebrows rose. 'What are you planning on having done?'

'It's all right, Harry, I'm not going to knock your flat about. I want to find out who owned the cottage in Nethergate.'

'Hang on, I'm not sure I know about the cottage in Nethergate,' said Harry, looking confused.

Fran and Libby filled him in, leaving him only slightly better informed. He emptied the bottle into their glasses and stood up.

'Well, I'll leave you to sort it out, then,' he said. 'I've got me first bookings in about ten minutes. There's a table free later on, if you want it.'

'No thanks, Harry,' said Libby, 'Ben's coming over.'

'Oooh.' Harry struck a pose. 'Another night of passion?'

'I will, though, Harry,' said Fran deflecting Libby's obvious chagrin and embarrassment.

'What happened to not wanting to rely on me?' said Harry. 'Come down when ever you're ready after about 8.30.'

'Go on, then, ring him,' said Libby, when Harry had returned to Donna in the kitchen.

'Oh, yes.' Fran took out her mobile and stared at it.

'It won't bite you, Fran.'

'No. Oh, well, here goes, then.' Fran picked it up and pressed a few buttons.

'Voice mail,' she mouthed at Libby. 'Yes, hello, Charles, it's Fran. Could you ring me when you get this? Just wanted to know whether you'd heard from the solicitor. OK, bye.'

'Was that his mobile or his landline?'

'Er–' Fran held the phone away and peered. 'Oh, mobile.'

'Try the land line, then.'

'OK,' said Fran and repeated the procedure.

'Well, I hope that doesn't mean he's back in the arms of the law,' said Libby, draining her glass. 'I'm off. Phone me when you hear from him.'

By the time Fran went down to the restaurant she still hadn't heard anything from Charles and was beginning to get worried. Harry put her in the corner by the counter and kept up an intermittent conversation with her in between customers.

'I think Libby's right, you know,' he said, after serving the last diners their stultifyingly sweet dessert. 'Much as I hate to admit it, the old trout can be right sometimes. You ought to look for those pictures of Mummy's. Might bring it all back.'

'I can't bear the thought of going all the way back up to London, though,' said Fran, sipping coffee.

'Oh, come on. Pete does it almost every day.'

'That's different, somehow,' said Fran, feeling wimpish.

'Oh? What about all the other people in this village who commute? Not to mention all the DFLs?'

'DFLs?'

'Down from Londons. All the weekenders who pushed the prices up so the kids can't afford anywhere to live.' Harry's pleasant face looked vicious for a moment. 'Worse in Nethergate.'

Fran looked at him for a moment. 'But you're a DFL yourself,' she said.

Harry looked startled. 'No, I'm not! I live with a Steeple Martonian born and bred. That doesn't count.'

'OK, OK. So what about me? That's what I'll be, won't I?'

'Yes, but you're different, too. Anyway, you probably won't be able to afford anywhere, either.'

'Oh, thanks. Just what I need to cheer me up.'

'Oh, never mind. You can stay upstairs for as long as you want, you know that.'

'Not rent free, I can't,' said Fran. 'And now, please may I have my bill?'

Harry reluctantly allowed her to pay, and sent

her up the back stairs, saying you never knew what might be lurking in the high street.

Taking her mobile out of her bag to ring Charles again, Fran was surprised to see she had received a message. She certainly hadn't heard the discreet beep, but then, Harry's diners tended to be a noisy lot.

'Sol left messg,' she read, 'call tomorrow. C.'

Fran forwarded this to Libby's mobile, guessing a phone call wouldn't be appreciated if Ben was with her, and was further surprised when Libby rang her straight back.

'Ben's just told me,' she said, 'he's been using your builder for years. But now he's retired, so no wonder he wasn't answering the office phone!'

'Does he know where to find him?' asked Fran.

'Not off hand, but he says he'll find out at the office,' said Libby. 'So that's two exciting things to follow up tomorrow, isn't it?'

## Chapter Twenty-four

Libby was already up when Fran phoned early the following morning. Ben had left even earlier to go and change into suitable going-to-the-office clothes, so she was sitting with a cup of tea and Sidney, wrapped in her old dressing gown and yet another post-coital glow.

'You sound a bit x-rated this morning,' commented Fran.

'I feel it,' said Libby. 'Disgustingly.'

'Well, if you can come down to earth for a bit, I'm going to leave the builder to you, at least for today.'

'Oh? Why?'

'Peter called this morning and offered to take me up to town with him.'

'Oh, did he, now?' Libby laughed. 'I sense Harry's fine Italian hand in this.'

'Quite right,' said Fran, and explained. 'So the upshot was, he told Peter all about me being such a wimp, and Peter decided to take me in hand. All I've got to do is be downstairs in five minutes, and I will duly be delivered home at 7 this evening.'

'So you'll unearth Mum's pictures?'

'That's the idea. And maybe see Charles, as well.'

'Do you think he might be at work?'

'No idea. He told me he had a failed career, but I don't even know what he did. Or does.'

'Time to find out, although as you're not interested in him, it doesn't matter, does it?' Libby yawned. 'When Ben phones through the builder info, I'll call you and see what you want me to do, if anything. Meanwhile, I'm going to see if I can get hold of Redding again.'

Libby finished her tea, thought about breakfast and decided it could wait. After as quick a shower as the water system could manage, she dressed, went downstairs and phoned Nurse Redding's number again. Then remembered that this week she was on earlies. So that left the builder. But it was still too early to expect Ben to have found out where he was, so now, what to do. She went into the conservatory and looked at the painting on the easel, wrinkled her nose, and went out again.

There was always shopping. August had turned grey and unappealing, so Libby tucked an umbrella into her basket and let herself out.

The village was quiet. In the butcher's, Libby met Hetty, Ben's mother, and in the post office his Uncle Lenny and Auntie Flo, who invited her back to Flo's little house for coffee.

'So, what you up to now, gel?' asked Flo, settling her in a chair by the fireplace. Lenny pottered off to the kitchen to make coffee, and Flo sat down on the other side of the hearth and lit a cigarette.

'Oh, this and that,' said Libby. 'My friend Fran's down here, staying in the flat over The Pink Geranium.'

'I know all that. And her old Auntie died, didn't she? Murdered, Hetty said.'

'Oh.' Libby was surprised. 'I didn't realise Ben had told her.'

'Course he did. Can't keep anything secret here, you ought to know that.'

'I don't know about that,' said Libby dubiously, remembering the secrets that had been kept in Hetty's family.

Lenny reappeared with a tray. 'Don't you go gettin' involved, young Libby,' he said, 'police'll look after it.'

'I know, I know. But it's difficult not to when a friend's involved.'

'So what's the story, then?' asked Flo. 'Who do they reckon did it?'

Libby gave them an edited version of all she knew, dwelling on the lighter aspects, including Harry's conviction that Nurse Redding was a witch.

'That's not so silly, gel,' said Flo, at this point. 'Lot o' women around her age go to these devil worship things. You read about it in the papers.'

'Oh, I know, and all the cults that suck people in and make them do awful things.' Libby nodded and took a sip of milky coffee. 'But how do you know what age she is?'

'I guessed. Stands to reason. Middle aged, is she?' said Flo, blowing on her own cup.

'Bit younger than me, perhaps. I don't really know.'

'There you are, then. I remember a few years ago they had a bit of trouble up at the old chapel. Holding their meetings up there, an' that.'

'What old chapel?'

'Over beyond Steeple Mount in the woods. Used to be a private chapel for the big house.'

'What big house?' asked Lenny.

'Oh, it's gone, now,' said Flo. 'Army used it in the war and the family didn't come back. Then there was a fire and it was left to fall down. Folk said the family couldn't afford it.'

'So sad when that happens, isn't it?' said Libby. 'Who were the family, do you know?'

'Can't say as I remember. Sir someone. Anyway, the chapel was still standing and these people were usin' it for their what-d'you-call-its–'

'Black mass?' asked Libby.

'Might be. They found blood and feathers and such up there.'

'Golly! So what happened?'

'Don't rightly know. There was a lot of talk about it, and it all died down. Some bloke was arrested, I think. Haven't heard nothin' since.'

'What was it called, do you remember?'

'Tyne Hall, far as I recall.'

'I wonder if it's still going on?'

'Now, young Libby, I told yer, don't you go pokin' yer nose in,' said Lenny. 'All them funny people, devil worshippers an' that. Nasty stuff.'

'I know,' sighed Libby. 'Sorry.' She put down her cup. 'So tell me. How are you two getting on?'

Lenny and Flo outdid each other telling her how happy they were. Libby reflected happily on her own part in bringing the two old people back together as she made her way back to Allhallow's Lane, and as the first spots of rain fell, opened the door to hear the phone ringing.

'Found him!' said Ben's voice triumphantly.

'The builder?' Libby sat down on Sidney's step.

'Yep. I called him, I hope you didn't mind, and after he'd moaned at me saying he didn't do any work any more, then moaned some more saying he didn't know what to do with himself these days, he said you could call him, or better still, go and see him.'

'Golly,' said Libby, for the second time in an hour. 'Did you tell him why?'

'Not really. I said it was about some property he might know about.'

'Right. Where is he? Could I go today?'

'How about I come with you? I'm finished here. I could come home and pick you up.'

Libby thought about talking to yet another old

person today and decided that having Ben with her would be an asset.

'I'll be with you in about half an hour, then,' he said.

Awash with milky coffee and biscuits, Libby didn't bother with lunch, and was waiting by the door when Ben drew up outside.

'So where does he live and what's his name?' Libby asked, as they turned into the high street.

'Jim Butler. Lives just outside Nethergate in a bungalow he built himself. His wife died a few years ago, and I think he's a bit lonely.'

'And bored, by the sound of it,' said Libby.

Their route took them past Steeple Mount and Libby found herself wondering where the Tyne chapel was. She nearly asked Ben, but thought he might react the same way as Lenny and Flo. The road wound through fields towards the sea, until Ben turned off into a well kept, newly tarmaced road lined with neat new bungalows on either side. At the end, a much larger and grander bungalow looked out over a terraced garden to the sea.

'Here we are.' Ben got out and came round to help Libby out. Before they could go any further, the front door opened, revealing a large, bald man in old corduroys and shirtsleeves, accompanied by an elderly black dog, whose tail waved in welcome.

'Here you are, then, mate. How are yer?' he held out his hand.

'Hello, Jim.' Ben shook the hand. 'This is my friend Libby Sarjeant, who I told you about.'

Jim Butler turned to Libby. 'How are yer, then,

ma'am?' he said.

'Oh, please call me Libby, Jim,' said Libby. 'And who's this?' She bent to hold out a hand for the dog to sniff.

'That's Lady. Silly bloody name, pardon me, Ma – Libby – but the wife liked it. Gettin' old now, like me.'

Old wasn't the word she'd apply to Jim Butler, thought Libby, as they followed him through an over furnished hall into a modern conservatory with a wonderful view. He couldn't have been more than a few years older than Libby herself, so his wife must have died very young, poor soul.

'Great view, Jim,' said Ben.

'Built it for the wife,' said Jim gloomily, 'then she up and died just after it got finished. Spend most of me time here, nowadays. Lady can get straight out to the garden, see.'

When they were seated and had refused tea or coffee, he said; 'So what did you want to ask me about, then?'

Libby looked at Ben, who gave her a slight nod.

'Well,' she said, 'a friend of mine thinks a cottage in Nethergate might have once belonged to her family, and she wanted to find out.'

'Where do I come into it?' asked Jim.

'Apparently the owners bought it from you, so she wondered who you bought it from.'

'Which one is it, then? I had quite a few properties in Nethergate. Used to let 'em out for holidays.'

'It's on Harbour Street. I don't think Fran told me what it was called.'

'Had a couple on Harbour Street,' said Jim un-helpfully. 'Which one?'

'It's got very thick walls and nearer The Sloop than the other end,' said Ben.

'Oh, ah. That'd be Coastguard Cottage. Least-ways, that's what they call it now. Sold it a coupla years back to a London couple. They use it in summer. Let it the rest of the time.'

'Oh, have you kept in touch?' asked Libby.

'Nah. I got a coupla cottages left and the agency lets 'em out for me. They do the same for Coastguard Cottage.'

'Right.' Libby waited to see if any more was forthcoming, and as it wasn't, asked again. 'So, do you remember who you bought it from?'

'Course I do,' said Jim, looking affronted. 'Not the name, mind, but it was someone to do with them Stones.'

'Stones?' Libby felt her scalp tingle. 'Barbara Stone?'

'Barbara? Don't remember no Barbara. Old Joe Stone. His family. They used to own it, then someone took it over from them.'

'Bought it, you mean?' said Ben.

'Yeah, course. But in the family, like.' Lady sud-denly surged to her feet and went to the sliding doors. 'Hang on a minute – got to let 'er out.' Jim got up and opened the doors. 'I'll leave 'em open if yer don't mind. Then she can come in when she wants.' He looked after her fondly. 'Gawd, I'll miss 'er when she goes.'

Libby swallowed and blinked. Ben reached out and squeezed her arm.

'Anyway,' said Jim, coming to sit down again,

'that's about all I know. Bought it from the Stones, or near enough. Sure yer don't want no tea?'

'Well, if you're going to have a cup,' said Ben, and Libby's insides quailed.

'Oh, I 'ave the kettle on all day, me,' said Jim, getting up. 'You wait here. Won't be two shakes.'

'What now?' said Ben, after he'd gone. 'Are we any further forward?'

'Well, yes,' said Libby, 'and certainly if it's the same family. Was Auntie Eleanor a Stone, do you suppose? Barbara is her blood relative, I think, so it looks like it, doesn't it? Do you think Uncle Frank rented the cottage from Eleanor's father, or something, and that's how he met her?'

'Could be. I still can't understand how Fran didn't remember staying there, though. Given her peculiar talents.' Ben leaned across and planted a quick kiss on Libby's lips. 'Sorry, couldn't resist it.'

Libby found herself blushing as she noticed Jim standing in the doorway with a broad smile on his face.

'Don't mind me,' he said, coming forward with a tray that looked suspiciously like the twin of the one in Flo's house.

After Ben had accepted a cup of what Libby referred to as "builder's" and she had managed to refuse without giving offence, Lady strolled back in and fell on Libby's feet.

'She likes you,' said Jim. 'Don't take to many people.'

Libby smiled and patted Lady's head, wondering what Sidney was going to say about this when he got a whiff of her legs.

243

'So you bought it from the Stone family,' prompted Ben.

'Not exactly from them, from a connection, like. Married into the family, 'e 'ad.'

'Uncle Frank,' said Libby and Ben together.

'Frank?' said Jim.

'Frank Bridges. Could it have been him?' said Libby.

'Oh, ah. Rings a bell.' Jim wrinkled his brow. 'Come to think of it, 'e married one of old Joe's girls.'

'Eleanor?' suggested Libby, almost holding her breath.

'Could 'a been,' said Jim slowly, 'I don't rightly remember their names.'

'Were there several daughters?' asked Libby.

'Two girls and a boy,' said Jim.

'Could Barbara have been the son's daughter?' asked Ben.

'Could 'a been. Didn't really know the family.'

This appeared to be the end of Jim's knowledge of the Stones and Coastguard Cottage, and although Libby was keen to leave and let Fran know of these exciting developments, Ben embarked on a discussion of old friends in the business and, according to Jim, the falling standards of local builders.

'I had to,' he said, as they left Jim and Lady on the front steps. 'He would have been hurt if we'd left as soon as we got the information out of him.'

'Yes, of course,' said Libby. 'Nice old boy.'

'Hey, not so old. Not much older than us.'

Libby grinned. 'Well, you're a nice old boy, too.'

Peter drove Fran to the station, got them both on the train and settled back in his seat.

'See?' he said, beaming at her. 'Easy.'

She nodded. 'I know,' she said, 'but you do it every day. It's an event for me.'

'Oh, come on, Fran. You've gone up and down since May. It's hardly a new experience.'

'All right.' She sighed. 'And thank you for forcing me into it. And for the lift.'

'No problem.' Peter crossed his elegant legs and opened his laptop. 'You don't mind if I do some work, do you?'

'Not at all,' said Fran, politely and truthfully, for she was happy to have the opportunity to think through her plans for today. First, she would go to her flat and search for the photographs, then she would call Charles and see if he'd heard anything from the solicitor. If there was time, she would see if Lucy was free to meet her for lunch or a cup of tea. It was unlikely, as Rachel and Tom would still be on holiday from school and nursery respectively, but guiltily Fran realised that she had paid her daughter very little attention recently, and she should at least try.

The journey didn't seem to take as long as usual, although by the time they reached Victoria, the train was packed. Stiffly, Fran climbed out of the carriage and followed Peter, who wove along the platform with the ease of familiarity. As she made for the tube entrance, he caught her by the arm and propelled her towards the taxi rank.

'It's all right, Peter,' she said, breathless at the speed with which he'd marched through the

245

crowds. 'I'll go by tube.'

'We'll share a taxi,' said Peter firmly, and kept hold of her until they reached the head of the queue.

'What's your address?' he asked as he pushed her inside the cab. He relayed it to the cab driver and sat back in the corner. 'Still one of my favourite luxuries,' he said, with a sigh, 'a cab in London.'

'I think I agree,' said Fran, staring out at the milling workers and the gridlocked traffic, 'although I'm not sure it's any faster.'

'No, it isn't,' said Peter, 'but much, much nicer, darling.'

He refused to take her share of the fare when they pulled up outside her flat, looking the building up and down with a rather disparaging air. 'Glad you moved down with us,' he said. 'See you at Victoria in time for the six o'clock. Got my mobile number?'

'Yes, thank you.'

'Don't be late, and keep me informed.'

'Yes, Peter,' she said obediently, and waved him off.

Climbing the stairs up to the Betjeman flat, she agreed with Peter. She was glad she'd moved, too. Even if the future was uncertain, her temporary quarters were streets ahead, she thought, pardoning herself the pun.

The cupboard built into the eaves where Fran had stored all that remained of her mother's possessions, was draughty, damp and cobwebby. Crawling on hands and knees and wishing she hadn't worn a skirt, she managed to drag several cardboard boxes in severe danger of disintegration out into the bedroom, sat back on her heels and brushed cobwebs off her hair and face, hoping no spiders had come with them.

Half an hour later she had found all sorts of things; old school reports, a few drawings from pre-school years and several photograph albums. These, however, dated from Margaret's own childhood and included pictures of her own parents and grandparents, severely posed ladies and gentlemen in Victorian attire and serious expressions. There were some of Fran, but these were taken when her father was alive.

Before she ventured back into the cupboard, she made herself a cup of tea and phoned Charles.

'I was just going to call you,' he said, 'the solicitor just called me.'

'And?'

'The only will he knows about is the one we found. He didn't know anything about me having Power of Attorney or even that she'd moved to The Laurels.'

'Well, I suppose there was no reason he would, was there? Eleanor wouldn't have thought to tell him, if she wasn't quite compos mentis...'

'Oh, she had most of her marbles,' said Charles, 'that's what's so puzzling. If she made a new will or a codicil, she knew what she was doing.'

'So Marion Headlam couldn't have conned her into it?'

'No! I still can't believe she would have done anything like that. I know you don't like her–'

'She wasn't exactly your favourite person when

we went there last week,' Fran reminded him.

'No, well, I was upset,' said Charles, sounding sulky.

'Anyway, what did he say about it? The codicil, I mean.'

'He will proceed with the original will until something turns up. He can't go on hearsay without concrete proof.'

'Well, that should please you and the Denvers. The Laurels won't get whatever she promised.'

'We could make a goodwill payment to them,' said Charles, 'the solicitor suggested that.'

'I bet it wouldn't be as much as Marion Headlam expected,' said Fran.

'Anyway, apparently we can't do anything until the police have finished their investigations.'

'Oh?' Fran frowned out of the window. 'I wonder what happens when a case is left unsolved? Does the person's estate just sit in limbo?'

'No idea, but let's hope it doesn't happen in this case,' said Charles. 'Did you say you were in London?'

'Yes, I'm just sorting out a few more things in the flat,' Fran said evasively.

'Would you like lunch? We could go to La Poule au Pot again,' said Charles, sounding hopeful.

'I can't afford it, I'm afraid, Charles,' said Fran, 'and I'm supposed to be seeing Lucy, anyway. And how come you've got so much time free? I've never asked you what you do, have I?'

'Ah – well, nothing at the moment, I'm afraid.'

'Libby said something about business commitments when you phoned the other day.'

'An interview, that's all.'

'For what, though? What was your career?'

She heard Charles sigh. 'I was a salesman,' he said. 'But not a very good one. I couldn't keep pace with the aggressive attitudes that seem to be wanted these days.'

Despite herself, Fran sympathised. 'I know what you mean. I couldn't sell a heater to an Eskimo, let alone talk someone into something they didn't really want.'

'I'm glad you understand,' said Charles, sounding gloomy, 'but it doesn't help. I can't get arrested now.'

There was a short silence while they both reflected on this rather apposite statement.

'Sorry,' said Charles, 'that wasn't intended.'

'I don't suppose it was,' said Fran, with a slight laugh. 'But chin up, Charles. You might have enough soon not to worry.'

Charles sighed again. 'I doubt it. I'll have to replace all the money I borrowed, won't I?'

'But there'll be more than that, won't there? There's the house.'

'Oh, I don't know,' said Charles. 'All I had access to was her bank. I didn't bother to look into anything else. So, anyway, lunch is off, is it?'

'I can't do it, really, Charles,' said Fran with a distinct sense of relief. 'I've still got a lot to do, and as I said, I'm supposed to be calling Lucy.' That wasn't a lie, she told herself, she had intended to phone Lucy.

'OK. Well, keep me posted if you hear anything.'

'And you,' said Fran, and switched off the phone. Well, that didn't get them any further forward, did it. She swallowed the rest of her tea and rinsed the mug before going back into the bedroom and crawling once more into the attic cupboard.

Peering into a couple more boxes, she discovered nothing more interesting than some old china that she thought she remembered from her childhood. A tea service that she'd bought her mother a couple of years after they moved out of Mountville Road to replace the one they'd left behind, an old tablecloth in blue checks, with a suspicious stain on the edge, and tucked right at the back, a box with some loose photographs on top of what looked like a framed picture. She pulled it out into the bedroom.

The photographs were fading and curled at the edges, but Fran's heart lurched under her ribcage as she felt a shock of recognition. There they were, she and her mother, sitting on the harbour wall, her mother's hair blowing about her face, and the sky behind them looking grey and cloudy. How she knew that, she wasn't sure, as the photographs, naturally, were in black and white. Next there was one of Uncle Frank and Fran on donkeys on the beach, Uncle Frank's feet almost touching the ground.

'Poor donkey,' murmured Fran, and took out the framed picture. This time, her heart didn't lurch so much as stop dead. For the picture was almost identical to those she had seen in Libby's studio.

Taking a deep breath and sitting back on her heels, Fran steeled herself to look further into the box. Wrapped in what looked like crocheted doilies were a couple of ornaments. Fran lifted them out and carefully unwrapped them.

And found herself looking at two china ponies.

# Chapter Twenty-five

## 1964

Fran lay on her back and gazed out of the window at the moon. If she sat up, she would see it reflected in the sea like a shining pathway to the sky, but now it was pleasant just to lie here and look at the moon, listening to the faint slap of waves against the harbour wall, which meant that the tide was in.

It was lovely to be here, even if it was autumn half term and most of the shops were shut for winter. They had arrived today, Thursday, the first day of half term, and were to go home Sunday in time for school on Monday, but it wasn't the same without Uncle Frank. Fran sighed and sat up. Things had been different since the wedding.

Frank and Eleanor had arrived back from their honeymoon in Brighton late one night, and Fran hadn't seen them. When she got home from school the next afternoon, Uncle Frank was sitting with her mother.

'Not as good as our holidays in Nethergate, though, poppet,' he said, tweaking Fran's plait, when he'd finished telling them all about

Brighton. Fran privately agreed, for they didn't seem to have done any of the things they normally liked to do on holiday.

'Tell you what, though,' said Frank, 'now I've bought the cottage from your Aunt Eleanor's dad, we can all use it whenever we like. I thought you and your Mum might like to go down for half term. What do you think, Margaret?'

Fran's mother looked dubious. 'It all depends if I can get the time off work,' she said.

'Course you can,' said Frank. 'If you can't, perhaps Eleanor and I could take Franny down.'

Fran tried not to look horrified, and sent her mother a pleading look.

'No, I'm sure I'll be able to manage it,' she said, giving Fran the ghost of a wink. 'We don't want to trouble Eleanor when she's only just got married.'

Fran didn't miss the slightly brittle tone in her mother's voice.

Frank smiled, although Fran didn't think he meant it. 'Good, good,' he said. 'Let me know when it is, eh, Franny?' He stood up. 'And now I'd better get back upstairs.'

'Aren't you staying for tea?' asked Fran.

'No, darling, Uncle Frank's got to go upstairs. Aunt Eleanor's cooking his dinner,' said Margaret, standing up herself. 'And you've got homework to do.'

And that set the pattern of the days and weeks to follow. Occasionally, Fran would find Frank sitting with her mother when she came home, but he would always go back upstairs very soon afterwards, and the visits became fewer and farther between. Eleanor never came down, and only once

252

or twice were Margaret and Fran asked to the upstairs flat. Margaret never complained, and when Fran did, patiently explained that Uncle Frank's life was different now, and she couldn't expect him to pay as much attention to them.

'We were very lucky he was here for us after your father died,' she said, 'but we couldn't expect it to go on for ever.'

Fran didn't see why not, but as she cordially disliked Eleanor, she supposed seeing Frank infrequently was better than seeing him more often but with his wife. He did, however remember his promise about sending them to Nethergate for half term, and so here they were.

Fran could hear the television downstairs, for when Frank had bought the cottage, he had installed the latest television and gramophone, which was good for Margaret, now she had no company after Fran had gone to bed. Not that she made Fran go to bed particularly early on holiday.

Fran got up and went to the window. It was almost the same view from up here as it was from downstairs. She could see the little boats bobbing in the harbour, and somewhere over to her left, the lighthouse intermittently swept the sea with bright white light to rival the moon. On the windowsill, two of her very own china ponies now sat, for this room was now hers for ever, or so Uncle Frank said. What would happen when he and Eleanor stayed here, she didn't know, although she couldn't see why they would, when Eleanor's parents and brother and sister still lived here. Why wouldn't they go and stay with them?

She was just going back to bed when she heard the front door. Turning back to the window, she opened it and peered out, but was too late to see who had just arrived. She couldn't think who it could be, for apart from a few families they met regularly in the summer, they knew no one in Nethergate.

But there was no sound of voices other than the murmur of the television, so she concluded that her mother must have opened the door for some reason and went back to bed.

She must have slept, for she awoke suddenly, her heart beating heavily. For a moment, she was disoriented, then, as she heard a male voice, remembered where she was. Uncle Frank? Coming fully awake, she realised that she shouldn't have heard his voice, but sure enough, it was his. Sounding angry. She sat up and got out of bed, frozen to the spot when she heard another, less familiar voice screaming.

Something crashed against the outside of her door, and she heard her mother's cry of pain.

'Mum!' She stumbled to the door and pulled it open.

'No, Fran!' Margaret whispered. She lay on the floor looking terrified, her arm reaching out to Fran. Then the screaming started again, almost in her ear, and she looked up to see Uncle Frank holding Eleanor by the arms, an Eleanor almost unrecognisable, her face twisted in fury, one hand still clutching a smashed china bowl.

It wasn't until much later that Fran remembered that Margaret had only been wearing a nightdress.

# Chapter Twenty-six

Before she met Peter at Victoria, Fran phoned Libby.

'What time are you seeing Ben tonight?' she asked.

'I needn't see him at all,' said Libby, with rare insight.

'I don't want you putting him off for me,' said Fran, 'but I would like to talk to you on your own.'

'Get Pete to drop you off at mine, then, and we can have supper. Ben won't be round till later.'

'Are you sure, Lib?'

'Of course I'm sure. And I've got some news for you, too, assuming this is because you've got news for me.'

'Well, yes. I think so.'

When Fran arrived at Victoria, Peter was already there, and they were able to make the ten to six train. Fran was quiet, and Peter, after a quizzical look or two, left her in peace. Getting back into Canterbury just before half past seven, Peter dropped Fran outside number 17 ten minutes later.

'See?' he said. 'No trouble at all.'

'It feels like a lifetime,' said Fran. 'I'd hate to do it every day.'

'Well, mind you tell me what's been going on. I'm a positive hive of seething curiosity.'

'I will,' said Fran, with a tired smile, 'when I've worked it all out myself.'

Libby settled her with a large gin and tonic, having learnt that her friend's favourite tipple was not the same as her own, brought Sidney in from the garden and dumped him on her lap.

'You look as if you need him,' she said, sitting on the sofa, and for once, avoiding the creak.

'Thanks, Lib.' Fran stroked Sidney, who butted her other hand and spilled gin and tonic on his nose.

'So? What did you want to tell me?' Libby lit a cigarette.

'I did stay in the cottage in Nethergate,' said Fran. 'In fact, my Uncle Frank owned it.'

And she recounted her search at the Betjeman flat, and the discovery of the photographs, the picture and the china ponies.

'So,' she concluded, 'Uncle Frank actually bought the cottage.'

'I hate to story cap,' said Libby, stubbing out her cigarette, 'but Ben and I found that out, too.'

She told Fran of the visit to Jim Butler, and his recollections of the sale of Coastguard Cottage.

'So we worked out that Barbara must be Eleanor's brother's child, and Charles the sister's son. Would that be right?'

'I suppose it must be. I never thought to ask Charles, but he hasn't said anything about the cottage.'

'Have you asked him?'

'No,' said Fran, surprised. 'Although we did talk about it, didn't we? When I said Charles lived in Steeple Mount.'

'He probably wouldn't have known anything about it, anyway, being a child at the time,' said Libby. 'But go on. What else?'

'I remembered,' said Fran, 'and it was horrible.'

Libby was silent when Fran finished. Eventually, she stood up and took Fran's glass to top it up.

'So Uncle Frank and your Mum were having an affair?' she said as she sat down again. 'And you knew about it?'

'Now I've remembered, I can put things together. I can only assume that that night at the cottage was so traumatic I blotted everything out. As soon as I saw the photographs of Mum and I and Uncle Frank it began to come back to me, then when I found the ponies, it was just as though I was reliving it all over again.' She shuddered. 'I hated it.'

Libby nodded. 'And presumably, they stopped when Frank got married, then he came down to the cottage that night and Eleanor followed him?'

Fran shrugged. 'I suppose so. I thought Eleanor was going to kill my mother.'

Libby thought for a moment. 'So, how did the whole business of Eleanor and the cottage come about?'

'We used to stay there every year, and I think Frank must have met Eleanor when we were down there, through her father, who owned the cottage at the time.'

'But if you were all down there, and he and your Mum were – um – together, how come he married Eleanor?'

'Now that I've remembered, there was one year when we left Uncle Frank down there, and we didn't see much of him when we got back. I remember wondering why, but if I asked Mum, I don't think she told me anything. They must have had a row.'

'I wonder why they never married? Your mum and Uncle Frank?'

'I wondered that, too. Perhaps they didn't think it would be right, Frank being my Dad's brother.'

'That's just plain stupid,' said Libby, snorting indignantly.

'Things were different then. Perhaps Mum didn't want any gossip.'

'Well, she didn't go about it in a very sensible way, did she? Going away on holiday with him every year. And you said you spent a lot of time together at home.'

'Oh, yes. It was as though he really *was* my father. He was there all the time.'

Libby eyed her curiously. 'I don't suppose he *actually* was your father?'

Fran's mouth opened in shock. 'Good Lord! I've never even considered it,' she said.

'I expect it's on your birth certificate.'

'Yes, and I'm sure it says Herbert,' said Fran. 'Anyway, why on earth would my mother have lied about that?'

'If she was married to Herbert, had an affair with Frank and became pregnant, she would have a very good reason to lie about it, wouldn't she?'

'Oh, hell, this is awful,' said Fran, dislodging Sidney and putting her head in her hands. 'I hate the thought of my mother having an affair.'

'Well, it would appear that she did,' said Libby, 'although it wasn't really a very sleazy one.'

'Except that apparently they carried it on after Frank and Eleanor got married.' Fran lifted her head and pushed her hair back. 'I don't understand any of it.'

'I certainly don't understand why the stupid bugger went down to the cottage when his wife knew about it,' said Libby. 'It had even belonged to her family. She must have known about your family holidays there.'

'At least I know now why we had to leave Mountville Road,' said Fran, 'and why we never spoke to Frank or Eleanor after that. Poor Mum.'

'And she never told you about any of it?'

Fran shook her head. 'Not a word. She never mentioned either of them, not even when she was ill at the end.'

'When did Frank die?' asked Libby. 'Did they tell you that?'

'No. I've no idea. I don't know how I know, but I'm pretty sure he died quite young. Perhaps someone did get in touch with Mum and tell her, and I found out, somehow. We kept up with a few of Frank's friends, but that all petered out because, as I see now, she was a single mother with a daughter, not a nice safe couple to go to dinner with. There was someone from the Conservative Club – or was it the golf club? Joe, his name was. He had a big old car, and he used to come and take us out sometimes, but his wife never came, and after a while that stopped, too.'

'You poor old thing,' said Libby.

'Oh, I was all right,' said Fran. 'I was growing up, and although we moved, I still went to the same school, and had the same friends. It's Mum

I'm sorry for. I never understood. No wonder she loved my children so much. She'd never had much of a family, had she?'

'No, I suppose not. I'd love to know what really happened that night, though.'

'You can make an educated guess. You already did. Eleanor followed him down.'

'But it could have been quite innocent. Perhaps, knowing you were down there, Frank and Eleanor came down to stay with her parents for a few days, and they popped in to see how you were getting on.'

'In which case, why was my mother undressed, and why was Eleanor trying to kill her?'

'That's the flaw in the argument,' said Libby.

'Oh – and I brought this for you to see,' said Fran, handing over a plastic bag.

Libby took out the little picture and gasped. 'That's my picture!'

'I remember it now. It hung in my room at the cottage, but it was a cheap print we bought in a gift shop. Your parents must have bought one, too.'

'I suppose so. But what a coincidence. And if I hadn't had it, you would never have found out – well, everything.'

'I know.' Fran looked solemn. 'The sort of coincidence that people say can't happen in real life.'

'If it was in a book it wouldn't be allowed,' agreed Libby.

'Good job you're not Miss Marple, then,' said Fran.

Libby grinned. 'Isn't it.' She stood up. 'I'd better

check on supper. Here, or in the kitchen?'

Ben arrived as they finished eating and Fran got up to go.

'Don't go on my account,' he said, squashing himself onto a chair between the table and the Rayburn.

'No, I want to get back,' said Fran. 'I've got a lot to think about, and it's been a long day. I don't know how people commute.'

'I'll walk you to the end of the lane, then,' said Ben, unsquashing himself.

'No need, honestly, I'll be fine. It's not late.' Fran went into the living room to retrieve her bag. 'Thanks for the supper, Lib. I'll talk to you tomorrow.'

'How much can I tell Ben?' asked Libby quietly, as she saw Fran to the door.

'As much as you like. I don't mind Ben knowing. And Peter wanted to know all the facts as well, but I think I might give them an edited version.'

'Very sensible,' said Libby, and kissed Fran's cheek. 'Let me know what you want to do next.'

'You were going to talk to Nurse Redding, weren't you?'

'Never got round to it after seeing Jim Butler,' said Libby, 'but I'll try tomorrow.'

Libby went back into the living room and found Ben sprawled on the sofa with his shoes off.

'Make yourself comfortable,' she said.

'Come here, then,' said Ben, holding out a hand.

Libby's stomach contracted and she walked forward. She and Sidney landed on Ben's lap at the same time. She won.

# Chapter Twenty-seven

Judging that being on earlies meant Nurse Redding would be home by two o'clock, Libby phoned at five past.

'It's Libby Sarjeant again,' she said when Redding answered. 'I do hope you don't mind my bothering you.'

'That's all right.' Nurse Redding sounded bored.

'It's a bit embarrassing, but it's something you said the other day. About sin.' Libby crossed her fingers and held her breath.

'Yes?' The voice sounded marginally more interested.

'I expect I got the wrong end of the stick, and I can't really understand what made me think of it,' or what made Harry think of it, anyway, she corrected mentally, 'but I've always been interested in–' oh, hell, interested in what? '–er, alternative religions. If you know what I mean.' She felt perspiration on her brow and her heartbeat hammering in her ears.

'Oh?' was the unpromising answer.

'Well, yes,' said Libby, aware that she was now going fast into waffle mode. 'And I don't know whether you've ever heard of it, but there's a chapel over in the woods near Tyne Hall – you know? The place outside Steeple Mount. And I was told – I heard – that there was – well, there *had* been – some sort of, er, meetings there. I just wondered.' Now her heart was going so fast she thought she might faint.

'I wouldn't know,' said Nurse Redding, sounding suddenly quite different, 'and I wouldn't advise you to find out, either.'

'Oh, why?' said Libby, feeling excitement rise.

'I just wouldn't, that's all.' There was a silence, and Libby wondered if she'd been cut off. But: 'You couldn't, anyway. It's confidential.'

'So you do know something about it?'

'I didn't say that. Now, if you don't mind, I've got things to do.' And this time, the phone really was switched off.

Well, that proves it, thought Libby. Now how do I check it? Her first idea was to phone Ben, but decided he might view delving into the Black Arts as a mite foolish. The thought that it perhaps *was* a mite foolish she thrust down. Fran might help, but Fran needed a bit of time to think through all she'd found out over the last few days. Peter would be disparaging and disbelieving. Which left Harry.

'You in this afternoon?' she asked, when he answered the phone.

'In where?'

'Home?'

'In about half an hour, yes. Why?'

'Is Peter there?'

'Yes. Is that a problem?'

'Why should you think that?'

'You wouldn't have asked, otherwise. Are you going to invite me for a cuppa?'

'Yes,' said Libby, 'please. I need your advice.'

'Gor blimey,' said Harry, 'that'll be a first.'

When he arrived, looking gorgeous in a short sleeved white T shirt and tight jeans, Libby fleetingly regretted his sexuality on behalf of her own sex. Then she reflected that if he wasn't gay, he probably wouldn't be her friend, and decided her own sex could fend for themselves.

'OK, then, what's it all about?' said Harry, once he was settled in the garden with a mug of tea.

'Nurse Redding and the Black Arts,' said Libby, and repeated her conversation.

'And you want to know whether you should try and find out more?'

'Yes.'

'Why?'

'Well—' began Libby, then stopped to think. 'I suppose because it might give her a motive. If she's a member of a coven, or something, she wouldn't baulk at murder, would she?'

'Oh, I don't know about that,' said Harry. 'I don't think they go that far. Isn't it more sticking pins and casting spells?'

'I haven't got a clue. I just thought she might have used her – oh, I don't know – her powers or whatever to protect Marion Headlam and The Laurels.'

'I'm confused. Protect them from what?'

'If the will, or codicil, was false, the witnesses might need to be eliminated, and old Auntie bumped off so the will came into effect.'

'I sort of see that, but the will's missing, so where's the point?'

'She didn't know the will was missing, did she?'

'I still think it's a bit of a leap in the dark,' said Harry, leaning back and crossing his ankles. 'And how would you try and find out more, anyway? She's told you off about being nosey already. Where would you go from here? It could be dangerous.'

'You just said they wouldn't go that far,' Libby reminded him.

'I didn't mean they'd hire a hit man, but they could make life uncomfortable, maybe.'

Libby looked at him thoughtfully. 'So you don't think I should go any further, then?'

'I don't see what good it would do.' Harry shrugged. 'But if it's just your satiable curiosity, go ahead. Nothing anyone can do to stop you.'

'You just said–'

'I meant nothing any of your friends could do,' said Harry testily.

'You wouldn't feel inclined to help me, then?' Libby looked up into the branches of the tree.

'No, I would not! The idea.' Harry poked her with a foot and grinned. 'What would our Ben say?'

Libby smiled back reluctantly. 'That we were both mad, I expect.'

'Wouldn't he forbid you to do it?'

'Forbid? What century are you living in, young Hal? Anyway, I don't know that there's enough to our relationship for him to comment on anything I do.'

'Why didn't you ring him, then? Or ask him when you see him tonight?'

Libby felt herself blushing. 'I didn't think he'd be interested,' she said.

'Gertcha! You were scared.' Harry poked her again. 'See, underneath it all, you're a sweet old fashioned girl, aren't you?'

'No, I'm not. I'm a free, emancipated woman, thank you very much.'

'Well, now you've had the benefit of my advice, I'll pick your brain.' Harry leant forward in his chair. 'What's left of it.'

'I don't know much to pick,' said Libby.

'Your opinion, then.' Harry stopped and stood up. After taking a turn round the garden, he came back and stood over her.

'Pete wants to get married,' he said.

Libby gaped at him. 'What?' she gasped. 'But you – he – you're–'

'To me, idiot,' said Harry, perching back on the edge of his chair. 'A civil partnership. At Christmas. What do you think?'

Libby flung her arms round him. 'I think it's wonderful.'

'Well, don't say anything to anyone yet. I think he wants to make a formal announcement. Will you be a bridesmaid?'

'Yes, please. Can I wear a long frilly frock?'

'You may, Cinderella.' Harry leant over and kissed her. 'You could even be my best woman. Except Pete might want you as his.'

Libby hugged him again. 'I think it's just wonderful,' she said. 'Go on, go off home to him, and try and get him to make a formal announcement as soon as possible. Give us something to celebrate.'

Libby decided she really needed a computer. Watching Harry stride off down the lane, she wanted to look up civil partnerships and see what happened. And where they could be held, and whether you had bridesmaids or best people. A computer would be useful for all sorts of things, wouldn't it? Emailing – her children were always complaining that she hadn't got email – looking up covens, or Tyne Hall, or what happened with wills.

She went out into the garden to collect the mugs. She knew she ought to let Fran know about her conversation with Nurse Redding, but for a while she needed to think about it and decide what to do. Harry had confirmed her belief that meddling any further would not meet with anyone's approval, and looked at from a sensible angle, there really didn't seem to be any reason for suspecting Nurse Redding of anything. And the police would have found out if she had any connections to the murder, wouldn't they? After all, they always seemed to be one step ahead of everything she and Fran found out. Libby washed the mugs and felt a bit stupid. That was it, really, wasn't it? Why on earth were they investigating? The police were much better at it than they were, and it would be far less dangerous if they just sat back and waited for results.

Except, she thought, as she went into the conservatory to stare at her easel, they wouldn't know about Coastguard Cottage. Not that she was sure how that affected the murder, but she was certain there was a connection somewhere. Perhaps, she reflected, as she wandered back into the front room, they ought to tell the police about it and let them work it out.

But what would they say? Inspector Murray might listen to Fran, but even he would find it difficult to get a handle on the information. And what with repressed memories, remote viewing and witches, the whole thing was becoming too far fetched for words. Much simpler, Libby decided, to lay the blame on the ubiquitous tramp and try and forget it.

Fran had come to the same conclusion as Libby, and that was to tell Chief Inspector Murray everything she'd learned. She could hardly be accused of withholding information, as a) she wasn't going to, and b) it would hardly have been seen as relevant.

She was surprised to be put through to Murray almost immediately.

'What have you got to tell me, Mrs Castle?' His voice sounded vaguely amused and avuncular, and Fran almost decided not to tell him anything. Gritting her teeth and swallowing her pride, she told him.

'So, you see, it may be nothing,' she said when she'd finished. 'It just seemed such a coincidence, and from my memory, if that's what it was, Eleanor Bridges was not very happy with my side of the family.'

'And you say Coastguard Cottage isn't in family ownership any longer?'

'No, it's been sold twice since then. I don't suppose it's got anything to do with Eleanor's death, but it's odd that no one else seemed to know anything about it.'

'Are you sure they don't?' said Murray.

'Oh!' Fran stopped and thought. 'No, I suppose I'm not. Charles Wade lived in Steeple Mount when he was a child, but I think Barbara lived in Nethergate. No one's ever said anything about it, though.'

'If it's all that long ago, and not owned by the family anyway, why should they?' said Murray. 'No, Mrs Castle, I think you were right. It's nothing to do with Mrs Bridges' death. But thank you for telling me, anyway.'

Feeling dismissed, Fran sat down in her chair by the window and looked out at the high street. Over the road, she could see Flo and Lenny walking slowly, hand-in-hand, and further down the street, Lenny's sister Hetty going into the butchers. How lovely, she thought, to belong so completely to such a community. As the Stones did to Nethergate, she supposed.

Despite Chief Inspector Murray's dismissal of her information, Fran still felt sure it had something to do with Eleanor's death. How it could, she was unable to work out, but somewhere, somehow, it fitted in. She wondered if she should go back to Nethergate and see if anything struck her. Perhaps she should go and see – what did Libby say his name was? – Jim Butler.

'Libby, it's me,' she said, when Libby answered her phone. 'Listen, I'm wondering whether that Jim Butler would see me. What do you think?'

'I don't see why not,' said Libby, 'but why?'

Fran explained. 'And I know Murray dismissed it, but I can't.'

'Do you know, that's exactly what I thought. Tell it all to the police and let them get on with it,' said Libby. 'But it seems they don't want to know.'

269

'No.' Fran sighed. 'I wish I could just forget it.'

'But you can't,' said Libby. 'Anyway, I called Nurse Redding again this afternoon.'

She told Fran about the conversation, and Harry's subsequent visit, although keeping his exciting news to herself. 'So what do you think?'

'About what? I think Harry's right. Stay out of it. I don't think she's got anything to do with it.'

'What about Tyne Hall?'

'What about it? Tyne Hall's a Red Herring you've pulled in yourself. Leave it, Libby. You go poking your nose into that sort of thing and you're liable to get hurt.'

'How?' scoffed Libby. 'According to everybody it's all a load of hooey.'

'Honestly, Lib, you're just like one of those stupid heroines in films who go off into the cellar with only a candle after they've heard suspicious noises. Northanger Abbey, here you come.'

'Ah, but Northanger Abbey was all in Catherine Morland's imagination, wasn't it?'

'No comment,' said Fran. 'Just don't go there.'

'So where *do* we go?' asked Libby. 'Or is that it?'

'I'd like to talk to Jim Butler, I told you.'

'But we've decided it's nothing to do with Eleanor's death, haven't we?'

'Even so, for my own satisfaction I'd like to. Would you like to come with me?'

'I'd have to ask Ben for the phone number. He arranged it last time.'

'Will you, then? Tonight? Or aren't you seeing him tonight?'

'I expect so,' said Libby, clearing her throat. 'He hasn't actually said.'

'But he'll turn up anyway?'

'Yeah, I guess,' said Libby gruffly. 'I'll have to warn the kids.'

'Oh, yes, you said they were coming. Is it this weekend? All of them, was it?'

'Bel and Ad in a few weeks,' said Libby. 'Dom's gone off to France.'

'And they don't know about Ben?'

'Well, sort of, but they might not like it if I have a man in every night.'

'No,' agreed Fran, 'they don't really like thinking of their parents having sex, do they?'

'They accepted Derek and the floosie all right.'

Fran laughed. 'Ah, but he didn't do it under their noses, did he?'

'Well, he does now. That's who Dom's with in France.'

'Why didn't the others go?'

'Only room for one, apparently.'

'So have you, in theory.'

'Oh, well, they don't mind bunking on the floor,' said Libby. 'So, I'll ask Ben for Jim's number tonight, and phone in the morning, shall I?'

Next, Fran phoned Charles.

'You must have known about Coastguard Cottage,' she said, 'you were still here at school when I was visiting.'

'I know my grandfather owned a couple of cottages,' he said, sounding bewildered, 'but nothing else.'

'And you don't know if Aunt Eleanor had anything to do with it?'

'No, I'm sure she didn't. Actually, no, I don't know, but I don't see how she could. I know she worked in her dad's office, though.'

'So she might have been involved in letting out the cottage?'

'I suppose so. I just don't know. For heaven's sake, Fran, I was a child. Eleanor was just my aunt, the same as Barbara's father was my uncle. I don't know anything about anything else.'

'So you never stayed there?'

'Fran!' Charles sounded exasperated. 'I've just told you, no. What is this, anyway?'

Fran gave him an edited version of the facts and he calmed down.

'Well, I can see that it's very interesting,' he said, 'but I don't see what it's got to do with Aunt Eleanor's murder.'

'Neither do I,' said Fran, 'but I wanted to find out for myself. Do you know when Uncle Frank died, by the way?'

'Why, don't you?'

'No, I told you, we never spoke again.'

'As far as I know, he died quite young. Must have done, because I never saw him after I grew up. I don't think they were married that long.'

'Poor Uncle Frank.' Fran's throat felt tight. 'He should never have married her.'

'Steady on!' said Charles. 'That's not a very nice thing to say.'

'I don't think she was a very nice woman, Charles.'

'No,' Charles sighed. 'She wasn't.'

'So why did you continue to visit her?'

'Duty,' said Charles. 'I hated to think of her down there all on her own.'

'She had your cousin Barbara and Paul.'

'I know, I know.' Charles sighed again.

'So, has the furniture turned up, yet?' Fran changed the subject.

'On its way, apparently. Should arrive tomorrow. I've actually had confirmation from the haulage company.'

'Well, that's a good thing, surely. And they'll have had a good look, so you can be sure the codicil isn't in any of it. I think you should forget about it.'

'How can I? I'm still the prime suspect,' said Charles. 'If I could find the codicil, perhaps I wouldn't be.'

But the following morning, Fran learnt that Charles was no longer chief suspect. Marion Headlam had been taken in for questioning.

## Chapter Twenty-eight

'How did you find out?' asked Libby, going into the kitchen to put the kettle back on the Rayburn.

'Charles phoned me. He'd phoned The Laurels to speak to her about something that was missing, apparently, and that little Nurse Warner answered, all of a tizzy, and blurted it out.' Fran perched on the edge of the table. 'Sorry to barge in like this.'

Libby grinned, and pulled her dressing gown slightly tighter. 'Ben was just going anyway,' she said.

'No, I wasn't,' said Ben, appearing now clad in jeans and a t-shirt. 'I was just going to ravish her again.'

Libby and Fran both blushed, and Ben apologised.

'Anyway,' he said, 'I've left Jim's number by the phone, if you want to go and see him. He's a nice old boy, isn't he, Lib?'

'Yes, he is, but he's not really old. Just gives that impression. He's got a lovely dog.'

'Who smells a bit,' said Ben. 'I must go. See you later, Lib.'

'So what was that about something missing?' asked Libby. 'I didn't quite get that bit.'

'Charles told me yesterday that the furniture would be arriving today, although I don't suppose he thought it would be this early, and when it came, there was an item missing. He phoned Barbara, who didn't know anything about it, then The Laurels.'

'What was missing?'

'Do you know, I never thought to ask,' said Fran, surprised. 'The Headlam put it out of my head.'

'Do you suppose she found the codicil?'

'No idea,' said Fran, accepting a mug of tea. 'But the police must have come to the same conclusion that we did, mustn't they? That there was something fishy about it?'

'Hmm.' Libby led the way into the sitting room. 'We might be jumping to conclusions.'

'That's rich, coming from you! Mistress of jumped conclusions.'

'All right, all right, but she could literally just be answering questions, couldn't she? Maybe she's in deadly earnest. Perhaps there really is a genuine codicil. After all, didn't that woman say her husband had received something from Aunt Eleanor?'

'But Marion Headlam could have sent that.'

'Now who's jumping to conclusions? Anyway, we'll hear soon enough. Or you will, anyway.' Libby picked up the phone. 'Shall I phone Jim Butler?'

'Oh, go on, then. Take my mind off it.'

Jim Butler professed himself delighted to receive guests, especially, Libby gathered, two ladies. Would they like to come to lunch?

'No, that's fine, thank you,' said Libby hastily. 'We don't want you to go to any trouble, and we have to go into Nethergate at lunchtime.'

'Do we?' asked Fran, when Libby put down the phone.

'I thought we'd pop in and see Guy as we'll be in the area. And you can have another look at Coastguard Cottage.'

It was nearly mid-day when they arrived at Jim Butler's bungalow, and Libby was worried in case he might still press them to lunch.

'Just in time for elevenses,' said Jim, leading them into his conservatory. 'You won't want much if you're going to lunch, though, will you?'

Relieved, Libby agreed, and introduced Fran.

'Ah, you'll be the lady who used to stay in that cottage on Harbour Street, then,' said Jim. 'Well, I don't know as I can tell you any more than I told young Ben the other day. I didn't know the Stones very well.'

'We know that Frank Bridges bought the

cottage from the Stones,' said Fran, 'and it must have been he who sold it to you, but we don't know when or why.'

'Oh, it weren't long after 'e bought it. I don't remember ever meeting' 'im, like, it was all done through solicitors. Good job, 'e did, though, dying so soon after.'

'Dying?' said Libby and Fran together.

Jim looked surprised. 'Didn't yer know? I say soon, but it must'a been a year or so.'

'No, I didn't know,' said Fran, looking upset.

'How did you come to know he'd died,' asked Libby, 'if you didn't keep up with the family?'

'Oh, it were in the papers. 'Im bein' connected to the Stones. Accident, it were.'

'Accident?' Fran's voice was shrill.

'Don't remember what sort of accident. Just remember seein' it. Missus pointed it out to me in the paper. I wouldn't of noticed it otherwise.'

That was all Jim could tell them, and after drinking a suspicious cup of coffee each and making a fuss of Lady, they made their way into Nethergate to meet Guy in The Swan.

'I can't get over the fact that he died so soon after we moved out,' said Fran, as Libby drove down the hill towards the sea. 'Why did no one tell us?'

'You said you thought someone might have told your mother.'

'Only guessing. It's just awful. He'd been like a father to me all through my childhood.'

Libby looked sideways. Fran still looked upset. 'Well,' she said, 'you could always find out by looking up his death certificate. You know, trac-

276

ing your family like they do in those television programmes. Or even the local paper, if Jim meant that's where his death was reported. They keep everything on microfiche, don't they?'

'But we don't know when it was.'

'About a year after he sold the cottage to Jim, he said.'

'I don't know,' said Fran, and turned to look out of the window. Libby frowned, and edged into a parking space in the square. She wished now she hadn't rung Guy and arranged lunch if Fran was going to be like this.

Guy took one look as they went into the bar, stood immediately and put an arm round Fran, who promptly dived in her bag for a handkerchief. Much pleased by this evidence of affection, Libby smugly sat herself down at the bar and waved at Tony.

'I'll have a glass of mineral water, Tony, and my friend will have a gin and tonic,' she said.

'Looks as though she needs it, Mrs – er – Libby.' Tony turned down the corners of his mouth in sympathy and went off down the bar.

Guy had settled Fran at a little round table at the corner of the bar, and beckoned Libby to join them.

'So tell me what it's all about,' he said, as Tony came over with the drinks.

Fran told him, with frequent interruptions from Libby. 'And is this all connected with your aunt's death?' he asked when they'd finished.

Fran shook her head. 'We don't know, but I'm sure it is, somehow. I just can't get over losing Frank like that. He might have come back to us if only he hadn't died so soon.' She stopped, her drink half way to her mouth, her expression frozen. Libby and Guy glanced at each other.

'He was,' she said, putting her glass down. 'He was coming back to us.' Her face crumpled again, and Guy rushed into the breach with his comforting arm, while Libby handed over a rather creased, but clean, tissue.

'Doesn't this put a different complexion on things?' said Libby, after a decent interval. 'I mean – accident? Sounds suspicious to me.'

Guy nodded and looked at Fran. 'And me. Where was this accident?'

'I don't know,' said Fran. 'Jim didn't say. He just said it was in the papers, and we assumed he meant the local papers.'

'That was because he said he was connected with the Stones,' said Libby. 'That must mean the local paper, but it doesn't follow that it happened here.'

'So what are we saying,' said Guy, waving a menu at Tony. 'Somebody bumped off Uncle Frank to prevent him coming back to you and your Mum?'

Tony appeared with a pad and pencil and they all ordered lunch.

'That can only mean Aunt Eleanor,' said Libby, when Tony had gone.

Fran nodded. 'It was the cellar steps,' she said, matter-of-factly.

'You saw it?' asked Libby. Guy just stared.

'Yes. Like I saw Eleanor being smothered.'

'I don't think we need to tell DCI Murray about this,' said Libby, with a worried frown.

278

'Why not?' Fran looked surprised. 'Surely it must have some connection with her death, now?'

'That's exactly what Libby means,' said Guy, 'and the connection is you.'

Fran looked at him with her mouth open.

'Oh, God,' she said.

'Precisely.' Libby rummaged in her basket for her cigarettes. 'Murray's reasonably sympathetic about your moments, but if you go telling him about having seen Eleanor push Frank down some cellar steps, and follow it up with a graphic account of *her* death – what's he going to think?'

'That I did it for revenge,' nodded Fran. 'God, I'm so angry.' Her expression was indeed ferocious, and Libby moved her glass out of reach. 'That bloody woman. It's so frustrating. There's nothing I can do about it.'

'No,' said Libby, 'and as you didn't do it, it gets us no further forward, does it?'

Fran looked up, surprised. 'No.'

Guy looked relieved. 'So you can let it all go, now. Just let the police get on with it.'

'Yes.' Fran looked down as Tony placed a plate in front of her. 'I suppose so.'

'Won't know what to do with ourselves, will we,' said Libby, only half humorously.

'You could get on with doing some more paintings,' said Guy, nodding his thanks to Tony. 'I've got a nice little cheque for you. Those that I picked up the other night walked straight out of the shop.'

'But they weren't even of Fran's cottage,' said Libby.

'The punters aren't wedded to those pictures. They seem to like them, but they like most things you do. And don't forget, we're nearly at the end of the season, so if you've got any more, I'll take them all. Then you can concentrate on getting some more up for next year.'

'I'm not a bloody production line,' said Libby.

'No, but we're not talking fine art, here, are we?' Guy reached over and patted her arm. 'Don't get bolshie with me, just be grateful that you sell.'

'Hmm,' said Libby, and addressed herself to her jacket potato.

They went back to the gallery after lunch and Guy gave Libby her cheque, and on the pretext of letting her have another look at the cottage, took Fran outside. Libby raised her eyes at Sophie.

'Oh, I got Sue Warner's parents' address,' said Sophie, 'but I don't think she's living there any more. From what I hear, she's got herself a new boyfriend, and I think she might have moved in with him.'

'Oh, well, it was worth a try,' sighed Libby. 'But I think we're going to stop sleuthing, now, and leave it to the professionals. All we do is go round in circles and make wild assumptions.'

'I didn't realise it was proper sleuthing you were doing,' said Sophie, looking interested.

'It wasn't,' said Libby, with a grin.

Fran was quiet on the drive back to Steeple Martin.

'Did Guy ask you out?' said Libby, eventually.

'Yes.' It came out on a sigh.

'You don't sound very pleased. I thought you

liked him.'

'I do.' Fran looked at Libby. 'But it's difficult. You know what it's like.'

'Go out with him. Where did he want to go?'

'He said dinner. But I don't want to go to Harry's. Or the pub.'

'There are plenty of other places, you know.' Libby changed gear as they went up the hill round Steeple Mount. 'I hope you said yes.'

'Yes. He's coming over on Saturday,' said Fran, and turned back to the window.

Ben took Libby to The Pink Geranium that evening, despite Libby protesting that she'd already eaten out once today. There was no table when they arrived, so they sat on the sofa in the window and drank Harry's best Sancerre while Libby filled him in on the day's events.

'So that's it, really. We're giving up. It was all a bit pointless, anyway,' said Libby.

'Well, I can't say I'm sorry,' said Ben, taking her hand and squeezing it. 'You never know what you might have run in to. But how sad for poor old Fran. You think she's right about Eleanor and Frank?'

'About her killing him? Well, she seems to get things right, doesn't she? And she seemed certain he was going to go back to them.'

'Horrible. No wonder she's frustrated.'

'Well, let's hope Guy can help in that department,' said Libby innocently, caught Ben's eye and blushed. 'Sorry. That wasn't in the best of taste, was it?'

He leant across and kissed her cheek. 'No,' he said.

'Oi. None of that there here,' said Harry, looming over them in his whites and checks. 'Your table's ready.'

## Chapter Twenty-nine

Over the next few days Libby got bored. She heard nothing more about the police investigation, or what'd happened to Marion Headlam. Fran went off to a job in London for Goodall and Smythe, after reporting on her dinner date with Guy.

'Lovely restaurant,' she told Libby dreamily, over a lunchtime drink in the pub. 'Beautiful country house.'

'And?' said Libby.

'He brought me home, and went home himself.' Fran laughed at Libby's expression. 'Sorry, Lib.'

'Is he gay?' Libby was indignant.

'No, of course not. Just a gentleman. And I'm not exactly the sort to inspire uncontrollable lust, am I?'

'Hmm.'

'Come on, Lib. Just be grateful that there are nice men out there who don't have unrealistic expectations.'

'I have to say,' said Libby, after giving it a moment's thought, 'that Guy usually attracts the younger element. I've seen him with some real glamour in the past.'

'What the hell's he taking me out for, then?'

said Fran, looking as though she'd gone down suddenly in a lift.

'I don't know,' said Libby simply. 'But he's attracted to you. Otherwise I wouldn't have pushed you together.'

'Are you saying that this is entirely due to your intervention?' Fran was now looking amused.

'Well, partly,' said Libby, attempting to look modest.

'Don't forget he was chatting me up in The Swan before he knew we were friends.'

'I did say partly,' said Libby.

But now Fran was in London, Ben was clearing out his flat in Canterbury prior to moving permanently to The Manor and Libby had nothing to do. She painted in the mornings, finishing her autumn picture, starting a new pretty peep of Nethergate Harbour, not worrying too much about accuracy. The people who bought the paintings wanted an idealised interpretation of an idyll, not a photographic rendition.

After lunch, she sat in the garden, rejoined the library, and one day drove to the supermarket just to pass the time. The weather was changing, going from the unnatural warmth of the early summer to the normal grey of early autumn, so time in the garden was limited, and Sidney began to spend more and more time indoors.

Towards the end of the week, Libby woke to a beautiful day. Two things occurred to her. One, she ought to check whether Guy's cheque had cleared in her bank account so she could buy the computer she had now set her heart on, and two, it would be a lovely day to go and see Tyne Hall and its chapel. She reassured herself that it was a purely aesthetic trip, and nothing to do with any sort of investigation.

She checked her bank account at the ATM inside the village post office, and was so excited by the sight of her balance she nearly abandoned her sightseeing plans to rush off to Canterbury and buy a computer. Deciding, however, it would preferable to have an experienced computer user by her side when she did so, she put Romeo the Renault in gear and set off for Tyne Hall.

It hadn't occurred to her that there might be a problem in getting access to the chapel. Following signs to Tyne Hall – not easy, as there were no brown and white signposts and only one or two wooden ones – she finally came upon two large iron gates set into a crumbling brick wall, where an old notice hung on a gatepost informed the public that this was Tyne Hall, and there was no entry.

Realising that she should have done a little more research before setting out on this trip, Libby fished out her mobile and rang Ben.

'I just thought I'd come and have a look at it,' she said, after listening to his forcibly expressed exasperation. 'It was such a lovely day. But I can't find an entrance.'

'Tyne Hall isn't open to the public, Libby,' said Ben, 'so you won't find an entrance. If it's the chapel you particularly want to see, you can get to it another way. But I think you're mad.'

'It's a beautiful day, and I only want to have a look. What could happen?'

'Oh, all right,' said Ben with a sigh, and gave

her directions.

A little lane led past a few cottages and a wide stream, where Libby was enchanted to see crested grebe. She parked on a grassy verge, and crossed a small stone footbridge which lead to a track between overhanging beech trees. This lead out onto one side of a shallow grassy valley, at the top of the other side of which, surrounded by more trees, already turning golden and red, stood the chapel. In the same colour stone as the bridge, all Libby could see of it was the gothic arch of the door set into a short tower. Away to her left, the glint of water told her the stream had reappeared, and walking a little way down the slope, she saw that a lake spread away towards the ruins of the main house. The grass was already dotted with fallen leaves, yet the day was warm enough for Libby to be wearing summer clothes. Wishing she'd worn slightly more sensible shoes, she set off down one slope and up the other, until she was in front of the chapel. Now she could see that the trees pressed hard up against the walls of the chapel and a path led off to her right from the front door. The door itself was typical arched, planked oak, with enormous iron hinges. Libby was surprised that there were no extra bars or padlocks on it if there had been trouble there, but there was nothing, and when she ventured to turn the great iron handle, it moved easily and without a sound. It must have been bolted inside, however, because it refused to budge. Suddenly nervous, she stepped back and looked round. It seemed such a peaceful place, it was hard to imagine anything remotely evil happening, but unless Flo had got it wrong, it had.

She walked a little way along the path to her right, and saw that down the side of the chapel there were three stained glass windows almost obscured by the trees, and, she was sure, another door, although she couldn't be certain. The path led only to a barbed wire fence, half hidden by undergrowth, which looked as though it hadn't been disturbed for years. If Satan worshippers, or cult or coven members met here, they must have flown in, thought Libby. She began to retrace her steps.

After a further examination of the door and the tower, she gave up, and walked back towards the track between the beech trees. As she got to the bottom of the slope, she looked back, and stopped.

In front of the chapel door stood three figures, all in black, watching her.

She fled.

Fran got back to the Betjeman flat, glad that she hadn't yet given it up. Three days of wandering round an old manor house, its mews and stable yard had exhausted her, especially as all sorts of strange images had presented themselves to her, most of which she discounted as they obviously belonged to incidents far in the past. Goodall and Smythe's client, a property developer, had been delighted with her, and planned to use some of her information in his publicity, although Fran couldn't see why anyone would want to buy a remodelled mews flat with the exciting knowledge that a stable lad had once been beaten to death there.

Tomorrow she would go back to Steeple Martin, but tonight she'd phone Charles. Not that she was interested in getting involved with any more investigations, of course. Just to see how he was. She'd told him briefly about Uncle Frank owning Coastguard Cottage, but he'd been surprised, and professed to know nothing at all about it.

'Just wondered if there was any news,' she said, after they'd greeted one another with a wary friendliness.

'Not that I've heard,' said Charles. 'I gather Marion Headlam was let off the hook, but I still don't know why she was taken in. I haven't heard from Barbara, either.'

'Now, why doesn't that surprise me?'

'You're not still investigating, are you?' asked Charles.

'No, Charles. And I wouldn't exactly call it investigating. The police are quite capable of doing that without our help.' Even if they don't know everything we know, she added silently.

'Your friend Libby didn't give me that impression,' said Charles.

'Well, she isn't doing anything now,' said Fran, crossing her fingers. True, Libby had said she wasn't going to do any more nosing about, but you never knew with Libby.

'Tell me,' said Charles, with a heavy-handed air of changing the subject, 'how did you come by the information that Frank Bridges owned that cottage?'

287

Fran's mind went blank. Then, 'I thought I told you. I found a box of photographs and things when I was clearing out my flat.' Well, that was true.

'Yes, you did, but what did they actually tell you? I suppose,' said Charles, with the suspicion of a snort in his voice, 'there wasn't a picture of him signing a contract?'

'No, of course not,' said Fran irritably, 'but when I saw the photographs, I remembered we used to go there on holiday, and he bought the cottage from the person who let it. That was your grandfather.'

'Oh, I see.' Charles still sounded doubtful. 'So is that how he met Eleanor?'

'I suppose so,' said Fran, not certain herself. 'Don't you remember your grandfather owning property in Nethergate?'

'No. I lived in Steeple Mount, remember, and only went to school in Nethergate. I know we visited my grandparents, and Barbara's family, but I wouldn't have known anything about any businesses they might have had. I do remember, though,' he said, with a hint of renewed interest, 'that Eleanor was always called "poor Eleanor". I think they were all surprised when she married.'

'What was she like before she was married?'

'All right. Not much interested in us children. Oh, she gave us an obligatory present at Christmas and birthdays, but that was about all. She lived at home with our grandparents. I don't know what sort of social life she had.'

Not much, thought Fran. Not back then. Frank must have come as a godsend. No wonder she flipped when she found out about Margaret.

'So have you heard anything more about the will?'

'No,' said Charles gloomily. 'I don't know quite what happens there. Will I be prosecuted for fraud, do you think?'

Privately, Fran thought he would. 'I don't know Charles. Can't you ask the solicitor? If you're the executor, you've got the right to ask him. Mind you – if you've defrauded the estate, perhaps you can't be executor?'

'Oh, Fran, don't say that! I will get done, won't I?'

'Charles, just ask the solicitor. I'm going back to Steeple Martin tomorrow, but if you need me for anything, just ring.'

Later that night, Fran lay in her bed and reflected how much nicer it was living in Steeple Martin. She really must see about finding a flat to rent somewhere in the area before Harry got fed up with her cluttering up his upstairs. Pity, she thought, as she turned over and began to drift away, that she couldn't afford to buy somewhere like Libby's cottage.

# Chapter Thirty

The following morning, Fran packed quickly and locked up the flat. As she went down the stairs, she met Dahlia coming up, and told her that she would be giving notice. Dahlia, easily moved, showed a tendency to weep at this news, then remembered her cousin's daughter who was currently looking for a flat, and cheered up.

'Post for you, this mornin' Miz Castle,' she said. 'I would'a brought it up if I'd 'a known.'

Prepared for a slew of junk mail, Fran was surprised to find a letter franked with the name and address of a firm of solicitors. Wondering if it was from Aunt Eleanor's, but if so, why, she slit open the envelope and began to read.

A minute later, she was sitting on the bottom step, heart pounding, trying to catch her breath while making a mull of punching in Charles's number on her mobile.

'Calm down, Fran,' he said, after listening to her garbled explanation for a few seconds. 'I can't make head or tail of this. Where are you? Shall I come and get you?'

'No, Charles, I'm fine, I'm just about to go home – back to Steeple Martin. I just thought you ought to know. And whether it's the same firm of solicitors.'

'No, it isn't. I wonder how they knew she was dead? I wonder what else we're going to find out?'

Fran re-read the letter after she'd switched off. Frank, it said, had put the money from the sale of Coastguard Cottage, or 34 Harbour Street, Nethergate, as it was unromantically referred to, into a trust fund for her, Fran, only to be released on the death of Eleanor Bridges. As the under-signed believed this had now taken place, would she please make an appointment to come into the office of Messrs Hallbert and Dunkin to discuss the winding up of the trust.

Trying to calm her still unruly breathing, Fran punched in the number at the top of the letter and asked for John Meade.

'Mr Meade's not in until Monday, I'm afraid,' said the voice which answered. 'Can anyone else help you?'

Fran explained her mission. 'Oh, well, then, I'm afraid it will have to be Mr Meade. May I ask him to ring you as soon as he gets in on Monday?' asked the voice.

Fran agreed, and gave her number. And now to contain her soul in patience until Mr Meade got in touch and put her out of her misery.

'I'm sure it must be a mistake of some kind,' she said to Libby, whom she called the minute she arrived back at Harry's flat.

'Of course it isn't,' said Libby. 'It makes perfect sense. You've pieced together all the information so far, and this confirms it. Frank wanted you to have the cottage, but he couldn't do that, because of its connection with Eleanor's family, so he sold it and put the money in trust for you. I expect he meant to give it to you on your twenty-first birthday or something.'

'But it said not to be released until Eleanor's death,' said Fran.

'Well, in that case, he probably thought she'd kick up a fuss and try and get it overturned or something – you know, doing her out of her just desserts.'

'I expect she would. After all, she would expect to inherit everything from him, wouldn't she?'

'And that's why he did it this way. Clever, I call it,' said Libby. 'I wonder how much it's worth now?'

'I don't suppose it's grown along with the property prices,' said Fran, 'so I don't expect I'll have enough to buy anywhere.'

'You could put down a deposit, though, couldn't you?'

'Yes, but I'm not likely to get a mortgage, am I? I'm self employed, and only work intermittently.'

'Oh, yes. But if you had it invested and it paid out interest monthly, you could afford to get a better rented place.'

'So I could,' said Fran, much taken with this idea. 'Who'd know about that sort of thing?'

'It pains me to say it, but Paul Denver would,' said Libby. 'He might not be much cop as an estate agent, but I expect he knows all about that sort of thing.'

'No, I'm not telling him,' said Fran, a decided note in her voice. 'But I will go and see Barbara, and ask her what she knows about Coastguard Cottage. I bet she knows more than Charles.'

'Good idea,' said Libby. 'Do you want any back up?'

'No, I'll be fine on my own, thanks, Lib.'

'Would you like to borrow Romeo, then?'

'Oh, Lib, I'd love to! I wasn't sure how I'd get there, otherwise.'

'OK, then. When do you want to go?'

'I'll phone Barbara and see when it's convenient and ring you back,' said Fran, and switching off the phone, thought again how lucky she was to have landed here with such lovely people.

Barbara, although obviously surprised to hear from her, agreed to see her tomorrow morning, which suited Fran, as, having come all the way down from London she didn't really feel like setting off again. Next, she phoned Guy.

'I'm going to see Barbara Denver tomorrow morning,' she said. 'What's happening about the sculpture?'

'Nothing,' said Guy. 'We've got it on hold. It's far too over the top, anyway, so maybe she'll change her mind.'

'As long as the sculptor doesn't mind,' said Fran, 'because it isn't Barbara's decision anyway, and I think Charles would prefer not to have it. Eleanor was an old cow, anyway.'

'So I gather,' said Guy, sounding amused. 'So, you'll be here tomorrow morning? How about lunch after the devilish Barbara?'

'That would be nice,' said Fran, feeling a bit hot under the collar. 'But I shall have Libby's car, so I won't be able to drink.'

Libby, when she heard that Romeo would be out on the following day, immediately rang Ben to ask for his advice.

'You see,' she said, 'I want to buy a computer. I told you, didn't I? But you haven't been around, so I couldn't ask for your help.'

'I'm still not around,' he said, 'so how can I help?'

'I thought I'd come into Canterbury tomorrow, and perhaps you could come with me to choose one? The only thing is, I've lent the car to Fran, so I'll have to come in by bus.'

'You've never seen the flat, have you?' said Ben.

'No,' said Libby slowly.

'Well, this is your last chance. I shall be moved out completely by Saturday, so why don't you come and have lunch there tomorrow, then we'll go and buy a computer.'

'OK.' Libby felt squirmish under her ribcage. 'What time and how do I find it?'

Ben gave her directions, and she agreed to be there as near as possible to half past twelve, buses permitting. Hugging herself with excitement because she hadn't seen him since Monday, Libby went into the kitchen to tell Sidney all about it.

Arriving in Canterbury the following morning, Libby made her way through the narrow back streets behind the high street and The Marlowe theatre to the building, beautifully converted, where Ben had his flat.

'Did you do this conversion?' she asked, as he led her up the stairs.

'Of course.' He grinned back at her. 'I own the building, so I'll just let this out when I've finished clearing out.'

'You don't seem to have done much yet,' said Libby surveying the comfortably furnished living room.

'Oh, I have. I've packed all my clothes and

personal stuff. I shall let this furnished.'

'Oh, pity. I was thinking perhaps Fran could have rented it.' Libby wandered over to the window, which looked out over the river.

'Frankly, Lib, I don't think she could afford it,' said Ben coming over to join her and handing her a glass of red wine. 'I'd love to be able to let her have it at a reduced rate, but it wouldn't be fair on the other tenants, apart from any other considerations.'

'No, I suppose not,' said Libby, and sighed. 'But it's a lovely flat.'

'Perhaps Fran doesn't want to live in Canterbury.'

'No, but I think she might be able to afford it.' Libby turned to look at him. 'She's just heard about an inheritance.'

Libby told him about Fran's surprising news while he seated her at a little table and served up soup.

'It depends on how the trust was invested,' he said, offering french bread. 'As long as it's been administered by someone reputable and not milked, she should have a tidy sum.'

Libby thought about Charles.

'Fran's cousin Charles did that, you know,' she said, sampling the soup. 'Hey, good soup!'

'Don't sound so surprised,' said Ben. 'I can cook, you know. How do you think I survived all those years on my own? Anyway, Charles did what?'

Libby explained about Charles and the Power of Attorney.

'Oh, dear. No wonder the police had him in.'

295

'But it takes away his motive, surely? He would want her alive, because if she died, it would all come out. I don't know what happens now, but I expect the estate will sue him or something, won't it?'

'You say he's executor?' Ben leant back in his chair. 'I'm not sure what the legal position is in that case. Do you want me to find out?'

'No, thanks.' Libby shook her head and tipped her soup plate to scoop up the last of the soup. 'There are enough solicitors lurking about the place in this case.'

'Case? Libby, I thought you'd given up?' Ben narrowed his eyes at her.

Libby flushed. 'I have. I just meant the police case. And that's why I don't want you finding anything out.'

They finished lunch, and Ben took her on a tour of the flat. The kitchen was shiny, functional and small, the bathroom the same, and the bedroom masculine.

'It's a big bed,' said Libby, surveying the dominant feature of the room, covered in a dark brown quilt.

'That's coming with me,' said Ben.

'To your mother's?'

'Yes, although I won't use it until we get my permanent quarters sorted out. I'm still using the spare bedroom.'

'Was it yours when you were a child?'

'The bed or the bedroom?'

'The bedroom.'

'Yes. I'm still in the single bed.'

Libby giggled. 'Oh, dear!'

'Now you can see why I've never invited you to stay at The Manor.' He moved behind her and his arm came round her waist. 'Might be your last chance to try it out for a long time.' He lowered his lips to her neck and Libby felt a rush of pure desire.

It was some time later that Libby emerged from the shower to get dressed. Ben was sitting in the kitchen waiting for her, and looked up when she appeared.

'Sure we're going to get a computer?' he asked, grinning at her.

'Yes,' said Libby firmly. 'I've decided I need one, and anyway, Guy's money's burning a hole in my bank account.'

'I'll come and help you if you invite me round this evening,' he said, pulling her down onto his lap.

'I thought you were staying here?'

'Nah – changed my mind. I've more-or-less finished here now. Anyway, I've missed you.' He nuzzled her neck, and she shivered.

'Now don't start that again,' she said, struggling to stand up. 'You can come whenever you want, you know that.'

Ben raised his eyebrows and she blushed again. 'Oh, you know what I mean!'

They spent a happy hour at a large computer supermarket, and Ben persuaded her to buy a small laptop which, although more expensive than most, he assured her was easily the best. And the prettiest, thought Libby, as she stroked its glossy white lid admiringly.

'Come on, I'll drive you home and we'll get it

set up,' said Ben. 'You won't be able to connect to the internet yet, because that'll take a few days, but we'll put everything in motion.'

'Oh, really?' Libby was disappointed. 'I wanted to look things up.'

'Well, if we find a hotspot, as this is wireless, we might be able to log on.'

Libby stared at him open-mouthed. 'Sorry?' she said.

Ben opened the car door for her to climb in, and put the precious boxed computer on the back seat. 'I'll explain later,' he said.

Libby was surprised to find Romeo parked in his normal position under the trees across from No 17. She found the keys on the mat when she opened the door, and after settling Ben at the little table in the sitting room and putting the kettle on the Rayburn, she found her mobile and phoned Fran, as Ben seemed to be busy with the landline telephone socket.

'Was everything OK?' she asked. 'I didn't expect you back so soon.'

'I got home about half an hour ago,' said Fran. 'It's not that early. And I had lunch with Guy, as well.'

'That's nice,' said Libby. 'I had lunch with Ben, too.'

'Oh?'

'At his flat in Canterbury.' Libby smiled dreamily.

'Ah.'

'Yes,' said Libby. 'Anyway, I don't suppose your lunch with Guy was quite like that, was it? Even if you would have liked it to be?'

'Libby!' said Fran. 'Behave. I thought you wanted to know about Barbara Denver?'

'I do, I do,' said Libby. 'Hang on, I'm pouring water onto teabags.'

'Oh, is Ben with you?'

'Yes. You see,' she said proudly, 'I bought a computer this afternoon.'

'Oh, well done you. Can I borrow it?'

'If you help me with how to use it, yes. Anyway, come on. Tell me what happened this morning.'

Barbara had been far more relaxed than the last time Fran saw her. Fran wondered if it was because it was just the two of them, without Paul or Charles.

'So what can I do for you?' asked Barbara, after ushering Fran once more into the green and grey sitting room.

'I just wanted to know if you remembered anything about Aunt Eleanor when she was young, really, and whether you remember how she met my Uncle Frank.'

'Is it relevant?'

'Relevant?' Fran was startled. 'How do you mean?'

'Relevant to Eleanor's – er – murder.' Barbara was looking wary now.

'Not at all.' Fran allowed herself a small laugh. 'No, it's just that all this has naturally brought up a lot of memories from the past for me, including remembering my holidays in Nethergate with my mother and Uncle Frank.'

'Oh?' It was Barbara's turn to look startled. 'I didn't know you'd ever been here before.'

'I'd forgotten all about it,' said Fran, not mentioning how deeply the memories had been buried. 'But obviously, as I said, this has brought it all back, and I dug out our old photographs. I just wondered if you remembered anything from those times. After all, we're about the same age.'

'No, I don't think so. I never met your mother. Did you come here after Frank and Eleanor married?'

'Yes,' said Fran casually. 'We stayed in Harbour Street, as usual.'

'Harbour Street? In one of my grandfather's cottages?'

Ah, thought Fran. She does know.

'That's right, except that by that time, my Uncle Frank had bought it.'

'Had he?' Fran could see the calculations going on in Barbara's mind. 'I don't remember seeing any mention...'

'Of it in the will?' asked Fran gently.

'Well, yes.' Barbara rallied quickly. 'I'd seen the will, of course, when she told me where she kept it.'

'In the bureau.' Fran nodded.

'Yes.' A slight flush stained Barbara's pale cheeks.

'You wouldn't have seen any mention of the cottage,' said Fran. 'Uncle Frank sold it on not long after he bought it.'

'Ah.' Barbara nodded, looking faintly relieved. 'So, did you come down here after that?'

'No,' said Fran. 'We rather lost touch.'

'And of course, Frank had his accident not that

300

long after they were married,' said Barbara. 'Horrid for you.'

'It is now, but I didn't know about it then,' said Fran. 'Whether my mother did, and kept it from me, I don't know.'

'Perhaps she thought it was kinder if you had been very close.'

'Possibly. We were, you see, very close.' Fran was still debating whether to tell Barbara about the trust fund.

'Oh?' Barbara was watching her intently, now. 'I'm afraid I didn't know Frank well at all. Eleanor moved to London with him after they married, then he died.'

'Yes, I know. What I don't know,' said Fran, 'is exactly how he died.'

'An accident.' Barbara looked surprised.

'Yes. The cellar steps, wasn't it?'

'You *do* know,' Barbara said accusingly.

'Only that he fell down the cellar steps. I assume it was the cellar steps at home in London?'

'I suppose so. I don't think I knew it was cellar steps. I thought he'd fallen downstairs. I was only young, you know.'

'Yes, I know. Charles doesn't remember anything about it.'

'Charles never saw them. He and his parents lived in Steeple Mount. Thought they were a cut above the rest of us.' Barbara looked mean for a moment, until a smug expression crossed her face. Fran correctly read it to mean 'I showed 'em.'

'I didn't know that,' she said aloud. 'Was Charles's father well off, then?'

'I don't know about that, but they lived in a nice house, and he was in business of some kind.'

'Charles didn't follow him into the business, then?'

Barbara looked surprised, as well she might, thought Fran.

'Considering I don't know what the business was, I have no idea. I didn't see Charles for years after we'd grown up. Not until Eleanor came down here to The Laurels, in fact.' Barbara was beginning to look restless now. 'And I don't really see what it's got to do with you. She wasn't your relative.'

'No, that's true. But she wanted to see me, didn't she? At least, that's what Charles said.'

'I'm sure I don't know,' said Barbara huffily. 'I don't think you had any claim on the estate, did you?'

'If most of it came from my Uncle Frank, I probably did, actually,' said Fran, not knowing whether this was true or not, but it startled Barbara again. 'However,' Fran continued, herself feeling rather smug now, 'as Frank left me a trust fund, I don't suppose it matters.'

Barbara gaped. 'A trust fund? What for?'

'Because I was his niece, I suppose.' Fran looked Barbara squarely in the eye. 'I have to tell you, Barbara, that your aunt was a most unpleasant woman who came between me and my mother and my Uncle Frank. So that she couldn't touch this money, he had it put into a trust fund for me.' Fran knew she was assuming, but she agreed with Libby, it seemed right.

'But that money should have gone to his wife!'

'No, it should have come to me. It's a good job she didn't know about it before he died, isn't it? Perhaps, after all, a good job he died when he did.' Fran didn't believe this for one second, as she was sure Frank would have come back to her and Margaret if he had lived.

'And what right have you to tell me Aunt Eleanor was an unpleasant woman?' Barbara was working herself up, now, thought Fran, probably at the thought of being deprived of a half share of all that money in the trust fund.

'None.' Fran shrugged. 'But she was. I saw her being more than unpleasant.' She stood up. 'Well, as you don't remember anything more, I'll leave you in peace.'

Barbara didn't say another word as she followed Fran into the hall, but at the door, Fran turned to her.

'What happened about Mrs Headlam?' she asked. 'I heard she was arrested?'

Colour came swiftly into Barbara's face. 'Of course she wasn't. She was merely helping with enquiries. I believe the police thought she was lying about this other will, or whatever it was.'

'I see.' Fran nodded. 'Well, thank you, Barbara. I expect I shall see you at the funeral – whenever that is.'

On impulse, as she drove Romeo out of the Blagstock House drive, Fran turned towards The Laurels. Pushing down the thought that she was turning into Libby, she decided it was time to ask Marion Headlam a few more questions.

There were a few dry leaves blowing across the lawns as Fran drove up towards the house. She had an even more vivid picture of the little old ladies flitting across the gardens, this time with their hair blowing behind them like an Arthur Rackham drawing.

'Oh, Mrs Castle, I'm so pleased to see you!' Marion Headlam appeared like a genie almost as soon as Fran set foot inside the hall. 'Come into my sitting room.'

She looked a lot better than the last time Libby and she had visited. Perhaps police interrogation suited her.

Sitting Fran down on a comfortable sofa, she sat down opposite, perching on the edge of a chair with her hands clasped in her lap.

'Mrs Castle,' she said, 'you'll never believe it. We've found it!'

## Chapter Thirty-one

Fran sat open mouthed for a long moment.

'Found it?' she said. 'The will?'

Marion Headlam nodded, excitement shining out of her face. 'The will *and* the codicil!'

'Good heavens.' Fran was astounded, and all sorts of new scenarios chased themselves through her mind.

'It was amazing.' Mrs Headlam was still nodding, then looked doubtful. 'I'm sorry, did you want something particular?'

'No, I just wanted to see how you were after – well, you know.' Well, that was fairly truthful.

'Would you like some tea?' Mrs Headlam half rose.

'No, no thanks, I'm on my way to lunch with someone,' said Fran, wondering whether she should phone Guy and warn him she might be late. But it would look rude if she interrupted Mrs Headlam, so she just smiled. 'Please, go on.'

'Well, apparently,' the woman began, at last leaning back in her chair, 'the police were very suspicious about the whole business of the lost will and the codicil. I was the only person who had seen it, and the two witnesses were both killed in road accidents.'

'Yes, I know that,' said Fran. 'You gave us their addresses, and when we tried to get in touch we found out.'

'Oh, right.' Marion Headlam nodded again. 'Well, anyway, I can't quite work out whether they thought I was lying about the codicil, or that I'd killed poor Mrs Bridges to inherit.' She shook her head. 'As if I would. And it would be stupid, wouldn't it, to kill her if I was lying about the codicil?'

'Yes, but perhaps they thought you'd *faked* the codicil.'

Marion looked bewildered. 'But we couldn't find it. How would anyone know?'

'I expect that's what they thought,' said Fran. 'Anyway, they sent you home. What happened next?'

'That Inspector – what's his name?'

'DCI Murray.'

'That's him. He rang me and said someone had

305

found the original will, which had been verified.'

'Yes, Mr Wade and I found the original will at Mrs Bridges' old home.'

'Well, that was it, I thought, especially as I wouldn't have expected there to be more than one copy, but she definitely had a copy here, because we added the codicil to it. And I know Mr and Mrs Denver had looked for it.'

'Yes – in the bureau.'

'They took it away the very next morning, you know.'

'I know they did, and it was empty. It's arrived at her old home now.'

'Well, I didn't think to look for it anywhere but in her room. The police searched, too.' Marion Headlam sighed. 'It was very upsetting, especially for the other residents.'

'OK,' said Fran, beginning to get impatient, 'so where was it found?'

'That's the funny thing,' said Marion. 'Our Nurse Redding – you remember Nurse Redding? Oh, of course you do. Weren't you trying to get in touch with her? Or your – er – colleague was, anyway.'

'Oh, yes, we know Nurse Redding,' said Fran.

'Well, Nurse Redding found it. Wasn't that amazing? And somewhere where we were sure we'd searched, and the police, too.'

'Oh?' said Fran, already knowing the answer to her next question as clearly as if she'd been there. 'Where was it?'

'Where she used to like to sit in the day room. She'd tucked it down the side of an armchair. I just can't understand why it wasn't found before.

The chairs are checked daily for – er–' Marion looked uncomfortable.

'Leakages?' suggested Fran.

'Exactly. Anyway, there it was.'

'When was this?' asked Fran. 'I would have thought Mr Wade would have been told, as executor.'

'Oh, only yesterday. I phoned the police immediately. I think they were rather suspicious that it had turned up, but I'm just relieved. Of course, they can't confirm it with the witnesses, but they've contacted the solicitor, apparently.'

'Well, congratulations,' said Fran. 'And did it confirm that she'd left money to The Laurels?'

'Oh, yes,' said Marion, her colour rising. 'A proportion of her estate.'

That won't please Barbara and Paul, thought Fran. 'Well, good luck,' she said, standing up. 'I hope the police don't make any more trouble for you.'

They will, though, she thought, as she went back to the car.

Guy took her to The Sloop for lunch and she gave him an abbreviated version of her morning's visits.

'So, you're investigating again, are you?' Guy's brown eyes twinkled at her.

'No, I'm not at all. I merely went to see Barbara to see if she knew anything about my childhood, and I went to see Mrs Headlam–'

'Yes?' prompted Guy.

'Because I was curious,' admitted Fran.

'And now things have changed, haven't they?'

'Well, of course they have. This will business

307

changes everything,' said Fran.

'So what are you going to do?'

'Nothing much I can do,' said Fran, 'but I'll phone Charles and ask what he's heard. The police must have notified him, surely, as executor?'

'I would have thought so.' Guy looked down at the table and smoothed his discarded napkin. 'Are you very close? You and Charles?'

'Eh?' Fran was shocked. 'We've only just met. I told you, didn't I?'

'But you've seen a lot of him in the last couple of weeks.'

'Well, yes, but only because of this whole business. He's a bit of a wimp.'

Guy looked up. 'Good,' he said.

Fran felt suddenly breathless, and bent down to retrieve her bag.

'I must get going,' she said.

'So soon?'

'I've got to get Romeo back.'

'Romeo?'

'Libby's car.'

'Don't tell me she's actually got a name for her car?' Guy threw his head back and laughed. 'Well, I'd never have thought it.'

'I must admit I was surprised. It seems a bit twee for Libby, doesn't it?'

'I suppose you never know with old Lib,' said Guy. 'She's a bit—'

'Mad?' suggested Fran.

'Impulsive. Liable to do exactly what she wants without thinking of the consequences.'

'Oh, I think she does think about the consequences, but her thinking's slightly skewed.' Fran stood up. 'But I'm being disloyal. She's been an amazing friend to me since I met her.'

'And to me. Especially now you're here.' Guy stood and twinkled at her. Fran felt breathless again.

'I must go,' she reiterated. He nodded and stood back for her to go past him towards the door. He paused at the bar to pay their bill, and Fran wondered if she should offer her share.

'You must come and have dinner at The Pink Geranium,' she said as he joined her. 'My treat. As I only live upstairs.'

'I'd love to,' he said. 'When?'

'Oh,' said Fran, flustered, 'I don't know. What's today?'

'Friday. What are you doing tonight?'

'Um – nothing.'

'Eight o'clock? Shall I ring on your doorbell?'

Fran swallowed. 'I'll meet you in the restaurant,' she said.

She related most of this to Libby, leaving out the conversations with Guy.

'That's a turn up for the books, isn't it?' said Libby. 'Very suspicious, that will turning up like that.'

'I really don't think Marion Headlam had anything to do with it. She was almost girlishly excited.'

'Yuck,' said Libby.

'Anyway, I knew before she told me it was Redding. She took it out of a pocket and pretended to find it down the side of a chair.'

'You saw her?'

'In my head, yes. Just like the cellar steps. I wonder why?'

'Why you saw her, or why did she do it? I can't think. She's not affected by the will one way or another, is she?' Libby got down stiffly from her perch on the kitchen table.

'Perhaps she is,' said Fran thoughtfully, 'if The Laurels can't keep going she loses her job.'

'Oh, yes. But she'd easily get another job, wouldn't she? Nurses are in such demand.'

'Perhaps she doesn't think she can, for some reason.'

'This really needs talking through, Fran,' said Libby. 'Why don't you come over for a drink tonight?'

'Guy's coming over for dinner at Harry's tonight,' said Fran, after a pause.

'Hey!' Libby was delighted. 'Way to go, Franny.'

'Don't call me that,' said Fran.

'Sorry. Well, OK, then, how about now?'

'Libby, I've been out practically all day. I want to relax a bit before having to doll myself up for tonight.'

'OK.' Libby looked over at Ben. 'Can I tell Ben?'

'Yes, of course. Talk it through with him.'

'I will. Have a lovely evening.'

Libby went and peered over Ben's shoulder. 'How's it going?'

'Fine. There's actually another wireless user near here, and I've asked permission to use it while yours is being set up.'

'What does that mean?'

Ben explained. Libby understood that she could, at least some of the time, use the internet, but beyond that the finer details escaped her.

'Are you staying for supper?' she asked.

'I did ask if I could come round tonight, remember.' Ben peered over his glasses at her.

'You didn't mention food, though.'

Ben leered at her. 'Oh, no?'

'Stop it!' Libby laughed. 'So I'll throw something together, shall I? I want to talk to you, anyway.'

Ben groaned. 'This would be to do with the marathon conversation you've just had with Fran, I take it?'

'Yes.'

'Fine. You cook, I'll play with the computer, we'll light the fire, and you can talk me to death.'

Libby grinned. 'Done,' she said.

## Chapter Thirty-two

Harry leered suggestively at Fran when Guy appeared to join her at the restaurant. He settled them on the sofa in the window to wait for their table, and raised an eyebrow at Guy's request for mineral water.

'I've got to drive back to Nethergate tonight,' said Guy.

'Pity,' said Harry.

Fran, with flaming cheeks, asked for a glass of

311

red wine.

'I think Harry wants to promote my cause,' said Guy, as he watched the tall elegant figure weaving its way through the other tables.

Fran opened her mouth to ask what cause, then thought better of it.

'So, what did Libby have to say about your revelations?'

'She wanted to talk it through. I told her to discuss it with Ben. Not that it's got anything to do with her.'

Guy smiled. 'That doesn't usually stop her,' he said.

'No, and it's been good to have someone to talk things over with, but the police are on the case, and we mustn't interfere.'

'Even if you know something they don't?'

Fran shook her head. 'They wouldn't believe what I know.'

Guy looked thoughtful. 'I let it go at the time, and you haven't brought it up since, but you mentioned something about "seeing" something which you couldn't have seen, and Libby referred to it as one of your "moments".' He looked at her. 'Can I ask now what it was about?'

Fran sighed. 'I suppose so. It's how I earn a meagre living, and the police know about it, so there's no reason for you not to, but I quite understand if you're sceptical.'

'Who am I to doubt the word of the police?' Guy covered her hand with his and squeezed. 'Tell away.'

Fran explained briefly about her job with Goodall and Smythe and DCI Murray's interest.

'I think quite a lot of police forces use people like me occasionally,' she finished. 'Not very openly, it's true, but if something helps it's worth trying, isn't it?'

'And what is it you've seen that he won't believe now?'

'Nurse Redding concealing the new will. Or rather, planting it. Which means she had been concealing it before.'

'Well, you've got to tell the police,' said Guy. 'It puts a whole new complexion on the matter.'

'Yes, I know,' Fran sighed again, 'but they can hardly go and charge her with something because I've had some sort of a vision, can they? And then there's Eleanor and the cellar steps.'

Guy looked slightly bemused by the time Donna came to take them to their table.

'I think you should have talked it over with Libby,' he said. 'I'm having difficulty following it all.'

'But you were coming over,' said Fran. 'She wanted me to go for a drink this evening.'

'We could go round after dinner,' suggested Guy.

'Oh,' said Fran, trying not to sound disappointed.

'If you really wanted to, that is. I'd prefer to have you to myself, but this sounds urgent.'

Fran smiled with relief. 'Oh, no. It'll keep. After all, now the police know the will's been found, they'll look again at Mrs Headlam and Nurse Redding, I should think. They'll find anything there is to find.'

'Oh, I meant to tell you,' said Guy, as Donna

set their first courses in front of them, 'Sophie said she saw her old school friend, the other nurse, yesterday with her boyfriend.'

'Really? I think Libby gave up on trying to talk to her. I expect the police will, though.'

'Will they?'

'Oh, yes. Now the will's turned up, they'll ask everything all over again.'

'God, how boring.' Guy turned his attention to his food. 'This is good, Fran. Why have I never been here before?'

Fran realised she was getting used to dining with Guy by the ease with which they maintained both conversation and comfortable silences throughout the meal. Harry was on hand – far too frequently – to top up glasses and enquire about the food, until Guy gave him a charming smile and an explicit instruction. Harry roared with laughter and took himself off to the kitchen.

It wasn't until Guy had pushed away his dessert plate with a satisfied sigh that Fran became aware of a curling sensation in the pit of her stomach. What now?

'Wondering whether to invite me up for coffee?' said Guy, cocking his head on one side like an inquisitive blackbird.

'Are you getting in on my act?' Fran asked.

'Yes, as a matter of fact, I was. Coffee's not a euphemism, though.'

'Of course not.' Guy pretended to be shocked. 'As if I would think it was!'

'Well,' said Fran, confused, 'you might. Although I can't see why.'

'Now you really are confusing me,' said Guy, shaking his head. 'Come on. Let's sneak out without Harry noticing.'

'I've got to pay,' said Fran.

'He knows where you are.'

'Yes, and he'll probably come leaping up the back stairs demanding his money.'

'Oh, all right. Anything to prevent that.'

Fran went over to Donna at the table they used for a cash desk and paid, just in time before Harry reappeared as they left.

'Very nice,' said Guy, as Fran showed him into the living room before going to put the kettle on.

'Did you want coffee? Or something stronger?' she called from the kitchen.

'Coffee's fine. I'm driving, remember?'

'Yes,' she said gratefully, coming back into the living room.

'Thank you for a lovely meal, by the way.' Guy sat on the sofa and smiled up at her. 'Harry's a good cook.'

'A great chef, I think he would prefer,' said Fran, laughing.

'Then he shouldn't refer to his restaurant as "the caff" should he?'

'I'll tell him,' said Fran, 'but not tonight.'

'No, not tonight,' said Guy, reaching for her hand. 'Come and sit beside me.'

'I'll go and get the coffee,' said Fran hastily, pulling her hand away. 'Sorry.'

When she returned with mugs and cafetière, she apologised again. 'I'm out of practice,' she said.

315

'I'm glad to hear it,' said Guy. 'Shall we start again?'

An hour later, when he left, refusing to let Fran come downstairs with him, they'd not only started, but gone quite a way towards the finishing line, and Fran was in a state of delighted confusion. Clearing the coffee things away, she was aware of a sort of tingling, bubbly feeling that almost took her breath away. Coming to live here, meeting Libby, Harry and Peter, the sudden and surprising acquisition of a legacy and finally, meeting Guy were all rather too much for someone who'd not had the best life or luck over the past few years. Climbing into bed, she thanked Uncle Frank, and whoever else was up there looking after her, and looked forward to discussing everything with Libby in the morning.

Libby called her in the morning before Fran had even gathered her thoughts together.

'I was going to call you,' she said, yawning.

'That sounds like a good night,' said Libby, a question in her voice.

'I'll tell you all about it later,' said Fran. 'What did you want?'

'A chat. I think you should tell the Inspector what you know.'

'That's what Guy said.'

'There you are then. And I think we should see what Nurse Warner knows, too.'

'Oh, yes. Guy said his daughter Sophie saw her with her boyfriend the other day.'

'Really? Where?'

'I don't know. Look, Lib, I'll come round when

316

I've woken up properly and we can discuss everything. Anyway, I want to look at your computer.'

'OK. I'll have the kettle on. Don't be too long.'

'All right, all right,' said Fran, exasperated. 'I'll
be as quick as I can.'

In fact, it was over an hour before she arrived at
Libby's, coat collar turned up against a sharp
wind.

Libby sat her down in front of the new computer while she made tea.

'So, what happened last night?' she asked.

Fran gave her an expurgated version of the
night's events and made her laugh about Harry's
obvious nosiness.

'A proper relationship, then?' said Libby, when
she'd finished.

'The beginning of one, perhaps,' said Fran
uncertainly, 'but I know now what you felt like
about Ben, back in the spring.'

'And a couple of weeks ago, don't forget,' said
Libby. 'Being middle aged and starting a
relationship's absolute hell, in my opinion. Much
worse than when you're young.'

'I don't know what I'll do if I ever get to the
point of taking my clothes off,' said Fran, staring
out of the window.

'Oh, so you didn't get that far last night?' said
Libby, grinning.

'No,' said Fran, blushing and trying not to
think about Guy's enterprising hands.

'Hopefully, by that stage, you'll be too far gone
to be thinking,' said Libby.

'Let's change the subject,' said Fran, coming
away from the computer and sitting in the arm-

chair. Sidney appeared immediately and jumped onto the arm.

'Right. Nurse Warner. Bet you she's got a story.'

'Bet you so has Nurse Redding.'

'Well, of course she has, but she put me off pretty conclusively over the Satanists, didn't she?'

'I suppose I could try,' said Fran, looking thoughtful. 'I've a legitimate reason to ask her questions, now, haven't I?'

'The will, you mean? But you aren't in it.'

'She doesn't know that.' Fran thought for a moment. 'Oh, yes, she does, doesn't she? If she had the will, she'll have read it. I still can't think why she wanted it.'

'Perhaps she didn't. Perhaps she just found it.'

'I can still ask her about it.'

'I thought,' said Libby, 'you weren't going to do any more. Leave it to the police, you said.'

'You said I ought to go to the police, and we ought to discuss it.'

'Oh, well, whatever.' Libby waved a dismissive hand. 'Tell DCI Murray what you've seen.'

'You think so?' Fran looked doubtful.

'Yes, I do. And about Aunt Eleanor.'

'Let's not over-egg the pudding,' said Fran. 'He might not be like the White Queen.'

'Eh?' said Libby.

'In Alice. Believing six impossible things before breakfast.'

'Oh.'

'I'll ring him.' Fran heaved a sigh and dragged her mobile out of her bag.

'I've told you, use the land line, or he'll be able to get hold of you anytime.' Libby handed over the phone.

Fran, hoping that DCI Murray would be un-available, was disappointed.

'What have you got for me, Mrs Castle?' he said, sounding much more friendly than the last time they'd met.

Fran, with much hesitation, explained.

'Yes,' he said, when she'd finished, 'we sus-pected something of the sort. Our scenes of crime people are very thorough, and we'd even searched the other residents' rooms. Didn't go down too well.'

'I wouldn't imagine it would,' said Fran. 'So you searched the staff quarters, too?'

'Except Marion Headlam, they all live out,' said Murray, 'but we searched all the staff rooms and lockers. We're quite competent, you know, Mrs Castle.'

'I know.' Fran cleared her throat. 'Actually, there's something else I ought to tell you, In-spector. As a result of Mrs Bridges' death, I've come into a legacy.' And she explained about the trust.

'And you knew nothing about this?' Murray sounded suspicious.

'No, I promise you. I've got the name of the solicitor who told me. He's ringing me back on Monday. John Meade of Hallbert and Dunkin.'

'I'll phone him first thing,' muttered Murray. 'This is getting too complicated.'

'There was something else, too,' said Fran, feel-ing that she might as well burn her boats.

'Yes? What? More visions?' DCI Murray sighed heavily.

319

'Well, yes, actually,' said Fran, and explained about the cellar steps.

'When was this?' he sounded quite bright, now, thought Fran, as she explained that she didn't actually know, but it must have been 1964 or possibly 1965.

'So you weren't living in the house, then?'

'No, we moved away after he married Eleanor,' said Fran, wondering how many more times she was going to have to explain her family details.

'We've got the address of the property, haven't we?' he said. 'It's where Mr Wade lives now.'

'Yes, it is. Is that all Inspector? Only I'm using my friend's phone.'

'*Chief* Inspector, *Mrs* Castle,' he said. 'Yes. I'll come back to you if I need anything else.'

'That's that, then,' said Libby, as Fran handed her back the phone. 'Now what?'

'Redding,' said Fran. 'I can talk to her on the pretext of warning her about the police wanting to question her again.'

'Shall I ring her?'

'We don't know what shift she's on, do we? Or even if she works at weekends. It *is* Saturday.'

'I'll risk it and go to The Laurels,' said Fran.

'Marion Headlam'll be surprised,' said Libby. 'You were only there yesterday.'

Fran shrugged. 'I'll think of something,' she said.

In fact, she didn't have to. Borrowing Romeo once again, and deciding that, if the trust materialised, the first thing she would do would be to buy a car – a nice, clean environmentally friendly one – she was just about to turn into the drive of The Laurels, when a car, almost as ancient as Romeo, drove out, and Fran, whose distance eyesight was excellent, recognised Nurse Redding driving it. As she turned away from Fran, Fran was able to follow her without looking suspicious, and as Nurse Redding was a careful, not to say over-cautious, driver, following her was easy. She parked eventually in front of a large detached house near the hospital in Canterbury, and Fran was able to park in a space just beyond, and catch her up just as she walked up the path to the front door.

'I'm so glad I caught you,' panted Fran, skidding to a halt on some early fallen leaves.

'What do you want now?' Redding glared at her.

'Just to say that the police want to talk to you again. I heard this morning.'

'And why would they tell you?' Nurse Redding's eyes narrowed under her heavy brows.

'Because of the will.' Fran narrowed her eyes back, and hoped she wasn't squinting.

'You're not in it,' said Redding, then looked horrified.

Fran didn't bother to conceal her triumph. 'Exactly,' she said. 'You had it. You read it. That's why they want to talk to you.'

'How did they know?' The stuffing had leached out of Redding and she stood, limp, leaning against a wall.

'It was obvious, wasn't it?' said Fran. 'It wasn't there when they searched, so it had to have been taken off the premises, and brought back by someone. Someone who had access to the whole place – not just a visitor.' She eyed Redding thoughtfully. 'Come on. Let's get you inside. You've had a shock.'

To her surprise, Nurse Redding didn't demur, and led Fran into a large downstairs flat that appeared scrupulously neat and tidy, and curiously soul-less. The one thing of any character was the large and rather unpleasant picture over the bricked up hearth.

'You're into Satanism, I see,' said Fran, in a conversational tone, and trying not to look too interested.

'Yes.' Redding sank down into a armchair. 'So's your friend.'

Fran raised her eyebrows. 'Libby? Yes,' she said.

'Phoned me asking about Tyne Chapel, she did. I put her off.'

'I'm sure,' said Fran. 'It's still used then?' Of course it was. She could see it. Torches and black robes. Tonight. Her heart banged frighteningly, and she sat up straight and tried to ignore it.

Nurse Redding shrugged. 'Might be,' she said.

'So tell me why you took the will,' said Fran.

'Why should I?'

'You're going to have to tell the police. And although I'm not a legatee in Mrs Bridges' will, I am in her late husband's,' said Fran, crossing her fingers in her lap. Well, it was almost true.

'I don't see that it has anything to do with you.' Nurse Redding looked truculent. Any minute now she's going to ask me to leave, thought Fran, unless I can come up with something.

'But it has to do with Charles Wade,' she said, 'and Mr and Mrs Denver.'

To her surprise, Redding's face took on an alarmingly malevolent expression. 'Him,' she said, a globule of spittle landing on her hand.

'Charles?' said Fran.

'Paul bloody Denver.' Redding's head poked forward like a snake about to strike, and Fran felt a trickle of fear down her spine and raising the hair on the back of her neck.

'The police ought to ask him about his fucking aunt's death.' Suddenly, Redding surged up out of her chair and loomed over Fran.

Keep calm, Fran told herself, aware that her heart was banging so hard, Redding could probably see it. 'But Paul didn't arrive until after his aunt died,' she said.

'Oh, no? You ask that stupid bitch Warner where he was. With his auntie outside the french windows in her wheelchair.'

'Where was *he*, then?'

'In her room, wasn't he? With Warner. Fucking the life out of her.'

## Chapter Thirty-three

Fran just stared. Redding flung herself back in her chair and started chewing a nail.

'Have you told the police?' Fran was surprised that her voice came out sounding normal.

'No.'

'Why on earth not? It changes the whole case.'

'I've got something on him, haven't I? And he

knows it.'

'Is that why you took the will?'

Redding's face took on a cunning expression. She's mad, thought Fran.

'They were really worried about that will. I heard them talking.' She looked at Fran. 'He used to tell me things when we were in bed.'

'You?' Fran gasped.

'Oh, yes. I know what you're thinking. Why me.' She laughed. 'That's what they thought before.'

'Who thought what before?'

'At work. I was a sister.'

Fran was now finding it hard to follow this barrage of information, but this made sense. 'This is where you lived when you worked at the hospital?' she said. 'You said something about that the first time we met at The Laurels.'

Redding stood up again. 'You'd better go now,' she said. 'I've been on all night. I need sleep.'

Fran went willingly to the door.

'Thank you,' she said, before it was slammed in her face.

She was shaking as she walked to the car. Her first thought was to phone the police, but after this morning's call, she wondered if it would be construed as pestering. Resting her head on the steering wheel after getting into Romeo, she took a calming breath and decided to call Guy.

'I'm sorry to bother you on a Saturday,' she said, 'it must be your busiest day.'

'Bother away,' he said. 'I tried to call you earlier, but your phone wasn't switched on. So I called Libby.'

'Did you?' Fran was ridiculously pleased.

'Yes. She said you'd spoken to Murray, and you were going to see Nurse Redding.'

'That's what I wanted to talk to you about,' said Fran, and embarked on a rather garbled version of her visit to Nurse Redding.

'Where are you now?' asked Guy.

'Sitting outside her flat. She lives in one of those big houses near the hospital in Canterbury.'

'And she used to work there?'

'Yes, and there's obviously something funny about that, too. It sounds as if she might have had an affair there, but I could be wrong.'

'How could you find out?'

'I couldn't. I don't know anyone who works there. Anyway, what does it matter? The thing is she seems to have had an affair with Paul Denver.' Fran shuddered. 'Awful.'

'And with this other one, too, Sophie's friend.'

'Yes.' Fran shuddered again. 'You should have heard her. It was horrible.'

'Look, we can't talk about this on the phone. Why don't you go home and I'll come over.'

'Oh, no. You can't leave your shop on a Saturday. Anyway, I've got to take the car back to Libby. I'll talk to her.'

'I'll come over later, then. Ring me if there are any developments.'

Soothed and slightly happier, Fran put Romeo in gear, and with an ominous grinding turned him homewards. Once or twice on the way back to Steeple Martin, Fran found herself wondering whether she'd actually jumped any red lights, her mind was so full of what she'd learned from Nurse Redding. She arrived safely outside 17,

Allhallow's Lane, and was relieved to find Libby still at home, although making preparations to go and meet Ben for a Saturday lunchtime drink.

'Doesn't matter about that,' she said, sitting Fran down and dumping Sidney on her lap. 'I'll ring him and put him off. You look awful.'

'Gee, thanks.' Fran leaned back in the chair and closed her eyes. 'I was terrified.'

'What happened?'

Once again, Fran recounted the morning's events, while Libby's eyes grew wider and wider and her jaw dropped lower and lower.

'Go to the police.' Libby was firm. 'This is no time to worry about what they're going to think. She's got to be the murderer.'

'I still don't know what to think about her hiding the will, though. What on earth for? And what about Paul and Nurse Warner?'

'Goodness knows. Just phone the police. It doesn't have to be Murray, it can be anyone.' Libby handed over the phone. 'Here.'

It wasn't Murray, it was, in fact, DS Cole, who listened with obvious impatience, then informed Fran that DCI Murray and DC Bulstrode were on their way to interview Nurse Redding as he spoke. No doubt she would give them the information herself.

'I wouldn't bet on it,' said Fran, ringing off. 'Did I tell you she admitted to belonging to some sort of coven? Horrible picture over her mantelpiece. And I'm sure she's going to a meeting tonight.'

'At the chapel?' said Libby.

'It seemed like it.'

'Is it worth asking how you know?'

'No.'

'I thought not. I went to have a look at it the other day. I forgot to tell you.' Libby recounted her unnerving experience at the chapel. 'Do you think it was members of the coven, or whatever it is?'

'Sounds like it,' said Fran. 'Good job they only saw you from a distance.'

'So what do we do now?' asked Libby. 'I don't trust Redding to tell them anything.'

'I think she might drop Paul in it, now. I can't understand why she didn't do it before. She was obviously furious with Warner. And that explains why Warner seemed so scared when I met them both the day after the death.'

'Funny that she's still living where she used to when she worked in Canterbury,' said Libby. 'I would have thought those flats were reserved for their own nurses.'

'That's another thing,' said Fran, 'she said "that's what they thought before". When I was surprised about her and Paul.'

'She must have had some sort of affair while she was there, then,' said Libby. 'How could we find out?'

'We can't, Lib. There's nothing we can do now. Leave it to the police. That's what you advised me to do, isn't it?'

Libby looked at her thoughtfully. 'OK. Until I think of something. Come on, come and have a drink with Ben and me.'

Before they could leave, Fran's mobile rang.

327

'Fran, it's Charles. You'll never believe this, but I've had a letter from a development company. They think they're buying this house.'

'What?'

'You remember that the houses either side have been bought up and they wanted this one as well? Well, apparently, bloody Paul Denver approached them on the basis of being Eleanor's beneficiary and somehow convinced them that I could sell it to them.'

Fran sat down with a thump. Libby followed suit.

'I don't believe it. When's the letter dated?'

'Beginning of the week. They obviously didn't know she'd died.'

'No, because you certainly can't do it now, until her estate's sorted out. Bloody Paul. What a cheek!'

'I bet Barbara was behind it,' said Charles. 'Anyway, do you think I should tell the police? It probably gives Paul a motive.'

Fran thought for a moment. 'On the contrary, it removes it,' she said. 'You could only sell it with power of attorney, not after she was dead.'

'I could. Or we could. Once probate is granted.'

'Oh, yes.' Fran sighed. 'And do we know if that's held up in a case of murder?'

'Probably,' said Charles gloomily. 'I could do with the money.'

'Obviously, so could Barbara and Paul,' said Fran. 'Oh, well, tell the police anyway. DCI Murray's gone to see Nurse Redding now, I happen to know, so you'll have to talk to someone else.'

'How do you know?'

'It's a long story, Charles,' said Fran wearily. 'I'll tell you all about it another time.'

'So what was that all about?' asked Libby, after Fran had rung off. Fran told her.

'Did he ask about the codicil?' said Libby.

'Oh, no. I didn't think to mention it. He must know, surely?'

'The police will have told him. Funny he didn't mention it, though. He really needs to know, doesn't he?'

'He's bound to phone me again. I'll ask him then.'

'I say, it's all happening, isn't it?' Libby beamed. 'Let's go and tell Ben.'

Fran allowed herself to be persuaded into one drink, then returned to the flat to think things through. She still couldn't understand why Redding had concealed the will, unless it was a purely childish reaction in order to hurt him after what she saw as his betrayal with Nurse Warner.

Fran lay on her back on the sofa and gazed at the ceiling. So who now became the most likely suspect? Paul, because he was there before he said he was? No, because he would have left after Redding burst in. Warner? Highly unlikely. Redding, after the other two had left?

No, it had to be Barbara. She was on her own in the room for several minutes before calling for help, during which time she said she hadn't realised that Eleanor was dead. Phooey, thought Fran, and tried to focus her mind on the suffocating blackness she'd felt that day on the train, and then again in Eleanor's room. But it was no good. Nothing was coming through.

And, she asked herself, sitting up, what about the witnesses? Both killed in road accidents. Could Barbara have done that? She realised that she had no idea whether or not Barbara drove, but surely, these days, everyone drove, especially if you lived as far out of town as Blagstock House. So Barbara could have bumped off the two witnesses to prevent them being called upon to prove there had been a codicil, then it would be just her word against Marion Headlam's. And then, Nurse Redding's position became clear. She knew a codicil had been written. She might not have seen it, but she knew it existed, and she was obviously aware that Paul and Barbara knew it, too, and were unhappy about it. So first, she took it, in order to frustrate them, then planted it to confound them. It would also make the police look more closely at the Denvers, who had every reason to want the codicil suppressed.

Her mobile rang again.

'Charles again,' he said. 'You'll never guess what. I just called the developers.'

'On a Saturday?'

'I thought I'd give it a try. And sure enough there was somebody there, apparently to take enquiries from prospective purchasers.'

'And did they know anything?'

'Oh, yes. They were able to look up the file immediately.'

'And?'

'They've only paid Paul a deposit.'

'No!' Fran was stunned. 'No wonder he wanted to find that will.'

'Anyway, I've just called him and told him he has to return it. The house will have to be sold to divide up the estate and give The Laurels its share, so they can still have it, but they'll have to buy it from the estate.'

'And what did he say?'

'I wouldn't repeat it, but I got the impression that the deposit was no more.'

'There'll be hell to pay. No wonder Barbara was so scared. But surely, then, she and Paul wouldn't have wanted her to die any more than you would, as all this would come out?'

'I would think so,' said Charles. 'I wonder how many more shocks we're going to get?'

'Well, you obviously know about the codicil. How much of her estate goes to The Laurels?'

'Two thirds,' said Charles, gloomily. 'No wonder it – er – got lost. Paul and Barbara wouldn't want to lose out on that.'

'Neither would you. How much would that be, do you suppose?'

'Well, the house is probably all there is in the estate, and don't forget it'll be over the inheritance tax limit, so anything above that will be taxed at forty percent, but even so, I expect we're talking a lot of money after the solicitors have taken their cut.'

After Charles had rung off, Fran sat thinking for a while longer, then took a deep breath and called Blagstock House.

'I'm afraid he's not here, Frances,' said Barbara. 'He's gone to the office.'

'Oh?'

'He usually does on a Saturday. It's the one day

people come out house hunting here, it seems.'

'I see.' Fran frowned. 'Could I have the office number, do you think?'

'Why? Can't you talk to me?' Barbara's voice was sharp.

'It was something he said to Charles,' said Fran.

'Charles? When?'

'This morning, I think. Charles just phoned me.'

'What was it about?'

'Legal stuff,' said Fran. 'Nothing to do with you.'

'If it's to do with Aunt Eleanor it's very definitely to do with me.'

'I'm afraid not,' said Fran sweetly. 'I've already told you about my trust. Don't bother with the number. I'll find it.'

And now Barbara will ring Paul to find out what's going on, thought Fran. And maybe by now, the police have talked to Nurse Redding and they've been in touch with Paul.

But within five minutes, her phone rang again, and this time it was DCI Murray.

'How did you get this number?' asked Fran indignantly.

'From your cousin Charles,' said Murray abruptly, 'and now would you tell me what this nonsense was you were telling DS Cole earlier on? I've just been talking to Nurse Redding and she denied every word.'

# Chapter Thirty-four

'What?'

'According to you, she concealed the will, and on the day of the murder found Paul Denver and Nurse Warner in Mrs Bridges' room before Mrs Denver arrived.'

'That's right. She told me so this morning.'

'Well, I can't prove that she told you or she didn't, but *I'm* telling you – she denied it all.'

Fran sat, stunned. 'Why?' she said eventually.

'Don't ask me,' said Murray irritably, 'I'm only the bloody investigating officer. And I ask myself why you would tell me this information if it wasn't true. It doesn't seem like you.'

'It isn't,' said Fran. 'You know that. I might give you some strange information sometimes, but I always believe it's true.'

'Exactly,' sighed Murray, 'so now I'm forced to try and prove what Miss perishing Joan Redding tells me.'

'Did she say she found Nurse Warner in the room, and that Marion Headlam asked her to go and get the birthday cake?'

'Birthday cake? What birthday cake?'

'All the residents have one, apparently.'

Murray exploded. 'So why didn't I know? Why has no one thought to tell me any of these nice little tit-bits? Don't they know concealing evidence is a crime?'

'I don't suppose they thought of it like that,' said Fran, consolingly.

'Well, go on then,' said Murray, breathing heavily, 'now *you* tell me something I don't know.'

'Nurse Redding belongs to some kind of Satanist cult. I believe she's going to a meeting tonight.'

'Don't tell me,' groaned Murray, 'and all the others are going with her.'

'I don't think so,' said Fran, amused. 'I just thought you ought to know. It's illegal, isn't it?'

'Depends what they're doing. Can be a breach of the peace.'

'Well, I think it's at Tyne Chapel. You had some problems there before, didn't you?'

'Tyne Chapel? What do you know about that?' Murray's voice had changed.

'Only local gossip. Someone said whatever trouble there was had been stopped, but perhaps it hasn't.'

'And how do you know there's a meeting tonight?'

'Well – I don't, for certain.'

'Ah. One of those.' Murray sighed. 'I think we might just check it out, though. Nasty goings on up there, there were. And don't you go poking your nose in.'

'No, Inspector,' said Fran, demurely.

'*Chief* Inspector, *Mrs* Castle,' he said and rang off.

Now what, thought Fran. What a muddle. She wandered into the kitchen to fill the kettle. Presumably, Murray would ask Paul and Warner to confirm or deny what she, Fran, had told them.

334

And what would they say? Paul would deny it, of course. But Warner?

She dialled the number of Guy's shop. Sophie answered.

'He's with a customer, Fran,' she said.

'It's all right, Sophie, it was you I wanted. Did you find out for Libby where your friend Sue Warner lived?'

'Not really, I think she's moved out to be with her boyfriend. I did see them together the other day, did Dad tell you?'

'Yes, he did,' said Fran, remembering. 'Where was it? Did you speak?'

'No, she was too far away, but I'm certain it was her. And I'm not so certain, but the chap she was with – well, it looked like that Paul Denver.'

Fran's eyebrows rose. Result! she thought, and, after thanking Sophie, ran down the back stairs to see if Harry was still on the premises. He looked up in surprise and stopped chopping onions.

'What's the problem, ducks?' He came forward, wiping his hands on his apron.

'Have you got a telephone directory here, Harry?'

'Yeah, over there in the drawer of the desk. Both sorts, I think. Why?'

'I need to look up Paul Denver's number,' said Fran, going towards the desk.

'Paul Denver. Hang on, he's the estate agent, isn't he?'

Fran nodded, leafing through the business section of the directory. 'Here he is.' She punched the number into her phone, saved it, and called. A mechanical voice asked her to leave a message.

'Paul, I need to know what you were doing with Nurse Warner before Aunt Eleanor died. You were there before you said you arrived. Please ring me on this number.'

Harry leant his elbows on the desk and grinned. 'Even more intriguing, this, isn't it?' he said. 'Are you going to take it up professionally?'

'Take what up?' Fran was looking through the private section now.

'Detecting,' said Harry. 'Between the two of you, your instinct and Lib's nosiness would make a great team, I reckon.'

'Don't be daft, Harry.' Fran closed the book. 'Damn. No private number listed.'

'You don't know that. You don't know what address you were looking for.'

'There's only one Denver in the book. And that's Barbara.'

'Oh.' Harry straightened up. 'Well, perhaps he still lives there.'

'Oh, come on. He must be thirty. Still living with his mother?'

'She's got a big house. He's got a business, he's broke. Why not?'

Fran stared at him. 'Could be. But Sophie said–'

'Who's Sophie?'

'Guy's daughter.'

'What's she got to do with the price of fish?'

'Oh, Harry,' said Fran, exasperated, 'it doesn't matter. I just thought he might live somewhere with a girlfriend, that's all.'

'OK, keep your hair on. Want a coffee?'

'No, thanks. I've got a couple more calls to make. Thanks for the directory.'

'Any time. Be good.' Harry ushered her out of the kitchen and watched her go up the stairs.

Libby was still out, so Fran left a message on the answerphone and tried the mobile. From the background noise when she answered, it was clear that she was still in the pub.

'I just thought I'd let you know about a couple of developments. Sorry to interrupt your lunch.'

'Not exactly lunch, Fran! It's nearly half past three. Peter came in, and he and Ben are deep in family conversations. What's happened?'

Fran explained.

'Shall I come up?' asked Libby. 'They won't miss me, and Ben can always phone me if he wants me.'

'OK, if you like. It's all so puzzling, I felt I had to talk to someone.'

'And who better than your partner in crime,' said Libby triumphantly. 'See you in a minute.'

The distance between the pub and The Pink Geranium being only a matter of metres, she was, in fact, slightly less than a minute.

'So what do you think will happen now?' she asked, when Fran had finished telling her.

'Murray will try and question Warner and Paul, I suppose, and probably go back to Nurse Redding. Did you know her name was Joan?'

'No. Doesn't suit her. Mind you, it might give us a handle on what went on at the hospital.'

'How do you mean?' asked Fran.

'Now we know her name is Joan Redding we could ask a couple of people at the hospital.'

'Like who? Do you know anybody?'

Libby wrinkled her brow. 'Not off hand. Pity

David isn't alive.'

They both sat in silence for a moment, remembering Ben's brother-in-law David, the village doctor who had died tragically back in the spring.

'I know,' said Libby suddenly. 'My friend Tricia.'

'Sounds like a pony book,' said Fran. 'Who's your friend Tricia?'

'She's a medical secretary at the hospital. She's worked for several departments over the years. I bet she knows.'

'How do you know her?'

'Oh, she works back stage at my old drama society. Hang on, I'll find her number.' Libby began scrolling through the address book on her phone.

'That's efficient of you,' said Fran, 'considering you're always leaving your phone behind or switched off.'

'Pots and kettles,' said Libby. 'Ah, here we are.'

Fran went and made a pot of tea while Libby talked to the surprised Tricia, having to catch up on a lot of gossip before she reached the point of her phone call. Finally, she switched off and picked up the mug Fran offered.

'Apparently, Joan Redding had a relationship with a doctor a few years ago, although Tricia says general opinion was that she must have forced him into it, and when he broke it off she started up a sort "Fatal Attraction" stalking operation. Very nasty, it got. She was asked to leave.'

'There you are, then. That's why she was worried about her job. Marion Headlam must have known about it when she took her on, but it would be difficult for her to get a job anywhere else.'

'I wonder why Headlam took her on?' mused Libby. 'She's hardly the comforting type. More like a prison warder.'

'Perhaps that's what she needs. To stop the old dears getting out.'

'Tricia didn't know anything about Satanism, though. Still I suppose that's not the sort of thing you boast about, is it? More a dodgy handshake sort of thing.'

'I told Murray about Tyne Chapel. He's going to look into it,' said Fran.

'Oh. You didn't tell him I'd been up there, did you?' Libby looked nervous.

'No, I didn't. Why?'

'He'd have my guts for garters. He doesn't like me at all.'

'I think he just gets annoyed with us both for interfering. The police always do in books, don't they?'

'He's willing to listen to your moments,' said Libby.

'Only because I've surprised him by being right once or twice.'

'Why don't we try and find Nurse Warner?' said Libby, after a minute.

'I don't see how we can,' said Fran. 'Marion Headlam won't give us her address, and you said there were too many Warners in the book to trawl through.'

'You found Redding this morning, didn't you?'

'Yes, but that was sheer luck. It's hardly going to happen again, is it?'

'Suppose not. Oh, well, we'll just have to wait for the police, won't we?'

But it wasn't the police who next rang Fran's mobile.

'Paul?' she said, her eyebrows shooting up. Libby almost choked on her tea.

'What do you want now?' he asked, obviously abandoning the polite family member act.

'If you got my message, as you must have done, you'll know.'

'And what's it to you?'

'I'm just warning you, that's all,' said Fran, ostentatiously crossing her fingers, 'the police know about this, or think they do, and they'll be coming after you.'

'Oh, yeah? And who told them?' Fran could hear the sneer in Paul's voice.

'Well, I did, but Nurse Redding told me.'

He laughed. 'Oh, and they'll believe you, will they? Well, what if I told you I happen to know she won't corroborate any such story, and anyway, there is a witness who's already sworn he saw me arriving when I said I did.'

'Who's that?'

'I don't see why I should tell you, but on the other hand, perhaps it'll keep you off my back. It was the gardener. Not to mention Sue Warner, of course. She saw me, too.'

'Do the police know that?' asked Fran.

'Of course. They found out when they questioned the gardener. I didn't point them in his direction. Now, please, I've got work to do. And I'd appreciate it if you kept out of our business. This has nothing to do with you, as I believe my mother has already told you.'

'So that's that,' she said to Libby, switching her phone off. 'Exit Paul as a suspect. I wonder if Redding was lying to me?'

'Couldn't you tell?' asked Libby.

'No, of course I couldn't. All that I got from her this morning was the business about Tyne Chapel. It's quite possible that she was trying to shock me. Particularly when she said that about sleeping with Paul. I just can't imagine it, can you?'

'No. Urgh,' said Libby, shuddering. 'I've only ever seen Paul once, but the two of them together – it's creepy. Do you think she locked him in the linen cupboard?'

'I think it's quite serious, Libby,' said Fran. 'You didn't see her this morning. She was – oh, I don't know. She terrified me.'

'Do you think she might kill again, then?' Libby looked scared.

'Again? You've decided she's the murderer, then?'

'Well, who else? On her own admission she went into Aunt Eleanor's room before letting Barbara in, whether she saw Paul and Nurse Warner or not. And she nicked the will, for some confused reason of her own.'

'I don't see it,' said Fran. 'Marion Headlam was coming down that corridor, remember, to ask about the birthday cake. *She* could easily have slipped in and done it before Barbara got there.'

'She does have a motive,' said Libby. 'Redding doesn't really, neither does Warner.'

'I'm afraid my money's still on Barbara, though,' sighed Fran. 'The more I think about it, the more obvious it seems.'

'It's the will that's confused everything isn't it?' said Libby. 'Being stolen, or mislaid, or whatever.'

'I suppose so. If it had still been there, and Barbara or Paul had seen it, they wouldn't have tried to kill Eleanor, they'd have tried to make her change the codicil. They certainly wouldn't want her to die with that in place.' Fran frowned. 'So why did Redding take it?'

'Revenge on Paul?' Libby was looking confused. 'Oh, no, she would have to have taken it before she found Warner with Paul. Oh!' A light broke across her face. 'That's it!'

'What's it?'

'What happened! After she caught the two of them together, she took the will, killed Eleanor, all the time meaning to put the will back so that Paul wouldn't then inherit anything.'

Fran shook her head. 'Why take the will? She could just have killed Eleanor and let the will be found.'

'Oh.' Libby's face fell. 'Well, if it wasn't her, and it couldn't be Warner or Paul, it has to be either the Headlam or Barbara.'

'Or a passing tramp,' said Fran, gloomily. 'And I don't know why I'm bothered, it's nothing to do with me, as the Denvers keep telling me.'

'Well, it is, in a way. Especially now you've discovered everything about you and Uncle Frank and the cottage. You're bound to be interested.' Libby tucked her feet underneath her. 'And what's Cap'n Murray going to do about Eleanor killing Frank?'

'I don't know. There's nothing anyone can do about that, anyway. They're both dead now.'

Libby leaned over and patted her hand. 'And you're going to have a little bit of extra money so you can live down here with us all, go out with Guy and help me with the pantomime. Lots to look forward to.'

'And set up in business, Harry suggested,' said Fran with a smile.

'Eh? What business?'

'With my instinct and your nosiness – his words, not mine – we should set up in the detective business, he thinks.' Fran laughed at Libby's expression. 'Go on, he wasn't serious.'

'But it's a great idea!' said Libby, sitting bolt upright. 'Just think! You could do exactly what you do for Goodall and Smythe, and I could ferret things out. Way to go, Harry! Is he downstairs?' She scrambled to her feet.

'He was, but listen, Libby, it was a joke. Sit down.'

Libby sat down.

'I know it sounds great, but honestly, the only times we've been involved with anything like this it's because it's been very close to us. And that's coincidence enough. I never believed in all those amateur detectives who fall over bodies wherever they are.' She stood up and collected mugs. 'We know nothing about investigations, and we've both realised that the police get there before we do.'

'Except with your moments.'

'But they're frequently not relevant.'

'If you learnt to – oh, I don't know – channel them somehow–'

'Libby, leave it. I'm not going to channel anything. Now, are you staying for another cup of tea, or are you going back to Ben?'

Libby took herself off to the pub, and Frank pottered around the flat, cooking herself a meal, watching some television, reading, and looking out of her window on to the darkening high street. Guy rang and invited himself over, and Fran, with heightened colour, rushed round the flat tidying up, changed and put on some make-up.

Guy had barely arrived when Fran's mobile rang.

'Mrs Castle?' said a strange voice.

'Yes?' said Fran, raising her eyebrows at Guy and shaking her head.

'Detective Inspector Connell here. I believe you gave my colleague DCI Murray some information this afternoon?'

'Er – yes,' said Fran. 'Several pieces. Which bit?'

'About Tyne Chapel.'

'Oh. Oh, yes, right.'

'Can you tell me how you came by this information, please?'

'Which information exactly?' asked Fran.

'That there was to be a meeting tonight.'

'Oh, well – er – you'll have to ask Mr Murray,' said Fran, feeling uncomfortable. 'He knows.'

'I shall have to ask you to come to the station, Mrs Castle. This is a serious matter.'

'Oh, God,' said Fran. 'You'll never believe me.

Can't you ask Mr Murray? And why, anyway?'

'There was a meeting tonight, Mrs Castle.'

Fran felt a familiar suffocating blackness descending on her.

'And someone was killed. A Joan Redding.'

## Chapter Thirty-five

A police car was already standing outside The Pink Geranium. A young police constable knocked on Fran's door and asked politely if she would come with him. Guy, equally polite, insisted on accompanying her. To her surprise, as she was ushered into the back of the car, DCI Murray turned round to greet her.

'Am I being taken to the station?' asked Fran. 'An Inspector Connell says I have to go there.'

'No, you don't. He called me earlier and I happened to mention how I'd got the information. So then he called you, didn't he?'

'Yes, five minutes ago.'

'I thought he might. Good evening sir.' Murray acknowledged Guy, who had climbed in beside Fran.

'This is Guy Wolfe, Mr Murray,' said Fran.

'Oh, ah? The painter, would that be?'

'Yes,' said Guy, surprised.

'Mmm. Got one of yours. Only a print, of course. Got one of Mrs Sarjeant's, too. Anyway, Mrs Castle, I decided I'd pick you up on the way to Tyne chapel. I was sure you'd want to go and

345

see, and it'll save you the trouble of going in to the station to make a statement.'

'I'm not sure I want to go and see a murder,' said Fran, and Guy took her hand in a comforting clasp.

'A murder? Did Connell tell you that?' Murray's head swivelled round again.

'Yes. He said Nurse Redding had died.'

'He shouldn't have done that. Not if he was treating you as a suspect.'

'A suspect?' Fran almost shrieked.

Murray grinned at her. 'Well, you've got to admit, it's suspicious that someone passes on information about a meeting and there's a death almost immediately.'

'You don't believe it, though, do you?' said Guy, gripping Fran's hand tightly.

'Of course I don't. I shall explain Mrs Castle's involvement in this, and my own, of course.'

'Do you think it's linked to my Aunt's death?'

'Couldn't say, but under the circumstances you can't help wondering, can you?'

They approached Tyne Chapel from a different direction than Libby had some days previously. The darkness was already illuminated by police lamps, and to Fran's surprise, a white tent stood beyond the chapel itself.

'Weren't they inside?' she asked in a whisper, as they approached the blue and white tape.

'She wasn't,' said Murray. 'I'll find out in a minute.' He strode off and in a few moments, Fran saw a tall dark man emerge from the tent and greet him. Then, they both disappeared back inside.

'I don't understand why you're here,' said Guy. 'Surely, if they'd wanted a statement it would have been better to go to the station, as Connell said.'

'Murray wants to see if I'm going to pick anything up,' said Fran, looking at the shadowy figures standing around, and across at the denser darkness of the wood on the other side of the hill. Somewhere ahead glinted the lake.

'And are you?'

'Only fear and hatred. Normal in this sort of setting. No one's got guilt written all over their heads.'

Connell and Murray emerged from the tent and came towards them. Murray introduced Fran.

'I've explained your part in this, Mrs Castle,' he said, 'but Inspector Connell still wants to ask you a few questions.'

'I'd ask you to come inside, Mrs Castle, but we haven't yet opened the chapel. The meeting, or whatever it was, was being held out here, over by those trees.' He pointed to a rough circle on the other side of the chapel, where a fire could still be seen glowing. Fran nodded and shivered.

'When you spoke to Joan Redding about belonging to this cult, did she admit it?'

'I asked if she was interested. She said she was. But she wouldn't admit anything else.'

'So how did you know about Tyne Chapel?'

'Coincidence, really. A friend–' she looked at Murray '–in my village heard about it.'

Connell looked as though he was bursting to say something else.

'And Mrs Castle gets these sort of – intuitions

about things, Inspector,' said Murray. 'I've learnt to take them very seriously.'

Connell looked now as though he'd like to lock Fran up. He towered over all three of them like Lucifer, Fran thought.

'How well did you know Miss Redding, Mrs Castle?' he asked.

'Not well at all. She was merely one of the nurses attending my aunt when she died.'

'And was, up to now, a suspect for her murder,' said Murray. 'No, Inspector,' as Connell opened his mouth, 'I think that's enough. I just wanted to give Mrs Castle the opportunity of being here to see if she came up with anything.'

Now Connell was really angry. Fran could feel it coming off him in waves, but she stepped past him and made for the circle of trees. Inside stood several cloaked figures, huddled together in groups, their faces in partial shadow, flickering in the light of the fire. Around the edges stood impassive police constables, mainly women, Fran noticed. There was more fear here, but nothing else. No images came into her mind. Nothing since the blackness when Connell had phoned.

She went back to the men and shook her head. 'Nothing,' she said. 'Can I ask how it happened?'

Connell and Murray looked at each other. Murray nodded slightly.

'She was strangled. Garrotted, actually,' said Connell.

'God,' whispered Guy.

'Nasty,' nodded Murray. 'Well, come on, then. Let's get you two back to civilisation.'

348

'Aren't you coming with us?' said Fran, as he shut the car door after her.

'No, I shall be involved now. Another sleepless night, I expect.' He looked almost jaunty.

'I don't think he likes Mrs Murray very much,' said Fran under her breath, as she watched him step away from the car and wave.

'No?' said Guy.

'No. She calls him Donnie.'

They were silent on the journey home, mindful of the young constable driving.

'I must phone Libby,' said Fran, as they went up the stairs to her flat. 'It's not too late, is it?'

'Nearly half past ten. She won't be in bed yet, will she?'

'You never know,' said Fran absently, then blushed. 'Well, you know what I mean.'

Guy laughed. 'I think you ought to sit down with a large drink. You've had a shock. Can't Libby wait?'

Fran shook her head. 'She's been in on this from the beginning. It wouldn't be fair.'

Guy sighed. 'OK. Would you like a drink?'

Fran smiled up at him and nodded. He dropped a kiss on the top of her head and went to forage for drinks in the kitchen while Fran dialled Libby's number.

Libby, disturbed only from watching an old DVD with Sidney and Ben, was, in her own words, gobsmacked.

'So it definitely wasn't her, then.'

'Doesn't look like it. I'm going to talk to Barbara again tomorrow.'

'Fran, don't. If she's killed Redding, you'll be

in danger. Let the police handle it. They'll find out. Besides, it might be something to do with the coven thing – nothing to do with Aunt Eleanor.'

'No, it's connected. I know that much.'

'Will Murray tell you what's going on, do you think?'

'Only if I come up with a startling prediction for him. At least he's taking me seriously, but the other chap was furious.'

'I expect it was a bit hard for him to swallow, to have a psychic thrust upon him in the middle of a load of witches.'

Fran smiled. 'I suppose so,' she said. 'Now I'm going to have a drink and try and forget it. I'll talk to you tomorrow.'

Guy came and sat beside her on the sofa. 'What you need is a little life affirmation,' he said, putting an arm round her.

Fran smiled bleakly. 'I'm not sure I feel very affirming,' she said.

'Then just relax,' said Guy. 'Talk if you want to.'

'I'll shut up, I think, if you don't mind,' said Fran. 'I'll have to do enough talking with Libby tomorrow.'

She closed her eyes and leant back against his arm. 'Wake me if I fall asleep.'

After a night of turning things over in her head and smoking too many cigarettes, something she hadn't done recently, Libby rang Fran as early as she dared.

'Let's go and see Barbara together,' she said. 'She can't do much against two of us. Then we could go and see the Headlam, and we might get to see Warner.'

'It's Sunday,' said Fran, groggily.

'So what? Nursing homes don't close on Sundays. And as it's Sunday, we might get to see Paul, too.'

'All right,' sighed Fran, 'but let me get up and dressed first.'

'Are you alone?' asked Libby.

'Yes, I am. I'm not ready for anything else at the moment.'

'All right, all right. Don't get crotchety,' said Libby. 'I'll pick you up in an hour.'

As they drove past Steeple Mount, Fran averted her eyes, but Libby slowed down and tried to peer through the trees.

'No sign of anything,' she said.

'There wouldn't be. Come on, Lib.'

'All right. Don't be in a such a rush.'

'You were the one in a hurry earlier,' grumbled Fran. 'And I haven't had any breakfast.'

'What's that got to do with anything? We'll get you something after we've been to Blagstock House.'

The beautiful autumn morning did nothing for Blagstock House. It still looked grim and forbidding as Libby swung Romeo onto the drive in a scattering of gravel.

Paul answered the door.

'What do you want?' he said.

Fran looked at him, trying to decide whether or not Murray would have been in touch with him yet. Libby had no such reservations.

'It's about Joan Redding,' she said. 'When did

you last see her?'

Paul's eyebrows flew up. 'And what's it got to do with you? Who the hell are you?'

'My – er – colleague, Libby Sarjeant,' said Fran.

'With a J,' put in Libby.

'Look, we're all under suspicion, now, Paul,' said Fran, crossing her fingers behind her back. 'I thought we ought to talk about it.'

'You know, then?' said Paul, looking from Fran to Libby and back again.

'That she was murdered? Yes. I was dragged out to the scene last night by the police.'

'Why?' Paul looked astonished.

'I was a suspect, I suppose.' Fran hurried on, not wanting to get bogged down in just why she was a suspect. 'Look, can we come in and talk to you and Barbara? It might help all of us.'

'Why does she have to come in?' said Paul, nodding in Libby's direction.

'She's been helping me, and I was staying with her,' said Fran. 'Come on Lib.' She stepped firmly past Paul, with Libby on her heels and went straight into the eau-de-nil drawing room.

'This is Libby Sarjeant, Barbara,' she said, as Barbara rose, open-mouthed from an armchair. 'Barbara Denver, Libby. Stone, as was.'

'Yes, I remember you,' said Libby.

'Do you?'

'When I first moved down here with my husband. Yes.' Libby volunteered nothing else, which obviously confused Barbara.

'They're here about Nurse Redding, Mum,' said Paul.

'Oh? Why? We don't know anything about her.

Do we, Paul?'

Libby watched Paul's face. It gave nothing away.

'Except as one of Aunt Eleanor's nurses, no,' he said. 'Do sit down.'

'Do you live here, Paul?' asked Libby.

He laughed. 'You've certainly got a cheek,' he said. 'Yes, I do. Some of the time, anyway.'

'The rest of the time he stays with his girlfriend in Nethergate,' said Barbara.

'And is that Nurse Warner?' asked Fran.

'Yes.' Paul flicked a glance at his mother's surprised face. 'How did you know that?'

'I didn't know it was a secret,' said Fran. 'So when did you hear about Nurse Redding?'

'Last night. The police phoned me here at about, oh, I don't know, eleven, I suppose.'

'And you were here?'

'Obviously, I was, if I spoke to the police. Where were you?'

'I was at home.'

'In London?' said Barbara.

'No, she's staying down here now,' said Paul. 'Were you on your own?'

'No, I wasn't. Were you?'

'Oh, for goodness sake!' said Barbara. 'Paul was here earlier in the evening, then he went off to take Sue to work, came back here for the rest of the evening, slept here, then went back to collect Sue from work this morning. She's on nights. He's just come back to make sure I'm all right.'

'And in case you're wondering,' said Paul, with a malicious smile, 'my mother wasn't alone, either. She had her book group round here from seven thirty, and they were still here when I got back from taking Sue to work. So, you see, I'm afraid that any suspicion that our – *family* – might be suspects comes down to just you, cousin Frances.'

Two minutes later, Libby and Fran stood outside on the gravel. Fran swallowed down anger and disappointment and began to walk towards the car. Libby watched her.

'No point in asking for Warner's address?' she said.

Fran sighed an exasperated sigh. 'Libby!'

'Oh, well, it was a thought.' Libby followed her to the car and unlocked the door. 'Breakfast? Or The Laurels?'

'Breakfast. I can't see any reason to go to The Laurels. Sue Warner's in bed asleep, presumably.'

'What about the Headlam?'

'Oh, let's leave it to the police, like you said. Come on. Let's get some breakfast.'

In a little café on the Marine Parade in Nethergate, they both ordered the traditional Full English, and were brought thick white mugs of tea. The sky had clouded over, and the breeze had whipped the sea into meringue-like points.

'Marion Headlam, then?' said Libby gazing out at the unlit fairy lights swinging gaily over the neat promenade gardens.

'Must be,' Fran sighed. 'Although we don't know exactly when Redding died, do we?'

'It wouldn't have been before her book group, though, would it? What would Redding have been doing at her coven before dark?'

'I don't know.' Fran sighed again. 'I don't really know anything except that she was garrotted.'

The waitress, unfortunately arriving at that moment with their food, nearly deposited it in their laps. Libby smiled at her. 'Sorry,' she said. The girl departed, flustered.

A few people strolled along the promenade. Ladies in pale coloured zip up jackets, the occasional rain hood, and determined cream sandals; gentlemen in raincoats, flat caps and trilbies and slightly darker zip up jackets.

'I always thought I'd be like that,' said Libby, as they left the café and went to lean over the railings to look at the beach.

Fran laughed. 'Never!'

'I know that now. I'm doomed forever to be the eternal aging hippy. Do you think Ben's ashamed of me?'

'Considering the way he's been monopolising you recently, I hardly think so.'

'Yes,' said Libby, looking smug, 'he has, rather, hasn't he?'

'Come on, then, let's go home,' said Fran. 'We didn't come for a day out at the seaside.'

They walked back to where Libby had parked the car, in a road just off Marine Parade, lined with tall Victorian houses.

'All hotels and guest houses, now,' said Libby, 'but once, whole families would hire them for the entire summer.'

'Really? Sort of early self catering?'

'I suppose so. They brought their own servants with them.'

'Lucky servants.' Fran looked up at the attic

355

windows of 'Marine View'. 'They probably could see the sea from up there.'

'Hey, Fran, look!' Libby grabbed her arm. 'Sue Warner!'

Fran looked. Sure enough, at the end of the road, disappearing into the doorway of a rather down-at-heel redbrick villa, was the slight figure of Nurse Warner. Libby started to move after her, but Fran pulled her back.

'What do we need to speak to her for, Libby? We know Paul and Barbara are in the clear for Redding's murder. The poor kid's probably been shopping before she goes to sleep. Let's leave her alone.'

Uncertain, Libby watched the doorway for a moment, then shrugged, and crossed the road to where Romeo sat waiting for them. 'Doesn't hurt to know where she lives, though,' she said.

Fran shook her head and climbed into the passenger seat.

Just as Libby pulled up outside The Pink Geranium, DCI Murray rang Fran's mobile.

'I thought you'd want to know where we're up to, Mrs Castle,' he said.

Fran's eyes widened in surprise, and she silently beckoned Libby to come inside with her.

'With the investigation, Mr Murray?'

'Both, Mrs Castle. I know I probably shouldn't have taken you out there last night, but I hoped it might be helpful.'

'I know that, Chief Inspector, but, as I said, nothing came to me.' The scene rose up vividly in Fran's mind's eye, the circle of trees, the shadowy cloaked figures and the fire.

'I know. I thought you might be interested to know what happened, though. Are you free to talk for a minute?'

'Yes,' said Fran, waving Libby towards the kitchen and miming tea, 'but it's a bit unusual, isn't it?'

She heard Murray let out a long breath. 'Yes, it is, but see, Mrs Castle, I'm treating you, un-officially like, as an expert witness.'

'Eh?'

'I've been talking to a couple of blokes I know in the Met and Thames Valley, and they've both been helped by – er – well – er–'

'Mediums?' suggested Fran. 'Psychics?'

'Yes. Exactly. And I know you've been quite ac-curate, that is to say, very accurate. I just thought, perhaps, if you knew all the circumstances, you might – well–'

'Pick something up?' said Fran.

'Yes.'

'What about Inspector Connell?' Fran pictured his dark, frowning face and could almost feel disapproval radiating towards her.

'What about him? The investigations are linked, and I'm Senior Investigating Officer.'

'So you can do what you like?' Fran was amused. 'Go on, then. I'll see if I can help.'

Libby came in with the tea, her eyebrows raised hopefully. Fran nodded her to a chair.

'First of all,' began Murray, for all the world as though he was on Jackanory, 'we know that Joan Redding arrived at this cult meeting, or whatever they call it, somewhere after seven thirty and before eight o'clock. Like all the others, she was in a long black cloak, lined with green stuff. Some of the folk there think there was someone else with her, who was also wearing a cloak, and others aren't certain, because they all milled about a bit, apparently.

'Anyway, after a bit of chanting and what have you, they split up into – er – pairs. And sort of, slipped off, if you get my meaning. And then they all came back together again for a bit more chanting, and that's when someone realised Redding wasn't there.'

'If they weren't certain whether there was someone with her or not, how could they be sure?' asked Fran.

'They all had to say a name, or something.'

'Ashtaroth, Hecate and so on?'

'You know?'

'Guessed. Go on.'

'So, her name, whatever it was, didn't come out. So they started calling her, thinking she was, well, still – um – occupied. And then one of them tripped over her.'

'And no one saw anyone else?'

'Well, no. They were all a bit preoccupied, you might say. Someone had the sense to have a mobile in his cloak pocket and called us.'

'So it could have been any one of the other people there?'

'Or this extra person. I mean, none of them are going to admit going off with someone who turns up dead, are they?'

'No. You've questioned them all?'

'Oh, yes. At the time, and afterwards. Poor souls have been up all night,' said Murray, gleefully.

'And no one's guilty?'

'Well, what you have to understand here, is that they were all in couples. And each one was questioned on their own, and they all came up with the right answers. Each couple confirmed each other's story.'

'They could have organised that while they were waiting for you.'

'They could, they could. But there were a few things the lads had picked up which confirmed the stories.'

'And what were they?'

'Forensic stuff, Mrs Castle. You wouldn't be interested.'

Wrinkling her nose, Fran thought she probably wouldn't.

'You think, then, that there was this extra person with Nurse Redding? How would they have got hold of a cloak?'

'According to the leader of this group, lots of them have more than one. You know, one on, one off, one in the wash.' Murray chuckled. 'Like vests.'

Fran rolled her eyes at Libby, who was, by now, consumed with curiosity and sitting on the windowsill with her head out of the window, puffing furiously on her first cigarette since the middle of the night.

'So, someone she knew, to whom she'd lent the cloak.'

'Right. Now, because of her connection to your old auntie, and her hiding the will, or finding it, as she put it, we decided to talk to all the–'

'Suspects.' Fran helped him out.

'Yes. We wondered a bit about your cousin.'

'Mr Wade?'

'No, no. He was in London. Mr Denver.'

'He's not my cousin,' said Fran.

'No? Well, whatever he is, we'd heard Redding had a bit of a crush on him. And you probably won't know this, but she did a bit of a number on a doctor at the hospital where she worked previously. Asked to resign.'

All that work wasted, thought Fran.

'So we wondered if he might have got a bit fed up with her chasing him. Especially now he seems to have taken up with that pretty little nurse whatsit. Warner.'

They knew all this all the time, thought Fran. Why did she bother?

'But he was with his mother until seven thirty, when he left to pick up Nurse Warner and take her to work. She's on nights at The Laurels. And she confirmed it. We spoke to her last night. And Mrs Denver had group of highly respectable ladies with her all evening, and Mr Denver got back to them before nine. So they're out of it. And little Nurse Warner couldn't have done it.'

'Oh? Why?'

'She was getting ready for work, and as she hasn't got a car, could never have got to Tyne Chapel from Nethergate and back in the time.'

'But surely, Nurse Redding wouldn't have gone off into the bushes with a woman?' said Fran. 'I mean, I thought she was rather frighteningly heterosexual.'

'Ah, well,' said Murray, obviously warming to

his task and settling down for a good long chat, 'that's where it becomes interesting, you see. According to our information, the doctor at the hospital wasn't the only one. Oh, no.'

'No?'

'Swung both ways, did our Nurse Redding. She'd been disciplined once before because of an alleged assault on a young nurse. Sexual, of course.'

'Oh, of course.'

'So there we are. It wasn't you, we checked with Mr Wolfe, it wasn't Mr Wade, he was in London with his daughter, it wasn't Nurse Warner, Mr or Mrs Denver. So, who are we left with, Mrs Castle?'

'Mrs Headlam, Mr Murray.'

## Chapter Thirty-six

'I thought you'd say that,' said Murray, with smug self-congratulation. 'So what's the gut instinct about it?'

'Nothing, I'm afraid,' said Fran. 'The only times I've felt anything about these murders has been once when Inspector Connell told me over the telephone, and in Aunt Eleanor's room.' Her other moments weren't relevant here, Fran decided.

'Was Headlam there then?'

'No, Redding was, although Mrs Headlam came in afterwards.' Fran sighed. 'I didn't like

361

her much, but she does seem to have the best motive, doesn't she?'

'The business about the will, yes. Don't understand why it was taken, though, whoever took it.'

'It should have been Paul or Barbara Denver, they had most to lose, but they couldn't find it, either. All very confusing.'

'We had Mrs Headlam in for questioning about your Aunt's death, but there was no conclusive evidence.' Murray sounded disappointed.

'What about the two drivers?'

'Ah, yes. Both suspicious deaths. Both driven off the road. We've matched all the forensics, and we know what car it was, but nobody in the case has one like it, and we've had no reports of one being stolen. So dead end there. We're still working on it, though.'

'Could a woman have done that?' asked Fran doubtfully.

'Course she could. As long as she had the nerve. It's not the woman's strength that counts there, it's the car. And if she's a good driver, of course.'

'And is Marion Headlam a good driver?'

Fran could almost hear Murray's shrug. 'No idea. But she's got a very nice little sporty job.'

'And that's it, is it?' said Fran, after the silence had lengthened. 'What about other suspects? From her fellow witches, or Satanists, or whatever they are. And *who* are they?'

Murray laughed. 'Oh, a very respectable lot, they are, you wouldn't believe. There'll be a couple of dodgy marriages on the go after this. Some of their partners had no idea. The places they said they were going! Opera club, out with the lads, darts, night fishing, one even said she was going to Mrs Denver's book group!'

'And the cloak? You haven't found it?'

'No, that's long gone, I reckon. Well, there you are, Mrs Castle. Any thoughts about this, I'd be glad to have them. Don't you go phoning anyone else, mind.'

'You mean, don't tell Inspector Connell?'

'Well, he's young, poor lad. Doesn't have the experience yet.'

'He didn't look very young to me,' said Fran.

'Younger than me, any road,' said Murray. 'Can I leave it with you? I'll give you my mobile number.'

'So there you are,' said Fran, when she'd finished recounting this remarkable conversation to Libby, who, by this time, had smoked another cigarette and got very stiff sitting on the windowsill.

'We were right then. Marion Headlam.' Libby inched herself back on to firm ground.

'Looks like it.' Fran sighed. 'Why am I not convinced?'

'No idea. Why didn't you say that to Murray? That's what he was asking you for.'

'No, he was asking me to come up with a startling revelation, some kind of vision he could put to the test.'

'OK. So what now?' Libby collected empty mugs and went towards the kitchen.

'I'll have a think, and see if I can come up with anything. I suppose I ought to go to the various sites, as it's only on the ground, as it were, that I seem to get anything.'

'No, it isn't,' said Libby. 'You get it over the phone as well, and on the train.'

'Yes, but that was a dream. I can't dream to order.'

'Shall we go and have a look at the chapel, then?' suggested Libby hopefully.

'We wouldn't be allowed anywhere near it,' said Fran. 'No, I'll just sit here and think. I'll let you know if anything happens.'

'I'm going to lunch at the Manor,' said Libby, 'but I'll have my mobile with me. I might not be able to drive afterwards, though. Hetty keeps a good cellar, and Flo and Lenny are coming as well, so there'll be masses to drink.'

'I shan't go anywhere today, Lib, but thanks for telling me. Have a good time.'

Libby had a very good time. Peter and his brother James arrived, and at the end of the meal Harry staggered in with left-over desserts from the restaurant. As she had done before, Libby helped Ben load the dishwasher, leaving the 'pots' as Hetty called them, to Hetty herself. While they worked, Libby brought Ben up to date on Fran's sudden co-option onto the police force.

'So all your investigations turned out to be unnecessary,' said Ben. 'The police found it all out, too.'

Libby flicked a tea towel at him. 'Yes, but we *did* find out. Which is much cleverer of us, because we haven't got their resources. And this could be a very good thing for us.'

'How do you mean?'

'When we go into business,' said Libby, and told him about Harry's hare-brained suggestion. 'Fran's not keen, but I think it could work,' she finished defiantly.

Ben roared with laughter.

Libby bristled. 'I don't see what's so funny,' she said, banging the dishwasher door shut.

'Oh, my darling, no, you wouldn't,' said Ben, wrapping his arms round her and resting his cheek against hers. 'That's why I love you.'

Libby held her breath. Ben, too, had gone still, as though he belatedly realised what he'd said. Then, he eased her away from him.

'Sorry, Lib. That wasn't the way to do it, was it?' He kissed her nose and sighed. 'But I'm afraid I do.'

Libby tried to speak and discovered there was something in her throat. Swallowing hard, she nodded, and found her eyes were smarting, too.

'Hey, don't cry!' Ben pulled her back against him. 'Is it so terrible?'

'Eyeuffoo,' said Libby against his chest.

'Pardon?'

She pulled away and wiped her eyes. 'I love you, too,' she said.

After that, they forgot the dishwasher, the family and Fran's elevation to police informer. Much later, in bed at number 17, Allhallow's Lane, Libby remembered her mobile, and reaching across Ben, fished it out of her basket.

'Oh, dear, I forgot,' she said, switching it on. 'And there's a message from Fran, too. Bother.'

'cn I brro car in morn see Warner?' said the message.

365

'I'll drive u' replied Libby.

'Fran's thought of something,' she told Ben. 'See? I bet we could be detectives.'

The phone woke Libby just before seven o'clock.

'Why don't you get an upstairs phone?' grumbled Ben, as she stumbled out of the bedroom and fell down the first two steps. Sidney, delighted to see her so early, wound himself round her legs and nearly caused further disaster. The answerphone cut in, and she had to yell over the top of herself to make sure she was heard.

'All right, all right, I can hear you.'

'Fran. You're a bit early.'

'You said you'd drive me. I want to get to Sue Warner's before Paul leaves.'

'Paul?'

'Presumably he takes her home every morning, like he did yesterday.'

'OK, why?'

'I've thought of something.'

'What?'

'I'll tell you later.'

'Oh, all right. I'll get dressed. See you in about half an hour.'

'I'll walk round to you. I'm up and dressed already,' said Fran.

'Hmph,' said Libby.

By the time Fran arrived, Libby was showered and dressed, eating a slice of toast, and Ben was in the shower. She shouted goodbye, received a gargled reply and went out to the car.

'So what's all this about?' she asked, as she set

off on the now all too familiar road to Nethergate.

'Something's not right. It's Sue Warner. I want to see on her home ground and see if anything happens.'

'Warner?'

'She's lying. Trouble is, I don't know what about.'

'But you haven't even spoken to her. How on earth do you know that she's lying?'

Fran sighed. 'I don't know,' she said. 'I just know. Look, let's go over it again. Barbara and Paul both told us Paul left his mother to pick up Sue Warner after the book club people arrived at Blagstock House.'

'Yes,' agreed Libby, 'and Sue Warner confirmed it, apparently.'

'But how did she know when he left Blagstock House?'

'Oh.' Libby glanced sideways, startled. 'Well, I suppose by knowing how long it took to get to her place from there.'

'We know it only takes five minutes in a car, we did it yesterday,' said Fran, 'so he must have arrived at about – what? – twenty to or twenty-five to eight?'

'Yes.'

'And he got home just before nine. That's a long time.'

'Well, perhaps they didn't go straight to The Laurels. Perhaps they – er – well, you know.'

'Maybe,' said Fran. 'I just think there's something wrong somewhere.'

Libby sighed. 'I really don't know why. Paul left

his mum with her book group, drove to get his girlfriend, spent some time with her, took her to work and went straight back to mum and the book group. Mum's got an alibi, he's got an alibi, girlfriend's got an alibi. Headlam hasn't.'

'How do we know she hasn't?' asked Fran. 'For all we know, she'd gone off duty and was in the company of several unimpeachable witnesses.'

'Oh, I don't know,' said Libby grumpily. 'I still don't know why you think Warner's lying. About what, for goodness' sake?'

'I'll find out,' said Fran, and turned her face to the window.

They drove the rest of the way in silence and parked a little way from the red brick villa in a resident's parking place. 'If we get done, I'll make Murray pay the fine,' muttered Libby, locking Romeo and given him an encouraging pat.

'That's Paul's car,' said Fran. 'I saw it at Blagstock House.'

Libby eyed the low-slung silver sports car with distaste. 'Think how difficult they are to get out of,' she said.

Fran gave her a look, and rang the bell marked Warner.

Paul's face was a study as he opened the door.

'Sorry, Paul, but I need to ask your young lady a few questions,' said Fran, pushing past him, Libby gamely trundling behind. Too surprised to stop them, Paul followed them up the stairs, to where Sue Warner, still in uniform, stood looking terrified.

'Now, what's all this about?' said Paul, recovering and going to put an arm round her.

'Just a couple of questions,' said Fran.

'Who do you think you are?' said Paul, beginning to look angry. Libby noticed Nurse Warner flinch as his hand tightened on her shoulder. 'You're not the police!'

'All right, Paul, all right,' said Fran, showing remarkable composure under the circumstances, Libby thought. 'I just wanted to know what time you got here on Saturday night?'

'Well, why don't you ask me? What's it got to do with her?' Libby could swear Paul's eyes were glittering now.

'All right, I'm asking you. What time did you get here?'

'About twenty to eight,' said Paul.

'Half past seven,' said Nurse Warner.

They looked at each other.

'Somewhere around there, anyway,' said Paul.

Libby felt a horrible sinking sensation in her stomach and nearly jumped out of her skin when a voice behind her said: 'Not half past seven.'

Libby and Fran turned to see Barbara coming up the stairs behind them.

'Mum!' Paul let go of Nurse Warner and pushed between Libby and Fran to grasp his mother's arm.

'Silly little bitch,' said Barbara, conversationally. 'I knew what you'd been up to, you know.'

'What?' Fran stood between Barbara and Sue Warner and Libby tried to blend in with the wallpaper.

'She was with him in Eleanor's room, you know. The day she died.'

'I know,' said Fran, 'and Nurse Redding found them.'

'How do you know that?' asked Barbara.

'She told me,' said Fran. 'So, why couldn't it have been half past seven?'

'He was with me.' Barbara's eyes were looking a little wild.

'Yes, Nurse Warner, he was,' said Fran. 'All the other ladies confirm it.'

Nurse Warner looked as if she were going to faint. Libby thoughtfully pushed a chair towards her and she collapsed onto it.

'So, twenty to eight, Paul?' said Fran, watching him as he nodded. 'Did you go straight to The Laurels?'

'Yes,' said Nurse Warner.

'No,' said Paul, and looked at Sue Warner as though he'd never seen her before. She closed her eyes and bowed her head.

'That would appear to be that, then, Mrs Castle,' said a new voice, and DCI Murray now appeared on the stairs, followed by Inspector Connell. Libby caught a glimpse of uniform boots outside the front door and felt her breathing return to normal.

'Well, well. Not quite the same story then, eh, Miss Warner?' Murray bent over her solicitously. 'What time did you go on duty? Quarter to nine, wasn't it?'

Slowly, Sue Warner nodded.

'Took a long time to get to work, then, didn't it?'

He turned to Fran. 'Well, Mrs Castle?'

'If you could get someone to look in the wheelie bin, Mr Murray,' she said.

'They were checked,' growled Inspector Connell. Libby gazed at him admiringly.

'Near a hedge. A few doors down,' said Fran calmly.

DCI Murray frowned as Inspector Connell clattered down the stairs. 'Should have been more thorough,' he said.

Fran shook her head. 'It wasn't there before,' she said.

'Where was it?'

'I'm not absolutely sure,' said Fran. 'Perhaps Barbara could tell us?'

Libby gaped. Barbara began to make noises like a stranded fish. She certainly looked like one. Behind them, Inspector Connell came clattering back up the stairs.

'Here,' he said, holding out a grubby black object.

Barbara screamed.

'It wasn't half past seven, was it Mrs Denver?' said Murray quietly. 'Your ladies arrived at seven.'

Libby looked at Paul, who now stared at his mother, his face grey.

'And you arrived *here* at nearly half past eight, Paul,' said Fran. 'Where were you all that time?'

A silence that seemed to stretch the nerves was finally broken by another scream from Barbara, Nurse Warner slumping to the floor and Paul trying to run through the flat and out on to the fire escape. Fran moved over to Libby and collapsed against her friend. Libby gave her a hug and discovered that she was trembling.

Paul was brought back through the flat in handcuffs, Barbara and Nurse Warner were attended to by kind and sensible looking police constables, and Fran and Libby were escorted downstairs by Murray and Connell.

'Told you so,' said Murray to Connell, triumphantly. 'I said she'd come up trumps.'

Connell looked at Fran and suddenly held out his hand. He's really quite attractive, thought Libby.

'Thank you, Mrs Castle,' he said.

'So what exactly did you do and how did you do it,' said Libby, driving Romeo carefully out of Nethergate and feeling rather light-headed.

'I wondered if there was a discrepancy between the time Paul left Blagstock House and arrived at Sue Warner's. Then I wondered if Warner was lying to save her own skin. It was terribly confusing. And I kept seeing this cloak. That was the only thing I actually *saw*, in the way Murray wanted me to, and then, when I was asleep, I had that dream again, the one I had in the train, where I saw a face over Eleanor's shoulder. Remember, I told you?'

'Yes.'

'And it was Paul.'

'But why?'

'He was searching for the will, I suppose, and Eleanor had to be kept quiet.'

'And last night?'

'I expect he called Redding after I'd seen her on Saturday, or she called him, and he seduced her

372

into taking him along. I don't know. Murray'll tell us. Now, just let's go home. I could sleep for a week.'

## Chapter Thirty-seven

Fran held a little drinks party on the Tuesday night. She had refused to talk to anyone, except briefly to Guy and Libby to say she would tell them all about it together, as it would save breath, and anyway, she would be out most of Tuesday. Harry left Donna in charge of the restaurant, and he and Peter gave everyone champagne and then sat on the floor. Ben sat on the arm of Libby's chair, Guy sat next to Fran on the sofa and Libby was given dispensation to smoke.

'Later,' said Libby. 'Go on, Fran, tell us what happened.'

'This is pieced together from what Barbara, Paul, Warner and Headlam have said to the police. Murray seems to have got it more or less right.' She took a deep breath and a sip of champagne. 'Apparently, what happened was that Paul learnt from Sue Warner that Eleanor had made this codicil. He and his mother decided they would have to find it, and either get Eleanor to change her mind or destroy it. As far as anyone knew, there wasn't another copy. And there wasn't, by the way, but it was quite legal.

'Paul's habit was to push Eleanor outside the french windows "for a breath of air" and then search her room. According to Warner, Redding found him doing this, and he charmed her into submission. He wasn't above actually using Eleanor's bed if the need arose.'

Harry snorted. Everyone looked at him.

'Sorry.'

'So she began to pursue him, and because he still wanted her on his side, he went along with it, at the same time carrying on his affair with Warner. On Eleanor's birthday, Redding actually found the will and the codicil and took it, intending to give it to Paul, which is why she burst in on him with Warner, not knowing Warner was there. Furious, she ordered Warner out, then the bell rang and she went off to let Barbara in. Paul, still not knowing the will had been found, brought Eleanor back in and started a hasty search, but Eleanor must have kicked up a fuss. So he smothered her. Then left through the french windows, doubled back and was seen entering as if for the first time by the gardener.

'Neither of the nurses said anything about him being there because of the circumstances.'

'What about the two witnesses?' asked Ben.

'Warner had their names, so he tracked them down not long after the codicil was written.'

'How did the police connect him to their deaths?' asked Peter.

'Murray told me they'd done all the forensics and knew what sort of car had been used, but no one connected to the case had a car like it, and

374

nothing had been reported as stolen. Once they decided Paul was the murderer (before we did, Libby) they started to go through people he might have known who had that sort of car.'

'He wouldn't have borrowed a car, surely?' said Harry.

'No, but he did hire one,' said Fran.

'How bloody stupid,' said Peter. 'He must have known he'd be caught.'

'Apparently, there are some dubious car-hire operations who don't ask to see driving licences, but ask for huge deposits. He used one of those in London.'

'So how did the police find it? The hire firm, I mean?' said Libby.

'The indispensable police computer, I gather,' said Fran, grinning. 'When leant on, the owner didn't know nuffink, just tried to help people out, like.'

'So did they get DNA off it?' asked Harry.

'I think so. That sort of clinched it.'

'So the will was valid, was it?' said Libby, returning to the main theme.

'Oh, yes. The handwriting was Marion Headlam's, by the way, but signed properly by Eleanor.'

'Why couldn't anyone find it?' asked Guy.

'She'd hidden it down the side of a drawer, much like she'd hidden the will in London. Redding took it home with her after the murder. She put it back because she was still angry with Paul and suspected he and his mother might inherit. Her job was important to her after her disgrace at the hospital.'

'What disgrace?' asked Harry, looking interested.

Everyone looked at him again.

'Oh, all right,' he said, and sank back against the wall. Peter patted him on the leg.

'When I went to see her on Saturday morning – god, it seems a lifetime away – she decided on a bit of blackmail, Murray says. So she phoned him up, and he then went round to her flat, seduced her all over again, and asked if he could go to the meeting with her that night.'

'If he was in her flat, why didn't he kill her there?' asked Peter.

'It was daylight, he could have been seen going in or out, and he'd leave DNA.' Fran shrugged. 'That's what I think, anyway. So he left his mother's just after seven, when her ladies came – and why she thought they'd all agree that they didn't arrive until seven thirty, I don't know – went to pick Redding and the cloaks up, and off they went. They were naked under the cloaks, you know.'

Harry's face brightened and he opened his mouth. Everyone looked at him again.

'So, after he'd garrotted her–' Fran's audience shifted uncomfortably, '–he threw her clothes into the woods, put his own clothes on, and went off to pick up Nurse Warner and take her to work. Then home to mummy, where he hid the cloak.'

'Did mummy know any of this?' asked Libby.

'Murray thinks she knew most of it, which was why she was so scared.'

'So Warner was lying about him getting there at

seven thirty?' asked Peter, with the air of one manfully trying to keep up.

'Yes. That was what I'd picked up on, obviously, although I didn't actually know. After the police had asked Paul about his movements, they rang Nurse Warner at The Laurels.'

'On Saturday night?' asked Guy.

'Yes. But Paul got in first and asked her to lie for him.'

'Why on earth did she? She must have known then what was going on,' said Libby.

'Search me. I think she was frightened of him. And she was infatuated, of course. Oh – and she thought he was going to be rich.'

'So,' said Peter, frowning, 'let's get this straight. He left mummy just after seven, picked up Nurse Redding, took her to the woods, killed her and went to Nurse Warner's by twenty past eight, then back home just before nine. So both Barbara and Nurse Warner were lying to protect him.'

'And Barbara tried to implicate Nurse Warner,' said Libby. 'I was there when she did that.'

'That's right. Barbara found the cloak and wanted to incriminate somebody, so went and put it in a bin near Warner's flat, not thinking it would also incriminate her beloved Paul. I actually saw her do it. I mean, in my head.'

'You clever girl,' said Guy, and gave her a kiss.

'More champers,' said Peter, getting up and popping another cork.

'And so Marion Headlam inherits most of Eleanor's estate,' said Libby, finally lighting a cigarette and propping herself once again on the windowsill.

'Yes. Not that there's much of it,' said Fran.

'Oh, dear. Cousin Charles?' said Ben.

'Not exactly,' said Fran. 'My Uncle Frank.'

'What?'

'Apparently, according to this Mr Meade who telephoned me yesterday afternoon, my father and Uncle Frank owned the house in Mountville Road between them, and it was to be left to their heirs.'

A silence fell.

'So–' said Libby.

'I'm the only heir. Frank's will said Eleanor was allowed to live there for her lifetime, but it would revert to me when she died. I believe that's when she killed him, when she found out. Probably in a temper.'

'So it was all for nothing,' said Harry, in an awed voice.

Fran nodded.

'And you're a rich woman,' said Guy, scowling at her.

'And did it say anything about – well, you know, about Frank and–'

'My mum?' said Fran. 'No. It referred to me throughout as Herbert's daughter.'

'But it all comes to you?' said Peter.

'And you can buy somewhere to live!' said an overjoyed Libby. 'Oh, Fran, congratulations!'

'And where will that be?' asked Ben.

'Oh, down here, of course,' said Fran, to a delighted cheer.

'Brilliant,' said Peter.

'Fab,' said Harry.

'Where?' said Ben.

'I'm really pleased,' said Guy.

Fran twinkled at him.

'So was Inspector Connell,' she said.

This Large Print Book for the partially sighted, who cannot read normal print, is published under the auspices of

**THE ULVERSCROFT FOUNDATION**

V9